Private
PASSIONS
A Hideaway Novel

D1177133

NATIONAL BESTSELLING AUTHOR
ROCHELLE ALERS

Private
PASSIONS
A Hideaway Novel

ARABESQUE®

Recycling programs
for this product may
not exist in your area.

PRIVATE PASSIONS

ISBN-13: 978-0-373-53474-6

Copyright © 2012 by Rochelle Alers

First published by BET Publications, LLC in 2001

www.kimanipress.com

Printed in U.S.A.

Dear Reader,

Riddle: What do you get when you pair Joshua Kirkland's daughter with the stepson of Matthew Sterling?

Answer: *Private Passions.*

Private Passions is the perfect recipe for an all-nighter: beautiful, feisty heroine, sexy hero, exotic locales, dirty politics and a suspenseful plotline that will keep you guessing until the end.

In *Private Passions,* readers are reunited with characters they've come to love, as Emily Kirkland and Christopher Blackwell Delgado struggle to keep their relationship a secret from everyone, including their families. Settle down in a comfy chair with a beverage and your favorite playlist, and take the fast-paced journey that is a timely reminder of why readers have become so captivated with the Hideaway series.

Late 2012 brings a new bridal trilogy with the Hideaway Wedding series—*Summer Vows, Eternal Vows* and *Secret Vows.* This Cole family wedding wager pits Ana Cole, Nicholas Cole-Thomas and Jason Cole against one another in a bet to see who makes it to the altar first. The prize goes to the one who can pick the winner, but the real winners are Ana, her brother Jason and their cousin Nicholas, all of whom find love in the most surprisingly romantic ways.

Read, live and love romance.

Rochelle Alers

www.rochellealers.com

HIDEAWAY SERIES

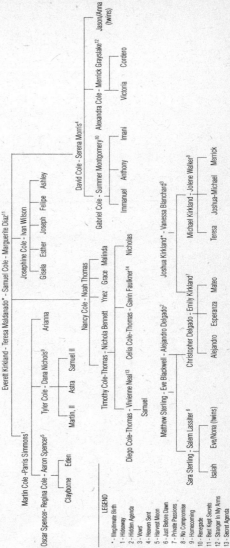

Everett Kirkland - Teresa Maldanado* - Samuel Cole - Marguerite Diaz[11]

Martin Cole - Parris Simmons[1]

Oscar Spencer - Regina Cole - Aaron Spencer[5]

Clayborne   Eden

Tyler Cole - Dana Nichols[9]

Arianna

Martin, II   Astra   Samuel II

Josephine Cole - Ivan Wilson

Gisela   Esther   Joseph   Felipe   Ashley

Nancy Cole - Noah Thomas

Timothy Cole-Thomas - Nichola Bennett

Diego Cole-Thomas - Vivienne Neal[13]

Samuel

Celia Cole-Thomas - Gavin Faulkner[14]

Ynez   Grace   Malinda

Nicholas

David Cole - Serena Morris[4]

Gabriel Cole - Summer Montgomery[10]

Immanuel   Anthony   Imani

Alexandra Cole - Merrick Grayslake[12]

Victoria   Cordero

Jason/Anna (twins)

Matthew Sterling - Eve Blackwell - Alejandro Delgado[2]

Sara Sterling - Salem Lassiter[6]

Isaiah   Eve/Nona (twins)

Christopher Delgado - Emily Kirkland[7]

Alejandro   Esperanza   Mateo

Joshua Kirkland* - Vanessa Blanchard[3]

Michael Kirkland* - Jolene Walker[8]

Teresa   Joshua-Michael   Merrick

LEGEND

* - Illegitimate Birth
1 - Hideaway
2 - Hidden Agenda
3 - Vows
4 - Heaven Sent
5 - Harvest Moon
6 - Just Before Dawn
7 - Private Passions
8 - No Compromise
9 - Homecoming
10 - Renegade
11 - Best Kept Secrets
12 - Stranger In My Arms
13 - Secret Agenda
14 - Breakaway

Part One
Secrets and Shadows

Chapter 1

December 23
Santa Fe, New Mexico

A late-model silver-gray Saab cruised silently along a remote road in a Santa Fe suburb, slowing and stopping at the gatehouse to a private community.

A uniformed guard slid back a window, leaned forward in the small booth and peered at the driver. "Happy holidays, Senator Delgado."

The driver smiled at the guard. "Thank you, Mr. Stewart. Happy holidays."

Jack Stewart pressed a button on the panel in front of him, then recorded the time of arrival next to the visitor's name. "Miss Kirkland is expecting you."

Waiting until the wooden arm lifted, New Mexico State Senator Christopher Blackwell Delgado drove slowly along the brightly lit path and maneuvered into the driveway leading to Emily Kirkland's two-story town house. Lights blazed brightly from the expansive windows, radiating warmth and welcome. He and Emily would share a pre-Christmas dinner, then exchange gifts. The ritual was one they'd established two years earlier.

He turned off the engine, opened the driver's side door, and stepped out of the convertible sports car. He lingered to slip on a suit jacket and retrieve a small decorative shopping bag from the rear seat, then made his way up three steps to the door and rang the bell.

Less than a minute later, the door opened to reveal a yawning space claiming a two-story foyer and a circular wrought-iron stairway leading to a dramatic loft. Gleaming wood floors, Palladian windows, skylights and a massive stone fireplace provided the backdrop for the tall, slender woman standing in the doorway.

Her luminous eyes crinkled in a friendly smile. "Hi."

Leaning down, Chris kissed her silken cheek, the seductive fragrance of her perfume lingering in his nostrils. "Hi, yourself."

Frigid air swept through the open door and Emily Kirkland shivered slightly. "It feels like snow."

Chris stepped into the foyer, returning his childhood friend's warm smile. "All of the meteorologists are predicting it."

Emily closed the door, her expression sobering. "I just hope it holds off until tomorrow afternoon."

"What time are you leaving for Florida?"

"We're scheduled for a ten-thirty departure."

She and her parents had made arrangements to spend Christmas in West Palm Beach with her father's relatives; however, Joshua and Vanessa Kirkland planned to remain in Florida for the winter season, while she would return to New Mexico on December 26. She was scheduled to attend a staff meeting the next day at KCNS-TV. She would've forgone the meeting, except that she was expecting a promotion to a position for which she had worked all her professional career.

Chris sniffed the air. "Something smells wonderful."

Emily looped her arm over the sleeve of his silk- and wool-blended charcoal-gray jacket, steering him into the living room. "It's glazed pork tenderloin."

He stopped, turning slightly to stare at her. Emily Kirkland had inherited her mother's raven-black hair and tall, slender body, and her father's coloring, eyes and features. She was one of the most beautiful women he had ever known. Her naturally curly hair was cut to frame her oval face. There was a time when she had worn the loose curls to her shoulders, but she now preferred shorter hair because she felt it made her appear more sophisticated for the television viewing audience. At thirty, the political analyst had garnered a legion of fans, and whenever she appeared in front of the camera the network's rating escalated appreciably.

It was Emily Kirkland's eyes that drew one's attention immediately. They were large, heavily lashed, a clear sage-green and a barometer of her moods. If she smiled they crinkled and her face lit up like a brilliant sunrise, but they could also become cold, forbidding and dispassionate.

Chris had known her for thirty of his thirty-five years, and he had always treated her like a sister. But lately it had become more difficult for him to think of her that way. Their parents were close friends, his sister Sara and Emily were best friends, and he and Emily were godparents to Sara and Salem Lassiter's young son, Isaiah.

He handed her the shopping bag. "Merry Christmas."

Emily extracted her arm and took the bag. "Thank you. Your gift is on the armchair."

While his gaze shifted to the large, gaily wrapped box on the chair, Emily studied her dinner guest. Christopher Delgado was a man who would only grow more attractive as he aged. He claimed a sensual, masculine beauty that usually elicited inaudible gasps whenever he trained his penetrating gaze on women who had managed to garner his rapt attention.

An even six feet in height, his weight fluctuated between 160 and 175 pounds, depending upon his work schedule. Those close to him were aware that once he involved himself in a project there were days when he subsisted almost entirely on strong black coffee.

She noticed his face was leaner, almost gaunt. The elegant ridge of cheekbones under his khaki coloring verifying his African and Mexican ancestry were more pronounced, confirming that he had not been eating or sleeping enough.

Her gaze shifted from his close-cropped graying black hair to his straight nose, a pair of firm, sculpted lips, and down to the attractive cleft in his strong chin. Emily had stopped asking herself why she had fallen in love with Chris. It was just that she could not remember when she had not been in love with him.

He raised his curving black eyebrows. "Do you want me to open it now?"

She glanced at her watch and gave him back the shopping

bag. "We still have some time before we'll sit down to eat. Why don't you fix us a drink while I check on the roast? Then we'll open our gifts together."

Chris stared at her departing figure as she made her way in the direction of the kitchen. His velvet black eyes darkened with an unnamable emotion. Emily wore a white silk blouse with black piping around the collar and short sleeves with a pair of tailored wool crepe slacks that fit her slender body with impeccable precision. Like himself, Emily did not buy her clothes off the rack. At five foot nine, she was taller than the average woman, and there were times when some people mistook her for a fashion model.

He dropped the bag on the chair with his gift from her, then made his way over to a portable bar and opened a door concealing a small refrigerator. Crystal decanters held an array of premium liquors. Selecting two martini glasses, he quickly and expertly blended a gin martini for himself and a manhattan for Emily. He placed the glasses on the table next to a stack of linen napkins, small plates and several silver serving pieces.

Emily returned to the living room with a platter filled with an assortment of hot hors d'oeuvres. He took the platter from her and placed it on the coffee table. He waited for her to sit before sitting down beside her on a love seat covered in Haitian cotton.

She picked up a napkin, spread it over her knees and handed him a plate. He filled the plate with bite-size pieces of puffed pastries covering spicy shrimp, sweet and sour pork, chicken and peppery ground beef, handing it back to her before he repeated the process for himself.

They reached for their glasses. Tilting his head, Chris stared at her, absorbing everything that made Emily Kirkland who she was. He flashed a slow, sensual smile, displaying his straight white teeth, and raised his glass.

"Here's to a joyous Christmas, festive Kwanzaa and a new year filled with everything your heart desires."

Her lashes came down, concealing her innermost feelings from him. She concentrated on the chilled red-gold liquid and cherry in her glass. "To Christopher Delgado." Her beautifully modulated voice was a seductive contralto. "Our next governor of New Mexico."

He leaned closer and she glanced up at him. There was no movement except for the measured rhythm of breathing. Angling his head, he touched his mouth to hers, increasing the pressure until she responded. The mere brushing of their mouths lasted seconds.

Emily took a sip of the manhattan, welcoming the chill before a warmth spread throughout her chest. "If you ever decide to give up politics, you can go back to tending bar," she teased.

Tiny lines fanned out at the corners of his eyes when Chris laughed. He had worked as a bartender for private parties on weekends when he attended college. Even though he had not needed the money, the job provided him with the entrée he needed to meet people whose influence he sought after he decided on a career in politics. He tasted his martini. It was perfect. He had not lost his touch.

His gaze was fixed on the shape of Emily's lush mouth, outlined in vermilion red, watching as she took small bites of fluffy pastries, while he ate several himself.

"If I decided to give up politics and you journalism, we could go into business together as restaurateurs. I'll work the bar and you can supervise the kitchen."

"Bite your tongue," she chided. "Work in a *kitchen*." She shook her head. "I don't think I'll ever be that domesticated."

His expression changed, becoming impassive. "Do you ever think of combining marriage with your career?"

Emily went completely still. She examined the man sitting inches away—his stark white custom-made shirt, charcoal-gray suit, burgundy silk tie and imported black oxfords. He was asking her a question she was unable to answer because it was too general. If he had asked if she would marry him while continuing with her career as a television journalist, she would say yes without hesitation.

"It would depend on who I'd marry," she said instead.

"Does that who include Keith Norris?"

No, her heart whispered. "Keith and I see each other occasionally."

"You didn't answer my question, Emily."

Her spine stiffened. "And I don't have to answer your question. After all, I don't ask you who you sleep with."

Chris's eyes darkened dangerously as he struggled to control his temper. Emily Kirkland was the only woman who made him feel things he did not want to feel. She was the only woman who knew exactly what button to push to make him lose control. Unwittingly, she had scaled the wall he had erected to monitor every phase of his personality and existence.

Whenever she called, he came. He could not deny her anything—and that included himself. But he found himself competing with men she dated even though she refused to commit to a future with them. Only superstar baseball player Keith Norris was different. Norris and Emily had recently celebrated their first year together.

He forced a smile. "You're right, Emily. Forgive me for meddling."

Emily cursed herself for the sharp retort. Chris did not deserve to be the recipient of her frustration. It was he she wanted to date, he whom she wanted to kiss her with passion, and it was he she wanted to marry.

Smiling up at him through her lashes, she leaned closer and kissed his smooth-shaven brown cheek. His body's masculine scent was the perfect blend for the haunting citrus-based aftershave on his jaw.

"I'm not going to marry Keith," she said close to his ear.

He wanted to believe her, but a popular journalist whose tattletale columns were syndicated in Santa Fe and Denver dailies had reported sightings of the multimillion-dollar ballplayer at upscale jewelry stores, examining diamond engagement rings.

"Good for you. You could do a lot better than a pompous jock."

Pulling back, she stared numbly at him. "You sound like Michael."

Chris nodded. "Your brother is a very bright man."

"Whenever it concerns me, my brother is quite biased."

"So am I. I'd hate for you to marry the wrong man."

A slight frown creased her high, smooth forehead. "Not you, too. I'll be thirty-one in eight weeks, and my father still questions me about the men I date."

"That's because of his Latino machismo. He feels it's his duty to protect the women in his life."

She knew Chris was right. Her African-Cuban-American father was resolute when it came to protecting his wife and daughter. And Michael Kirkland had become as inflexible as his father. Her blood had run cold, shaking her to the core, after Michael confessed that if the police hadn't killed a man who had stalked her, he would have. The crazed man had begun following her because she had not responded to his online marriage proposals. He had come close to killing her when he fired a couple of rounds at her from a high-powered rifle. One bullet had shattered the windshield of the car she was driving. Even though the sliver of glass was removed along her hairline, a minute scar remained. It was a constant reminder of how close she had come to being murdered.

Chris saw Emily pull her lower lip between her teeth, and he knew her well enough to realize that she was uneasy about something. "Are you all right?"

Her expression brightened when she offered him a smile. "I'm okay."

Reaching for her fingers, he held them gently within his larger hand. He examined her long, slender hand and professionally manicured nails. His head came up slowly and he gave her a penetrating stare that made him appear to Emily more stranger than friend.

"You know I'll always look out for you, Emily." His voice was low, mysterious. Her eyes widened until he could see their jade depths.

"And you know I don't need another father or brother, Chris."

He held her gaze, and there was a tingling in the pit of her stomach. She tried curbing the dizzying currents of trepidation racing through her. There was something in his eyes that unnerved her. Something that told her that the man sitting next to her had become a complete stranger.

Glancing away, he stared over her head. "You're right about that." She eased her hand from his loose grip, and even though they sat only inches apart he felt her withdrawal. Pushing off the love seat, he walked several feet to the armchair and gathered up the gifts. He handed Emily the shopping bag, then retook his seat.

Emily withdrew a square package, removed a black velvet bow and ribbon, then methodically peeled off the silver foil paper, revealing a black velvet box. Without opening the box, she knew it contained a piece of jewelry.

"Open it," Chris urged, seeing her hesitation.

She smiled at him. "Open yours."

The sound of tearing paper competed with the soft gasp of surprise from Emily as she stared at a yellow bangle bracelet banded all around with a profusion of sparkling diamonds. She picked it up, reading the engraved inscription on the underside: *Merry Christmas, Love always, Chris.*

Chris opened an ebony lacquered box to reveal a set of exquisitely carved chess pieces in pale and dark green jade. He was an avid chess player and had also become a collector of chess sets. His collection included pieces made of pewter, brass and teak. However, none were as elegant as these smooth jade pieces. His stunned gaze shifted from the chess pieces to Emily's perfect profile. As if on cue, they turned and looked at each other, smiling.

Emily shifted her expertly waxed eyebrows in a questioning expression. "I hope you like them."

Nodding his head, he replied, "They are beyond description. Thank you."

She lowered her lashes in a demure gesture. "You're welcome. The bracelet is beautiful."

"I hope you like it," Chris said, winking at her.

Her brilliant smile reached her luminous eyes, reminding him of sparkling, clear emeralds. "I love it. I love you," she added. She held out her right arm. "Please put it on."

He took the bracelet, opened the clasp, then slipped it on her tiny wrist. She watched his long, well-groomed fingers as he managed to secure the safety catch with a minimum of effort. His hands were as elegant as the rest of him.

Chris did not react to her declaration of affection because he had grown up hearing Emily tell him that she loved him—loved him fondly, not passionately.

They sat side by side, sipping their drinks and staring at the flickering flames behind the decorative screen in the fireplace, each lost in their own thoughts.

Ten minutes later, Emily placed her half-empty glass on the coffee table and stood up. "Everything should be ready now."

Without waiting to see whether Chris followed her, she made her way to the dining area. The table was covered with an antique embroidered linen cloth and set with china, crystal and shiny sterling silver pieces. She stopped, dimmed the lights in an overhead chandelier, and lit several beeswax candles.

She had told Chris she loved him for what seemed like the hundredth time in her life. And, again there was no reaction from him. Closing her eyes, she made herself a solemn promise. She would never again tell him that she loved him.

Chapter 2

December 27
Santa Fe

KCNS-TV News Director Richard Adams's penetrating gaze swept around the conference room, lingering momentarily on the impassive expression of Emily Teresa Kirkland.

"This concludes our last staff meeting for the year. I want to thank all of you for your ongoing cooperation. I'd like to wish everyone a wonderful New Year, and for those of you who have scheduled vacation leave—enjoy. Emily, could you please give me a few more minutes," he added as she gathered her leather-bound day planner.

The eight people who made up the political news staff pushed back from the oak conference table and stood up, offered one another warm smiles, and congratulated Calvin Robinson, while Emily remained seated.

She stared numbly at her boss; she had successfully concealed the anger and resentment racing through her rigid body, threatening to explode. She knew why she'd been passed over for a promotion, and it had nothing to do with her job performance and everything to do with her refusal to accept Richard's very subtle advances. Any respect she'd had for him was suddenly swept away because he had waited less than half an hour before she was to take vacation to announce his decision.

Richard Adams had been careful—very, very careful—not to step over the line where she could charge him with sexual harassment when he had asked her to share an intimate dinner meeting at his home to discuss her future at the all-news cable television station.

She had left KHRP a year ago, after network executives at KCNS approached her with an offer she could not refuse; they had hired her with a promise that she would take over as lead anchor of the weekend political desk within a month of the network's popular veteran anchor's impending retirement. The man had officially retired six weeks earlier.

She had chided herself for not securing the pledge in writing; but then, she had told herself that she could trust Richard. He had offered her what she had spent most of her professional life pursuing: the position of assistant political analyst for a national television network.

His decision to select Calvin Robinson for the anchor slot had momentarily stunned her. Calvin had come to KCNS three months after her, and they were the only two African-Americans in front of the camera. She tried rationalizing why she had not been given the position: she was only thirty, hardly what could be called a veteran correspondent, and she was a *woman.* However, female television journalists had come a long way since Barbara Walters had been hired by ABC's Roone Arledge.

Emily and her contemporaries still had a never-ending journey ahead of them within a male bastion that had reluctantly and grudgingly allowed members of the opposite sex into their coveted profession. She and many other women had become the recipients of the 1964 Civil Rights Act and a 1971 Federal Communications Commission ruling mandating equal employment regardless of gender. The result was that more women were hired in TV newsrooms all over the country, even though legislation was not going to change her current status.

Richard waited until the others filed out of the conference room, then gave Emily his full attention. He had to admire her. She had not reacted visibly to his decision not to promote her. But then, he admired everything about her. When meeting her for the first time he had been awed by her intelligence and stunned by her beauty.

Seeing her close up and in person verified what the camera always revealed—it loved her. Soft, flattering light illuminated her large, heavily lashed eyes and their vibrant color—reminiscent of early spring leaves. They were a brilliant contrast to a flawless complexion in a hue of heated honey. Her straight, delicate nose; full, lush, curving mouth and naturally curly, professionally coiffed black hair completed her winning professional persona. However, after working closely with her, he thought her reserved and inhibited—much too reserved for her age.

He glanced down at the printed schedule in front of him, feeling the heat from the laser-green eyes on his bowed head. "I've decided to reassign you for the gubernatorial campaign. I want you to cover Savoy instead of Delgado."

There was a pulse beat of silence before Emily was able to respond to Richard's second surprise announcement. "Why?"

A slight smile curved his mouth as he glanced at her without raising his head. "I've changed my mind after being apprised of your relationship with Senator Delgado."

Her gaze narrowed. "What relationship?" There was a tremor of annoyance in her voice when it lowered half an octave. The only relationship she shared with Christopher Blackwell Delgado was friendship.

Richard's head came up. "I need impartiality in this gubernatorial race, and I don't feel comfortable assigning you to cover the campaign of a man whom you know personally. It's a known fact that you and Delgado are godparents to his sister's son."

Emily gripped the arms of her chair as she leaned forward. "Are you questioning my professional ethics?"

"I'm not questioning anything," Richard retorted. A flush of bright pink color crept swiftly up his neck and face to his ill-fitting toupee. "I've made my decision." Steepling his fingers, he brought them to his mouth, a forefinger stroking the neatly barbered hair covering his upper lip. "You can accept the assignment, or…" His words trailed off.

She shifted an eyebrow. "Or what?"

He met her direct stare. "You can edit copy."

A sense of strength replaced her simmering anger. The egg-sucking dog wanted to punish her only because she hadn't been receptive to his advances. Perhaps if she didn't work directly for him, and if he considered removing the ratty nest doubling as a toupee she would have reconsidered and shared an occasional dinner or movie with him. He would simply join the other men she dated but refused to commit to. Richard claimed an angular face with even features, and had married and divorced thrice while earning a reputation as a brilliant television journalist.

However, she had no intention of becoming wife number four. There was only one man she wanted to marry—a man she had known all her life, a man who continued to treat her as if she were his younger sister.

She forced a smile, chilling him with the icy-cold glare shrouding her luminous eyes. If Richard Adams thought she was going to allow him to demote her because she did not like her assignment, then he did not know her competitive spirit. She had another year left on her contract, and the coming twelve months would give her the time she needed to assess whether she would remain with the network.

"Do I have the option of selecting my camera team?"

Richard's jaw went slack. He hadn't expected her to accept the reassignment without an exchange of dialogue. He did not know how he knew it, but after observing Emily Kirkland and State Senator Christopher Delgado together at a recent social gathering at the governor's mansion, he was certain he had detected a silent intimacy between the attractive young couple. He needed objective views from his correspondents, and he felt Emily's oversight of her childhood friend's campaign would not yield the unbiased reporting KCNS expected from its reporters. He would grant her every wish except that she cover the Delgado campaign.

"Put your request in writing and I'll make certain you get your team," he confirmed.

She glanced at her watch. "Is there anything else, Mr. Adams?"

Richard flinched visibly, as he always did whenever she addressed him as "Mr. Adams" instead of "Richard." There had been an occasion when Emily had hinted that he was too old for her. He was only forty-two—hardly what he would think of as an old man or too old for a woman in her early thirties. A mask of hardness settled on to his features before he glanced away.

"No. Enjoy your vacation."

Rising to her feet, Emily resisted the urge to reach across the table and rip the offending hairpiece from her boss's head. If she had been younger and more reckless she would have done it without compunction, but her reputation as a professional news correspondent was much more important to her than humiliating Richard Adams. He knew she wanted to be assigned to cover Chris's campaign. She had been the likely choice because both she and the candidate were bilingual. She was the only political correspondent at KCNS who was fluent in Spanish.

What Richard did not know was that her lifelong association with her best friend's half brother would not compromise her standards even if she were to cover his election campaign. The fact that she had been in love with Christopher Blackwell Delgado for more than eighteen years would not eclipse her reporting the facts as she saw them.

"I'll see you in a month." The six words were barely audible as she turned and walked out of the opulent conference room, closing the door softly behind her.

Richard's head came up and he stared at the solid mahogany door. "Dammit!" The word exploded from between his teeth.

Emily walked into her office and read the telephone message on her desk. Sara Sterling-Lassiter had returned her call. Over the past two months she had promised her best friend that she would come to Las Cruces for a weekend visit yet had not found the time. Now that she had a month off she would be able to spend more than a weekend with her friend and sixteen-month-old godson. She planned to spend the first two weeks of her vacation in Ocho Rios, Jamaica, and the last two in Las Cruces, New Mexico.

She would leave the States that afternoon and return to KCNS on January 29. William Savoy would officially begin his campaign with a $2500-a-plate fundraising gala on February 4. An event she would now be expected to attend.

Reaching for the telephone, she buzzed an administrative assistant, dictated an intra-office memorandum giving the name of the person she wanted as her cameraman, then gave the efficient woman authorization to sign her name.

Opening a desk drawer, she gathered her handbag, turned off the desk lamp, retrieved a Pullman case she had left near the door, then walked out of her office. Three minutes later she stood in front of the modern office building where the offices of KCNS were housed, waiting for Keith Norris's arrival. She spied his Lamborghini as it eased to the curb like a silent, sleek black cat.

Keith Norris slipped from behind the wheel of the sports car, ignoring the curious stares of passersby. His admiring gaze was fixed on Emily Kirkland's smiling face. He had offered to drive her from Santa Fe to Albuquerque because he would not see her for four weeks—much too much time to be separated from a woman he had fallen in love with.

"Hello, beautiful," he crooned, lowering his head to brush his lips with hers.

"Hi," she whispered.

"Have you been waiting long?"

She shook her head. "No."

Taking her Pullman, he guided her to his car and helped her into the low-slung vehicle.

Several pedestrians stopped, staring and pointing at the couple. They had recognized Keith Norris, the National League's Most Valuable Player, and Emily Kirkland of KCNS-TV. The Colorado Rockies outfielder had graced the cover of most major sports and several men's fashion magazines during the past year. It was reported that the image of his sensually brooding face on the cover of *GQ* sold as many copies as the *Sports Illustrated* swimsuit issue. Individually and as a couple, he and Emily were acknowledged as one of *People* Magazine's "50 Most Beautiful."

Keith stored Emily's suitcase in the trunk, slipped into the driver's seat and shifted into gear. Smoothly, expertly, he maneuvered the powerful sports car into the flow of downtown Santa Fe's late-morning traffic. Emily closed her eyes and pressed her head against the headrest, her chest rising and falling gently. A mysterious smile curved his strong, masculine mouth when he took a surreptitious glance at her enchanting profile.

"How was your meeting?"

Emily inhaled, then let out her breath slowly. "Enlightening, to say the least."

"How?"

"Calvin Robinson will be lead anchor for the weekend segment, and I was reassigned to cover William Savoy's campaign." Her voice was soft, even.

Keith's head snapped around before he returned his attention to the road in front of him. "You're kidding me, aren't you?"

Her eyes opened and she stared through the windshield. "No, Keith, I'm not kidding."

He shook his head, totally confused. Emily had returned to Santa Fe after spending Christmas with her parents, grandparents and cousins in West Palm Beach, bubbling over with enthusiasm because she had expected to be named anchor for the network's weekend political desk.

"I'm sorry—"

"That's all right," she interrupted. What she did not want or need was his pity.

"It's not all right," Keith countered.

"And I said it is."

"But, Emily—"

"It's my career, Keith," she retorted angrily, "and it's my business."

He clamped his jaw tightly to keep from spewing acerbic words. Emily had her career, but what she failed to realize was that she had become his business from the moment he had fallen in love with her. And before she boarded the private jet that would fly her from Albuquerque to Kingston, Jamaica, he would demonstrate just how much he loved her.

Their exchange of dialogue ended, both content to listen to the music flowing from the speakers in the car during the hour-long drive, each lost in private musings.

In the past when Emily encountered disappointment or failure in her life she had sought her father and poured out her heart to him as he held her in his strong, comforting embrace. He had pampered and protected her, telling her that she could accomplish anything. Joshua Kirkland had only been half right. The position she coveted most was still beyond her grasp, and the man she had fallen in love with was also beyond her.

Keith spied the signs indicating the airport and slowed down to move into the lane that led to a terminal near a private airfield where a corporate Gulfstream jet sat on the tarmac, fueled and waiting for Emily Teresa Kirkland's arrival.

Parking in the short-term lot, Keith escorted Emily to the area of the airport where she would be cleared through customs. He smiled down at her, his penetrating gaze committing everything about her to memory.

"I'm going to miss you," he stated simply.

She peered up at him through her lashes. Keith Norris was the consummate sports superstar. It was rumored that he'd earned more in one year from endorsements than his pay for his five-year, multimillion-dollar contract. And there was no doubt that his engaging personality and good looks were bankable assets he would be able to exploit even after his baseball career ended.

He flashed a perfect smile, eliciting a smile from her. "Are you sure you don't want me to join you in Jamaica?"

"I'm sure, Keith. Thank you for dropping me off."

His golden-flecked brown eyes crinkled as he pulled her into the circle of his strong arms. "I want to give you a little something before you leave. It's a Kwanzaa gift."

Her eyebrows lifted, her gaze surveying his handsome face. Keith stood six-four, and his 208 pounds was evenly distributed over a perfectly sculpted physique of velvet, sable-brown flesh. He had already given her a pair of natural gray twelve-millimeter cultured pearl earrings from the South Seas for Christmas. The exquisite jewels were suspended from a graceful curve of brilliant diamonds. She had dated Keith Norris off and on for a year—more off than on, due to his baseball schedule.

Reaching into the breast pocket of his cashmere jacket, Keith withdrew a flawless emerald-cut diamond ring and slipped it on the third finger of her left hand. The large stone with its platinum setting shimmered against her golden-brown skin.

Stunned, Emily shook her head. "Oh, no."

He gripped her hand firmly as she attempted to wrest the ring from her slender finger. "You don't have to give me an answer now. I'll talk to you when you get back." She held on to the sleeve of his jacket, but he was too quick and too strong when he escaped her grasp.

"Keith Norris!" Her shout reverberated throughout the terminal.

A small group of passengers, several airport personnel and members of a flight crew stopped and stared at her. A rush of heat suffused her face as she stared after Keith's departing figure as he disappeared from sight. He had just proposed to her.

Biting down on her lower lip, she tried composing herself. Keith was willing to wait a month for her answer, but she would not change her mind. Her answer was and would continue to be a resounding *no.* Trancelike, she passed through customs, then made her way to the gate that led to the ColeDiz International Ltd. corporate jet. It had become a family mandate that anyone who claimed Cole or Kirkland blood was expected to use the corporate jet for air travel. The decree had gone into effect after Martin Cole's eldest daughter had been kidnapped.

Her father and uncle had transferred control of the family-owned conglomerate to the next generation of Coles but continued to attend monthly board meetings to provide indirect oversight of the many coffee plantations in Belize, Puerto Rico and Jamaica, as well as vacation properties throughout the Caribbean.

The copilot took her luggage and assisted her into the luxurious aircraft, waiting until she was seated and belted in before he returned to the cockpit. Fifteen minutes later the jet taxied down the runway in preparation for liftoff. Emily sat motionless, staring at the brilliant stone on her left hand. It was only after the plane was airborne that she twisted the ring off her finger and dropped it into the cavernous depths of her handbag.

Chapter 3

December 28
Las Cruces, New Mexico

Christopher Delgado sat on his favorite chair in the family room in his parents' ranch house, watching a Christmas movie he had seen at least a dozen times. He would've gone to bed soon after his parents had bid him good-night, but he chose to stay up to catch the late edition of the nightly news.

He had celebrated his thirty-fifth birthday on Christmas Day with his mother, stepfather, sister, brother-in-law, nephew, long-time Sterling Farms resident employees, horse trainer Joseph Russell and housekeeper Marisa Hall.

There had been the usual exchange of gifts, but this year's celebration had become more momentous. Matthew Sterling had raised his glass of champagne, his brilliant gold-green gaze shimmering with unabashed pride when he toasted his stepson as the next governor of New Mexico. Everyone had followed suit, raising their glasses—everyone except his mother, Eve Blackwell-Sterling. She had verbalized her apprehension when he had announced his candidacy for state senator two years earlier, because she'd feared the secrets she and Matthew Sterling had put to rest regarding Chris's biological father would surface during her son's campaign against William Savoy. Her fears were temporarily allayed when the name of Alejandro Delgado-Quintero was never mentioned.

Chris did not attempt to belie his mother's consternation, because Eve had stubbornly refused to discuss it with him. She had voiced her opinion, and nothing he could say would make her change her mind.

The telephone rang, and he reached over and picked up the cordless instrument. "Hello?"

"This is Grant."

Chris sat up straighter. Why was his fraternity brother and campaign manager calling him at his parents' home?

"What's up, Grant?"

"A source told me that Savoy uncovered some information about your father."

Vertical lines appeared between Chris's black eyes. "Matthew Sterling?"

"I said *father,* not stepfather." Grant had stressed the word.

Chris inhaled, unable to move or breathe. "Who's the source?" he asked when he finally let out his breath. He hadn't realized how fast his heart was beating when the name Alejandro Delgado-Quintero—the man who had been responsible for giving him life—whispered in his head.

"I can't reveal my source."

His fingers tightened on the telephone. "Do I have to remind you that you work for me, Grant?"

There was a prolonged pause before Grant said, "No. But I do know that I don't have to reveal my source. You're going to have to trust me with this, Chris. He's reliable, and I promised him that I would never compromise his anonymity."

Closing his eyes, he ran his free hand over his graying hair. "I suppose I don't have a choice with this one. You know I don't want a campaign run on smut and lies."

Grant Carsons had run a squeaky clean campaign for him in his state senatorial bid, but had verbalized his doubts whether it would be the same in the gubernatorial race.

"What did your source tell you about my father?" he continued, not recognizing his own voice. It sounded old—tired.

"He's returned to Mexico," Grant said softly, "to die. The Mexican authorities received his request to return home six months ago and finally granted it last week."

Chris opened his eyes. The movie had ended and the familiar image of a news anchor appeared on the screen. "Where is he?" The three words came out flat, emotionless.

"He was permitted to return to his family's estate in Puerto Escondido."

There was a pregnant pause—a full sixty seconds—before Chris spoke again. "Thanks for the information."

"What do you want me to do?" Grant asked.

"Nothing right now. I'll handle it."

There was another pause. "How?"

"I have to decide whether I'm going to see him."

"When do you think you'll know?"

"Probably next week."

"Whatever you decide to do, just be ready for the kickoff fundraiser on February seventeenth."

An expression of implacable determination crossed Chris's face. "I'll be ready. Thanks, buddy."

"Thank me when you're governor. Good night."

"Good night, Grant." The call was over. His no-nonsense campaign manager had hung up. Pressing a button, Chris replaced the instrument on the table.

He sat motionless, staring at the television screen. He could not believe that his life was suddenly spinning out of control.

The moment Chris had announced his decision to seek the office of governor of New Mexico he'd known he had embarked on an odyssey that would permit the residents of the state to dissect every infinitesimal fact of his past.

Representing an election district as state senator would be far different from assuming the responsibility of handling the affairs of an entire state. He had won his senatorial seat in a hard-fought campaign and a hotly contested election when he'd opposed William Savoy. Savoy, still smarting at his loss to a virtual unknown who had had no prior political experience, reluctantly conceded, then promised that the next time they faced off it would be very different from their initial encounter.

Christopher Blackwell Delgado and William Alan Savoy had been given two years to plan strategies for the gubernatorial race, and the time had provided the incumbent governor's son the opportunity to delve deeply into his opponent's past to unearth a scandal that had besmirched the Delgado name.

The professional investigators hired by Savoy had deliberately leaked the news that terminally ill Alejandro Delgado-Quintero, who had fled Mexico thirty-two years earlier to live in an undisclosed South American country after informing on several corrupt Mexican officials, had returned to the country of his birth—to die.

Chris knew Savoy was waiting for him to begin his campaign tour; then everyone in New Mexico would become privy to a family secret Matthew Sterling de Arroyo and Eve Blackwell-Sterling had buried more than three decades ago.

He did not remember the man whose genes and surname he shared, because Matthew Sterling had become the only father he knew, loved and respected. Now his mother's worst fear after he'd decided on a political career was about to be realized: her life with Alejandro Delgado would be played out before the residents of New Mexico and the entire United States.

How had she known? What special powers did his mother possess to see into the future? *The ghost of Alejandro Delgado will rise up and destroy you.*

Her premonition echoed in his ears, drowning out the sound of the sportscaster's voice recapping the day's sporting events. The images of Keith Norris and Emily Kirkland flashed across the screen, superimposed with a logo of interlocking wedding bands. Chris sat dazed, his heart pumping painfully in his chest. He felt as if someone had slammed a hammer into his chest, had pierced his heart with a dagger, leaving him to hemorrhage unchecked.

"No!" he whispered aloud. "She can't." How many more shocks would he be faced with before the year ended and a new one began?

He could not believe Emily was going to marry Keith Norris. He had had dinner with her at her Santa Fe home the day before she left to celebrate Christmas in Florida, and she had said she wasn't going to marry the ballplayer. He had left her home before midnight, kissing her gently on her lips, with the promise that they would see each other in the new year.

The phone on the side table chimed again, and he reached over and picked up the receiver before it rang a second time.

"Hello."

"Chris!" The sound of Sara Sterling-Lassiter's strident voice brought him out of his paralyzing stupor. His sister had married their parents' neighbor, and within her first year of marriage had made Matthew and Eve Sterling grandparents for the first time.

"Sara? What's the matter?"

"Did you see it, Chris? Turn the television on to Channel—"

"I'm watching it," he countered, interrupting her, knowing what she was referring to.

"When? When did Emmie decide to do this?"

"You didn't know?"

"Of course I didn't know. When I spoke to her this morning, she never mentioned that she was getting married."

"Where is she now?"

"She's in Ocho Rios at her parents' vacation home. She's going to be there for two weeks, then she's coming here."

Closing his eyes, Chris whispered, "Is she alone?"

"Of course she's alone!" Sara snapped. "You're going to lose her, Chris," his sister warned, this time in a softer tone.

It wasn't the first time Sara had warned him about Emily Kirkland. He had known Emily all his life and had always treated her like a sister. But with each passing year it had become more difficult for him to think of her or interact with her as if she were family. And he wasn't even certain when he realized his feelings for her had changed.

But what Sara failed to understand was that he couldn't lose Emily because he had never had her. Whenever she dated she usually saw several men at the same time, refusing to commit to any of them. Most seemed content to wait until she was able to fit them into her busy schedule—all except the Colorado Rockies persistent outfielder.

"What are you going to do, bro?"

A frown appeared between his dramatic black eyes. "What am I supposed to do?"

"Go after her."

In a moment of weakness, Chris had confessed to his sister that he was in love with Emily—had been in love with her for a long time. He saw other women, slept with a few of them, but not once had he ever permitted any of them to see the real Christopher Delgado.

He'd tried discerning what had drawn him to Emily, aside from the fact that their parents were lifelong friends, and it was only recently that he had concluded that she was his female counterpart. They were more alike than dissimilar: organized, goal-oriented and very ambitious. While he was compassionate, generous, loyal and dependable, he was also controlling and a workaholic. And so was Emily Kirkland.

"I'm going to tell you something I promised Emily I would never tell you," Sara continued in a hushed whisper.

"What is it, Sara?"

"She's in love with you."

There was a pregnant pause before Chris was able to respond. "She can't be."

"Why not?"

"She sees other men."

"You *sleep* with other women."

"Careful, Sara!" The lethal warning in his voice was like the crack of a whip.

"Shut up, Christopher Delgado, and listen to me," Sara ordered. "After I hang up I want you to call the airport and reserve a flight to Jamaica. Then rent a car—anyone in Ocho Rios will be able to direct you to the house and property the locals call Sunderland. Be a man, Chris. Get up off your ass and go after her, because I don't want to see you or speak to you again until you've settled your business with Emily Kirkland. Goodbye, brother."

He sat there, listening to the drone of the dial tone in his ear. His sister had hung up on him. A slow smile eased the lines of tension ringing his generous mouth as he depressed the button on the telephone, then dialed information for the number of any carrier that flew to Jamaica. Sara's revelation that Emily was in love with him was even more shocking than Grant's or the sportscaster's announcement.

It was an hour later—after he had reserved a red-eye flight from the Las Cruces International Airport to Miami, with a connecting one to Kingston—that he remembered his younger sister's unwarranted reference to his masculinity. He would settle with her—after he returned from Ocho Rios.

He made his way out of the family room and into Matt Sterling's office. He scribbled a note to his parents, explaining that he was going to Ocho Rios. What he did not write was that he was going to try to convince a woman he had fallen in love with not to marry another man. He taped the sheet of paper to the telephone receiver, then retreated to the bedroom he'd occupied when growing up to shower and shave. A car service was expected to arrive at Sterling Farms within three-quarters of an hour to take him to the airport. He was ready—ready to challenge William Savoy again, ready to reunite with Alejandro Delgado and ready to bare his soul to Emily Kirkland.

Chapter 4

Emily swam out into the clear blue-green waters of the Caribbean, glorying in its warmth and the healing rays of the tropical sun on her back and shoulders. It was only her second day in Ocho Rios, and when she arose that morning to the scent of lush fruit and tropical flowers drifting in through the open windows she could not believe it had been seven years since she had taken advantage of her family's Caribbean retreat. The last time she had come to the house was the spring her parents renewed their marriage vows for their twenty-fifth wedding anniversary.

Her former career army officer father had taken over as CEO of ColeDiz International Ltd. after his younger brother, David Cole, resigned to set up his own recording company. Joshua and his older half brother, Martin Cole, who had assumed the responsibility as Chief Operating Officer of ColeDiz, diversified and expanded the empire their father, Samuel Cole, had set up more than a half century earlier. Earlier in the year, Joshua and Martin, at sixty-eight and seventy-four respectively, had successfully turned the day-to-day operation of ColeDiz over to their sisters' sons, who had inherited the business acumen of their elderly grandfather, Samuel Claridge Cole.

Emily's brother Michael had followed in his father's footsteps when he attended and graduated from the U.S. Military Academy at West Point, then joined the same branch of the army from which their father had retired as colonel and former Associate Coordinating Chief of the Defense Intelligence Agency. Michael had also inherited his father's proficiency with languages. He had mastered Spanish, French, Italian, Portuguese, German, Arabic and Japanese.

Her certified public accountant mother had left the world of finance for motherhood but continued to manage her husband's investments. After a number of extraordinary ventures resulted in phenomenal windfall profits, Vanessa Blanchard-Kirkland had become the ColeDiz investment guru.

Turning over on her back, Emily closed her eyes and floated with the gentle rise and fall of the tide. Her semiretired parents had elected not to return to Santa Fe with her. They claimed they wanted to take advantage of the warmer Florida temperatures, but Emily suspected her father hadn't wanted to leave Samuel Cole. At one hundred and three, the Cole patriarch barely clung to life as he drifted in and out of lucidity. When he was rational he demanded his illegitimate son's presence. Joshua usually spent hours at Samuel's bedside, reassuring him that he loved him and would remain with him until he drew his last breath.

She got to see the members of her extended New Mexico family on a regular basis—her mother's sister, Connie, her husband, Roger, and their two sons, both of whom were married and had started their own families. However, whenever she traveled across the country to visit with her Florida relatives it was usually for a festive occasion. Her cousin, Regina Cole-Spencer, had invited her to come to Bahia to spend time with her, her husband, Aaron, and their son and daughter, Clay and Eden. Emily had never been to Brazil, and even though she had found the offer very tempting, she had not found the time to accept their invitation.

Kicking her feet gently, she floated toward the shore until she found herself in shallow water, then stood and walked back to the beach. Sitting down on a large towel, she leaned over and brushed the minute particles of white sand off her damp feet. A gentle northerly breeze ruffled the fronds from a nearby palm tree and the distinctive fragrance of bougainvillea hung in the warm air. Droplets of water dotted her brown shoulders and raven-black hair. Smiling, she picked up a pair of sunglasses, perched them on the bridge of her nose, then lay down on her belly to sleep.

Chris thanked the young man who told him that he was only a few kilometers from Sunderland. He had been traveling for fourteen hours and had managed only two hours of sleep during that time. He had boarded a jet in Las Cruces at 2:20 a.m. Mountain Time for a nonstop flight to Miami International. However, the four-hour layover in Miami turned into six, and when the Air Jamaica jet touched down in Kingston all he craved was a shower and a bed. It wasn't until he slipped behind the wheel of the rental car and headed west through the historic community of Spanish Town that he realized the intense fatigue was due to his body's circadian rhythm's inability to adjust to the different time zone.

The verdant beauty of the island overwhelmed him: the mountain ranges, waterfalls and beautiful beaches with pristine white sand and clear turquoise waters. One winter his parents and sister had joined the Kirklands in Ocho Rios during a school recess; however, he had opted to go to Switzerland with his high school ski team.

He'd learned to ski at six, and the first time he strapped on a pairs of skis it became an obsession. By the time he was sixteen he was ranked an expert and his coach urged his parents to let him try out for the U.S. Olympic Ski Team. However, his passion for the sport waned once he entered college. Law and politics replaced skiing, dismissing a recreational sport in favor of a competitive one.

It had been more than two years since he'd been skiing. An accident had left him with a dislocated shoulder and broken leg. Now his workout regimen consisted of lifting weights and exercising on a treadmill and rowing machine within the boundaries of a gym set up in his Santa Fe loft apartment.

A wry smile curved Chris's mouth. Even though he and Sara had grown up on a horse farm in desertlike Las Cruces, while Emily and her brother Michael had grown up less than an hour from the Taos Ski Valley, their recreational interests were as different as their personalities. Sara loved riding horses, Emily preferred swimming, Michael riflery, while he favored skiing. The offspring of Matthew and Eve Sterling and Joshua and Vanessa Kirkland had grown up secure and protected, which afforded the four of them a quiet assurance years before they entered adulthood.

He slowed the rental car, coming to a fork in the road, then turned left. Less than a quarter of a mile later he saw the house. It was a two-storied white stucco structure that was completely West Indian in character: red-tiled Spanish roof, white-tiled floors surrounding the house and Creole jalousie shutters. Exotic flowers and trees added to the lushness of the property. He maneuvered the rental car around to the back of the house, parking next to a late-model Mustang convertible.

All vestiges of exhaustion vanished as Chris slowly pushed open the driver's-side door and stepped out onto a sand-littered path. *She's in love with you.* Sara's revelation sang in his head, in his heart and in his veins.

How had she fooled him? How had he missed the signs—or had Emily become such an accomplished actress that she was able to successfully hide her innermost emotions? Had he felt so comfortable with her that he saw only what he wanted to see?

The questions continued to taunt him as he walked around to the front of the house and peered through a screen door. An entryway opened out to a parlor decorated with furnishings from a bygone era. Reaching out, he grasped a length of rope attached to a brass bell and pulled it. The melodious sound echoed in the sultry stillness of the afternoon. He waited, then pulled it again.

When there was no sign of Emily, Chris strolled around the gallery to the back of the house. Branches of fruit trees, pregnant with their heavy yield, swayed gently. Squinting through the lenses of his sunglasses, he noted that there wasn't another structure in sight as a stretch of white sand and the blue-green ribbon of the Caribbean in the distance served as the backdrop for the exotic setting. The sight of the ocean and the beach beckoned him, and he headed in that direction.

The heat of the sun burned his flesh through the linen fabric of his shirt, but as he neared the ocean the gentle breezes cooled his fevered body. A copse of palm trees acted as a barrier between the beach and the lush vegetation surrounding the large house, and as soon as he stepped out onto the beach he saw her.

Clad in a black one-piece swimsuit, Emily lay facedown on a colorful towel, her head cradled on folded arms, her eyes shielded from the sun by a pair of sunglasses—asleep.

Slowly moving closer, Chris surveyed the length of her long, shapely legs and incredibly narrow feet. The hot tropical sun had darkened her exposed flesh to a rich chestnut brown. There was a tightening in his groin as his gaze moved slowly and intimately over her body. The rush of heaviness surprised him; it was the first time he had permitted himself to feel the passion for her that he had consciously repressed all his life. He stared at her, gorging on her exotic beauty.

She belonged here—among the flowers and fruit growing in wild abandonment—because she was as fragile and enchanting as a delicate orchid. He wanted to lie beside her and inhale the feminine scent that was exclusively Emily Kirkland's. He wanted to trail his fingertips over her velvety skin, committing every dip and curve to memory; he wanted to lose himself in the depths of her mysterious green eyes when he fused his body with hers—making them one for all time.

Retreating slightly, he walked over to a palm tree, sat down and waited for her to wake up.

The sun had passed overhead when Emily stirred and woke up. Blinking slowly, she removed her sunglasses and rolled over on her side. A soft gasp escaped her when she saw the familiar figure of Christopher Delgado sitting under a palm tree, his back pressed against the solid trunk.

Her heart was pounding so loudly that it became a roar in her ears. Her legs were shaking as she stood, her gaze widening when she saw Chris push to his feet and close the distance between them within seconds. He stood less than three feet away, his dark gaze capturing hers and making her his unwilling prisoner.

He stared at her with a strange expression that made her aware that even though she had known him all her life, she really did not know him at all. He was dressed for the tropical weather: a banded-collar white linen shirt, tan linen slacks and a pair of brown woven leather loafers.

"What's wrong, Chris?" Closing her eyes, she swallowed back the arid taste of fear rising in her throat. Emily did not recognize her own voice. When she opened her eyes they were brimming with unshed tears. "Why are you here? How did you know where to find me?" She hadn't told him that she would be vacationing in Ocho Rios.

He gave her a half smile, his gaze shifting from her feathery, curly hair down to the soft swell of golden-brown breasts rising and falling heavily above the bodice of her black maillot suit.

Extending his arms, he tilted his head at an angle. "Nothing's wrong, Emily. Is this the kind of welcome I get the first time I come to Jamaica?"

She felt weak with relief as her fear subsided, replaced by anger. Placing a hand over her heart, she glared at him. "What the hell is wrong with you? You show up here unexpected and all I could think of was that someone had…" Her words trailed off. Chris's unexpected arrival had caught her off guard. There was one thing Emily never wanted to be, and that was not in control of herself or her environment.

Chris pushed his hands into the pockets of his slacks, successfully concealing his uneasiness. "Which question do you want me to answer first?"

"All of them," she shouted at him.

"Sara told me where to find you, and I came to congratulate you."

"On what?"

"Your engagement."

Closing her eyes, she swayed slightly, then righted herself as Chris took a step forward. She held up a slender hand, stopping him. "What did you say?"

"There was a televised announcement on the late edition of

yesterday's news that you and Keith Norris are engaged to be married."

Her delicate jaw dropped, her expression was one of disbelief. "You're kidding, aren't you?"

"No, I'm not. Are you or are you not engaged to Keith Norris?"

"Of course not."

"Did he give you a ring?"

"Yes, he gave me a ring."

"Then you're engaged."

Emily ran her fingers through her hair. "I am not engaged. Keith drove me to the airport, and before I went through Customs he slipped a ring on my finger."

"You didn't give the ring back to him?"

"No. It all happened too quickly." Her brow creased in worry. "He'd given me no clue that he was going to propose."

Moving closer, Chris rested his hands on her bared shoulders. "I suppose the poor man was desperate."

"I can understand desperation, but not deception."

Lowering his gaze, Chris studied her moist face. The sun had darkened her skin. It had also brought out a spray of freckles across the bridge of her nose. Her eyes glowed like precious jewels in a bare face that radiated good health and a fragile beauty that sucked the breath from his lungs.

"What are you going to do?" he asked in a quiet voice.

She frowned. "I'm certainly not going to marry Keith."

He mumbled a silent prayer of thanks. "What are you going to do about his leaking the news to the press that he's engaged to you?"

"Nothing until I return to the States. Then I'm going to give him his ring and suggest he issue a statement that the engagement is off. If anyone asks me about it, my response will be no comment."

She smiled for the first time and kissed his cheek. The emerging stubble on his jaw grazed her delicate lips. "I can't believe you came all this way because you believed I was engaged to marry another man."

"That's not the only reason I'm here."

Emily shivered in spite of the heat. Chris's face was expressionless, and a part of her wondered when he had changed into someone she recognized but did not know.

"What's the other reason?"

"My father."

She gave him a questioning look. "Uncle Matt?" She and Michael had grown up calling Matt and Eve Sterling Uncle Matt and Aunt Eve, and Chris and Sara referred to her parents as Uncle Josh and Aunt Vanessa.

Chris shook his head slowly. "My biological father, Alejandro Delgado."

Her eyelids fluttered rapidly. "I thought he was dead." She had heard the elder Sterlings whisper the name of Alejandro Delgado on occasion, but it was Eve Sterling who had stated vehemently that her first husband and the father of her son had died a long time ago. It was apparent that she had only symbolically buried him when she divorced him.

Cradling her face between his palms, Chris stared directly at her. "No, Emily, he's not dead. He's alive, but he's dying."

"Where is he?" she whispered, even though they were the only two people standing on the private beach.

"He's returned to Mexico."

Vertical lines appeared between Emily's eyes, her perceptive gaze noticing the fatigue ringing his generous mouth. There were tiny lines around Chris's eyes that should not have been apparent in a man his age. It was as if he had spent too many hours squinting into the sun. She saw all of the signs of his visible stress but felt something in the man she had fallen in love with that she had never felt before—vulnerability.

He was State Senator Christopher Delgado, stepson of an eminent New Mexico horse breeder. He had graduated from law school in the top one percent of his class before clerking for a state supreme court justice. It was at the urging of that judge that he had considered a career in politics. He had become the perfect candidate because he had it all: looks, intelligence, money and charisma. He had it all, yet he was hurting.

"We'll go back to the house," she said. "After you've gotten some rest we'll talk."

Chris shook his head. "No. I need to talk now."

"You need sleep. We'll talk later." There was a hint of steel in her voice.

"You're a hard woman, Emily Kirkland."

She flashed a saucy smile. "You didn't know? I once had a man refer to me as 'that pit bull bitch in a skirt.'" Reaching up, she curved her fingers around his wrists, pulling his hands from her face and looping her arm through his. "How long do you intend to hang out with me?"

He gave her a sidelong glance. "A couple of days."

"You can't stay a couple of days."

"Why not?"

"That's hardly enough time for me to show you Ocho Rios."

He shrugged a broad shoulder. "Okay—a week."

"You're a hard man, Christopher Delgado."

He laughed for the first time in more than fourteen hours. "What am I? A rottweiler in a jock strap?"

Emily gave him the dazzling smile he had come to look for from her. He waited until she picked up the towel and her sunglasses, then followed her back to the house where he would stay during his unplanned vacation in Jamaica.

Chapter 5

Chris opened the shuttered windows in the bedroom and stepped out onto the second-story veranda. The panorama unfolding before his stunned gaze was awe-inspiring. He had an unobstructed view of the beach and the ocean. The house was perfect, his bedroom perfect, and the woman with whom he would share the Caribbean retreat was perfect.

He had selected the first bedroom at the top of the narrow, winding staircase, and when he walked into the sparsely furnished space he felt as if he had stepped back in time. The expansive room claimed an antique mahogany four-poster bed draped in a sheer creamy white fabric. A massive matching mahogany armoire, a rocker with plump cushions embroidered with primitive African masks in earth tones of beige, brown and ocher, and two chairs with chintz-covered seats pulled up under a pedestal table covered with a linen tablecloth had beckoned him when Emily opened the wood-carved door.

Turning, he walked back into the bedroom and closed the shutters to keep out the heat. He flipped a switch on the wall and the ceiling fan turned slowly as it worked to dispel the buildup of tropical air.

He opened his carry-on bag, withdrew a toiletry kit and made his way to the bathroom. A weighted fatigue swept over him and he wondered if he could remain awake long enough to shave and shower.

Emily showered, lingering under the spray of warm water and rinsing the salt and sand out of her short hair. She stepped out of the shower stall and blotted the moisture from her body before she covered her arms and legs with a scented moisturizer.

Frowning, she noticed she had chipped a particle of deep rose-pink color off the big toe of her right foot, and made a mental note to give herself both a manicure and a pedicure. Her beauty regimen consisted of weekly manicures, biweekly pedicures, monthly facials, massages and haircuts.

From the first time she appeared in front of the television camera, her physical appearance had become as vital to her as the gathering and dissemination of political information she offered her viewing audience. Some of her colleagues felt she had become obsessive about her looks, but she ignored them because the network's ratings usually escalated whenever she filled in for the regular anchor.

Squeezing a small amount of mousse onto her hand, she rubbed her palms together before massaging it into her damp hair. Then she brushed the raven-black strands off her forehead and over her ears. Streams of sunlight pouring into the bathroom glinted off the diamonds in her pierced lobes. She had screwed the rare yellow stones her parents had given her in her pierced lobes the day she celebrated her eighteenth birthday and had never removed them.

Ten minutes later she left her bedroom, dressed in a pair of loose-fitting white cotton slacks and matching tank top, her feet pushed into a pair of colorful striped espadrilles, and headed for the kitchen.

She hummed to herself as she mixed a pitcher of lemon verbena iced tea, then prepared a Mediterranean salad platter of thinly sliced zucchini, red pepper, tomato, Spanish onion, feta cheese, capers, black Kalamata and green olives tossed with a light, fragrant olive-oil-and-balsamic dressing. Covering the colorful concoction with plastic, she placed it in the refrigerator next to a bowl filled with clean, chilled shrimp. She would wait for Chris to wake up, then share the light repast with him.

She filled a tall glass with the tea, walked out of the kitchen, and made her way to the rear of the house and to the gazebo containing an oversized hammock. The paperback romance novel she'd begun reading during the flight from Albuquerque to Kingston lay on a low rattan table. She picked it up, settled herself on the hammock, then quickly lost herself in the lives of the characters her favorite novelist had created.

Night had fallen over the island, and Emily turned on the light above a massive, scarred mahogany table in the large kitchen, adding more light to the expansive space. All of the rooms in the house had remained virtually untouched, with the exception of the addition of electricity and indoor plumbing. The kitchen and the parlor were her favorite rooms in the early-nineteenth-century structure. She'd realized, after swimming in the ocean and sunbathing on the beach, away from the curious gazes of the nearest neighbor, who lived more than a mile away, why her father had purchased the house and surrounding property, and why he and her mother visited Ocho Rios several times a year. After only two days she'd found herself succumbing to its healing and restorative powers.

However, her cloistered existence was disturbed by the man sleeping in one of the bedrooms on the second level. She had come to the Ocho Rios retreat to be alone, to discover the real Emily Kirkland. Like Alice in Lewis Carroll's *Through the Looking-Glass,* she wanted to escape to a world of make-believe. A world where there were no Keith Norrises, Richard Adamses and most of all no Christopher Delgados—men who affected her, touched her life, men who, each in their own way, had transformed her into someone she did not want to become.

Keith had lied about being engaged to her. Richard continued to pursue her and, because she was not receptive to his advances, had subtly manipulated her professional career. And Christopher Delgado—the man she loved with all her heart. A man who refused to acknowledge that she had grown up, that she was a woman—a woman who had and continued to repress her sexuality because she had chosen instead to live in a fairy-tale world. Because at thirty she still believed that princes married princesses and made them their queens.

A wry smile tilted the corners of her mouth when she realized that this was the first time Chris had come to her with a problem. In the past it had always been the reverse.

Sprinkling a light coating of flour over a smooth wooden cutting board, she turned out a mixture of yeast-filled dough. She was so totally absorbed in kneading the dough that she neither heard nor saw the man standing under the arched entrance, watching her. It wasn't until she had placed the dough in a large bowl and covered it with a moist cotton towel that she registered movement behind her.

"Can I help with anything?"

Spinning around, she saw Chris leaning in the doorway, muscular hair-covered brown arms folded over his chest. He was casually dressed in a pair of black cotton slacks with a drawstring waist and a matching tank top. Her gaze widened as she surveyed his broad shoulders and bare feet.

"No, thank you. How was your siesta?"

He smiled, not moving. "Wonderful. It's amazing what a little nap can do."

Emily turned back to the table. "A little nap? You were asleep for five hours."

Pushing himself off the wall, Chris made his way into the kitchen. "I forced myself to get out of bed, otherwise I'd wind up prowling the house half the night."

She glanced at him over her shoulder, noticing the moisture clinging to the strands of his salt-and-pepper black hair. He had begun graying prematurely at the age of twenty-eight and probably would be completely gray by the time he turned forty.

"Are you hungry?"

Taking two long strides, Chris pressed his chest to her back, trapping her between his body and the table. "Starved."

Swallowing to relieve the sudden dryness in her throat, Emily closed her eyes. "We'll eat out."

Chris's hands went to her bare shoulders, gently turning her around to face him. Her eyes opened, her gaze widening and fusing with his. The sensual scent of her perfumed flesh wafted in his nostrils and he curbed the urge to lower his head and kiss her lush mouth. Not the chaste kisses they usually shared, but ones that would denote the passion he had successfully concealed from her for years.

His thumb grazed her left cheekbone. "You have flour on your face," he explained in a quiet voice.

She gave him a bright smile. "Thank you."

Seeing her smile reminded him of Vanessa Kirkland. Like her mother's, Emily's expression was usually solemn, closed, until she smiled. The gesture lit up her face and fired her mesmerizing green eyes. She was undeniably Vanessa's daughter, with the exception of her eyes. The green orbs were Joshua Kirkland's. Only his were lighter, colder, nearly transparent, while hers were dark, warm and less intimidating.

"What time do you want to go out?"

Emily glanced around his shoulder at a clock on a shelf of a massive built-in pine cupboard. "Can you be ready in half an hour?" It was apparent he had already showered.

"Yes," he whispered, leaning down to kiss her cheek. "I'll see you later."

She watched Chris walk out of the kitchen, and suddenly she was able to breathe normally. Staring at the space where he'd been made her aware that she had made a mistake in asking him to stay. Even though he would occupy a second-floor bedroom, the fact remained that they were together—isolated—for the first time in their lives. For one week they would reside under the same roof in a remote section of Ocho Rios. Whispering a silent prayer, she cleaned up the kitchen before she retreated to her bedroom to prepare to share dinner with her houseguest.

Chris sat on a deep-cushioned armchair in the parlor, staring at the soft light shining through the delicate Waterford crystal base of a lamp on a nearby table. Crossing one leg gracefully over the opposite knee, his gaze shifted to the golden light from the lamp spilling over the toe of his Italian-made loafer.

A gentle peace feathered through his mind and body, easing some of the anxiety he'd felt before boarding his flight in Las Cruces. He'd been hard-pressed not to exhibit his relief once Emily revealed she was not going to marry Keith Norris, although the predicament surrounding Alejandro Delgado's return to Mexico still had to be resolved.

His serene expression changed and a muscle in his lean jaw quivered noticeably when he silently cursed William Savoy. The man had challenged him for a senate seat—and lost. Two years later Savoy was back, challenging him for the highest elected office in the state of New Mexico. Their first campaign had been virtually free of scandal and personal attacks, but all of that would change because the man would not accept losing to Christopher Blackwell Delgado for a second time.

But Emily Kirkland was not about political ideology or a thirst for power. She differed from William Savoy and the life of politics he'd embraced because she represented a bright light and love—a love of a lifetime.

The subject of his musings walked into the parlor, the haunting scent of lilies trailing in her wake. Chris uncrossed his legs and rose to his feet, his gaze scanning her critically and beaming his approval. A lazy smile crinkled his eyes and he inclined his head, as if bowing to a person of royal rank.

"You look incredible," he crooned.

The deep rose color on her lush mouth was the perfect match for slashes of pink crisscrossing the delicate silk fabric of a lime-green wrap skirt she had paired with a matching green silk shell and slip. The airy garment floated around her long legs, ending at mid-calf. Her footwear was a pair of high-heeled mules in a shocking pink fabric.

She offered him a dazzling smile as she admired his light-weight taupe suit, white shirt and dark brown tie. "Thank you."

Chris forced himself to move. Trancelike, he closed the space between them, his dark gaze studying her intently. He wanted to take her into his arms and make her feel what he was feeling, had been feeling for years. He'd repressed his love for her for so long that he had begun responding to her like an automaton. He'd kissed her mouth without the passion he knew he was capable of offering. Any other woman he had ever become involved with had been a meaningless substitute for the woman standing before him; he was finally able to acknowledge that Emily Kirkland appealed to his maleness in a way no woman had ever been able to do.

His protective instincts had surfaced so quickly that it left him reeling. The awesome need to make certain she was safe— at any cost—frightened Chris more than it surprised him; he knew he would forfeit everything he possessed to protect her from danger—seen and unseen.

Emily felt a slow warmth spread over her face, down to her throat, chest and even lower to a pulsing spot between her thighs. Chris had complimented her many, many times, but there was something different about him now—different in the way he looked at her.

Reaching for her hand, he held it gently within his large, protective grasp. "Where are we going?"

"Not far," she said mysteriously.

Chris smiled, the gesture as intimate as a kiss. "Good."

He had assuaged some of his exhaustion with more than five hours of uninterrupted sleep, but a gnawing hunger had reminded him that he needed to eat. He detested airline cuisine and had only drunk a cup of coffee on each of the carriers.

They walked out of the house and into the warm, sultry Jamaican night. A sprinkling of stars littered the navy-blue nighttime sky. A hint of a full moon illuminated the tropical landscape. The cloying smell of damp earth, salt water, vegetation and perfumed flowers hung in the air, an olfactory feast.

Sand grated under the leather soles of Chris's shoes as he preceded Emily, opened the driver's-side door to the racy white Mustang convertible, waited for her to slip behind the wheel, then circled the automobile and sat beside her. She turned on the ignition, shifted into gear, and within minutes they left the house, beach and ocean behind.

Chapter 6

Emily downshifted, slowly maneuvering into a parking space in a large clearing where more than a dozen bungalows painted in tropical pastel pinks, yellows and blues stood under a copse of towering palm trees. Each structure claimed white-shuttered windows and a red-tiled roof.

Chris stared at the colorful buildings, nodding his approval. "Very nice," he said in a quiet voice.

Emily stared at his strong profile, a knowing smile curving her lush mouth. "The restaurant is near the beach." She turned off the engine and dropped the key into her small crocheted shoulder bag.

She waited for Chris to help her out of the car; then, hand in hand, they walked along a slate path through what looked like a small village. Strategically placed streetlamps that resembled late-nineteenth-century gaslights cast a golden glow throughout the impeccably maintained property.

The distinctive sound of steel pans playing an upbeat tune drifted from the open windows of a large lime-green stucco building. Chris caught himself nodding his head in time to the driving, pulsing island rhythm.

Pulling his hand out of Emily's silken grasp, he leaned in close to her ear. With her heels, her towering height came very close to his own. "Is dancing allowed?"

"Yes."

"If that's the case, then will you save me a dance tonight, Miss Kirkland?"

Turning her head, she stared at him. "Yes."

He returned her direct gaze, unable to look away. And it wasn't for the first time that Chris acknowledged that Emily

Kirkland had a wonderful voice. It was low-pitched but soft, and as warm as the cashmere sweaters she favored during the winter months.

A white-jacketed waiter met them when they stepped into the waiting area. A middle-aged man inclined his head, offering an open, friendly smile. His eyebrows shifted slightly as his smile widened. He'd recognized the young woman he had not seen in years.

"It's good seeing you again, Miss Kirkland. How long has it been?"

"Seven years." She looped her arm over the sleeve of Chris's jacket and smiled at the restaurant's manager. "Mr. Alton, I would like you to meet my guest, Christopher Delgado. Chris, Lindsay Alton."

The two men shook hands, exchanging pleasantries before the older man signaled a passing waiter to show them to their table.

Chris was totally charmed by his surroundings. The restaurant's interior was much larger than it appeared from the outside. There were dozens of tables, all of them crowded, a bar, an area set aside for dancing and an elevated stage where a sextet played a rocking rendition of a popular calypso tune.

The rattan furniture, potted palms, banana trees and orchids hanging from poles rising high above the wooden floor were all in keeping with the tropical locale, while the mouthwatering aroma of food wafting from passing trays carried by silent, efficient waiters intensified his hunger.

When they reached their table, the waiter stepped back politely and permitted Chris to seat Emily. He waited for Chris to sit, then said, "May I bring you something to drink?" His British-accented voice was crisp and exacting.

Emily gave her dining partner a questioning look, and he nodded. She would order for both of them. "We'll have a passion punch."

Chris waited until the waiter walked away to place their beverage order, then glanced at Emily. "Passion punch?"

Her eyes crinkled slightly. "It's a wonderful concoction made with carrot, pear, apple, pineapple and cherry juices. Even though it's nonalcoholic, it can be just a little wicked."

He shifted his eyebrows, his expression mirroring disbelief. "Wicked?"

She nodded. "The locals say it acts much like an aphrodisiac. Women drink it when they want to conceive."

A mysterious smile parted Chris's lips as he picked up one of the menus lying on the table, perusing it leisurely. "What effect does it usually have on you?" he asked, not looking at her.

Staring at his bowed head, Emily's face creased into a sudden smile. "I suppose you can say that I experience a tad bit of wickedness."

His head came up. "Only a tad?"

She gave him a direct stare, noticing a silent expectation flowing from his large, deep-set, dark eyes. Her chest rose and fell heavily, bringing his penetrating gaze to linger briefly on her breasts.

"The level of wickedness increases with the number consumed." Her velvety voice had lowered to an enticing timbre.

He leaned closer, covered her fragile hand with his, tightening his strong grip on her delicate fingers. "Will I have to be the designated driver tonight?"

Emily's heart pounded an erratic rhythm when she felt the electricity of his touch. Chris had held her hands more times than she could count or remember, but this time she registered something—something very different. His thumb caressed the back of her hand in a soothing, erotic motion. She was transfixed by the shape of his large, strong, masculine hand: long fingers with well-groomed, square-cut nails, and covered with a feathering of short black hair that made them appear darker than they actually were.

"No," she finally answered after a comfortable silence.

"Too bad," he countered softly. Pulling his hand away, he glanced at the menu again. "What do you recommend?"

She studied her own menu. "Every selection is excellent."

"How's the snapper?" The menu listed stuffed, baked red snapper in a piquant garlic sauce.

"Wonderfully spicy." They shared a knowing smile. Both had developed a penchant for hot, spicy dishes.

Minutes later, they were served the punch in fresh pineapple shells, along with a platter containing a cold fish salad, marinated vegetables and bite-sized portions of batter-fried chicken, beef and pork.

Chris leaned back on his chair, studying Emily. "After I leave Jamaica I'm going to Mexico," he said without preamble.

Emily's expression was impassive. "You're going to see your dad?"

His expression changed as a mask of hardness descended, distorting his handsome face. "He's not my dad. He never earned the right to be acknowledged as such. And to answer your question—yes. I'm going to see my *father*."

"Why?"

"Because I have to put my personal life in order. I have to tie up all of the loose ends from my past before I hit the campaign trail."

Emily knew he was right. She had read about too many candidates seeking public office who lost or had to drop out because their opponents had uncovered a secret or scandal that was certain to spell political doom.

"Do you remember anything about him?"

Exhaling audibly, he wagged his head. "No."

"How old were you when he and your mother divorced?"

"I wasn't quite two." He glanced at a spot over her head. "My mother met Alejandro Delgado and married him after a whirlwind courtship, then divorced him before they celebrated their third anniversary. As a condition of their divorce, she was granted sole custody of me, but the judge allowed her ex-husband liberal visitation privileges. He picked me up one Friday afternoon with the intention of taking me to a Halloween party, but we never made it. He had his driver take us to the airport and we boarded a flight for Mexico City."

Emily's gaze widened in astonishment. "How did he get you out of the country?"

"He was assigned to the D.C. consulate at the time."

She sat back, shocked by this disclosure. "He used his diplomatic immunity to kidnap his own son. Why?"

"It was quite simple, Emily. He wanted to punish my mother for divorcing him."

It was simple to Chris, but not to her. He'd just confessed that his father had kidnapped him, taken him to a foreign country, no doubt causing his mother pain and suffering, while he sat across the table from her concealing his feelings behind a facade of indifference.

"He hated her that much?"

He nodded once. "I'm ashamed to say he did."

"How were you and your mother reunited?"

He wanted to tell Emily the truth, every sordid detail as to how his mother met and married Matthew Sterling—the man he called dad. His mother, stepfather and sister had sworn an oath never to reveal Matthew Sterling's former clandestine lifestyle to anyone outside their immediate family. However, her father knew, and so did Salem Lassiter, because he had married Sara Sterling.

"She went to Mexico, met Matt Sterling, married him, and, through his connections and influence, he negotiated with the Mexican government to assist in my return."

Emily wanted to believe Chris, but she couldn't. She had overheard whispered variations of this explanation so many times that she felt Chris had rehearsed it. She had to respect his right for privacy because her own family had its share of secrets and scandals, the most profound one surrounding her father. Fewer than half a dozen people outside of their family knew that he was Samuel Claridge Cole's illegitimate son.

She put the straw in the large pineapple shell to her lips and took a swallow of the icy-cold drink, enjoying the distinctive blend of fruits on her discerning palate.

"Does he know you're coming?" she asked, her voice soft, soothing.

Chris let out an audible sigh. "No. I suppose it will be as much a surprise for me to see him as it will be for him to see me after thirty-two years."

It was Emily's turn to reach across the space separating them and hold his hand. "Everything will work out."

He stared at her again, raw hurt glittering in the depths of eyes so dark that no light would ever penetrate them. "I hope you're right." He flashed a wry grin. "Billy Savoy must be spinning like a whirling dervish. He's finally found something to attack me with."

A soft gasp escaped her. "William Savoy? What does he have to do with this?"

"It was his investigators who uncovered that Alejandro Delgado is my biological father and that he has been living in hiding in South America."

Pulling her hand away, Emily slumped back against the tufted cushion on the rattan chair, shaking her head. "Why now, Chris? Why didn't he reveal this information two years ago when he opposed you for the senate seat?"

Chris shifted his eyebrows. "I don't know. Maybe he hadn't known about it, or perhaps he was so cocksure that he'd win because his father is the governor."

"He's a fool," she spat out angrily. "He ran a clean campaign the first time, and now he's resorted to slinging mud. I hope I'll be able to make it through the next ten months covering his campaign and remain unbiased."

Chris registered her last statement, the words hitting him in his gut with the force of a well-aimed punch. "What did you say?"

Emily took another sip of her fruit punch to relieve the dryness in her throat. She had planned to call Chris and tell him that she would not be covering his own campaign when she returned to New Mexico. Now there was no reason to wait two weeks.

"I've been reassigned."

"Why?" The single word was harsh, cutting.

"Richard Adams claims…" She paused, trying to recall her boss's exact words. "He said, 'I've decided to reassign you for the gubernatorial campaign. I've changed my mind after being apprised of your relationship with Senator Delgado.' End of quote."

"What the hell is he talking about, Emily? What relationship? Does he think we're sleeping together?"

Chris was looking forward to having Emily join his campaign as a part of the press corps when he began touring New Mexico. As it was he did not see her enough. He was lucky if he met with her more than twice a month. His permanent residence was in Las Cruces, even though he maintained an expansive loft apartment in an industrial section of Santa Fe.

She shrugged a narrow shoulder. "I don't know what he thinks or believes when it concerns us. What he's become is a spiteful man who has a problem accepting rejection." Chris's expression had changed from shock to anger and, finally, to amusement. Her quick temper flared. "You think it's funny?"

He sobered. "No, Emily, I don't think it's funny. What I don't understand is your naïveté. How many men have to either lose their lives or their minds when it comes to you?"

"What are you talking about?"

"Take a look in the mirror and you'll know what I'm talking about, Emily Teresa Kirkland. You're an incredibly beautiful woman and you have the perfect combination of looks and brains. Of course a man—any man—would have the hots for you. And I'm no exception," he stated after a pause.

It was her turn to smile. "You?" How could he, when he shared his bed with another woman?

"You think it's funny, Emily?"

"I find it amusing."

"I don't," he countered.

She waved a hand. "We're friends, Chris. We've always been friends."

He stared at her until she lowered her gaze. "I'm not debating our friendship. But I will admit that I'm just as enthralled with you as your boss and the millions of Keith Norrises who lust after you."

Emily held up her right hand. "Chris—"

"Let me have my say," he said, interrupting her. "I came to Ocho Rios because I was frightened. More frightened than I'd ever been in my life."

There was a soporific silence as they sat motionless, staring at each other, shutting out the sounds of the band playing a seductive ballad, the soft conversations going on around them and the clink of utensils against plates. It was as if they were strangers seeing each other for the first time.

And it was the first time that Emily saw Christopher Blackwell Delgado not as a friend she had known all her life, but as a man—a man who finally saw her as a woman.

"Why?"

The sound of her query reminded him of a cloaking fog, sweeping around his face like moist, caressing fingers. "Why, Emily?" She nodded slowly. "Because I thought I was going to lose you."

Her gaze widened. "To what? To whom?"

"Keith Norris."

"But I told you that I'm not marrying Keith."

His lids lowered, a fringe of long black lashes touching his high cheekbones. "Something wouldn't permit me to believe you."

"What I can't believe is that you're jealous of Keith."

"I'm jealous of Keith Norris and any other man you've ever been involved with."

Her shock was complete. If he was jealous of the men she dated, then that meant that his feelings for her ran deeper than mere friendship, and that the bond between them went further than their parents being lifelong friends, than she and his sister were best friends, and than they were godparents to Sara and Salem's son.

Her heart was pumping so wildly that she was certain it was noticeable under the delicate fabric of her silk shell. She had waited years—more than half her life—to hear the words Christopher Delgado had just uttered. And now that she heard them, she was totally unprepared to respond.

She had earned an undergraduate degree in communications and a graduate degree in journalism, yet she was unable to communicate with the man sitting a few feet across from her. She earned a generous salary because of her verbal ability, but at the

moment she was too dazed, too stunned to speak. Closing her
eyes, she swallowed several times, helpless to halt her embarrassment.

Chris was aware that he had shocked Emily, but now that the
words were out he could not retract them any more than he could
change how he felt about her.

"I love you, Emily," he said simply. "I don't know when it happened, but I do know that I've been in love with you for a long
time."

Her lids fluttered wildly as she struggled to control her emotions. Covering her mouth with a trembling hand, her eyes filled
with unshed tears. The moisture turned them into shimmering
pools of brilliant peridot.

"But...but you see other women," she whispered through her
fingers.

A sensual smile lifted the corners of his strong mouth. "And
you've seen other men," he countered softly.

Emily lowered her hand. "Touché, Chris." She had dated a
number of men, but what Chris did not know was that she hadn't
slept with any of them. She was certain Keith Norris had proposed marriage because he thought she would agree to share his
bed if she wore his engagement ring.

Emily wanted to tell Chris that she loved him, had been in
love with him since he kissed her for the first time in her grandparents' garden after her cousin's wedding the year she turned
twelve.

She'd been a preteen girl who had physically become a woman
but had been experiencing the gamut of strange emotions that
changed her moods from highs to lows within seconds. And it
was during one of her elated moods that she and Chris found
themselves in the cloistered seclusion of the formal boxwood
garden. Still enthralled with the ethereal beauty of Aaron and
Regina Spencer's wedding ceremony, she had asked Chris to kiss
her.

He had hesitated, then placed his mouth over hers for her first
kiss. A passion she had never known before or since ignited a
fire within her. At seventeen, Chris claimed a dark, masculine

beauty that turned the heads of much older women whenever they surveyed his tall, slender body, rakishly long, wavy black hair, deeply tanned tawny skin and penetrating dark eyes that tilted upward in the most beguiling smile.

She'd felt the warmth of his moist breath, inhaled the sensual scent of his flesh and aftershave, and felt the lean hardness of his body as he pressed closer. The kiss lasted only seconds, but everything that was Christopher Blackwell Delgado had lingered. Every boy and man she'd ever met or dated paled when she compared them to the young man who had captured her heart with a single kiss.

Chris saw the sweep of emotions cross Emily's incredibly beautiful face. She knew. He had bared his soul and confessed his love for her, and now he would wait—wait for her to verbalize what she had told his sister. A look of tenderness filled his eyes when she lowered her gaze shyly, making his heart turn over with the demure gesture. He stared at the length of her slender neck, the velvet skin he wanted to touch, to kiss.

She glanced up and slowly let out her breath. "What's going to happen to us?" Her query was a breathless whisper.

Chris covered both her hands with one of his. "Nothing," he whispered in return. A reggae version of Marc Anthony's blockbuster hit "I Need To Know" floated through the restaurant and he tightened his grip on her fingers. "Come, dance with me." Apprehension made it impossible for him to sit still.

Emily waited for Chris to come around the table to pull back her chair and within seconds found herself on the dance floor and in his arms. The pulsing Latin rhythm and the melodious sound of his voice in her ear as he sang along with the band's lead singer sent a torrent of fire throughout her body. He spun her around, swung her out, then pulled her up close to his chest, their lower bodies fused from belly to knees.

Chris was an excellent dancer, and although they had danced together in the past, she knew this time it was different. Neither was aware of the other couples on the dance floor as they shared a smile, a smile reserved only for lovers, when their gazes met.

The song ended amid rousing applause, Emily and Chris join-

ing the others as they made their way back to their table. He
pulled out her chair, seated her, then leaned over and dropped
a light kiss on her mouth when she tilted her head to stare up
at him. Curving his fingers around the column of her neck, he
pressed a kiss on her silken throat before moving to her mouth.

"Emelia," he crooned against her moist lips, using the Spanish derivative of her name.

Her lids lowered as she smiled up at him through her lashes.
"Sí," she replied, lapsing easily into the same language.

"Dímelo."

He wanted to know, needed to know. And she knew exactly
what he wanted. He needed to know how she felt about him. He
wanted to hear the words she had locked away in her heart for
years.

Her smile faded and her eyes darkened with passion. *"Te
amo, Cristobal."* The confession flowed out of its own volition,
reminding her that she had broken her promise that she would
never tell Chris that she loved him again.

Hunkering down beside her chair, he ran a forefinger down
the length of her nose. Leaning closer, he winked at her. "Thank
you."

She pressed her lips to his. "You're welcome."

Chris retook his seat, a soaring joy making him feel light-
headed. The trepidation he had felt when he boarded the jet in
Las Cruces had vanished completely. Even if he lost the upcoming election, it would never be as traumatic as if he lost Emily
Kirkland.

She had become his everything; if he lost her, he surely would
lose himself.

Chapter 7

"**P**ut me down, Chris." Emily clutched her shoes to her chest as Chris carried her out of the car, around the house, and headed for the gazebo.

He tightened his grip under her knees. "I'll put you down in a little while."

Resting her head on his solid shoulder, she closed her eyes. It was a few minutes after midnight, and the food and drink she had consumed left her feeling a bit too full and very drowsy. And it hadn't helped that she and Christ had spent more than ninety minutes on the dance floor once they'd finished eating dinner.

The reflective paint on the white structure shone like a beacon in the darkness as Chris walked up the two steps that led to the gazebo. He deposited Emily on the oversized hammock, then climbed in beside her. His greater weight caused it to dip lower as she moved over to give him more room to stretch out his long legs.

Turning on her right side, she laid her head on his shoulder. "I knew I shouldn't have had that second passion punch. I think you were trying to get me drunk so you could take advantage of me."

Chris tried making out her features in the darkness. "I thought you said it was nonalcoholic."

"It is," she confirmed. "It must be the combination of the ingredients that make it so potent."

He chuckled deep in his chest, causing her to glance up at him. "I would never deliberately get you drunk so that I could take advantage of you. I will not touch you, Emelia, unless you want me to. That choice will have to be yours, not mine."

Her left arm curved around his slim waist. "You're going to have to be patient with me."

The fingers of his left hand played with the short, silken curls sweeping over her ear. "Take all the time you need."

"We don't have a lot of time, Chris."

"Why do you say that?"

"I join Savoy's campaign February fourth. After that my contact with you will have to be kept to a minimum. We can't be seen in public together. I don't want to compromise myself."

Chris cursed to himself. Raw, crude expletives. He had forgotten that she would be traveling with his opponent's campaign team. "We can always make arrangements through Sara to see one another," he suggested.

"No, Chris. I don't want to sneak around to see you."

The muscles in his body tensed, then eased. "Do you have a better suggestion?"

"No." Her voice was muffled against his chest. "I'll think of something."

That was the last thing she said as her lids fluttered before they closed. Chris held her to his heart while she slept, trying to think of a way he and Emily could see each other over the next ten months.

He hadn't even slept with her, yet his protective and possessive instincts were in full throttle. What he refused to think about was William Savoy coming on to Emily.

Thirty-eight-year-old, never-married William Alan Savoy had become one of New Mexico's most eligible bachelors. Women found him attractive and extremely intelligent, while both men and women applauded his political intellect. Yet he had one defect in his nearly flawless character: he had a proclivity for women—married or single. Chris had heard rumors that Billy preferred married women because of his unwillingness or inability to commit.

Now that he knew the woman he loved would be traveling

from city to city with Billy Savoy, he would have to make arrangements to keep her out of the man's clutches.

A peaceful expression softened the lines of tension around his mobile mouth as he closed his eyes. The soft sounds of Emily's breathing whispered under his ear. She had fallen asleep in his arms like a trusting child.

Fifteen minutes later he welcomed the arms of Morpheus calling him to sleep—a sleep wherein he dreamt of Emily Kirkland-Delgado—her belly swollen with his child.

Emily walked halfway up the staircase leading to the second floor. "Hurry, Chris, or we're going to be late."

"I'm coming," he called back.

She glanced down at her watch, retracing her steps to the parlor to wait for him. They had spent the night in the hammock, waking before dawn, but only to retreat to their respective bedrooms, where they slept until the sun was high in the heavens.

It was Sunday, and Emily had planned to attend mass at a quaint little church ten miles away. She heard footsteps and turned to find Chris standing under the arched doorway, smiling at her. He was casually dressed in a finely woven off-white short-sleeved linen shirt and coffee-colored linen slacks. A matching jacket dangled from the forefinger of his right hand while he clutched a tie in the other hand.

"Will I need a jacket or tie?"

"No," she replied. "Everyone's always informal."

She wore a loose-fitting, sleeveless, yellow shift dress with a squared neckline. Picking up a soft straw hat, matching purse and a pair of sunglasses from a drop-leaf table, she preceded Chris out of the parlor and to her car.

He deposited the jacket and tie on the table, followed her, then held his hand out for her key. "I'll drive."

She dropped the key in his outstretched palm, hiding a smile. "What's the matter, darling? You don't trust my driving?"

Curving an arm around her waist, he opened the passenger-side door of the Mustang and waited until she was seated on the leather seat. "You still drive too fast." He closed the door with a resounding slam.

She managed to look insulted. "I was only going seventy-five."

He slipped behind the wheel next to her, vertical lines appearing between his eyes. "Seventy-five at night on a road without lights."

"Don't be such a ninny, Chris. I've traveled that road hundreds of times. I can navigate it with my eyes closed."

Snorting under his breath, he put on his sunglasses, started up the car and backed out of the driveway. "Which road do I take?"

"Take a right and continue until you see the sign for Shrewsbury. Then make a left. The steeple of the church will be visible from the road."

Emily stared at his profile. He could have been carved out of stone. There was no doubt her speeding had rankled him. She did not know why, but she had a penchant for speed. There was a time when she owned a motorcycle—a Harley-Davidson. She had ridden up to her parents' house on the bike to share a Sunday dinner with them, and they had refused to let her come in.

She returned to her apartment with tears streaming down her face, and when she called her mother, Vanessa Kirkland refused to come to the phone. Michael had delivered the message that Mom and Dad would not talk to her or welcome her into their home again until she got rid of the bike. The impasse lasted two weeks before she sold the Harley for a fraction of its value. She could not accept the alienation—especially from her family.

Chris drank in the sensual beauty of Jamaica's topography behind the dark lenses of his sunglasses. Its verdant lushness was breathtaking, and he realized why the elder Kirklands returned to visit the Caribbean island several times each year.

Slowing the sports car around a sharp curve, he glanced down at a valley dotted with what appeared to be thousands of tiny trees. "What's down there?"

Emily looked out her window. "That's a coffee plantation. They're growing an arabica blend known as San Ramon."

He gave her a quick glance. "It's enormous. I didn't know they grew that much coffee in Jamaica."

"There are quite a few coffee plantations here. Jamaica Blue Mountain happens to be the most expensive coffee in the world."

"Why? Is the taste that much superior to Brazilian or Colombian blends?"

"All coffee growers admit it's one of the very best coffees available, but the price doesn't reflect the better flavor as much as the premium that some people are prepared to pay to secure supplies of it. To enjoy its full flavor you have to use more beans per cup than for other coffees. If you don't, then the flavor can seem a little hollow. So, the real cost of the flavor is the difference between it and the next most expensive coffee, plus ten or fifteen percent for the extra beans needed."

He glanced at her again. "How do you know so much about coffee?"

It was her turn to stare at him. "My family owns that plantation," she said in a quiet voice. "And a few others near Maggotty, Mandeville and Wallenford."

"Your family?"

"ColeDiz International Limited."

"I thought they only had coffee plantations in Belize and Puerto Rico."

There was a time when the Coles owned and operated coffee and banana plantations in at least half a dozen countries and islands throughout Central America and the Caribbean, but the company had begun selling them off to consortiums twenty years earlier.

"Daddy and Uncle Martin own resorts in Montego Bay, Port Antonio, Ocho Rios and—"

"The restaurant we went to last night is your father's?" Chris asked, interrupting her. Emily had not permitted him to pay for their dinner, but had signed a chit for their food and beverages.

She flashed a smug grin. "Yes. My father owns the house, all of the surrounding land, and holds private rights to the beach."

"How long has he owned the house?"

"He purchased it before I was born. Daddy came to Jamaica

for a vacation about thirty-five years ago and loved it so much that he decided he wanted to buy property here. Someone told him about the house and surrounding property. He took one look at the house and made up his mind on the spot.

"The house was built in 1836 as a honeymoon retreat for the members of a well-to-do British family. However, every woman who married into the family and spent her honeymoon at the retreat died within the first year of her wedding."

Chris gave her an incredulous look. "You're kidding."

Emily shook her head. "No, I'm not. There were rumors floating around that they were poisoned."

"By whom?"

"No one really knows. When Daddy told me about the superstition I decided to research the property's history. I went through microfiche of thousands of old newspapers, scanning the obituaries. I managed to come up with the names of at least three women. Afterward, I interviewed a few of the locals whose families have inhabited the region for several centuries."

"What did they say?"

"They alleged that the original owner's eldest son had taken a beautiful mulatto slave girl as his mistress, and she bore him several children. He freed their children, even though he never offered her her freedom because he feared losing her to another man. A hurricane hit the island that summer, ruining the sugarcane crop, so the son was forced to take a wife from a wealthy family to offset his family's losses.

"His mistress was devastated when a pale woman from across the ocean supplanted her as her lover's favorite. The rumor was that she went to a woman who had been a voodoo queen in her native Africa before she was sold into servitude in the Americas, and paid the old woman a generous sum to help her get her lover back."

Chris saw the sign pointing the way to Shrewsbury. "Are you saying the old woman placed a spell on the house?"

"I believe the word *curse* would be more appropriate. The planter's wife became pregnant and within months she began craving a particular fruit indigenous to the island. Unfortunately, the fruit contained properties that are toxic only to pregnant women, and within days of eating the fruit the young bride died."

"Did he remarry?"

"No. He lived out the rest of his life as a widower, but his relationship with his former mistress was never the same. The curse had rendered him impotent."

Throwing back his head, Chris let out a great peal of laughter. "I don't believe it."

"Neither did I, until someone else told me that around the turn of the century a distant cousin used the house for his honeymoon retreat, and his bride also died from eating the fruit."

Sobering quickly, he gave Emily a questioning look. "You're saying that the curse was still in effect seventy years later?"

She nodded. "It happened a third time in the late nineteen-fifties. Rumors of the curse had spread throughout the island, and the property was abandoned. It went into receivership for back taxes and Daddy bought it with most of its original furnishings still in it. The curse finally ended once the name on the deed changed from Abington to Kirkland."

Chris shook his head. "It sounds too absurd to be true."

"Fact is always stranger than fiction." There was a soft gentleness in her voice that indicated that she believed in the curse.

He knew Emily was right about fact being stranger than fiction. The circumstances surrounding his own abduction and subsequent rescue were bizarre enough to provide a conceivable plot for a big-budget action film.

Reaching over, he placed a hand on her thigh. The touch of his fingers through the light fabric of her dress added to the heat of her flesh from the warm rays of the sun coming through the windshield. Her blood heated, rushing through her system like a sirocco, leaving a film of moisture glistening on her face and between her breasts. The gesture was both innocent and erotic.

Emily closed her eyes and breathed through parted lips. She reveled in his touch, wondering how it would be if he touched her—without the barrier of fabric separating flesh from flesh.

I will not touch you unless you want me to. That choice will have to be yours, not mine. His words came rushing back with crystal clarity. She knew he wanted to sleep with her, and she wanted to lie with him. At that very moment!

Opening her eyes, she turned her head and stared at Chris; then she saw it. The tall, white steeple of the church came into view. It was too late to tell him to turn around and drive back to the house.

Placing her left hand over the one resting on her thigh, she held his hand until he maneuvered into the parking lot at the back of the simply constructed wooden structure. He removed his hand, shifted into park, and, despite the tropical heat, Emily felt a chill. It was as if some sixth sense had told her that she had kept every man out of her bed because she had been waiting for the man sitting beside her. That he would be the one to bear witness as to why she had been born female.

She sat motionless until Chris stepped out of the car, came around and opened the door for her. She blinked once, placed her hand in his and permitted him to assist her from the automobile. Looping her arm through his, they made their way to the entrance of the church.

All of the windows in the church were open to avail the interior of an occasional breeze flowing through the valley. It was late morning, but nearly every pew was filled with parishioners in lightweight clothing. Emily placed the straw hat on her head, dipped her fingers in the holy water in a small dish near the entrance and crossed herself. Chris duplicated her motions as he made the sign of the cross over his chest. He looked around the small church for a pew that would provide enough space for them to sit next to each other. A beautiful young Jamaican woman who looked barely out of her teens smiled at Chris. She patted the empty space beside her.

"You can sit here," she crooned to Chris.

Lowering his head, Chris whispered to Emily, "Take it." She shifted her eyebrows and he nodded. She slipped onto the pew beside the flirtatious woman, whose expression had turned from a leer to a frown within seconds.

He sat in a pew behind Emily, staring at the back of her head until everyone stood up to acknowledge the entrance of the priest.

A slight smile tilted his slanting eyes upward as he reached for a hymnal. Emily Kirkland affected him in a way no other woman ever had. Unlike her, he wasn't a regular churchgoer, but whenever they met for Sunday brunch it was usually preceded by their attending mass. And this Sunday's service would prove to be a special one because he had a lot to be thankful for—thankful that another one of his prayers has been answered.

Bowing his head, he thanked God for the gift of love—and that the gift was the woman with whom he had promised to live for the next five days.

Chapter 8

Chris rolled over on his flat belly and smiled at Emily. She lay on the blanket beside him, her head cradled on folded arms. "Hi," he crooned.

She returned his smile, wrinkling her delicate nose. "Hi, yourself."

Moving closer, he dropped a kiss on the tip of her nose. "How are you feeling?"

She closed her eyes. "Lazy. Very, very lazy."

They'd returned from church, changed into swimwear and shared a quickly prepared lunch of mixed salad greens with grilled chicken, freshly baked bread from the dough Emily had put up the day before and glasses of iced herbal tea while picnicking on the beach.

A soothing chuckle rumbled in his chest. "This has to be a first."

She opened her eyes. "What?"

"Emily Kirkland doing absolutely nothing."

"Bite your tongue, Chris. I'm not the only workaholic."

"The taxpayers of New Mexico are entitled to no less from me." He combed his fingers through her hair, rubbing the curling ends between his fingertips. His gaze caressed her face as lovingly as a gentle kiss.

Emily placed a slender leg over his, snuggling against his bare chest. She inhaled the hypnotic scent of the lime-based cologne clinging to the coarse black hair starting below his throat, spreading over his breasts and ending with a narrow line at the waistband of his swim trunks.

"There are forty-one other senators and seventy members of the house and none of them work as hard as you do," she chided softly. "The legislature meets for either a sixty- or thirty-day session every other year, yet you work pro bono, defending youthful offenders and mentoring high school students. Why must you try to fill up every hour of the day with work?"

He kissed her nose again. "Why, Emelia? Because I didn't have someone as wonderfully distracting as you in my life."

She flashed a saucy smile. "I'm a distraction? Should I be flattered?"

"Yes, you should, because you happen to be a very beautiful, sexy distraction." He punctuated each word.

Angling his head, Chris pressed his mouth to hers, increasing the pressure until her lips parted. Moist breaths mingled, fused, cemented. Without warning, his kiss changed, becoming more demanding.

Emily's respiration speeded up, her nerve endings short-circuiting. She gasped, her lips parting, and his tongue sampled the purity she had withheld from him. Everything she had dreamed of feeling, all of the love she had had for Christopher Delgado was manifested when she curved her arms around his neck, releasing the passions she had repressed for more than half her life.

Chris shifted her slight body effortlessly until she lay over his chest, her legs cradled between his. He inhaled her—her feminine scent, the soft, fragrant curls covering her well-shaped head, the velvety texture of her skin and the honeyed sweetness of her lush mouth. The searing heat at the apex of her thighs burned his groin through the spandex of his swim briefs, increasing the inferno scorching and searing his sex.

He wanted her—he wanted her so much that he feared exploding into tiny cinders of erotic ecstasy before he was given the opportunity to enter her body. His hands gripped her shoulders, making her his prisoner as he plundered her mouth, throat and ears before he returned to recapture the well of moist confection of her lush lips. He had spent so many years craving her, so many years when he had fantasized kissing Emily passionately, making love to her.

Like a sculptor reveling in the texture of his greatest creation, Chris closed his eyes and traced his fingertips down the column of her neck, over the bones of her clavicle, down and around the outline of her breasts, his thumbs sweeping over the distended nipples straining under the top of her bathing suit. His fingers continued their journey, outlining the indentation where her waist curved inward before flaring out to her hips. He registered the soft sounds of her quickened breathing in his ear when he reached between their bodies and cupped the expanse between her legs.

Emily felt the heat, the increasing pressure and a rising passion she was helpless to control. Men had kissed her, touched her before, but they had never been able to excite her. Now she lay on a private beach in Ocho Ríos, atop a man she had loved all her life, savoring his caress and kiss. Desire awoke, stirring like hot, slow-moving lava from a volcano that had lain dormant for years.

The heat from the sun overhead competed with the fire spreading through the hidden space between her thighs. She writhed sensuously against the solid bulge throbbing against her belly. She wanted Chris Delgado—more than anything she had ever wanted in her life.

Cradling his lean face between her hands, she opened her eyes and stared at the carnality gripping his sensual features, unaware of the control it took for him not to strip her naked and take her on the beach in full view of nature and all its wondrous majesty.

Roles reversed, she became the sculptress, a forefinger tracing the outline of his sweeping black eyebrows, the elegant ridge of cheekbones, the length of his nose, the outline of the masculine mouth with its full, passionate lower lip and down to linger at the slight indentation in his strong chin.

Lowering her head, she pressed her nose to his shoulder, inhaling the distinctive scent of his skin. He shuddered, gasping audibly, when her tongue left a trace of moisture on the taut brown skin covering muscle and sinew. Her tongue moved lower—over the crisp, curling hair on his chest, drawing tiny circles around one nipple, then the other.

How could she have known? How did she know where to

touch him to send him into a quivering mass of trembling lust? The questions penetrated the fog of rushing arousal that would not allow Chris to move or speak. The very air around them seemed electrified, vibrating with a repressed passion that threatened to swallow them alive, whole.

His fingers, curled into tight fists, were anchored in the sand. He feared touching her, because for the first time in his life he was close to losing complete control of himself and everything around him. He wanted his first time with her, their first time together, to be one of gentle passion, not unbridled lust. And it was lust—a straining, tumultuous and frenzied lust that threatened to escape and erupt without regard to anything or anyone except his own sexual gratification.

He uncurled his fingers, and his hands moved with blinding speed to manacle her wrists. Emily went completely still, her eyes widening in surprise. "No," he whispered in a shaking voice. Lowering his gaze, he stared at the erratically beating pulse in her throat. There was no mistaking the uncertainty in her luminous eyes. He forced a smile. "I don't want our first time together to be here on the beach."

Even though Emily was not as sexually experienced as Chris, she had been with enough men to know that he was close to going over the edge where he would not be able to stop himself from making love to her. She had noted the change in his breathing when she kissed his breasts, the contraction of his stomach muscles, the throbbing hardness of his sex straining against the constricting fabric of his swim trunks and pulsing against her belly.

His touch and kisses had aroused her, but she had also aroused him. A mysterious light darkened her eyes to an emerald green when she smiled down at him.

"You're right. I don't want *my* first time to be on a beach." Her voice was soft and soothing as wisps of cotton.

Vertical lines formed between his eyes, his sharp mind quickly analyzing her statement. "What did you say?"

She shifted an eyebrow. "About what?"

Chris released her wrists and curved an arm around her waist, reversing their positions. Supporting his greater weight on his elbows, he stared down at her deeply tanned face. "About it being your first time." She averted her gaze, silently answering his query. He cradled her closer. "Oh, baby," he crooned softly near her ear.

Closing her eyes, Emily felt the rapid pounding of her heart keeping tempo with his. She hadn't meant to tell him now, but if he was to become her lover, then he had the right to know, to know that she had waited for him.

"I couldn't…not with the others," she confessed, her voice much shakier than she wanted it to be.

It was Chris's turn to close his eyes. He couldn't believe it. Emily had dated Keith Norris for a year, yet their relationship had remained platonic. And now she was willing to sleep with him and give him the most precious gift a woman could offer any man. A gift she would only offer up once in her lifetime.

"I will never dishonor you, Emelia." There was a faint tremor in his voice, as though some deep emotion had touched him. "I will treasure you always."

What he did not say was that he would never be unfaithful to her. Unlike Alejandro Delgado, who'd slept with his wife and any other woman he'd found himself attracted to.

Emily smiled. "Thank you."

They lay together until their passions cooled, then rose and made their way down to the water. Chris swung Emily up in his arms and carried her out where gentle waves lapped against his chest. Lowering his head, he kissed her gently on the lips as she slid down the length of his body. Her arms circled his strong neck, her full breasts flattening against his chest.

Pulling back, he smiled at her. He wasn't disappointed when she returned it with a sensual one of her own. "I love you, baby," he whispered against her moist lips.

Burying her face in his neck, Emily breathed a kiss under his ear. "And I you."

Their simple declaration of love stayed with them as they cooled their passions in the clear, azure waters of what had become their private retreat. They tired of swimming and returned to the beach to lie under the tropical sun until the heat absorbed the moisture from their hair, skin and clothing.

Emily lay across the four-poster bed, peering through the swathing of sheer gauze drapery. The rumble of thunder disturbed the solitude as fat drops of rain beat against the shuttered windows in a rhythmic tapping. The distinctive smell of rain wafted into the bedroom, mingling with the haunting, cloying scent of tropical flowers and fruit.

She and Chris had cleaned up the remains of their lunch, then returned to the house for a siesta. Both were silent, each lost in their own private thoughts. It was if they were loath to speak because their respect for each other's privacy had become paramount to them.

She had fallen in love with Christopher Delgado almost eighteen years earlier. Now she lay on a bed in a house on a sensual tropical island in the Caribbean, while Chris lay on a similar bed less than two minutes from her, filled with a dizzying anticipation of what she knew she would come to share with him.

Offering him her virginal body did not frighten her as much as she feared she could satisfy him. Turning over on her belly, she pounded the pillow under her head.

"I'm too old for this," she mumbled against the embroidered antique fabric.

She should have been like some of the other girls she had gone to high school and college with. She should have relinquished her virginity when she had her first serious boyfriend, instead of waiting for a man who knew she existed but chose to interact with her in the same manner as he did his own sister.

The other girls never knew she was saving herself for one man—none except Sara Sterling. Sara was the one who listened to her most prized secret, a secret she could not tell her parish priest. Her best friend had listened while she poured out her heart when rumors were circulating that Christopher had considered proposing marriage to a fellow law student. The rumors ended abruptly when the young woman eloped with one of their law school professors less than a month after their graduation.

"Would you like company?"

Emily's head came up quickly and she shifted on the bed to find the subject of her musings standing in the doorway, dressed only in a pair of walking shorts.

Her pulse raced uncontrollably as she surveyed his tall, lean body. The sun had quickly darkened his skin to a rich mahogany brown. It was as if she were seeing him for the very first time. His short hair, usually brushed neatly against his scalp, was tousled in sexy waves. Hairy, muscular forearms were crossed over his equally muscled, hair-matted chest, making it difficult for her to draw a normal breath. Years of skiing had given him a magnificently developed upper body.

Rising up on an elbow, she parted the mosquito draping, moved over and patted the mattress. "Come."

Chris strolled into the bedroom, lay down beside Emily and pulled the sheer draping around the bed. His sensitive nostrils caught the familiar scent of lilies clinging to her skin, the delicate nightgown she wore to cover her nakedness and the bed linen. Turning on his side to face her, he felt a familiar stirring in his loins, wondering if he had made the right decision to come to her bedroom. He had spent an uneasy half hour in his own bed, tossing and turning, his mind filled with the images of their passionate coupling on the beach.

His obsidian gaze lingered on her suntanned face. The freckles across the bridge of her delicate nose were no longer visible, and the added color made her eyes appear much lighter than they actually were.

He placed a hand on her velvety cheek. "Are you using a sunscreen?" She nodded. "You've gotten a lot of sun in just a few days. You're going to ruin you skin."

She closed her eyes tightly. "Do you see any crow's-feet around my eyes?"

Chris forced himself not to smile. "No." His hand moved up to her already mussed hair, smoothing back the raven curls.

Her eyes opened and she stared at him staring back at her. "Will you still love me when I'm wrinkled and gray?"

He heard the apprehension in her voice. This was an Emily

Kirkland he did not know. The woman he knew had always presented herself with supreme confidence and self-assurance. Even when he had come to her after the police shot the man who had been stalking her, she had exhibited a calm that was almost unnatural. She'd teased him, saying it was better that the police captured the crazed man rather than her father or brother. His gaze narrowed. Where had her uncertainty come from? Why this fear of him not loving her?

"Will you continue to love me even though I am wrinkled and gray?" he asked, answering her question with one of his own.

"You're not wrinkled and gray," she countered quickly.

"I have lines around my eyes when I smile and I'm graying at an alarming rate. I'm willing to bet that I'll be completely white before I'm forty."

She touched the corner of one of his eyes with her forefinger. "They are called character lines. And your salt-and-pepper hair is sexy."

"Not hardly."

"Yes, hardly." She ran her fingers through his hair, lifting the strands. "You should wear your hair like this. It would make you look less staid, less severe." A roll of thunder shook the earth, followed by a flash of lightning, and Emily jumped slightly.

A slight smile curved his mouth. "You sound like Reanna."

She lifted a questioning eyebrow. "Reanna?"

Chris nodded. "Reanna Benton. She's my publicist. Two weeks ago I had a session for a complete image makeover. I sat for official photographs in formal and informal dress, and she selected the two poses that will go on the campaign buttons."

"Are you ready for this campaign?"

Anticipation fired his dark eyes. "I was ready two years ago after I defeated Billy Savoy by only sixty-four votes."

"If you defeat Savoy—"

"There are no *ifs*, Emily," Chris said arrogantly, interrupting her. "I will defeat the man again—this time by more than sixty-four votes." His unwavering stare matched his resolute declaration.

She met his accusing gaze without flinching. "After four years as governor, what are you going to do? You know you'll be ineligible for a state elective position for four years thereafter."

He glanced over her shoulder, staring through the sheer drape shrouding the bed. "Sara and I have talked about opening a practice together. We haven't decided whether it will be Delgado and Lassiter, or Lassiter and Delgado."

"You're going to give up your apartment in Santa Fe and move back to Las Cruces?"

His gaze returned to hers. He nodded. "More than likely I will. Dad said he'll wait until after the election before he decides what he's going to do with the horse farm. Salem has approached him with the idea that Sterling Farms become a registered stud farm."

Salem Lassiter, his veterinarian brother-in-law, owned the property abutting Sterling Farms, and he and Matthew Sterling had shared many hours discussing the future of the horse farm. Matthew had spent nearly thirty-five years breeding and training champion Thoroughbreds, but at seventy years of age planned to move to a much smaller house with his wife. Matt and Eve looked forward to occasional visits from their children and grandchildren in between the other activities they had planned for themselves.

Closing her eyes, Emily buried her face against his bare chest. Chris professed that he loved her, but not once had he spoken of a future together. Swallowing back her disappointment, she settled against his body and willed her mind blank.

"Do you mind going out in the rain?" His soothing voice caressed her ear.

"No," she answered, her voice muffled against his shoulder. "Where do you want to go?"

"It doesn't matter. I'd like to do a little shopping."

"We can go into the center of the city. There are a few malls and dozens of stalls where you can buy handmade crafts."

Chris brushed a gentle kiss across her forehead. "Do you have a date for New Year's Eve, Miss Kirkland?"

Easing back, her eyes crinkled in a smile. "Why do you ask, Mr. Delgado?"

He grinned down at her. "Will you honor me by going out with me tomorrow evening?"

Emily ran the tip of her tongue over her lower lip, bringing his fiery gaze to linger on her mouth. "I'll let you know after I check my book," she teased.

Curving a hand around her neck, he lowered his head and brushed his mouth over hers. "Whoever he is had better find himself another date. You belong to *me*."

Emily stared at him, complete surprise on her face. "What's going on with you?"

Chris's expression changed, becoming suddenly grim. "Nothing," he mumbled angrily. "I don't plan on sharing you with Keith Norris, or any other man, for that matter."

She went completely still, nothing moving—not even her eyes, which had paled to a forbidding pale green. "Let's get something straight, Christopher Delgado. You don't own me. No man owns me. I see who I want, whenever I want," she continued recklessly.

A silence ensued, bristling with tension, while they regarded each other like wary strangers. Chris knew he had made a great faux pas. He could not treat Emily like the others because she was nothing like the other women in his past. Perhaps that was why he had been so drawn to her, because she was totally impervious when it came to catering to his every whim, unlike the one or two women who had campaigned vigorously to become Mrs. Christopher Delgado.

It hadn't mattered to Emily that he was the doted-upon son of one of Las Cruces's prominent families, or that once he entered adolescence members of the opposite sex were drawn to him. The fact that he claimed above-average intelligence and that his parents owned a multimillion-dollar horse farm meant nothing to Emily Kirkland. She had grown up relating to him as if he were her older brother. There were occasions when they argued like siblings, and one or two times when her quick temper had gotten the better of her, when she came at him spitting and clawing like a ferocious cat. He'd always managed to subdue her by holding her wrists or placing his body over hers until she submitted to his superior strength.

If any other woman had said to him what Emily had just said, he would've gotten up and walked away from her—forever. But he could not walk away now; he had bared his soul and confessed his love for her. He loved her and she loved him. Their families and destinies were linked since before their birth.

His hands fell away and he moved off the bed, his gaze never leaving her face. "I'd better get dressed if we're going out." His voice was deceptively calm, masking the rage he had successfully repressed.

Emily lay back on the pile of pillows cradling her shoulders, staring up at the ceiling. She did not know what had possessed her to challenge Chris with the threat that she would see other men, but she refused to begin a liaison with him in which he would dictate what she could and could not do.

She loved him, but she refused to surrender her will. And if he thought he knew her, he had just made the biggest mistake of his life.

No one knew Emily Teresa Kirkland that well. Not even her parents.

Chapter 9

Wakefulness did not rest easy for Emily. It was the last day of the year and the thunderstorms of the previous day had given way to a thick haze that blanketed the coast, making visibility nearly impossible.

She struggled to open her eyes, her lids fluttering several times before she was able to focus clearly on the jalousie-shuttered windows. Diffused light filtered through the slats, giving no indication of the hour.

Turning over on her back, she closed her eyes again. She and Chris had established a temporary truce. After her verbal reprimand they had driven into town without exchanging more than half a dozen overly polite words. She'd waited in the car while he visited several shops to purchase souvenirs for his parents, sister, brother-in-law and nephew.

Their silent impasse continued until they shared dinner at the Almond Tree. The popular restaurant boasted an extensive à la carte menu featuring Jamaican specialties, as well as seafood and steaks. They were served by candlelight on a terrace overlooking the sea. Several cruise ships had docked, and the disembarking passengers crowded the streets, shops and restaurants, adding a boisterousness to Ocho Rios's normal carefree frivolity.

Chris had sampled a dish made with ackee and codfish—Jamaica's national dish—discovering it much to his liking. However, he'd confessed that he found it difficult to understand some of the local dialect, known as Jamaica Talk. She had lapsed easily into the dialect, then translated what she'd said for him. He tried it, bungling the words, and she'd laughed at his attempt, saying it was easier to learn than Spanish. Chris's parents were fluent in Spanish, while her father had taught her the language. Her laughter dispelled their strained mood, and they'd spent the rest of the evening exchanging flirtatious smiles.

She opened her eyes. Pushing back the mosquito netting, she sat up and swung her long, tanned legs over the edge of the bed. A minute later, she left the bed and made her way across the room to the adjoining bath.

Emily walked into the kitchen and was met by the smell of brewing coffee and the sight of Chris standing at the sink. Two large bananas and a pineapple rested on a counter near his left hand. She stood motionless, charmed by his attempt to prepare breakfast; she had always teased him about his inability to cook. Crossing her arms under her breasts, she surveyed his muscular, athletic legs under a pair of cutoff jeans. A startlingly white T-shirt stretched over his broad shoulders, emphasizing the sun-browned darkness of his skin.

"Would you like some help?"

Chris glanced over his shoulder at the sound of Emily's voice, juggling a mango he had picked from one of the trees earlier that morning and catching it before it fell into the sink.

"Not yet," he replied. Turning around, he flashed a warm smile. His gaze cast an approving glance at her scantily clad body in a pair of shorts, tank top and bare feet. "Are you hungry?"

She walked into the kitchen and leaned against the countertop, staring at his well-defined profile. The scent of soap lingered on his skin, indicating that he had showered, although the stubble on his lean cheeks revealed he hadn't shaved. The slight puffiness under his penetrating dark eyes showed that he hadn't had a restful night's sleep.

"No."

And she wasn't hungry. She'd found herself eating more often here than she did in Santa Fe. Her diet in Ocho Rios included a lot of fresh fruits, vegetables and seafood. Her exercise regimen was swimming several times a day in the ocean instead of trying to schedule swimming laps in an indoor pool at a local sports club.

"Are you sure you don't need help?" she asked, grimacing slightly as he began to practically mutilate the mango, peeling away too much fruit as he wielded a small, sharp knife over the firm skin.

Chris handed Emily the knife. "Let me watch you." She deftly peeled the mango, her slender fingers making quick work of the task. "You make it look so easy," he murmured.

"Practice, Chris."

"I never had to practice."

"That's because you were spoiled by a live-in cook."

"And you're not spoiled" he asked, rinsing his hands.

"No. At least I learned to cook, Christopher Blackwell Delgado. I don't fill up on coffee whenever I get hungry."

Moving behind her, he gathered her into his arms, holding her gently and making her his prisoner. "You didn't have to go there, Miss Kirkland," he growled near her ear.

It was difficult for her to breathe as she felt the pressure of his body against hers. She stared down at the dark brown arms cradled beneath her breasts.

"Chris." His name came out in a shivering whisper.

Burying his face against her damp, sweet-smelling hair, Chris savored the delicate curves of her body. He had spent a restless night tossing and turning on the large bed until he finally left it to spend the night sitting on the veranda, where he watched the fog roll in off the water to blanket the entire area with a heavy haze.

You don't own me. No man owns me.

Her words had tortured him relentlessly. He did not want to own her. All he wanted to do was love her—now and for all eternity.

He had wasted years not letting her into his life, watching her interact with other men. Even though she'd been in love with him, she'd still dated others. One had even proposed marriage. And even if she had slept with any of them, it still would not have mattered to Chris. What was important was now, not the past.

"Yes, baby?" he crooned, pressing his groin against the fullness of her hips.

"What…what are you doing?" Her voice came out in a strangled gurgling.

He tightened his arms around her body. "It's what I want to do."

Closing her eyes, she went pliant in his embrace. "What do you want?"

"I want you," he whispered, his breath hot against her ear.

Emily covered his hands with hers, pulling his arms from around her waist. Slowly she turned and stared up at him as he lowered his chin slightly, then met her gaze. His stare, though calm, was lethal. Lethal enough to elicit a feeling of extreme apprehension in her. And it was not for the first time that she thought Chris was hiding something. Was there a dark side that he camouflaged with a practiced smile and impeccable manners?

Chris noticed the slight fluttering in her throat and wondered whether he was moving too quickly. He had told her that the decision to sleep together would be hers. But he did not know how long he could continue to sleep under the same roof with Emily and not go a little crazy. How many more nights could he go without sleep until sheer exhaustion took over?

Reaching up, she looped her arms around his neck. "And I want you."

He stood completely still, his hands at his sides. "Are you sure, *mi amor?*"

"More sure than I've ever been in my life." And she was. She had waited eighteen years for this moment. A moment wherein she would willingly offer him her love and body.

Rising on tiptoe, she pressed her breasts to his chest as her lips searched for his. Her kiss was as soft as a whisper—a breath of wind across his mouth.

A rush of heat raced through Chris, eliciting a throbbing in his groin that he was helpless to control. His world stood still. Nothing mattered—nothing except Emily Kirkland. He had spent so many years loving her, wanting her, that he feared moving because he did not want this to be a dream wherein he'd wake to find himself alone with just his fantasies.

Her mouth tasted, teased, tantalized until the blood roared in his head, until he was nearly blinded by the lust spinning out of control.

His hands moved up and cupped her shoulders, bringing her closer. He wanted to drown in her feminine fragrance as he tightened his hold on her body. Her seduction ended when his tongue plunged into her open mouth, staking its claim.

He did not kiss her mouth but devoured it. And as his kisses became more demanding, Emily felt herself succumbing to the mastery of his lovemaking. His hunger was communicated to her and her hands moved from his neck, under his shoulders, her fingers gripping the fabric of his T-shirt so she could maintain her balance.

She returned his kiss with reckless abandon, her tongue meeting and curling around his, moving in and out of his mouth in a slow, rhythmic, erotic cadence.

A rush of liquid bathed the hidden place between Emily's legs, signaling that she was ready for his possession. Her arousal was so swift that she would have collapsed to the floor if Chris hadn't tightened his grip on her shoulders.

Pulling back, he stared at her flushed face. Desire had added a sheen to her dewy skin and darkened her luminous eyes to a jade green. Bending slightly, Chris swung Emily up in his arms and walked out of the kitchen in the direction of her bedroom as she buried her face against his shoulder.

It's her first time. She's never been with another man. The words swirled in his head as he entered her bedroom and placed her on the bed. The imprint of her head on one pillow was still visible. His gaze swept over the embroidered sheet folded back at the foot of the large bed. The sheets on Emily's bed weren't rumpled and twisted, unlike his own. She had spent the time sleeping, while he hadn't.

He lay down beside her, then pulled the sheer netting around them to create a cloistered, sensual retreat. She offered him a shy smile, lowering her gaze demurely. The gesture was so enthralling that it sucked the air from his lungs.

Pulling her against his chest, he pressed his lips to her forehead. "I don't want to frighten you or hurt you, Emelia."

"I'm not frightened," she mumbled against his throat. And she wasn't. Not when she'd waited so long for him. Not when she loved him so much.

"Good." Anchoring his forefinger under her chin, he raised her face to his. "If I do something that makes you feel uncomfortable, then I want you to tell me to stop. Okay?"

She nodded, smiling. "Okay."

That was the last word she remembered as she closed her eyes and gave herself up to the man who was sharing her bed. She felt his gentle touch when his fingers searched under her tank top and covered her breasts. The sheer fabric of her bra was like a second skin as her nipples sprang into prominence under his sensual ministration. She caught her breath, then let it out slowly when he deftly unhooked the snap and bared the mounds of flesh. He cradled them gently between his palms, seemingly assessing their firmness and weight, as if he were examining pieces of lush, ripe fruit to purchase.

Lowering his head, his mouth replaced his hands, causing her to arch off the mattress. Chris told Emily he didn't want to frighten her when he was frightened, frightened that it had become his responsibility to introduce her to a world of sexual pleasure. It was up to him to teach her to become familiar with her own body in order for her to derive the ultimate sexual fulfillment.

He kissed her taut nipples, teased them between his teeth, then drew circles around the areola with his tongue. She moaned softly, her breathing quickening. She attempted to touch him, but he held her wrists.

"Don't touch me," he ordered softly. "Not yet."

Swallowing to relieve the dryness in her throat, Emily nodded through a haze of rising desire. "Okay," she gasped when she finally recovered her voice.

Everything seemed to unfold in slow motion as Chris relieved her of her top, bra and shorts. There was a slight hesitation when he hooked his fingers in the waistband of her bikini panties and eased them off her hips and down her legs.

Emily opened her eyes and found him sitting back on folded knees, staring at her naked body. Every place his obsidian gaze touched brought a wave of heat and lingering fire.

"You're magnificent." There was no mistaking the awe in his voice. His lids fluttered closed. "You're more perfect than I could've ever imagined." He opened his eyes, his enraptured gaze meeting hers.

Her gaze widened when he reached down and pulled his T-shirt over his head, baring a broad chest covered with a profusion of thick, dark, curling hair. The power in his upper arms was apparent by the smooth flexing of muscles with the gesture. His hands went to the waistband of his cutoffs, and in one smooth motion the denim fabric and his briefs had settled around his knees.

Fluidly, and with a minimum of motion, Chris divested himself of his clothes and lowered his body over Emily's, supporting his weight on his elbows. He settled her legs between his, his hardening sex pressing against the mound hiding her femininity from him. She gasped slightly as he increased the pressure until their bodies were joined from chest to knees.

He wanted her to get used to his greater weight, the texture of his skin, and the difference between their bodies. Reaching down, he caught her left hand and placed it over his hip.

"Touch me, Emelia."

Her fingers traced the curve of his firm buttocks, a smile curving her lush mouth. "I like the way you feel."

"You feel a lot nicer than I do," he countered, his fingers feathering down her chest, over a breast and to her belly.

"That's debatable," she whispered against his mouth. Curving her arms around his neck, she pressed a kiss against his firm lips, closing her eyes and reveling in the sensations coursing through her body. She kissed his upper lip, then caught the lower one between her teeth, pulling it gently into her mouth before her tongue traced the outline of his strong, masculine mouth.

A noticeable shudder racked Chris from head to toe when the fire from Emily's lips was transferred to his. Her mouth was doing things to him that he did not want to feel—not yet. He wanted their first time together to be special, her first time to be wonderful, but if he didn't stop her, it would become a libidinous coupling instead of a gentle session of lovemaking.

He loved her, loved her too much to take her without tenderness.

He tore his mouth from her tantalizing lips and moved down her body, tasting flesh in his journey southward. Her fingers gripped his hair, but the shortened strands did not allow her a firm hold. He moaned softly when her fingernails sank into his scalp, but he forgot the discomfort once he parted her knees. Then he buried his face against the soft down at the juncture of her thighs.

Her soft whimpers of rising passion fired his blood. His rapacious tongue searched and found the small, engorged nodule of flesh and he worshipped it, alternating flicking his tongue over it with catching the nectar flowing from her virginal well of sensual delight.

Emily felt as if she had stepped outside herself and become a reluctant observer instead of a willing participant. Nothing she had ever shared with any man came close to what she was experiencing with Christopher Delgado. After she had recovered from the fact that he had put his head between her thighs, she was quickly assailed by the rush of desire shattering her dormant sexuality. Shivers of delight shook her body, and there was no way she could disguise the moans of ecstasy slipping through her compressed lips. Her whole being was flooded with a desire that threatened to drown her.

Her body vibrated with a fire that swept away all her doubts and fears that the man lying between her legs did not love her as much as she loved him. Her body went completely limp as she surrendered completely to his masterful seduction. Tears leaked from under her tightly closed lids, staining her flushed cheeks.

Without warning it happened; the soft pulsing grew stronger, more intense. The measured vibrations shook her, and she arched off the mattress.

Chris realized Emily was reaching the point of no return and slid up the length of her body, a finger replacing his tongue. He held her tightly, his hand motionless, feeling the throbbing flesh around his finger abate slightly.

Emily's tear-filled eyes opened and she stared at him. There was no mistaking her puzzlement. Chris pressed his lips to her thoroughly kissed mouth, permitting her to taste herself.

"I want to teach you to control your body so you can prolong fulfillment to the last possible moment." He moved his finger slightly in the tight opening. A sensual smile crinkled his eyes when she closed hers, gasping. "That's it, baby." He increased the rhythm, taking her to the point where she cried out for release, but he would not relent.

Emily's chest heaved as she labored for each breath, writhing against his hand in an ancient rhythm as old as time itself. Her emotions whirled; her senses exploded as her passion escalated. "No more," she pleaded. "Please, no more."

Chris wanted to join her in her dance of desire, but decided not to. Not this time. He would sacrifice himself and not pour out his passions in her soft, scented body in order to offer her a selfless pleasure. The next time would be his—theirs.

He increased the rhythm and she pulled back, trying to escape. He eased another finger into her narrow opening. She opened her mouth to scream, but he covered it with his own, capturing and swallowing her breath as she breathed her ardor into his mouth.

His hand was sandwiched between their moist bodies, fingers coated with the liquid flowing from her still-pulsating flesh. The turbulence of her passion had shocked him. Emily would become an extraordinary lover.

Withdrawing his fingers, he reversed their positions and she lay over his chest. Curving his arms around her narrow waist, he closed his eyes. A slight smile curved his lips when he felt her snuggle for a more comfortable position.

Her moist breath swept over his ear when she buried her face between his neck and shoulder. "Why, Chris?" she whispered softly. "Why didn't you—"

"The next time," he said, interrupting her.

She smiled, pressing her mouth to the side of his strong neck. "I'm looking forward to it." There was a hint of laughter in her voice.

Shifting his head, Chris kissed her damp forehead. "No more than I, *mi amor.* No more than I," he repeated.

Chris smiled, closing his eyes. Within minutes he had fallen asleep, while the woman in his arms stared at the serenity softening his features until she, too, joined him in a dreamless slumber.

Chapter 10

Emily and Chris walked into the restaurant at the resort and were quickly swallowed up by a lively crowd dancing and gyrating to the late Bob Marley's "I Shot the Sheriff." All of the tables in the restaurant were positioned close to the walls, allowing for a larger dancing area, while long tables covered with tablecloths in the colors of black, green and gold held trays of steaming dishes. White-jacketed servers stood behind the tables where a sumptuous buffet awaited the revelers.

Curving an arm around Emily's waist, Chris steered her through the crowd and over to the bar. Shielding her body with his to protect her from the throng lining the solid mahogany bar, he raised his right hand to capture a waiter's attention.

A young man with a mouth filled with perfect straight teeth approached, offering them a friendly smile. "Yeah, mon?"

"Two rum punches." Reaching into the pockets of his slacks, he placed a bill on the highly polished surface.

The bartender worked quickly, mixing the drinks. "A rum punch for the pretty lady, and one for her gentleman friend."

Emily smiled, her luminous eyes crinkling attractively. "Thank you."

"Thanks," Chris mumbled under his breath, successfully controlling his temper. He couldn't believe the man was openly flirting with Emily, as if he did not exist.

Turning to face Chris, Emily touched her glass to his. "Here's to a special night."

He inclined his head. "To love and passion."

She felt a rush of heat warm her cheeks with his toast. They had spent the morning in bed, rising to eat what had become a late breakfast of fruit, coffee and several slices of toast topped with an imported British strawberry-and-champagne-blended jam.

The haze had lifted by midafternoon, and they walked down to the beach and lingered in the water for nearly an hour. Afterward, they retreated to the gazebo and lay on the hammock, laughing and talking about the predicaments they had gotten into when growing up.

Emily refused to think about the time when Chris would leave Ocho Rios. This night would be their third night together, and within another three he would to fly to Mexico to meet his biological father.

She took a sip of the potent drink, closing her eyes briefly. When she opened them she found Chris staring at her with a strange expression on his face.

"Are you all right?"

She flashed a too-bright smile. "I'm wonderful."

Tightening his hold on her waist, he led her away from the bar and over to a table for two in a corner. Pulling out a chair, he seated her. Sitting opposite her, he studied her impassive expression. Instinctively, he knew she had not told him the truth. She wasn't all right. Something was bothering her, but he decided not to pry.

He had never seen her look more sensual than she did tonight. Her dress was a black fitted garment with capped sleeves, a squared neckline that revealed a hint of tanned breasts and a very short length that showed off her bare, well-shaped legs. She had added three inches to her statuesque height with a pair of black sling-back patent leather pumps. Her face was radiant, with a light cover of makeup that accentuated her jeweled eyes and full, lush mouth. Her hair shimmered from a styling gel that kept the raven curls off her face and ears. The flickering light from the small candle on the table reflected off the rare yellow diamond studs in her pierced lobes.

Seeing her earrings reminded him of the ones his mother wore. They were a pair of brilliant blue-white diamonds set in platinum in an antique design with levered backs that Matthew Sterling had given his wife on their wedding day. It had become a tradition with the Sterlings that the eldest son give the earrings to his wife after the birth of their first son. If there were no sons, then the eldest daughter passed them on to the first grandson.

Sara Lassiter had given his parents their first grandson, yet Eve Sterling had not relinquished the earrings. And when he questioned his mother about them she had revealed that Matt wanted him to have the earrings. Her explanation rendered him mute. He loved Matthew Sterling but had always acknowledged that he was his stepfather. Matt had never thought of him as his stepson, but the son who should have sprung from his own loins. The simple explanation changed how he viewed the man he called dad—forever. From that moment he had become Matthew Sterling's son.

He placed a hand over Emily's delicate fingers. "What if me get the pretty lady something to eat?" he questioned with a Jamaican accent. "Jerk chicken, jerk pork, jerk fish? What do you say if me get you some curry goat? Callaloo? Peas and rice?"

Throwing back her head, she laughed, the sensual sound of her voice bubbling up from her throat. "Me like it much."

Emily was still smiling as he rose to his feet and walked away to get her food. Her admiring gaze lingered on his tall, slim body. His navy blue tailored suit jacket fell with expert precision from his wide shoulders, while the matching slacks ended with the perfect break above his highly polished loafers. She knew that Chris had amassed an extensive wardrobe to accommodate the fluctuation in his weight. Tonight he had opted not to wear a tie when he selected a navy blue banded-collar silk shirt.

Good things come to those who wait. The caption beneath her photograph in her high school yearbook came to mind. She had waited a long time, but it was only now that she could acknowledge that the wait had been worth it.

Perfect. The single word summed up exactly who and what Christopher Blackwell Delgado was.

Emily felt a presence to her right and turned to stare up at a man she hadn't seen in years. He pulled back her chair and she rose to her feet, a wide grin creasing her face.

"Reginald!" He gathered her to his chest. The familiar fragrance of patchouli swept over her as she pressed her lips to his smooth ebony cheek.

"Emily Kirkland." His refined accent caressed her ear. "I had to look twice to make certain it was you." Easing back, his dark gray eyes surveyed her critically. "How long has it been?"

She calculated quickly. "At least ten years. My family had come down the Christmas before I celebrated my twenty-first birthday."

Holding her at arm's length, his gaze swept appreciatively up and down her slender body. "You've really grown up. The last time I saw you, you were still a little girl."

Emily shook her head. "I was a woman, Reginald," she reminded him in a gentle tone.

It was his turn to shake his head. "What was it that wouldn't permit me to see that?"

Emily affected an attractive moue. "I believe it was someone named Edwina Bramble."

"Who?"

"You men are all the same. How quickly you forget."

She had to admit that time had been very kind to Reginald Wallingford. Ten years her senior, he hadn't changed much. She was still stunned by his incredibly smooth, sable-brown skin. His coloring was the perfect foil for features usually attributed to one claiming European ancestry. Local rumor claimed that Reginald's mother had become pregnant during an extended vacation in England but had returned to Jamaica to give birth and raise her only child. At the beginning of each year a check arrived from London with enough money for Margaret Wallingford to live quite comfortably.

"I could never forget you, Emily Kirkland."

"Or I you, Reginald." There was a time when she had a crush on the tall man who taught British history at the University of the West Indies.

"How long will you be in Ocho Rios?" he asked her.

"I plan to leave here on the twelfth."

"Are you returning to the States?"

She nodded. "Yes."

"Are you here with your family?"

"No. I came without them."

Reaching for her left hand, he surveyed her bare fingers. "Would you mind if I come by and see you before you leave?"

"We'd love to have company, wouldn't we, *mi amor?*" said a male voice with a distinctive American Southwestern drawl.

Emily spun around to find Chris standing behind her. His smile was cold, lacking any trace of humor. He set a plate on the table, then extended his right hand to Reginald.

"Christopher Delgado."

Reginald took the hand, recovering quickly. When Emily said that her family hadn't come with her, he'd assumed that she had come to Jamaica alone.

"Reginald Wallingford."

Chris pumped the hand vigorously, adding to the other man's uneasiness. "When do you plan on visiting with us?"

"I'll call and let you know. The telephone number hasn't changed, has it?" Reginald asked, directing the question to Emily.

"It's the same," she confirmed.

Leaning forward, Reginald kissed her cheek. "I'll be in touch."

Emily knew his promise was an empty one. She had seen the silver gleam in his gray eyes dim with Chris's approach.

"I'll wait for your call, Reginald." He inclined his head, then turned and walked away.

Emily and Chris shared a knowing glance before they retook their seats. Both knew their chances of seeing Reginald Wallingford again during their stay in Ocho Rios were very slim.

She ignored the plate of food on the table and picked up her glass of rum punch. Taking a sip of the tropical concoction, she stared over the rim at Chris. The drink was liberally laced with rum, a little potent for her taste, yet she welcomed the warmth spreading through her chest. The realization that she and Chris were now a couple had not been apparent before Reginald's approach. In the past they went to mass, concerts and attended family gatherings together. But that had been before they declared their love for each other.

The tempo of the music changed, and a slow, sensual ballad filled the large space with its haunting melody. Emily smiled at Chris. "Will you dance with me?"

Rising, he rounded the table and pulled her gently to her feet. They joined the other couples on the dance floor, their bodies melding as they swayed to a classic love song that was usually played at wedding receptions.

Chris's warm breath swept over her ear when he lowered his head, his nose nuzzling the side of her scented neck. "I'm starving," he confessed in a raspy whisper, "and you look and smell good enough to eat."

A roaring heat swept through her, as if she had opened the door to a voracious furnace to feed it more coal. His erotic confession left her shaking, and she doubted she could remain standing without his aid.

"Not here, Chris."

He tightened his grip on her waist, pulling her closer. "Why not?"

"This is not the place." Her voice had lowered to a sultry whisper.

He swung her around and around, forcing her to put her arms around his neck to keep her balance. "I don't need a bed to make love to you, Emelia." He verified his assertion when he breathed a kiss under her ear.

Sinking against his cushioning embrace, Emily was conscious of everything that made Christopher Delgado the worldly, handsome, elegant and passionate man she had fallen in love with. It was apparent that he was much more sexually experienced than she was, yet he was a selfless lover.

"Am I embarrassing you?" he asked.

She nodded, her face pressed against his warm throat. "A little."

Pulling back slightly, he stared at her, his gaze narrowing. "You've had a long time to get used to us being together."

Emily glanced up, meeting his penetrating stare. "Knowing

each other is very different from us getting to know the other." His confusion was apparent when his curving black eyebrows lifted questioningly. "I know you," she explained, "because we've practically grown up together."

"Shouldn't that be enough?"

"No."

"Why not?" he shot back.

"Because there is a part of you I don't know. A part that makes you seem like a stranger."

He pulled her closer, burying his lips against her hair. "Which part?"

"The physical part. I don't know what I have to do to bring you pleasure."

The soft sound of his laughter vibrated in her ear. "You don't have to do anything, Emily. All you have to do is be yourself."

"But—"

"No buts," Chris interrupted quietly. "I've fallen in love with a woman who has been blessed with not only an incredible beauty but brains. A rare combination indeed. A woman who is so secure with her own femininity that I've found myself comparing every woman I meet with you."

It was her turn to laugh. "I was jealous of your women."

Closing his eyes, he smiled. "There was nothing for you to be jealous of, baby girl." Snuggling closer, Emily pressed her lips to his. He opened his eyes. "I think you must have cast a spell on me the day you asked me to kiss you in your grandparents' garden."

She went completely still, missing a step as he tightened his hold on her body. "You remember that?" Turning her head, she stared over his shoulder. "That was the most embarrassing day of my life."

"Why? Because your cousins saw us kissing?"

"That, and because I was so brazen."

"You were more curious than brazen."

Chris was only half right. She had been curious, but there were other young men she could have asked to kiss her. Young men who had been invited to Aaron and Regina Spencer's wedding, the sons of her uncles' business associates. But she had asked seventeen-year-old Christopher Delgado because she had felt comfortable with him. She hadn't yet realized that she had developed a serious crush on her best friend's brother.

Her gaze swung back, meeting his. There was a gleam of determination in her laser-green eyes. "Right now I'm going to be more than brazen. I want to go back to the house. I want you to make love to me," she stated with a confidence that hadn't been there before. "I want to be in your bed, in your arms and feel you in me when the clock strikes midnight to signal a new year."

It was Chris's turn to stumble at this erotic confession, but he recovered quickly, leading her through the throng of swaying couples. The silver-flecked eyes of Reginald Wallingford watched their retreat, a slight smile curving his mouth. The petite woman standing beside him noted the direction of his gaze and looped her arm through the sleeve of his suit jacket, recapturing his attention.

Emily felt as if she had been holding her breath until she sat beside Chris in his rental car. She didn't know where she had found the courage to utter the words she had buried in her heart, but now that they were out she felt free—freer than she had ever been in her life.

For almost two decades she had repressed her feelings and sexuality because she had been waiting for one man to acknowledge her as a woman. She had managed to control every phase of her existence, but there were times when she felt as if she had relegated herself to a prison without bars. She did not want to begin another year of her life denying her true feelings.

The year before she began seeing Keith Norris she had found herself accepting dates from men she had turned down in the past. It had reached a point when she did not want to spend a weekend alone, so she went out to dinner, shared brunch, attended sporting events and concerts with a lot of men with the hope that she would meet someone who could make her forget Chris.

After a while she had tired of trying to keep their names straight, so she began seeing Keith exclusively, and because his major league baseball schedule would not permit her to see him every week they were able to develop a comfortable relationship wherein they made the most of their limited time together.

Keith had waited two months to ask her to sleep with him. She'd turned him down, saying that she would let him know when she felt the time was right for them to take their relationship to another level. It was apparent that Keith had become impatient and, without her approval, had announced their engagement.

Keith and all of the others were her past, while Chris represented *now,* and she was mature enough not to project more into their relationship than that moment.

Chris's fingers tightened on the steering wheel as he navigated the unlit road. He replayed her erotic entreaty in his head, remembering the exact timbre of her sultry voice when she told him what she wanted. *I want to be in your bed, in your arms and feel you in me when the clock strikes midnight to signal a new year.*

A slight smile curved his mouth. He would fulfill her desire, and in doing so would also yield to his own.

There was a profound silence as they entered the house and climbed the narrow, winding staircase to the second floor. Chris pulled Emily gently into his bedroom, his gaze never leaving her face. The light from a bedside lamp cast a soft glow in the sparsely furnished space. The hands on his travel clock indicated that there was another twenty minutes before the advent of a new year, and at the stroke of midnight he intended to grant Emily her most fervent wish.

Her eyes glowed like a beacon, appearing large and trusting as she stared up at him, waiting—waiting for him to make the first move. Moving closer, his hands came up and curved around her upper arms, his fingers caressing the silken flesh.

Lowering his head, he brushed his mouth over hers, and her lips parted automatically. Moist breaths mingled, then fused, and tongues tasted, while banked passions stirred restlessly.

Emily placed her hands on Chris's chest, feeling the strong, steady pumping of his heart under her palms. She wanted to beg him to take her and assuage the flames of desire heating her thighs and groin. She wanted to climb the walls of ecstasy again and lose herself in the explosive currents that had taken her beyond herself.

Her hands moved across his chest to his shoulders. Deepening the kiss, she pushed his jacket off. Hearts pounding in unison, their hands were busy as they slowly, methodically, undressed each other, Emily taking an inordinate amount of time to slip each button on his shirt from its fastening. By the time she had relieved him of his belt and had unzipped his slacks she found herself clad in only her heels and panties. Her dress and demi-bra lay in a heap on the floor next to his shirt and jacket.

She inhaled audibly, the sound reverberating off the walls as his fingertips skimmed across her breasts in a slow, sweeping motion, bringing the nipples into prominence. His hands worked their magic, tracing every dip and curve of her body and molding her flesh like heated wax. Closing her eyes, she reveled in the tingling sensations coursing through her swollen breasts. His touch, his heat, the scent of cologne on his bared flesh transported Emily to another time and place.

Chris's right hand moved slowly down the length of her body to cradle her sex through a layer of silk and lace. Squeezing gently, he measured the slight pulsing against his palm. It matched the intense throbbing in his own blood-engorged sex—a throbbing that had him close to exploding.

His hand moved upward, cradling her face gently. "I love you," he whispered reverently. "I want you so much."

Emily answered his plea, her hands cradling the solid bulge straining against his briefs. Opening her eyes, she smiled. "I want and need you."

Chris returned her smile. "And you'll have me. *All* of me." Pulling out of her gentle grasp, he slipped out of his loafers, pushed his slacks down his legs and stepped out of them. His socks and briefs followed. He stood in front of her—proud, naked and magnificently aroused.

Her gaze lingered on his face, then moved lower, very slowly.

Her luminous eyes caressed his lean, muscled form as gently as a caress.

"Oh, Chris."

The awe in her voice nearly sent him over the edge, and he feared embarrassing himself by spilling his passions on the floor. He hadn't waited this long to have it end up with his not being able to complete the act, like an anxious adolescent during his first sexual encounter.

Bending down, Chris removed her heels, then slipped her black lace panties off her hips and down her long legs. Straightening in one smooth, continuous motion, he cradled her face, his mouth moving over hers and devouring its succulent sweetness.

Emily wasn't given the opportunity to catch her breath once she found herself in Chris's arms. He placed her on the bed, paused to protect her and then moved over her trembling limbs, supporting most of his weight on his arms.

Rising slightly, he reached down and positioned his sex at the entrance to her vestal body. "Easy, baby," he whispered.

Emily bit down on her lower lip until she tasted blood as her virginal flesh stretched inch by inch to accommodate her lover's rigid tumescence. The burning and the pain subsided once he was buried deep inside her; then the pleasure returned, the all-consuming passion she had experienced earlier that morning rushing back as he began moving in a slow, rocking motion that touched her womb.

The fists pressed against his back unclenched, her outstretched fingers sliding up and down his spine in an agonizing slowness that sent waves of heat throughout Chris's body. He kissed the pulsing hollow at the base of her throat, moved to the fragrant column of her long silken neck, then the moist sweetness of her lush mouth.

Emily felt his hardness sliding in and out in a strong, measured rhythm that took her higher and higher until she trembled in a shimmering desire that had her gasping for breath.

Her desire for him was uncontrollable, whirling, careening and tilting the earth on its axis. Looping her arms under his shoulders, she held him tightly and rode the waves of ecstasy buffeting her through a fire that completely swept her away.

The pleasure he offered her was pure and explosive, and she gasped in sweet agony. Love flowed through her like hot honey at the same time as she cried out her release, taking Chris with her in a shared free fall.

The sound of exploding fireworks reverberated in the stillness of the night; someone had used a more public way of celebrating the new year.

Emily lay in Chris's arms, listening to the thundering sounds and knowing that what they had just offered each other had changed them—forever.

Chapter 11

Streams of light slipped through the partially closed jalousie shutters framing the second-story veranda, inching their way across the floor and bed with the rising sun. The buildup of tropical heat intensified the redolence of ripening fruit and blooming flowers as a gentle breeze from the ocean carried the wafting scent for miles. Ocho Rios was wide awake with the raucous cries of colorful birds hopping nimbly from tree to tree while chattering noisily.

Shifting and turning to his left, Chris drew in a ragged breath, inhaling deeply. The soft crush of firm flesh against his bare chest reminded him of where he was and whom he was with, and he came awake immediately.

Emily lay curled against his body like a graceful feline, her full breasts grazing his chest, one hand cradled under her cheek; she had thrown a silken leg over his calf. A tender smile softened his features when he felt the soft whisper of her breathing feather over his throat. She had offered him her love, her virginal body and a passion that had left him trembling from its aftermath.

She had fallen asleep in his arms while he lay in the darkness, marveling at how her untutored body had elicited a raw lust within him that made him want to spend the entire night in her scented embrace.

He hadn't come to Emily a virgin, but he also hadn't come to her with a countless string of sexual conquests; he had forced himself to be very discriminating with women. Embarking on a career in politics had been a deciding factor, along with the fact that he did not want to become an Alejandro Delgado clone. His greatest fear was that he had inherited his biological father's proclivity for infidelity.

Grant Carson's revelation that Alejandro had returned to Mexico had given him the final piece he needed to complete the puzzle of his past. Even though he'd grown up thinking about the man who had fathered him, Alejandro Delgado-Quintero was not a man he had ever expected to meet again.

His mother had answered all his questions when he asked why his last name wasn't Sterling, and why he didn't look like her or the man he called dad. But it wasn't until he entered adolescence and felt the seductive pull of sexual desire that he understood his mother's explanation of why Alejandro could not be a faithful husband. It had taken a long time, but Chris had managed to successfully repress his strong sexual urges—until now.

Recalling the passion he had found in Emily's fragrant embrace elicited an immediate involuntary hardness in his groin. Closing his eyes, he let out his breath in an audible sigh. He couldn't make love to her again—not now. She was too newly opened. He would have to be patient until her tender flesh healed. Curving an arm around her waist, he pulled her closer and feasted on her fragility.

They had ten months to conceal their private passions; then he intended to introduce the woman he loved to the residents of New Mexico and the rest of the world.

Emily walked into the kitchen at the same time the phone chimed shrilly. Quickening her pace, she picked up the receiver of the wall phone.

"Hello."

"Happy New Year."

Her eyes shimmered with excitement when she recognized her mother's voice. "Happy New Year, Mom. How are you?"

There was a slight chuckle from Vanessa Kirkland. "I should be asking how you are. I called because I want to know if it's too early to begin listing names for invitations."

Vertical lines appeared between Emily's eyes. "Invitations for what?"

"Your wedding, of course."

She felt her heart lurch. It was apparent that her mother also thought she was going to marry Keith Norris. "I'm sorry, Mom, but there's not going to be a wedding."

There was a momentary pause before Vanessa's voice came through the wire again. "But...but it was announced on the news. Your father and I were *very* disappointed that you hadn't told us first."

Emily heard her mother's annoyance. Since Eve Sterling had become a grandmother, Vanessa had begun subtly hinting that it was time her son or daughter married and presented her with a grandchild.

"Momma," she drawled, "it's not going to happen."

It took her less than two minutes to explain Keith's subterfuge, and her plan to rebut his announcement once she returned to the States.

Vanessa emitted an audible sigh. "Well, I can honestly admit that even though I believe you can do better than marrying an athlete, I was looking forward to becoming the mother of the bride."

Emily laughed softly. "Maybe another time. Michael will probably marry before I do." What she didn't say was that she doubted if she would ever marry. If she did not marry Chris, she would remain single. She had slept with him, but their sharing a bed was not tantamount to a marriage proposal.

"Emily? Are you there?"

"Yes. I'm still here. How's Grandpa?" she asked, smoothly changing the subject.

"His condition hasn't changed much."

"Give him and Grandma a kiss for me."

"I will. Look, sweetheart, I'm going to let you go. I love you."

"I love you, too. Tell Daddy I love him."

"I will. Bye."

"Goodbye, Mom."

Hanging up, Emily stared at the telephone. There was no doubt she would have to do some serious damage control to alter her public image—now! She picked up the receiver again and dialed the area code for Denver, Colorado, then the number to Keith Norris's residence.

There was a break in the connection after the second ring. "Keith Norris," she said without preliminary after she heard his groggy greeting. "I want you to retract your announcement that we're engaged. And you have exactly twenty-four hours to do it. If not, it'll be my turn to make an announcement, and what I'll say will be quite detrimental to your impeccable image. Don't worry about your ring. I'll return it as soon as I return to the States. By the way…"

Her words trailed off as Chris strolled into the kitchen, his dark eyebrows slanting into a frown. She did not know how she had missed it over so many years, but she silently admired Chris's distinctive walk, with his straight spine and broad shoulders that swayed with each fluid stride.

Her hand was steady as she hung up the phone. If Chris hadn't come into the kitchen, she would've graced Keith with a few of the colorful expletives the Coles and Kirklands had become famous for.

Forcing a smile, she said, "Christopher Blackwell Delgado, this is your lucky day. I'm going to offer you your first cooking lesson."

He ignored her offer. "What's going on, Emily?"

Her false smile faded. "What are you talking about?"

"Did Norris call you?"

"No."

"I heard—"

"You heard nothing," she interrupted. "You were eavesdropping on a private telephone conversation. Let's get something straight, Chris, before we take whatever we've shared with each other further. There are things in my private life I have to resolve *for* myself and *by* myself. And I'd appreciate you not interfering. I will not question you about the women you've slept with, and I don't want you to question me about men from my past. What we have begins today—now. And if we can't agree, then it will end now—today."

Chris stared at Emily—completely stunned. He couldn't believe she'd turn her back on him because he was concerned about her well-being—concerned because Keith Norris had used his celebrity status for his own selfish purposes.

He took several steps, bringing them less than three feet apart. "Do you love me, Emily? Do you really love me?"

Tilting her chin in a defiant gesture, she gave him a direct stare. "Yes."

"I don't believe you. Do you know why? I don't believe you," he continued without waiting for her reply, "because you'd walk away from me simply because I want to help and protect you."

"I don't want your help. And I don't need your protection."

What Chris hadn't known was that she had spent years fighting for her independence—from both parents. They hadn't wanted her to move out and get her own apartment. They had alienated her when she bought the motorcycle, and her father sought to monitor every man she dated.

She was secure in her chosen profession, she was financially solvent, and at thirty she refused to permit anyone to regulate, limit, or control her life.

Chris stared down at her, a lethal coldness filling his gaze. "Then what the hell do you want from me?"

Emily returned his direct stare. Her eyes had become a frosty light green, chilling him until he couldn't look away even if he wanted to. *She's her father,* a voice whispered in his head. At that moment the woman he loved reminded him of Joshua Kirkland—a man whose cold, dispassionate, penetrating look could destroy the nerve of the bravest man.

How had he missed that part of her personality? He had known her all his life and this was the first time she had ever withdrawn from him, shut him out with only a glance.

"I want you to let me be Emily," she said softly.

"I don't want to change you," Chris countered.

"Then let me handle Keith Norris."

Nodding, he decided it would serve no purpose to argue with her. He wanted to love her, not alienate her. "Okay, baby. I'll let you take care him."

He would let her have her way—*this time.*

The impasse ended when Emily moved forward and curved her arms around his neck. Lowering his head, Chris kissed her waiting lips, drinking in the passion he had come to crave.

Chapter 12

Unconsciously, smoothly, Emily and Chris slipped into the routine of a couple who were committed to spending their lives together when they shared a bed, each other's bodies and cleaning and cooking duties.

They slept late, prepared monstrous breakfasts, strolled along the beach, swam in the Caribbean, toured the island and availed themselves of Jamaica's festive nightlife. A few nights they returned home in time to greet the rising sun.

They lay side by side on the oversized hammock in the gazebo, holding hands. An ocean breeze cooled their moist flesh as the hammock swayed slightly in the waning sunlight.

Not opening his eyes, Chris announced quietly, "I'm leaving on Thursday."

Emily felt her heart lurch in her chest. Two days—no, one day. They only had one full day together before he returned his rental car and boarded a flight in Kingston to Mexico City. She knew that Chris had only planned to stay in Jamaica a week, but she had hoped he would change his mind and stay longer.

"I'm going to miss you." She could not disguise the anguish in her voice.

"Come with me, Emelia."

She shook her head. "No."

"Why?"

"I can't."

Releasing her hand, Chris turned and looked at her. He had thought she could not become more beautiful, but it was as if her newly awakened sensuality had intensified her seductive femininity.

"Why not? You're still on vacation."

Emily smiled at her lover, her infatuation for him radiating from the depths of her luminous eyes. She ran a forefinger down the length of his nose before her mouth replaced her finger.

"What you have to handle with your father is too personal for me to be tagging along."

He arched a curving eyebrow. "Personal?"

"Yes, Chris, personal."

"What do you call personal?" he questioned, visibly annoyed. "If putting my face between your legs and tasting your flesh isn't personal, I don't know what is."

Heat and shame seared her face. "I'm not talking about that."

"I am," he countered. "I love you, Emily," Chris continued, this time in a softer tone, "and I want Señor Alejandro Delgado-Quintero to meet the woman I love *and* respect. And I want him to know that I will never do to you what he did to my mother."

Emily flinched at the ominous tone in his words. Why did he want to see his father? Was it to avenge his mother? Or did he want retaliation for his own abduction?

"I will not become a pawn for you because you want retribution for what happened to you and your mother more than thirty years ago."

His expression hardened, and a muscle throbbed noticeably in his jaw. "It has nothing to do with retribution. What I want to do is close a chapter on my life, never to reopen it again. I have to be prepared to answer any questions about Alejandro Delgado if they surface during the campaign. Answers I can't get from my parents. They have to come from Alejandro himself. And I intend to stay in Mexico until I get the truth from him."

This was the determination that made Christopher Delgado the dynamic, confident man who took charge of everything in his life with quiet assurance, that made him so sure of who he was. But for a second his confidence slipped, vulnerability filling his obsidian gaze.

"Please come with me," he pleaded in a broken whisper. Pulling her closer, he buried his face in her curly hair.

It was the first time she had known Chris to beg for anything. Why now? Did he fear coming face-to-face with his father? Was he not as confident as he appeared?

"Let me think about it," she whispered, unable and unwilling to commit to his request.

Later that evening, Chris stood under the cool spray of the shower in the bath in Emily's bedroom, singing loudly as he shampooed and rinsed the salt and sand from his hair. Opening the door to the stall, he reached for a towel on the bar over the door. His fingers groped in vain. He was certain he had left the towel on the bar.

"Looking for this, handsome?"

Emily stood off to his left, holding out the towel. She wore an ivory-colored robe. The silken garment clung to her slim curves and flowed out around her slender feet. His heated gaze inched up from her bare feet to the damp hair drying in wayward curls over her forehead.

He extended his left hand. "Give me the towel, Emily."

She pressed the terry-cloth fabric to her chest. "Come and let me dry your back."

Chris stared down at his dripping body. "That's all right. I can dry it."

Taking a step toward him, Emily crooned, "Don't be shy, Chris. You dried my back. It's my turn to spoil you a little." She had taken a leisurely bath and he had come into the bathroom to wash her body, rinse it, then spend an inordinate amount of time drying and moisturizing her skin with her favorite perfumed body cream.

He stared, complete surprise freezing his features. Of all the women he had known, Emily was the first to offer to do something for him. The others always wanted something from him: attention, sex or expensive gifts.

"Come," she urged, moving closer to him.

He stepped out of the shower stall, presenting her with his

back. Closing his eyes, he luxuriated in her gentle touch as she drew the towel down his spine, over his hips and down the back of his thighs and legs.

"Turn around," she ordered quietly.

Chris obeyed. Staring down at her, he suffered in silence as she blotted the moisture from his chest, shoulders, arms and belly, then drew the towel between his thighs, stopping short of his stirring sex. Her touch was soft, gentle and sensual.

Tilting her chin, Emily smiled up at him. "I think that just about does it."

He took the towel from her loose grip and dropped it to the worn, brick-lined floor. "I beg to differ. It's just beginning, baby."

She couldn't see the banked fires smoldering in his dark eyes. "What is?"

"This."

His fingers grasped her shoulders, pulling her to his chest. She opened her mouth, but whatever she was going to say was cut off when his mouth covered hers, stopping her words and her breath.

Chris lifted Emily effortlessly, carrying her out of the bathroom and into the bedroom. The dimmed light from a bedside lamp highlighted the four-poster bed draped in mosquito netting.

"Chris." Her voice was low, seductive.

"Hush, baby. It's my turn to spoil you."

Parting the netting, he placed her on the bed, lay down beside her, and closed the drapery around them. The dim glow from the lamp cast an eerie, shadowy light through the gauzy fabric.

Emily lay still, unmoving, as he untied the silken sash around her waist and parted the robe. Chills, then heat swept over her naked limbs as Chris drew the back of his hand over her breasts.

Her breath quickened. His hand traveled down her body until it cradled her womanhood before his fingers splayed and parted the folds hiding her femininity.

"Love me, please," she pleaded.

Leaning over, Chris kissed her deeply, his tongue searching the moist sweetness of her mouth. Emily repeated her litany, then more, shocking Chris with her passionate pleas. She was begging him to do things to her she had balked and blushed at when he'd first initiated them into their repertoire of lovemaking. She arched as his mouth followed the path of his fingers, drawing a moist path over her silken belly and still lower.

Chris smothered a savage curse because he thought it was going to be over before it began as Emily's hand closed on him in a swift stroking motion.

"No!" he cried hoarsely. Reversing his position, he reached for the latex protection in the small square package under his pillow. The momentary diversion gave him enough time to regain control of his runaway passions.

"Bruja!" he whispered, smiling as he placed his hardness at the entrance to her tight body.

Emily felt her flesh close around him and moaned softly. "Warlock," she countered through clenched teeth.

Chris began to push slowly, preparing her body to open and accept all of him. The hot, moist tightness of her sex sheathing his maleness had become akin to an erotic torture, but he did not want to take his pleasure before making certain Emily had achieved hers. Her legs curved around his waist and he pulled back, plunging deeply into her womb.

Emily felt like a budding flower, opening and giving of herself so her lover could taste, savor and possess what she willingly and freely offered him. He was making her feel things she never knew existed.

The coil of pleasure between her legs spread upward. Arching, she threw back her head. His name erupted from the back of her throat in a fevered whisper of wonder. Her hoarse cry faded to soft whimpers that took Chris higher and higher until he exploded, shaking him with the force of their ecstasy.

Broad shoulders convulsed and shuddered violently as he collapsed heavily on her slender frame, the roaring and spinning continuing to shake him with the ebbing passion. It took several more minutes for him to return from the dizzying heights as he sucked much-needed air into his lungs before he shifted to pull Emily's damp body over his until she lay on his chest. It had been much too quick. He had wanted it to last longer. Much longer.

She stirred once, her warm breath filtering over his hot throat. A slight snoring indicated that she had fallen asleep.

Chris pulled her closer. He seemed not to be able to get close enough. He was addicted to her and there was no known cure. He found himself too wound up to sleep.

I can't leave her. The realization haunted him. He couldn't leave Emily in Ocho Rios; at that moment he knew he would not be able to board a flight to Mexico City and not have her beside him.

The long legs nestled intimately between his thighs would not permit the fire between his own to die out. Though he had sampled the sweep rapture of her delightful body, a part of his own anatomy refused to follow the dictates of his brain. He was tense, exhausted, yet he continued to crave her.

His hand cradled the fullness of her buttocks, holding her prisoner when his hardness stirred and surged up against her belly. Damn! He was as hot and randy as an adolescent. He had never been this way with other women—only with Emily. The gentle caresses on her rounded hips changed, becoming stronger. He had to have her again. He reached for another condom.

Emily awakened to Chris filling every part of her, gasping from the primal force of his total possession. Before she could recover he withdrew, placing her legs over his shoulders. When he reentered her with a forceful thrust, it shattered all traces of her lingering somnolence.

Bracing his hands on either side of her head, Chris lowered his body and smiled down at Emily as she arched and brushed her swollen breasts against his chest. He went completely still. She was so moist and yielding that everything ceased to exist except the sexy, exciting woman writhing beneath him. He forgot about Alejandro Delgado, William Savoy and any and every thing that had ever touched his life.

He began to move, his hips setting a strong, driving, pumping rhythm. He shifted Emily's legs higher to allow him deeper access until he felt the contractions shaking her womb.

Emily's cries filled the room and his savage moans supplanted hers as his dammed-up passions broke, drowning her with liquid fire. She shivered violently, not so much from her own release but from Chris's primitive growl of complete satisfaction. He lowered her legs, sinking slowly down to the mattress.

His teeth closed gently on her shoulder before his tongue tasted the sweetness of her heaving breasts. Perspiration ran in rivulets from his quaking body, soaking the sheets.

Breathing heavily, he gathered her to his side. "Go back to sleep, darling." He pressed a kiss over her eyelids.

"I'll go," Emily gasped weakly. "I'll go to Mexico with you."

Chris whispered a silent prayer of thanks as he closed his eyes. This time when Emily was swept away in a sated slumber he joined her. He had gotten his fill of her—for now.

Chapter 13

Emily was awed by the natural beauty of Puerto Escondido as Chris maneuvered the rental car along Mexico's southern coast. The waters of the Pacific Ocean stretched out before them like an undulating blue carpet. It felt as if she had been traveling for weeks, even though it had only been four days since they had left Kingston.

Chris, aware of the Cole and Kirkland mandate against family members flying on commercial carriers, had chartered a private jet for their flight from Kingston to Miami. He overrode her protests that they use the ColeDiz corporate jet and reminded her that, as an elected official, the trip could be misinterpreted as a gift. They'd spent the night in a Miami hotel until arrangements for another private jet were confirmed for their trip to Mexico City.

The sight, size, noise and pollution of Mexico City had overwhelmed Emily, while the social contrasts were unimaginable to Chris. He had been disturbed by children begging barefoot on the streets, wizened old women slapping cornmeal into tortillas and roasting them in oil-filled caldrons over open fires and the obviously wealthy residents preening and trying to impress one another in their lavish homes and upscale restaurants. Their planned two-day stay in Mexico City was aborted, and the following morning they loaded the rental car with their luggage and headed southward.

The brilliant rays of the noon sun reflected off the large stone on the third finger of Emily's right hand, and she turned it around until only the band was visible. She hadn't wanted to wear Keith's ring, but she had decided it was safer on her finger than in her purse or luggage in case she became separated from the latter. However, when Chris noticed the ring on her hand, his expression was marked with cold loathing.

Chris glanced at the thin gold watch with the black lizard band circling his left wrist. He expected to see the Delgado property within minutes. The directions he had received from the owner of a marina near the harbor were excellent. At the end of the road was the residence where Alejandro Delgado had come to live out his last days. The home where he'd been born and raised would also become his final resting place.

The dusty road led to a paved path bordered by a thick undergrowth of ancient banana trees, which ended with a stone wall rising more than twenty feet above the ground in a towering arch. He slowed the car and maneuvered under the arch to an expansive courtyard. The stone entrance led to a flower-filled interior courtyard. Massive terra-cotta pots crowded the space with an overabundance of flowering plants. He stopped, then put the vehicle in park without turning off the engine.

Emily turned her head, staring at Chris's profile. His expression was closed, revealing none of the anxiety merging with the deep-seated hostility he had repressed for most of his life. She felt his tension as surely as if it were her own. He had flown thousands of miles to meet the man who had fathered him—a man who was a stranger—a stranger whose life was now being measured by each sunrise and sunset.

Chris stared through the windshield, not realizing he had been holding his breath until he felt the band of tightness around his chest. He had arrived. He had come to Mexico to meet the vengeful man whose genes he shared—the vindictive father who had used his wealth and influence to abduct his young son.

Reaching over, he covered Emily's left hand with his right one, squeezing gently. "I'll be right back," he said in Spanish. She offered him a comforting smile.

He removed his hand, feeling her loss immediately, then pushed open the door and stepped out of the cool automobile into the afternoon heat. He counted the steps it took him to reach a loggia.

The moment Chris raised his hand to lift the massive iron door knocker fashioned in the shape of a lion's head, he chided himself for leaving Emily in the comforting coolness of the automobile. She should be standing beside him when he met Alejandro for the first time. He didn't know why, but he wanted to silently taunt the elder Delgado and flaunt his love and devotion to a woman he had coveted for years.

The sound of the heavy knocker resounded dully in the quietness of the afternoon. If the grounds of the hacienda hadn't been so immaculately kept, Chris would've suspected that it had been abandoned. There wasn't a person, automobile or living creature in sight. There was only the lazy droning sound of invisible flying insects seeking the hypnotic sweetness as they darted in and out of the brilliantly colored blossoms.

He raised his hand to lift the knocker again but was thwarted when the door opened suddenly. The wizened face of an elderly woman appeared through the opening. Her dark eyes, faded with age, squinted through a network of lines that had recorded years of wars, civil unrest, corrupt administrations, poverty, prosperity and countless masses for baptisms, church holidays and funerals. The eyes had recorded more than three-quarters of a century of Mexican history, but she had never expected to see Señor Alejandro Delgado in his youth twice in her lifetime. Squeezing her eyes tightly, she shook her iron-gray head, a single braid swaying between her frail shoulder blades. The young man standing before her, with the exception of his graying hair, was an exact duplicate of her employer, who had disappeared without a trace more than thirty years earlier. She opened her eyes, staring mutely.

"I've come from the United States to see Alejandro Delgado," Chris said in Spanish, the words flowing fluidly from his lips.

"One moment, sir," the housekeeper replied. Her voice was weak, trembling. The three words came out like the sound of wind blowing through a profusion of thin reeds along a riverbank.

"Who are you talking to, Wilma?" asked a feminine voice, this one stronger and filled with a modicum of authority.

Wilma turned, glancing over her shoulder. "A gentleman wants to see Señor Delgado."

"What's his name?"

Wilma focused her attention on Chris. *"¿Cómo se llama, señor?"*

"Cristobal Delgado," he replied. A slight smile played at the corners of his mouth when the older woman reacted visibly to the name. However, his amusement was short-lived when the door opened wider and a younger, more elegantly attired and professionally coiffed woman stared at him as if he were an apparition.

Making the sign of the cross over her ample breasts, she laced her fingers together in a gesture of prayer. *"¡Dios mio!"*

Chris inclined his head in a respectful gesture. *"Buenas tardes, señora. Me llamo Cristobal Delgado."*

"You are Alejandro's son." The question came out as a statement. "You are the image of him before he…" Her words trailed off when she closed her eyes, as if she could will away the painful memories of another time. She opened her eyes. "I'm Sonia Medina de Delgado-Quintero. I'm your father's youngest sister and therefore your aunt."

A jumble of confused thoughts and feelings assailed Chris as he looked at the impeccably groomed, petite woman staring up at him. He had come to Puerto Escondido to confront Alejandro Delgado about his past, but not once had he thought that he would meet other relatives—people with whom he shared blood ties. Sonia Medina had announced that she was Alejandro's younger sister, as if that was an exalted honor.

Recovering quickly, smoothly, he leaned down and kissed her thin perfumed cheek. *"Mucho gusto en conocerle."* And he *was* pleased to meet her. It would help facilitate his imminent encounter with her brother. He refused to think of her brother as his father. Matthew Sterling was his father, not Alejandro Delgado.

Sonia opened the door wider. "Please come in."

"I did not come alone, señora. *Mi novia* is waiting in the car," Chris said smoothly. He had referred to Emily as his fiancée, as if it were something he had done many times before.

Nodding, Sonia offered him a warm smile, tiny lines fanning out at the corners of her golden brown eyes. "I would be honored if you would address me as *tía*. Please invite your *novia* to join us."

Turning, Chris made his way back across the loggia and the length of the courtyard, placing one determined foot in front of the other. He was grateful Alejandro Delgado had not come to the door, because it permitted him the time he needed to prepare for their inevitable encounter.

Emily's head came up quickly when the door opened. Her penetrating gaze took in everything about Chris in one glance. The stubborn set of his lean jaw and the shimmer of determination radiating from his midnight eyes indicated that he was in complete control of himself and his emotions.

Slipping behind the wheel, Chris flashed a lazy smile. "I'm going to park the car along the side of the house, then we're going in."

Emily nodded. She wanted to ask him if he had seen or spoken to Alejandro but decided against it. She had come along as a spectator and not a participant in a thirty-two-year-old, unresolved drama. And despite the level of intimacy she and Chris had shared, she felt what he had to discuss with his biological father was still too personal for her to become involved with.

Chris assisted her from the car, and together they made their way down the loggia with its floor of tiles laid out in hues of faded beige, brown and green. Potted palms, ferns and flowering plants in large clay pots lent a tropical flavor to the contemporary coffee table that added a modern touch to the centuries-old stone pilasters and *butacas,* leather sling chairs.

The elderly housekeeper opened the door at their approach, her gaze surveying the attractive sun-browned couple. "Please follow me. Señora Medina is in the *sala*."

Emily slipped her hand in Chris's, and she gave him a dazzling smile when he glanced down at her. His fingers tightened on hers as they followed Wilma through a spacious entry to the grandeur of a grand salon. She noticed twin elaborately decorated *vargueños,* traveling desks, flanking a set of massive oak doors leading to the salon. As they walked into the room, she forced herself not to stare at the antique pieces. She had inherited her love of antiques from her mother, who had furnished the home in which she had grown up in a Santa Fe suburb with a skill usually reserved for interior decorators.

A short woman with a rounded body swathed in gold silk rose from an armchair with an embroidered seat and cushioned back. Her liberally streaked gray hair was pulled off her face in an elaborate chignon. Tiny lines around her eyes crinkled in a friendly smile that parted her crimson lips. Emily estimated that she was in her sixties. She wasn't pretty, yet she would never be referred to as homely. Her jewelry was exquisite. A gold bracelet with precious and semiprecious stones graced her wrist, a pair of brilliant diamonds glittered in her pierced lobes and the third finger of her left hand boasted a gold band of glittering alternating diamonds and emeralds.

Curving his arm around Emily's waist, Chris pulled her closer to his side. *"Me gustaría presentarle a mi tía señora Sonia Medina de Delgado-Ouintero. Tía Sonia, éste es Emelia Kirkland."*

Emily successfully concealed her surprise. Chris had just introduced her to his aunt as if he had known Sonia Medina for years, instead of only minutes.

"Mucho gusto en conocerle," she replied politely.

Smiling, Sonia extended her tiny hands to Emily. "It's my pleasure to meet you, Emelia. How is it you speak perfect Spanish with a name like Kirkland?"

Emily smiled. It wasn't the first time someone had questioned her about her Anglo surname. "My father's mother was a *Cubana.*"

"My *sobrino* has chosen a beautiful *novia.*"

Novia? Emily turned and stared at Chris's impassive expression. What had he told his aunt? Did Sonia Medina believe they were engaged to be married?

Forcing a smile she did not feel and taking the older woman's hands, Emily mumbled a barely audible, *"Gracias."*

Keith Norris had perpetuated one lie about her being engaged to him, and it appeared that Christopher Delgado continued the prevarication with his own claim that they were to be married. What was it about her that prompted men to propose marriage? There were women who couldn't get one date, while she had lost count of the number of online proposals she had received since becoming a television news correspondent.

"Please sit down," Sonia urged, directing Emily to a chair positioned next to a small, round table. The highly polished surface of the table held a silver tray with a crystal pitcher filled with an icy beverage and a set of four matching goblets. She waited until Chris sat down, then said, "Do you mind serving, Emelia?"

Giving Chris a sidelong glance, Emily glared at him. She hadn't missed his mocking grin. She wasn't used to serving, but being served. However, she was in another country with customs that were not her own.

"Not at all," she said between clenched teeth.

She filled the goblets, serving Sonia first, then Chris. He lifted his curving eyebrows before winking at her. Taking a sip of the drink, she savored the tart taste of differing fruit juices as it slid down the back of her throat.

Emily and Chris had taken turns driving to Puerto Escondido. They had driven more than 400 kilometers from Mexico City to Acapulco, stopping to spend the night. After securing a bungalow with a private patio at Pierre Marqués, she had scheduled a session with a stylist, a manicurist and a masseur, while Chris opted for unwinding by swimming laps in one of the luxury hotel's three pools. They had fallen asleep without making love, content to savor the other's closeness and warmth in the air-cooled bedroom.

Looping his right leg over his left knee, Chris stared at the toe of his leather slip-on. His gaze shifted upward, lingering on his aunt.

"You must be very tired," she said perceptively.

"We've spent two days driving from Mexico City," he offered as an explanation.

"How long do you plan to stay?" Sonia asked.

Chris glanced at Emily, who raised her eyebrows in a questioning expression. He calculated quickly. She had said she wanted to return to New Mexico by the middle of the month. And that meant they could only afford to spend a few days in Puerto Escondido.

"No more than three days."

The older woman nodded. "I'll have Wilma show you to your rooms. Leave me the keys for your car and I'll arrange for your luggage to be brought up." She inhaled, her full breasts trembling noticeably under the silk fabric of her dress before she let out her breath. "I suppose you want to know about your father?" Chris's response was a slight lifting of one eyebrow. "He's not well," Sonia continued. "The infection takes all of his strength."

"What is the cause of the infection?"

"Acute myeloid leukemia. The infection stems from a delayed bone marrow transplant." Sonia's eyes filled with unshed tears. "The doctors couldn't find a donor match. They tested me and a few cousins, but…" she shook her head as her words trailed off and she valiantly composed herself. "Even though I knew Alejandro had a son, I had come to think of my brother as the last of the Delgado-Quinteros." Her expression hardened when she pursed her lips. "Alejandro probably will not live another three months, but our legacy will not die with him. The family name continues with you, Cristobal. You are a Delgado-Quintero."

Emily studied Chris's face, unable to believe that he had remained so composed. His aunt had just revealed that his father was dying of leukemia and he hadn't even blinked. It was as if the man she had fallen in love with had affected an expression of stone, an expression so unnerving that it chilled her blood.

"Did you tell him that I'm here?" Chris asked with an aloofness that indicated that he could have been asking about the weather.

Sonia shook her head. "No. The doctor left only minutes before you arrived. He gave Alejandro something to help him sleep."

"Is he in pain?" Again, his tone was neutral.

She lifted her shoulders in an elegant shrug. "It comes and goes. Today was not a good day for him."

Closing his eyes, Chris pressed his head to the cushioned soft-ness of his high-backed chair. The gesture was the first emotion he had exhibited since walking into the hacienda. He did not want to confront a terminally ill man—one who counted his days by the amount of pain he could endure when he did not mask it with a prescribed narcotic.

That meant he would have to wait—wait until Alejandro Del-gado surfaced from his drug-induced sleep to answer his ques-tions.

Sonia studied her nephew. He was an exact replica of his father at thirty-five years of age. The only exception was that Cristobal hadn't inherited his father's eyes, and the younger man's height eclipsed her brother's by at least four inches.

Placing her glass on the table, she rose to her feet, and Chris opened his eyes and stood up. "Come. It's time for siesta."

Wilma appeared, as if someone had rung a silent bell, sum-moning her. It was apparent that the housekeeper had been lis-tening outside the door.

"Wilma, please take Señorita Kirkland to the bedroom over-looking the sanctuary. Señor Delgado will occupy the room across from his father."

Emily felt the heat radiating from Chris's gaze on her back as she turned and followed the housekeeper. They would sleep under the same roof but would not share the same bed. How had it happened so quickly? How had she grown so used to falling asleep in his arms? How had she come to crave him in the same manner an addict craved a drug?

Not sleeping together in Puerto Escondido would prepare them for their eventual return to the States. And when they re-turned all she would be left with would be the memories of what they'd shared in Ocho Rios—memories of their private passions. Memories that would have to sustain her until after the election.

The stubborn set of her delicate jaw revealed her determi-nation. She could and would remain personally detached from Christopher Delgado. After all, she had had eighteen years of dress rehearsals.

Chapter 14

Chris followed Wilma and Emily as they made their way up a winding staircase with an elaborate wrought-iron railing. He hadn't missed the timeless elegance of the centuries-old hacienda or the opulence of its priceless furnishings, wondering who had assumed responsibility for the upkeep on the property during Alejandro's absence.

Wilma reached the top of the staircase and stopped. "Señor Delgado, your room." She pointed to a closed door on her right, then continued in a shuffling gait down the wide hallway. The thick, whitewashed stone walls countered the buildup of western Mexico's tropical heat.

Emily smiled at him over her shoulder, then followed the elderly woman to the end of the hall. He waited, watching Emily enter the room assigned to her. Wilma nodded at something Emily had said, then made her way down another staircase at the opposite end of the hall. Chris's gaze swung to the open door less than ten feet from where he stood. All he had to do was cross the hall, walk into the bedroom and come face-to-face with his past.

But he decided to wait—wait until Alejandro was lucid. He wanted to see the look on the elder Delgado's face when he stared up into a face from his past, a face he hadn't seen in thirty-two years, a face that would remind him of what he'd looked like when he had allowed revenge to control his very existence.

Emily walked around her room, awed by its contents. There was no doubt that the house had been constructed during Mexico's colonial period, but had been expanded and modernized with technological advances that had not diminished its original splendor.

Making her way across a terra-cotta floor to a casement window, she opened it and stepped out onto the second-story veranda. Resting her elbows on the wrought-iron railing, she gazed out on a small structure painted in bright yellow with a gleaming gold cross attached to its Baroque-style bell tower. It was probably the sanctuary Sonia had mentioned.

The sloping landscape, dotted with palm trees, led to the beach and the Pacific Ocean. She detected the smell of salt in the ocean breeze as she walked over to a cushioned rocker and sat down. Closing her eyes, she willed her mind blank, while experiencing an emotion of weightless peace. She felt as free as a feather floating on the wind.

The man she had loved for more than half her life had followed her to Jamaica, baring his soul. They had shared their love in the most intimate way possible, but what they'd shared over the past week would come to an abrupt end once they stepped foot onto U.S. soil. She would return to the TV station and Chris would begin what was certain to become a long, arduous and hard-fought campaign for the highest elected office in the state of New Mexico. Their lives would cross only in the political arena, while their private lives would be placed on hold until after the first Tuesday in November.

Could she wait that long for him? Could they wait that long for each other? Opening her eyes, she mumbled a silent prayer that she and Chris would be able to recapture what they'd discovered in Ocho Rios. What she refused to acknowledge was the possibility that if Chris became Governor Delgado he would change into someone she would not know nor want to know. Would his thirst for power make her regret ever loving him? And what might happen if he lost the election?

She spent her siesta on the veranda, sitting in the hot sun. When she returned to the bedroom she found her luggage by the bed. She unbuttoned her blouse and shrugged it off. She would shower, change her clothes, then seek out Chris.

A light rap on the door captured Chris's rapt attention. He rose from the chair where he'd sat reading *Don Quixote* in Spanish.

The last time he had been required to read Spanish had been as an undergraduate. He had faltered over the words, saying a few aloud, until he was able to grasp the language. The exercise reminded him of what lay ahead. His campaign manager had hired two speech writers: one for English, the other for Spanish. The fact that he was bilingual had given him a distinct advantage over his political opponent. There was no doubt that his senate victory by a mere sixty-four votes had been due to the heavier than usual turnout of Spanish-speaking voters. He had less than a month before he began campaigning actively, but he knew it would be a plus if he could read Spanish as well as he spoke and understood it.

A young woman in a nurse's uniform stood in the doorway staring at him. "Señor Delgado," she whispered hoarsely, after finding her voice, "your father is awake. You may see him now."

She moved aside as the tall, well-dressed American walked past her. Her admiring gaze lingered on his off-white raw silk shirt and the tailored precision of his coffee-brown slacks. Even his accessories were exquisite: the brown lizard belt circling his slim waist and a pair of brown woven leather loafers. His fluid elegant swagger was also in keeping with his being a Delgado-Quintero. Mexican history books had recorded the wealth and power of the Delgados—Spaniards who had come to the New World in search of gold.

The family also had its share of secrets and scandals. The nurse had grown up hearing her relatives gossip about Alejandro Delgado-Quintero's fall from grace, fleeing his family lands before she was born. The wagging tongues started up again when word circulated that Mexico's last Delgado-Quintero had returned to his familial hacienda to die.

But it appeared that the gossips were wrong. The Delgado-Quintero line would not end with Alejandro; there was no doubt his American son had come to claim his legacy.

Chris walked into the large, shady bedroom, his gaze fixed on a man who sat up in a massive bed with the aid of several pillows supporting his back. A lump rose in Chris's throat, not permitting him to swallow as he neared the bed. Despite the heat, a chill racked his body as he stared at his own face in the throes of late middle age.

He had inherited Alejandro's high, proud forehead, elegant cheekbones, nose, mouth and the cleft in his strong chin. Only the eyes and his coloring were different. The elder Delgado's eyes were dark, but not as dark as his, and they did not tilt upwards as his did. And despite his illness, he had not lost his hair. Straight, graying black hair was neatly combed and parted on the left side of his noble head. Now seeing the vain, selfish, wealthy, powerful and vindictive man, Chris knew why his mother had been attracted to him. There was an air of refinement in Alejandro Delgado that even age and illness had not diminished.

Alejandro ignored the spasm of pain gripping his body as he stared at the son he hadn't seen in over thirty years. It was as if he were looking in a mirror, and he saw things in his only child that no one else could see. He noted the slightest wave in his son's hair—the blending of his own straight hair with Eve Blackwell's curls. He felt as if he were looking into his ex-wife's eyes. Closing his eyes, he pictured the woman he had fallen in love with on sight. A woman he had claimed as wife, a woman he had made a mother, a woman he'd lost because of his own weakness of the flesh.

Opening his eyes, Alejandro managed a crooked smile. "Come, sit down." He had spoken English, a language he had only rarely used over the last three decades.

Chris moved closer and sat down on a chair beside the bed. He draped his right leg over his left knee in a smooth, continuous motion, resting his hands on the curved arms of the chair. Alejandro's alert gaze followed the motions. His smile widened, revealing a set of perfect teeth despite his age and debilitating illness. Not only did his son resemble him, but he had also inherited his body language. Their walk and the way they sat was identical.

"I can speak Spanish," Chris said in a terse tone.

"But I prefer speaking English," Alejandro countered. "It's been a long time since I've had the luxury of speaking the language," he said in British-accented English, while straightening a lightweight beige blanket over the pair of maroon silk pajamas concealing his wasting body.

A muscle twitched in Chris's jaw, indicating his annoyance. It was apparent that the man hadn't changed from the one his mother had told him about. Alejandro still wanted to control everything and everyone who came into contact with him.

"I've come because I want answers," Chris continued, deliberately speaking Spanish.

"Your mother should have given you the answers," Alejandro shot back in English.

Chris's fingers tightened on the intricately carved arms of the chair. "There are questions only you can answer. Why did you hate my mother so much that you tried to destroy her when you abducted your own son?" The Spanish words tumbled from his mouth like the staccato tapping of sleet assaulting glass. "Why did you see fit to shame her when you wallowed with every *puta* who would open her legs for you?"

A rush of color flooded Alejandro's pale face. *"¡Basta!"*

Shifting on the chair, Chris glared at Alejandro. "Oh, now you want to speak Spanish," he taunted. "It's not enough!"

The older man's right hand searched under the sheets, his fingers closing around the handle of a small bell. Gripping it tightly, he shook it violently. Within seconds the nurse appeared.

"Get him out of here!" he ordered in Spanish.

The nurse felt the swell of tension in the bedroom and trembled noticeably. "Señor, you must leave," she said apologetically.

Rising, Chris leaned over the bed. "You sniveling bastard," he ground out between his teeth. "I'll be back again, and I'll haunt you until you give me the answers I want."

Without a backward glance, he walked out of the room, not seeing the tears staining his father's cheeks. Rage so blinded him that he did not see Emily rise from the chair where she had sat waiting for him as he stalked into his bedroom. His gaze was wild as she closed the distance between them.

He jerked away from her, holding up a hand. "Don't! Just leave me alone."

Emily was totally bewildered at his behavior. Vertical lines appeared between her eyes. "What happened?"

"Nothing."

She refused to see his pain and anguish. All she knew was that he was pushing her away. Her quick temper flared. Resting her hands on her hips, she rose on tiptoe and pushed her flushed face close to his.

"Don't play yourself, Christopher Delgado. You were the one who begged me to come here when I didn't want to. Bark at me one more time and I'm out of here. All it takes is one phone call to West Palm and I'll be on a jet back to New Mexico so fast it'll make your head swim."

The red haze of rage that had blinded Chris until he couldn't form a rational thought cleared with Emily's threat. The fists at his sides unclenched and he gathered her close to his tense body. Burying his face against the column of her scented neck, he pressed a kiss to the silken flesh.

"I'm sorry, baby. I'm not angry with you. I'm ashamed to say it, but I lost it with him."

Running a hand up and down his back in a comforting gesture, Emily said, "You came here to reconcile with your father…"

"He's not my father," Chris interrupted.

She silently cursed his stubbornness. "He is your father whether you choose to acknowledge him or not. And if he goes to his grave without you getting the answers you need from him, you're going to spend the rest of your life disconnected from your past. You can't possibly know where you're going if you don't know where you've come from."

Pulling back, he stared at her. When had she become so wise? How did she know all the right things to say?

"My family has been where you are now," she said cryptically. Taking his hand, she led him over to a love seat in the sitting area of the bedroom. Sitting, she pulled him down next to her. "The Delgados aren't the only ones with family secrets."

Dropping an arm around her shoulder, Chris eased her head to his chest. "Every family has its secrets, baby girl."

"You're right about that. But what you can't do is allow your bitterness toward Alejandro Delgado to come between us."

"What I feel for him has nothing to do with you."

"Yes, it does, Chris. You're angry with him, and when I tried to reach out to you, you pushed me away. I'll never ask you to reveal what you discuss with your father, but I'm going to ask that you trust me enough to know that I'll support you in the bad times as well as the good. I love you. I've told you and showed you that much. Either we're in this together or we're not."

Anchoring a finger under her chin, he stared at the brilliant green lights in her incredible eyes. A slow smile crossed his handsome face. "It's too late for you to back out, Miss Kirkland. We are in this together."

"Good," she whispered seconds before his mouth covered hers. The kiss was sweet, healing—sealing their pledge to each other.

Chris's mouth moved from her lips to her neck. "I love the way you smell," he breathed out under her ear. "Just being next to you makes me so…"

Emily's mouth covered his, cutting off his erotic confession. Grasping her hand, he placed it over his groin. The evidence of his arousal throbbed under her palm. When would he ever not want her?

The harsh, uneven sound of Chris's breathing indicated that they were fast approaching the point of no return, and Emily tore her mouth away. Passion had dilated her pupils.

"Let's go for a walk." Her sultry voice trembled with lingering desire.

He ran a finger down the length of her nose. "You go. I need to be alone right now. There's a lot of damage control I have to do."

She kissed his chin. "I'll see you later."

Chris pushed to his feet. He extended his hand and pulled her up gently off the love seat. He watched as Emily left the bedroom, his gaze lingering on the space where she had been.

The lush scent of flowers filled the warm air when Emily stepped out onto the shaded loggia. She noticed the musical sound of a flowing fountain for the first time as she walked its length. She was startled when she bumped into Sonia carrying a basket of freshly cut flowers.

"Perdóneme," Emily said as she reached out to steady the wobbling basket.

"Lo siento mucho," Sonia exclaimed. "I didn't expect to see you."

Emily took the basket from her loose grip, examining its contents, flowers she had never seen before. "These are beautiful."

"Alejandro is very fortunate. He has the most talented gardener in Puerto Escondido tend his prize flowers."

"The hacienda is magnificent. Everything is magnificent."

Sonia nodded. "That it is," she confirmed without a hint of modesty. "Do you ever watch the Spanish *novelas* on television in your country?"

"Hardly ever," Emily confessed. She rarely watched television at all, and if she did it was the news segments.

"Well, if you had, then you probably would have recognized this house. Before Alejandro went away, he finalized a deal with a television producer to use the hacienda and the surrounding property as the setting for his *novelas.* They paid my brother well, while maintaining and protecting the property from vandals."

"You don't live here?"

"No, child. I haven't lived here in forty-three years. I married when I was twenty-one, then moved to Oaxaca with my husband. I'm here because my brother needs me." She peered closely at Emily. "Have you met with Alejandro?"

"Not yet."

"The nurse said it did not go well between Cristobal and Alejandro. What they don't realize is that they are too much alike— in looks and in temperament."

"Are you saying that there will never be peace between them?"

"That all depends," Sonia said cryptically.

"On what?"

She gave Emily a direct stare. "On you."

"Me?"

"Yes, you. You must become the peacemaker, *sobrina.* If you love your *novio,* then you must get him to soften his heart toward his father."

Shaking her head, Emily took a few steps, stopped, then turned to face Chris's aunt. "You're asking the impossible. You can't expect me to undo what has taken more than thirty years to fester."

"You love my nephew, and I love my brother. The two of them are all I have left of my family, and Alejandro has suffered enough. I will not let him go to his grave with enmity between him and his seed."

Emily replayed the older woman's words, her eyes narrowing in suspicion. "It was you," she whispered. "You were the one who informed on Chris to his political opponent."

Her expression hardened. "I would, as you say, 'inform on him' to the devil himself if it meant ending the breach in my family. Yes, I was the one," she stated arrogantly. "Before Alejandro left Mexico he paid someone to report to him on his son, and I made certain he knew everything that had happened in Cristobal's life. You were the only surprise. We didn't know the two of you planned to marry."

Staring at Sonia in stunned silence, Emily could not believe what she'd just heard. "You paid someone to spy on him."

"Alejandro paid."

"Same difference," she countered. "You're a meddler."

A slight smile softened Sonia's mouth and deepened the lines around her eyes as her gaze lingered on the flowers in the basket. "Call me names, Emelia, but one day you will thank me for meddling. I forwarded the information on Cristobal to someone in South America, who then made certain the letters were personally delivered to Alejandro. The couriers were well paid for their services. What I've just told you should remain between us. Will you give me your word that it will?"

Emily wanted to expose Sonia to Chris but knew she couldn't. Sonia had sought to heal the rift between father and son, while embracing her only surviving sibling. She had to give them a chance to become a family before Alejandro passed from this life to the next.

"You have my word," she said grudgingly.

Closing the space between them, Sonia kissed Emily's cheek. *"Gracias, sobrina."*

"De nada, Tía Sonia," she replied.

"Can you cook, Emelia?"

Emily's left eyebrow rose a fraction. "Yes, I can."

"Are you familiar with Mexican cooking? Not those vile concoctions the Anglos tout in your fast-food restaurants."

She forced back a grin. "There are quite a few authentic Mexican restaurants in New Mexico."

"Does Cristobal like Mexican cooking?"

Emily nodded. "Yes."

"Good. Come help me prepare dinner. I'm going to show you a few secrets that the women in my family have known for centuries, and before you leave Mexico I'm going to give you a book filled with recipes that only Delgado women have been privy to. After all, you will become a Delgado when you marry my *sobrino.*"

"You're right," Emily said, choosing her words carefully. She would become a Delgado *if* she and Chris married. What his aunt did not know was that the ring she'd removed from her finger and hidden in a drawer under her lingerie belonged to another man.

Chapter 15

It had gone badly, and Chris knew he was to blame. He had allowed his emotions to override his common sense. He had willfully attacked a sick man—a man whose face was uncannily like his own, a man whose genes he shared, a man he'd hated until now.

His loathing of his biological father had come from Eve Blackwell-Sterling's pain. Whenever Chris asked Eve about her first husband her tears flowed unchecked. When he was a young boy he thought she cried because she was still in love with Alejandro and that she missed him, even though she had married Matthew Sterling. But as he grew older he had come to understand the terror his mother had experienced when Alejandro abducted her firstborn, a fear it had taken years for her to overcome. Even after more than three decades Eve could not purchase a carton of milk with a missing child's picture on it.

He did not want to start a war with Alejandro—he just wanted and needed answers. Crucial answers, so that he'd be able to respond to and counter Savoy's attack on his personal life.

Three days. Emily had promised to remain in Mexico with him for three more days, then she would return to New Mexico. He hoped to get the answers he needed from Alejandro within that time, but if it didn't happen, he would remain behind.

The sound of Alejandro's voice raised in anger resounded in the hallway. He was screaming at his nurse. Taking long, determined strides, Chris walked out of his bedroom, crossed the hall and entered Alejandro's. The older man stood beside the bed, waving his arms wildly while the nurse tried to restrain him.

"What's the matter?"

Alejandro and the nurse went completely still, staring at Chris as if he were an apparition. "He's not permitted to leave the bed," the nurse said quickly.

"Has the doctor confined him to the bed, señorita?" Chris asked gently.

"No." The nurse and Alejandro had answered in unison.

Closing the space between them, Chris eased his father from the woman's grasp, picked him up as if he were a child, and placed him on a chair beside the bed. He was appalled at the frailty of the body concealed by the pair of pajamas, doubting whether Alejandro weighed more than 120 pounds.

Alejandro offered his son an appreciative smile. "*Gracias.* I hate that damn bed."

The pretty nurse glared at her patient. "The doctor says you're not to get out of bed after he gives you the sedative."

Alejandro waved his hand, dismissing her. "Leave me. I want to talk to my son."

The woman stared at Chris. He nodded. "It's all right. I'll look after him, señorita."

Closing his eyes, Alejandro compressed his lips tightly against a spasm of excruciating pain. "Go home, Señorita Rodriguez."

She glanced at her watch. "It is not time for me to leave, Don Alejandro. I'll leave after I feed you your dinner."

Alejandro opened his eyes, giving her a lethal stare. "My son will take care of me." There was a cold finality in the statement.

Again she looked at Chris for assistance, and he relieved her anxiety when he smiled. "Have a good evening."

Benita Rodriguez returned Cristobal Delgado's smile, her dark eyes sparkling. She worked twelve-hour shifts caring for Alejandro Delgado and was well paid for her nursing expertise. Most times there was little for her to do after the doctor came to medicate his patient. Her duties included changing the bed, helping Alejandro out of bed and assisting him with his personal hygiene, and she was also responsible for his IV feedings whenever he was too weak to chew and swallow food. He was normally an exemplary patient, except when he screamed at her. Señora Medina paid her well to care for her brother, and she did not want to lose her job. At least not before she lost her patient to the illness stealing his strength minute by minute.

"Buenas noches."

Waiting until the nurse walked out of the room, he glared down at the frail man slumped on the chair. "Was it necessary for you to shout at her?"

Alejandro stared at his bare feet resting on the highly polished wood floor. "She's being paid well for me to shout at her."

Pulling over a chair, Chris sat less than a foot away from his father. "She's being paid well to take care of you, not to be intimidated."

Alejandro's head came up slowly to meet his son's angry gaze. "I'm old—"

"You're not that old," Chris interrupted. "You're only sixty-eight—"

"And I'm dying," he continued, cutting off Chris.

"We're all dying," his son countered. "The moment we draw our first breath we're terminal. So don't use your age or your illness as an excuse to act like a son of a bitch."

Shaking his head slowly, Alejandro's eyes crinkled when he smiled. "You really think I'm a son of a bitch? I thought I was a sniveling bastard."

Chris affected a humorless smirk. "You're both."

They stared at each other, recognizing a common trait: willfulness. Not only did they share physical characteristics, but it was apparent they also shared personality traits.

Studying the younger man leisurely, feature by feature, a feeling of pride filled Alejandro's chest. His son radiated an air of authority that was evident the moment he entered a room. The last time he saw Chris it had been Christmas Eve—a day before the child celebrated his third birthday. He had abducted the boy and kept him for fifty-five days—nearly two months. And for more than half that time his son had cried himself to sleep every night because he missed his mother.

"There was a time when I would have agreed with you," he murmured softly. "But not now, Christopher."

"Why not now?"

"Living in exile for thirty-two years was the same as being imprisoned. I counted every day of every year I spent in that isolated jungle village. I'd lived there for more than a month before I realized the village wasn't in Bolivia, but Peru."

A scowl crossed Chris's face. *Liar!* How could he not know where he was going? Didn't he know in which country his plane was to touch down?

"A military transport plane took me from Mexico City to Caracas, Venezuela," Alejandro continued, switching smoothly to English. "From there I was driven southward. We arrived in Brazil, and after that I lost track of time and place. I'd come down with a fever during the trip down the Rio Orinoco, and it wasn't until after we'd crossed over the Andes that my fever broke. I looked into the mirror two weeks after I'd left Mexico and didn't recognize myself. I'd lost twenty pounds, my hair had begun to turn gray, and everyone I met spoke an Indian dialect that was impossible for me to understand."

"You mentioned a 'we.' Who were they?"

Alejandro closed his eyes, as if he could will away the memories, isolation and alienation. "The United States Government." Opening his eyes, he stared at the stunned expression on Chris's face. "The man responsible for seeing that I left Mexico with my head intact was your great-uncle, Harry Blackwell."

Chris remembered Uncle Harry, who had retired from the Federal Bureau of Investigation as an associate director after twenty-five years of service. Uncle Harry and Aunt Dorothy had lived in a Washington, D.C., suburb, and they visited Las Cruces once a year until they passed away. Harry Blackwell had died in his sleep the year Chris turned ten, and his wife joined her husband in death two years later.

"Why would Uncle Harry help you?"

"He didn't have a choice. I was his Mexican informant. I gathered information for your FBI uncle on Mexican drug traffickers, and he had promised to protect me. But he double-crossed me." A frown deepened the lines in his creased forehead.

"How did he double-cross you?"

Alejandro raised his right hand. "I'm tired, Christopher. We'll talk later."

Chris wanted to tell him that he didn't want to wait until later but knew he didn't have a choice. Rising to his feet, he leaned down, gathered the frail man off the chair, placed him on the bed and covered him with a sheet. His expression was impassive as he stared down at the older man. Within minutes he registered the soft sounds of snoring. Alejandro had fallen asleep.

He would wait. After all, he had been waiting thirty-two years.

Emily helped the elderly housekeeper spread a linen table-cloth over a large oval table on the loggia, admiring the exquisite hand-embroidered stitching. Sonia had revealed that Wilma had come to work for the Delgados as a young girl. Never married, Wilma Vasquez had remained at the hacienda even during Alejandro's exile.

Working quickly, she set the table with place settings for four while Wilma returned to the house to inform Alejandro and Chris that they would sit down to dinner within half an hour. Emily had to admit that Sonia's cooking skills were exceptional. They had prepared a modern, simpler version of Alejandro's favorite dish—*pollo en cuñete*—chicken in a clay pot. She had watched intently as Sonia cut up several whole chickens, washed and patted them dry, then rubbed the pieces with crushed cloves of garlic, coarse salt and freshly ground black pepper. Other spices were added after the chicken was sautéed in corn oil in a large skillet. The lightly browned pieces were transferred to a clay casserole and covered with a sealing layer of *masa*. Small bits of the corn mixture broke off and added a thickening texture to the vessel filled with small new potatoes in a sauce of red wine vinegar and olive oil flavored with bay leaves, thyme, marjoram and *chiles serranos*.

Emily's contribution to the meal was the Caribbean-influenced dish of *arroz blanco con plátanos fritos*—white rice with sweet, ripe plantains. A flavorful chicken soup and a colorful mixed salad with avocado dressing would also grace the table.

While working side by side in the kitchen with Sonia, Emily had been content to listen to the older woman extol her family's distinguished lineage. The first Delgados had come to Mexico with Hernán Cortés in the autumn of 1519. They settled in the Istmo de Tehuantepec for several decades, then received a land grant from Philip II of Spain in 1557 and established a sprawling estate along the Pacific Coast. The Delgados, taking advantage of the magnificent natural harbor, became sea merchants. They commissioned a fleet of galleons that sailed back and forth across the Pacific to the Philippines and the Far East, trading silver bullion and gold doubloons for silks, spices, ivory, perfumes and fine porcelain.

The New World Delgados quickly set their priorities: a shipping business and marriages to Spanish aristocrats. All marriages were arranged at birth, though there were a few renegades who fell in love with beautiful Indian women and produced scores of mixed-blood Delgados. The family's enormous wealth dwindled and came to an abrupt halt after the Mexican War for Independence ended in 1821, but they were able to salvage their status when a young, dashing Delgado caught the eye of Maria Dolores Quintero of Guanajuato. She was the only child of a man who had owned the largest and most profitable silver mine in Mexico's high, fertile, mineral-rich plateau.

New traditions were established once Maria Dolores Delgado-Quintero insisted that her sons learn English. British teachers were paid well to leave England for Mexico to duplicate the lessons the children received from their Spanish-speaking schoolmaster. Their schooling had become a precursor for bilingual education.

It was apparent that Sonia yearned to rejoin her architect husband, who had recently received a commission from the Mexican government for a municipal hospital to be constructed to replace one damaged by an earthquake. But her devotion to Alejandro was remarkable.

The door to the house opened, and Emily turned to see Chris

supporting the body of a frail man clad in a pair of loose-fitting slacks and matching shirt out to the loggia. She stood, amazed and shaken by the startling resemblance between Alejandro and Christopher Delgado. She had thought it uncanny that her brother and father looked so much alike, but it was as if Chris was a younger version of his father. For the first time Emily realized the perfect symmetry of her lover's features, which made him almost too handsome. Recovering quickly, she smiled and made her way toward the two men.

Alejandro studied the tall, graceful young woman. She had selected a sleeveless melon-green sheath that floated over the curves of her slender body. The deep rose-pink color of her toe-nails were visible in a pair of leather sandals.

Alejandro's sister had informed him that his son's intended had come to Mexico with him. Lowering his chin, he smiled. Like father, like son, he mused. Chris's *novia* was beautiful. His head came up and he met Emily's direct stare for the first time. His admiring gaze took in the raven-black hair and the radiant sheen of good health of her gold-brown face. The brilliant green sparks in her large eyes were mesmerizing. She was almost as beautiful as Eve Blackwell had been the first time he'd entered her elegant gift shop in Washington, D.C., so many years ago. No woman he'd ever met had come close to matching his ex-wife's exotic beauty.

Pride swelled in his narrow chest for the man he acknowledged as his son. There was no doubt Chris and his *novia* would beget magnificent children, the grandchildren he would never see or hold in his arms. Grandchildren who would carry on his family's name.

A hint of a smile played at the corners of Alejandro's mouth. "My son has chosen well. You are perfect."

An unwelcome blush swept over Emily's face with the compliment. The strong, masculine voice belied the older man's frail appearance. Her lashes lowered over her eyes in a demure gesture.

"Thank you…" Her words trailed off. She did not know how to address the elder Delgado. She gave Chris a beseeching look.

It was Chris's turn for words to die on his tongue. He could not address Alejandro as "dad." That title had been reserved exclusively for Matthew Sterling.

"Father, I'd like you to meet Emily Kirkland. Emily, Alejandro Delgado."

Extending a shaky hand, Alejandro grasped her fingers. Despite his fragile appearance, his handshake was firm. "There's no need to thank me. I merely state the truth."

Leaning forward, she pressed a light kiss on his cheek. "I'm honored to meet you. May I call you Father?"

Attractive lines fanned out around Alejandro's eyes. "With your face, you can call me anything you wish."

"Have you no shame, Alejandro?" Sonia chided softly as she stepped out onto the loggia. "Flirting with your future daughter-in-law."

Emily did not hear Alejandro's response because her complete attention was focused on Chris, who returned her penetrating gaze. It was one thing to attempt to mislead his aunt, but she did not want to be a party to blatant deception. It had not mattered what Alejandro had done in the past, but he deserved more than to be lied to as he counted down the days, hours and minutes of his life.

The seconds became a full minute as their questioning gazes fused and held. It was only when Sonia said that it was time to sit and eat that their soporific trance ended. They flanked Alejandro, leading him to the table. Chris helped him to sit in a chair with arms, then circled the table to pull out a chair for his aunt, then repeated the motion for Emily.

A secretive smile softened Sonia's crimson lips. Her instincts had been right when she sought to solicit Emelia's help to bring Alejandro and Cristobal together. It was apparent that her nephew was passionately in love with his *novia*. Whenever he and Emelia shared the same space, Sonia recognized the smoldering flame of desire in his midnight gaze. And it was also obvious that she had charmed his father.

Placing a cloth napkin over her lap, Sonia bowed her head, crossed herself and said grace.

Chapter 16

Chris took surreptitious glances at Alejandro, who was struggling to feed himself. He'd gripped the handle of the spoon like a small child as he tried to steady it. Most of the broth spilled back into his bowl before he was able to bring it to his mouth.

A wave of pity swept over him. *He's dying, and he's my father.* The realization nearly choked him, not permitting him to swallow his own soup. What had happened thirty-two years ago was in the past. He had to deal with today, and reality was that he had reunited with his biological father, although he knew the reunion would not be a long or lasting one. The man his mother told him about was not the same one she'd remembered. The Alejandro Delgado Eve knew had used his social status, wealth and diplomatic immunity as an attaché with the Mexican Embassy in Washington, D.C., to abduct his only child. Living in exile had left him a broken man.

Curving an arm around his father's thin shoulders, Chris eased the spoon from the unsteady hand. "Let me help you, Daddy," he whispered close to his ear.

Alejandro went completely still, his eyes filling with moisture. It was the second time that day that his son had brought him to tears. He hadn't been called Daddy in thirty-two years. Closing his eyes, he attempted to stem the hot rush of tears, but he was unsuccessful. They streamed down his face, staining his cheeks and shirt.

Chris reached into a pocket of his slacks, withdrew a handkerchief, and blotted his father's face. "I don't think the soup needs any more salt," he teased softly.

Nodding, Alejandro affected a trembling smile. "You're right."

The sight of the helpless man struck a chord so deep within

Chris that he leaned closer and brushed a kiss across Alejandro's forehead. The gesture was gentle and tender. Emily and Sonia stared in stunned silence, their soup spoons poised in midair.

The strained moment passed once the two women exchanged knowing looks. There was no need for them to interfere. It was apparent that father and son had established their own truce.

Chris patiently fed Alejandro, ignoring his own food as he alternated spooning food into Alejandro's mouth with wiping away minute pieces of shredded chicken that hadn't found their way between his parted lips.

"*Excelente,* Sonia," Alejandro stated, after he'd swallowed the last spoonful of the savory chicken soup. "You've surpassed Mama."

His sister beamed from the compliment. "*Gracias.* Cristobal will be a lucky man, because I'm going to give Emelia all our family recipes. The glorious foods will live on for another generation of Delgados."

Chris's head came up slowly and he stared across the table at the woman he'd fallen in love with. His aunt was talking about another generation of Delgados. It was up to him to carry on the name and the family traditions. But that would only be possible if he married and produced children.

His mercurial black eyes bore into the green ones staring back at him. The harder he tried ignoring the truth, the more it persisted. Emily Kirkland was the only woman he had opened himself and his heart to. She was the only woman he had confessed to loving and the only woman he wanted to share his life and his future with.

Thick black lashes came down and shadowed his gaze from the others at the table. It suddenly hit Chris that the last two surviving Delgado men were engaged in a race against time: Alejandro for his life, and he to become governor of New Mexico.

Leaning to his left, his shoulder pressing against Alejandro's, Chris whispered in his ear. His father's expression did not change as he nodded in agreement.

Alejandro pointed to the empty wineglass at his place setting. "Would someone please pour me a glass of wine?"

Sonia shook her head. "You know you're not permitted to drink."

He glared at his sister. "Then why is there a glass next to my plate?"

Emily felt a rush of heat in her face. She hadn't realized and had put out four wineglasses. "I set the table."

Placing his hand over his son's, he said softly, "Please serve me. It will help me to sleep."

His sister was right. He wasn't permitted to drink alcoholic beverages, but what did that matter? What would it do? Kill him? It didn't matter; he was dying. Once Sonia told him that she had contacted his son, he'd begun to pray—pray that he would not die until he saw Christopher's face once more. And now that he'd seen his son again he welcomed death.

He'd waited two days after his sister had informed him that she had contacted Christopher; then he notified his attorney. The lawyer had come to see him as he was experiencing the most excruciating pain since he'd been diagnosed with leukemia. He forbade the doctor to medicate him because he'd wanted to be of sound mind when he revised his will. The doctor and Sonia signed the legal document as witnesses; then he instructed the doctor to fill his veins with the powerful narcotic. Within seconds he'd lapsed into a deep, painless sleep that lasted nearly sixteen hours. When he awoke to bright sunlight pouring into his window, he'd offered a prayer of thanks that he'd been spared another sunrise.

His son had come to Mexico filled with anger, resentment and bitterness, but still he had come. Nothing Alejandro could say would reverse the pain and suffering he had inflicted on his wife and son, but he planned to make up for it—after his death.

Deliberately ignoring Sonia's scowl, Chris picked up the pitcher and half filled the glass with fruity wine. He held the glass to Alejandro's mouth and he took small sips, savoring each swallow.

Sonia served Alejandro a small portion of rice and fried bananas, letting out her breath in a sigh of relief after he chewed and swallowed the forkful Chris fed him. It had been a long time since he had been able to ingest solid foods. Satisfaction came into her eyes. Emelia had called her a meddler, but that no longer mattered. Her meddling would now allow her brother to die in peace.

The brilliant orange rays of the setting sun competed with the golden light spilling from the lanterns placed along the loggia. Nocturnal sounds were amplified with the onset of nightfall, and all conversation around the table ceased as the diners paused to listen to nature's unrehearsed symphony.

Feeling the calming effects from a glass of sangria, Emily leaned back in her chair. The piquant spices and refreshing blend of wine and fruit juices lingered on her tongue. A warm breeze caressed her bared flesh, bringing with it the lingering scent of salt water.

She stared at Chris through half-lowered lids, a slight smile softening her lush mouth. He gestured with one hand, while the other rested on the back of Alejandro's chair. Closing her eyes, she was content to listen to the musical sounds of the Spanish language punctuating the stillness of the warm tropical night. It wasn't until she felt a gentle shake that she realized she'd fallen asleep.

"Wake up, baby."

Stretching like a cat, a sensual smile parting her lips, Emily leaned forward and brushed her mouth over Chris's when he hunkered down beside her chair. His warmth and the scent of his clean-smelling cologne swirled around her like a cloaking mist.

"How long have I been asleep?" Her contralto voice had lowered half an octave.

He gathered her from the chair, swinging her up in his arms as if she weighed no more than a child. "Not long."

She glanced over his shoulder. "Where are your aunt and your father?"

"They've both retired for the night."

Curving her arms around his strong neck, Emily rested her head on his shoulder. "Your father is a very charming man."

Chris snorted under his breath. "He's a manipulative scoundrel who makes no attempt to conceal it."

"He's still charming."

Chris chuckled deep in his throat. "He's charming because you're a beautiful woman. And Alejandro Delgado could never resist a beautiful woman."

"That's obvious, he did marry your mother, after all."

Emily was right. Even at sixty-six, Eve Sterling was still stunningly beautiful. He'd noticed the gazes of men half his mother's age follow her whenever she walked into a room.

Tightening his grip under Emily's knees, Chris pushed open the door with his shoulder, let it close behind him, then made his way up the staircase to the second floor. Her moist breath feathered over his throat, reminding him of the times she'd lain over his chest after a passionate session of lovemaking. She had a habit of crawling atop him until she fell asleep. One or two times she'd managed to spend the entire night with her breasts pressed to his chest, her legs cradled inside his.

He walked the length of the hallway and entered her bedroom. Bending slightly, he lowered her feet to the floor, one arm clasped tightly around her waist. Reaching up, his hands moved to cradle her face, his velvet gaze caressing her face.

"I love you, Emily Teresa Kirkland, and I want you to marry me." She closed her eyes, swaying slightly. She whispered his name, her body stiffening in surprise. Gathering her closer, Chris pulled her against his chest. "Marry me before we go back to the States." The strong, measured beating of his heart kept tempo with her own.

She wanted to feel joy, but all she felt was fear and confusion because everything was happening too quickly. He had come to her on December 29 professing his love for her, and twelve days later he was proposing marriage.

Anchoring her hands against his chest, Emily backed out of his embrace, shaking her head.

"It's not going to work, Chris." Her voice vibrated with uncertainty. "We can't marry, then go back to New Mexico—"

"We won't tell anyone," he said, interrupting her.

Her gaze widened. "You want me to live a lie?"

"It won't be a lie if no one asks. We'll wait until after the elec-

tion, then make the announcement that we're husband and wife."
Closing the space between them, he pulled her against the length
of his solid frame. "I've loved you for so long that I can't even remember when I didn't love you." His dark eyes smoldered. "We
should've married years ago."

Reaching up, Emily looped her bare arms around his neck.
"We've waited this long, why not another year?"

"I don't want to wait another year." Realizing he'd come off
sounding like a self-indulgent lout, he said quickly, "I can't wait
another year, Emily. We don't have a year."

She went completely still in his protective embrace. "What
are you talking about?"

"He's dying, baby. He won't last long enough to see us married. Which means he'll never get to see or hold his grandchildren. I still think he's a son of a bitch for what he did to my
mother, but nothing I can say or do to him can change the past.
I have to deal not only with now, but *right now.*"

"You've forgiven him?"

"It's not about forgiveness, but about making certain his last
days on earth are not spent in pain. And it's also about allowing
him to die in peace. He wants to see us married."

Emily's mind was in turmoil. She loved Chris, wanted to
marry him, yet she wanted it on their own terms. She did not
want someone else dictating when, where and why they should
exchange vows.

"He's manipulating us."

"That's because he's a manipulator."

"You don't care?"

A deep laugh rumbled in his chest. "I care, baby. I care a lot.
However, it's not about Alejandro Delgado's manipulation. It's
about how I feel about you. Even before I slept with you I knew
I wanted you as my wife." Lowering his head, he placed a kiss
under her ear. "I want you to have my babies. I want to spend
the rest of my life with you, Emily, and I want to be in your arms
when it comes time for me to draw my last breath. I'm—"

Emily placed her fingertips over his lips, stopping his impassioned plea. "Don't, Chris. Please don't talk about dying. Death is in this house—all around us."

Capturing her wrist, he pulled her hand away from his mouth. "Marry me, Emily. Tomorrow!"

Closing her eyes, she shook her head. "I want to be married in a church."

"Alejandro said we can use the chapel."

"I want to be married by a priest."

"He will call a priest."

"I want my family with me," she continued, as if Chris hadn't spoken.

"We'll have family. My aunt and my father will be our witnesses."

Emily opened her mouth to counter his offer, but the words died on her tongue. She knew he was right. Everything she wanted for her wedding was right here: chapel, priest and family—Chris's family. And if she married him, they would also become her family.

"Can we do this, Chris?"

He stared down into her eyes, seeing a glazed look of despair shimmering in the green orbs. "Yes, we can, baby." Lowering his chin slightly, he flashed a sensual smile. "I'll make it up to you after the election. We can renew our vows with a big formal wedding and everything that goes with it, then honeymoon in any city or country that you choose."

A dying man was manipulating them. A man who had been exiled from his home for over thirty years had returned. And because he was a Delgado-Quintero, he still wielded enough influence to persuade a priest to marry his son without the customary posting of banns.

All she had to do was open her mouth and say yes, and within hours she would become Señora Emelia Delgado-Quintero. Hot tears welled up in her eyes, turning them into pools of sparkling peridot.

She was losing control—control of herself and her life. She was on a runaway roller coaster, unable to get off to regain her equilibrium. She'd challenged her parents for her independence, freely choosing who she wanted to date. But that no longer mattered. A man she had known all her life, loved for more than half her life, had professed his love for her and had turned her world upside down.

Christopher Delgado loved her, wanted to marry her, and she stood before him motionless, stunned, with tears filling her eyes and staining her cheeks. Leaning down, he kissed her tears, catching the moisture on the tip of his tongue.

"Baby," he crooned softly. "Please, don't cry." He breathed a kiss at the corner of her trembling mouth. "Everything will work out all right. Trust me."

Sniffling, she pressed her nose to his shoulder, nodding. "I'll try."

"Will you trust me enough to become my wife?"

"Yes. *Sí,* Cristobal," she repeated in Spanish. "I will marry you and bear your children."

Chapter 17

Emily awoke to find Chris sitting several feet from her bed, one leg looped over his knee and hands draped over the curved arms of the antique chair. She wasn't certain when he had entered her bedroom, though he hadn't been there when she finally fell asleep several hours before streaks of light pierced the sky. She had lain in bed, berating herself for agreeing to marry in Mexico. It was as if she and Chris were paralleling their parents' lives. Both Matthew and Eve Sterling and Joshua and Vanessa Kirkland had exchanged their vows in Mexico. What was it about the country that had roused passions they could not resist? And she did love Chris—more now that she had agreed to share her life with him. A slight smile softened her mouth when she realized that when the sun set to signal the end of the day she would be wife and lover to the man who had watched her while she slept.

"Hey," she whispered. Her sultry voice vibrated with a lingering somnolence.

Tilting his head, he regarded her, smiling. "Hey, yourself."

Emily returned his smile. He was casually dressed in a pale blue T-shirt and a pair of faded jeans. His tousled hair and the shadow of an emerging beard on his chin and lean jaw made him so sensually masculine that she sucked in her breath, holding it until she was forced to let it out. Her gaze followed him as he rose and made his way to the bed. The side of the mattress dipped as he sat down beside her.

Leaning against his shoulder, Emily closed her eyes. "Don't you think it's ironic that both our parents were married in Mexico? My mother met my father when she came here for a vacation, and your mother came to Mexico looking for her ex-husband and son, met Matthew Sterling and married him."

Chris stared at the mass of black curling hair covering her head. A few wayward curls fell over her forehead in seductive disarray. Unwittingly Emily had given him the opening he sought to make her privy to his stepfather's clandestine activities before he moved to New Mexico.

"How much do you know about Matthew Sterling?"

Shifting, she stared at Chris. "What do you mean by how much?"

"Do you have any idea what he did before he became a horse breeder?" She shook her head. "Your father never mentioned how he met him?"

A slight frown furrowed her forehead. "He said that he and Uncle Matt met when they were in the army."

"That's true. Dad joined the ROTC at the University of Texas at Arlington, graduated and fulfilled his military commitment with a tour in Vietnam. He was a member of an elite branch of the army that was the best when it came to rescue missions. After his military tour ended he taught political science for a few years after earning a graduate degree in international relations at Georgetown University. While there he ran into one of his former officers, who recruited him as an independent operative for the government."

Emily's eyes widened at this disclosure. "He was a spy?"

"He was a private citizen who had perfected rescue missions. Matthew Sterling was paid to marry my mother. It was a ruse to get Alejandro's attention, but what began as a marriage of convenience changed when they fell in love."

"Who paid him?"

Exhaling audibly, Chris stared across the room. "Harry Blackwell. Uncle Harry was an associate director of the FBI."

"What was the connection between your uncle and Alejandro?"

"Alejandro was marked for death by corrupt officials within the Mexican government. High-level officials he'd identified who were trafficking in drugs and stealing millions of dollars from U.S. companies doing business in Mexico."

"Where were you during this time?"

"Alejandro had contacted Uncle Harry and arranged for my return to Virginia a day before my third birthday, but I never made it back to the States. I was intercepted by a group of rogue Federales who held me hostage until they captured Alejandro. Dad negotiated with Mexican officials to release him. The U.S. Government paid nearly a million dollars to get their snitch out of Mexico alive."

Running her fingers through her short curls, Emily closed her eyes, unable to believe that the man she called Uncle Matt had once lived a double life. She knew he and her father had met when both were in the military, but she thought Matthew Sterling had always been a horse breeder. However, there were occasions when she'd heard her mother and Eve Sterling whisper about their husbands' *missions*. There was no doubt that her own father had been involved with classified military assignments, but she had never suspected Uncle Matt.

Opening her eyes, she stared across the room, her gaze fixed on a small wooden cross affixed to an otherwise bare whitewashed wall. "My father nearly lost his life here." Her voice was low, even. "He'd encountered my mother while on an assignment. They met on the flight down and married seven days later. Then Dad left to meet his contact but was stabbed or left for dead. Uncle Matt was responsible for getting him out of Mexico and back to the States. The army threatened to court-martial him because he'd disobeyed orders by becoming involved with a woman while on assignment. They were separated for a year before reconciling. I came along a year later."

Chris chuckled softly. "They probably had a wonderful time making up."

"Mom and Dad can be pretty intense," she said, flashing her own brilliant smile.

Sobering, Chris said, "Dad saved Uncle Josh's life because he'd saved his about ten years before, when both were in Central American on a so-called 'fact-finding' mission. Speaking of being intense," he continued, smoothly changing the subject, "Alejandro was very animated this morning. He called the local parish priest as soon as he woke up. Father Gonzalez has agreed to marry us this afternoon. Don't you think it's a little eerie that your parents, my parents and now the two of us will marry in Mexico?"

She nodded slowly. "There must be something about this country that the Kirklands, Sterlings and Coles can't resist. My cousin Regina lived here for eight years. She and Aaron still own property about a hundred miles south of Mexico City. Our marriage will finally unite the Sterlings, Kirklands and Coles."

"You're right. But things are going to change once we have children."

"Why?"

"Our children will be exempt from your family's mandate that they not fly commercial carriers."

"They'll be considered Coles," she insisted in a soft tone.

Even though Emily's last name was Kirkland, she was still a Cole. Her paternal grandfather, Samuel Claridge Cole, had engaged in an extramarital affair with a woman who worked for his company, and when she discovered she was carrying Samuel's child he paid Everett Kirkland, a vice-president at ColeDiz, to marry her. It had taken nearly forty years for the breach between father and son to heal, and now Joshua kept a constant vigil at the bedside of his elderly, dying father.

"Legally they'll carry my name. This will be one time when the Coles will not have things their way," Chris whispered in her ear. "Our children will be Delgados."

"I know they'll be Delgados, but they will also be Coles." There was a thread of annoyance in her voice.

Sitting up, he shifted on the bed and held her bare shoulders in a firm grip. "Wrong, Emily. If they're going to be anything, they'll be Delgados and Sterlings."

Her gaze widened, then narrowed. "Are you dismissing my family?"

"No, I'm not. I just want to let you know that I'm capable of protecting my wife and children. And I want all of us to be able to fly like normal people…"

"Are you saying I'm not normal?" she interrupted, her eyes darkening with her rising temper.

"Don't put words in my mouth."

"I'm not putting words in your mouth, Christopher Blackwell Delgado. I don't like being called abnormal, that's all."

Pulling away from her, he moved off the bed. His black eyes blazed with repressed fury, and the muscle in his lean jaw twitched noticeably when he clenched his teeth. He and Emily hadn't even exchanged vows and she had set down the rules for determining the lives of the children he hoped to share with her.

The Coles—one of the wealthiest African-American families in the United States—had established strict mandates for everyone born or married into their family. Mandates that were expected to be followed without question. But that would change with him and Emily. The Coles and Kirklands might have their own traditions, but he and Emily would establish new traditions for their children.

"I'll see you downstairs."

Emily watched Chris turn on his heel and walk out of her bedroom. She wasn't pregnant, they weren't even married, and they were already arguing about child-rearing.

She had known him all her life, but it was only now that she had become aware that she actually did not know Christopher Delgado. Easing back against the pillow, she closed her eyes. "He's a stranger," she whispered audibly. Hesitation plagued her as she vacillated. Swinging her legs over the side of the bed, the words she struggled to verbalize were lodged in her throat: *I hope I'm not making a mistake.*

Emily stood beside Chris in the small chapel, repeating her vows in Spanish. They had met with Father Gonzalez earlier that afternoon. The young priest was quick to inform the couple that what he intended to do was highly irregular, but his superior had directed him to offer the son of Alejandro Delgado and his *novia* the sacraments of Reconciliation and Holy Matrimony.

What Monsignor Ocasio hadn't told Father Gonzalez was that the elder Delgado planned to leave a sizable portion of his estate to the Church.

The hushed timbre of her voice belied the riot of emotions gripping her. She loved Chris and wanted to marry him—but not like this. She had spent years fantasizing walking down the aisle of the church where she had been baptized as an infant, a church filled with family and friends who had come to see her exchange vows with Christopher Blackwell Delgado. A rush of guilt and selfishness assailed her. She had given in to Alejandro's wish to see her and his son married, thereby cheating her parents of their right to attend her wedding.

Emily had lost count of the number of times she and Vanessa Kirkland had discussed her future. Her mother's only wish was to see her children secure in their careers and private lives. And on more than one occasion she hinted that she was ready to become a grandmother. The desire for grandchildren always followed a visit with Eve Sterling. Whenever Salem and Sara Lassiter left their young son Isaiah with Eve, Vanessa was enamored by the intelligent child who had inherited his attractive parents' best features.

Emily's head came up slowly, her gaze fusing with Chris's. Unabashed love shimmered from the depths of his raven-black eyes as he promised to forsake all others, to love and protect her until death parted them. Her gaze lowered when he slipped an exquisite gold band on her left hand. The ring fit her slender finger as if it had been made for her. After breakfast Sonia had given her a small antique box, stating that it was a wedding gift. Emily's shock was apparent when she'd gazed down at an assortment of exquisite rings, necklaces, bracelets and earrings. She had come to Mexico wearing another man's engagement ring but would leave with heirloom pieces that had once belonged to Chris's deceased paternal grandmother.

Flickering light from burning white tapers reflected off the flawless diamonds in an antique band of yellow gold as she wound her arms around Chris's neck when Father Gonzalez directed the groom to kiss his bride.

There was no soloist, no organist, no pews filled with her family members, Chris's family, and their friends when they turned to face the ancient wooden door at the back of the sanctuary. There was only Alejandro and Sonia, who sat together, holding hands. A shaft of sunlight coming through the stained-glass windows bathed the married couple in a shower of gold. The bright light picked up glints of red in Chris's black hair, highlighted the deep gold hues in Emily's sun-browned face, and accentuated the flattering contrast of her pale yellow dress against the olive-colored skin.

The fingers of her left hand rested lightly on the sleeve of Chris's navy blue suit as he turned to whisper in her ear, "I love you, Mrs. Christopher Delgado."

She nodded, smiling. "And I you, Mr. Delgado."

Sonia rose to her feet, her arms outstretched. *"Permítame ser el primero en felicitarle."*

Emily accepted Sonia's embrace and congratulations. "Thank you." She pulled away from Chris, handing him the small bouquet of white flowers bound with streamers of yellow, red, white and green ribbon, and walked to Alejandro.

Sitting down beside her father-in-law, she leaned over and kissed his cheek. "This is the happiest day of my life, Father." And it was. Even though she did not have her family and friends to witness her nuptials, she knew she would agree to marry Chris again, in any foreign land, because she loved him just that much.

Alejandro took her slender hand in his, squeezing her fingers gently. "This is only the beginning, Emelia. There will be many more happy ones." He closed his eyes briefly as a mysterious smile parted his lips. "May life offer you everything you've ever wished for. We must get back to the house and eat something before you and Cristobal share your wedding night."

Heat warmed her cheeks at the mention of her wedding night. She didn't think she could relax enough to make love with Chris with his father and aunt in the same house.

Chris and Father Gonzalez flanked Alejandro to help him from the sanctuary and back to the house, where a light repast awaited them. He had put up a brave front, enduring excruciating pain when he refused the nurse's recommendation that he take his prescribed sedative. He'd railed, saying he did not want to sleep through his son's wedding ceremony. But now that he'd seen Cristobal married, he'd willingly accept the two tiny pills.

January 12
Acapulco, Mexico

Emily pressed her face against Chris's throat, feeding on his warmth and strength. In less than fifteen minutes she would leave her husband and Mexico to board the ColeDiz Gulfstream jet for her return to the States. He tightened his grip on her waist, pulling her flush against his body.

"I'll call you later tonight," she vowed.

"I'm sorry I'm putting you through this, baby. I promise I'm going to make everything up to you when…"

She placed her fingertips over his mouth, stopping his apology. "Don't, Chris. We know it has to be this way."

He grasped her wrist, easing her hand from his lips. "It doesn't have to be this way."

"As long as I work for KCNS and cover Savoy's campaign, it will have to be this way." She pressed her open mouth to his ear, whispering, "We'll make it."

Chris closed his eyes. "I pray you're right."

So do I, she thought. "I have to go, darling, they're holding the plane for me." Her luggage in hand, the copilot stood a distance away, watching her.

Cradling her face between his palms, Chris placed light, moist kisses along her jaw, cheekbones and lips, increasing the pressure and devouring her mouth like a starving man who'd been deprived of food.

"I love you. I love you so much," he chanted over and over.

Emily wasn't certain where she found the strength, but she pulled out of his embrace and walked away from him.

She followed the copilot as he led the way through a narrow corridor, down a flight of stairs, then onto the tarmac. She made her way up the stairs to the jet, where the pilot had just received clearance from the air traffic controllers at the Juan N. Alvarez International Airport. They were scheduled to arrive in Las Cruces by noon.

The pilot greeted her with a friendly smile as she stepped aboard the aircraft. She took her seat, fastened her seat belt and closed her eyes as the plane pushed back in preparation for takeoff. The aircraft taxied, picked up speed, and within minutes they were airborne. She opened her eyes, staring down at the rapidly fading Mexican landscape as the jet increased its altitude. Bright sunlight poured through the windows, warming her face.

She wanted to cry but didn't. It was she, not Chris, who insisted they keep their relationship secret. They would be apart for ten months, and she rationalized that it wasn't a long time for them to conceal their private passions. Or was it?

Chris stood motionless, hands thrust into the pockets of his slacks, watching Emily's departing figure until she disappeared from his sight. He waited in the same spot for a full five minutes, unable to still an unexpected rush of foreboding. He forced himself to make his way to the terminal where he would board his own flight back to the States. He had a two-hour wait before he would board a jet for Albuquerque.

He'd called his campaign manager hours before he'd exchanged vows with Emily, and been read the riot act because he hadn't heard from his candidate in two weeks. Grant Carson's source had reported that William Savoy had planned a news conference, hinting that his investigators had uncovered additional information about Alejandro Delgado's background that could prove extremely detrimental to his candidate's political future.

Chris reassured Grant that he would be able to counter Savoy's attack. He'd terminated the call, then arranged for his return to New Mexico to coincide with Emily's. He would spend time with Grant in Albuquerque before flying down to Las Cruces to visit his family and reunite with his wife.

Part Two
Separate Lives

Chapter 18

The driver maneuvered into the driveway leading to the Lassiters' home, stopping several feet from a large wolf. Emily leaned forward, handing the driver the fare for her trip from the Las Cruces Airport.

The man's gaze was fixed on the animal staring back at him. "Will he attack?"

She smiled, shaking her head. "No. But, to be on the safe side, why don't you pop the trunk and I'll get my own luggage?"

The man let out an audible sigh, pulling the lever for the trunk. He shook his head, unable to understand why someone would keep a wolf for a pet. He watched from the safety of the automobile's interior while his passenger removed her bags from the trunk. Staring at the side-view mirror, he mumbled a soft oath under his breath when the wolf moved toward her and pressed his nose against the back of her hand. The trunk closed with a solid slam and he put the car in reverse and sped away with an ear-shattering screech of rubber hitting the paved driveway.

Emily smiled at the Lassiters' pet, scratching him behind his ears. "Hey, Shadow." Sara and Salem still had the best silent wireless security system in the Mesilla Valley. No one ventured onto their property without permission because of the wolf's presence.

The front door opened and the tall figure of Sara Sterling-Lassiter walked out into the bright sunshine. Marriage and motherhood had agreed with her. The jeans she had paired with a white cotton pullover blatantly displayed the feminine curves of her slender body. She wore her black wavy hair longer than she had when she'd worked as an assistant U.S. attorney in a New York federal court. She had brushed it off her face and secured it atop her head with an elastic band. Several wayward strands floated down around her long, slender neck.

Extending her arms, she embraced Emily. "Welcome home, Emmie." Pulling back, she surveyed her best friend, smiling broadly. Large gold-green eyes examined the tanned face and brilliant green eyes that sparkled like precious jewels. "You look fabulous. I must say Jamaica agreed with you."

"That's not all that agreed with me," Emily said cryptically.

Sara folded her arms under her breasts. "What else?"

"It's not a what but a who."

Giving her a critical squint, Sara said, "Chris?" She'd whispered even though there was no one around to hear them.

Flashing a smug grin, Emily nodded. Closing her eyes, Sara mumbled a silent prayer of thanks. It worked. Her brother had gone after Emily Kirkland. She hugged her again. "You're going to have to tell me all about it." The words tumbled over each other as they rushed out. "You don't have to tell me the most intimate details, but I want to know everything else."

Emily picked up one of her bags while Sara took the other. She couldn't tell Sara everything. She couldn't tell her that because she'd married her brother they were now sisters-in-law.

"Where are Salem and Isaiah?"

"Salem's in Carlsbad at the Living Desert Zoo. He should be back later tonight. As for Master Lassiter, I just put him down for his nap."

Emily followed Sara into the towering two-story structure and through an immense foyer reminiscent of a museum hall. Primitive-looking pieces of sculpture, each placed on its own freestanding block of wood, were displayed under dramatic lighting that cast shadows on the carved figures, which appeared to dance playfully along the smooth white backdrop of the walls. All of the pieces had come from Salem's parents' Taos-based art gallery.

Sara glanced at Emily over her shoulder as they climbed the

staircase to the second level. "I'll let you settle in before I begin the cross-examination," she teased. Before she'd resigned her position with the federal court, she had distinguished herself as an aggressive prosecutor who'd destroyed defense attorneys who opted to face her in the courtroom.

"I just might plead the fifth," Emily countered. Both women laughed as they entered the guest bedroom where Emily would sleep during her stay in Las Cruces.

Sara placed her bag on a cushioned bench at the foot of a queen-sized bed. "If you need anything, Emmie, just let me know."

"I'm going to shower and change my clothes, then I'll be down."

Sara nodded. "Take your time. I told Mom and Dad that you were expected today, so I hope you don't mind that I invited them to share dinner with us."

"Of course not. I always look forward to seeing them." What Emily could not say was that the man and woman she called Uncle Matt and Aunt Eve were now her mother- and father-in-law.

She waited until Sara walked out of the bedroom, then went about the task of unpacking. Sitting on the carpeted floor, she stared at the box containing Chris's grandmother's jewelry. The ring he had slipped on to her finger was nestled among the other priceless pieces. Reaching into the box, she withdrew Keith Norris's ring. Even if she had wanted to consider marrying Keith, she was now another man's wife. She would call Keith and arrange for the return of his ring, then call her parents to let them know she'd returned to the States.

Emily's damp hair curled over her forehead as she reclined on an overstuffed club chair on the Lassiters' sun porch, sock-covered feet stretched out in front of her. She took a sip from a cup filled with a fragrant blackberry herbal tea.

Sara sat on a matching chair, her legs folded under her body in a yoga position. "I can't believe you threatened Keith Norris with exposing him."

"I hated to go there, Sara. But my mother called me in Ocho Rios about a list of names for wedding invitations, and I wasn't about to perpetuate Keith's lie."

"Well, he had to know that you were serious. He had his agent issue a press release saying that he was calling off the engagement indefinitely for personal reasons."

Emily shook her head. "What I don't understand is why he didn't let his agent announce the engagement. Then he could've saved face by saying that his agent had misunderstood him. The problem is, he's beginning to believe his own hype."

"I'm not defending Keith, but I think he was intimidated by your threat."

She snorted delicately. "Not hardly, Sara. He's only concerned with his inflated ego."

Sara gave her a skeptical look. "You don't see yourself the way others do, Emmie. You're the only woman I know who can strip a man of his masculinity in ten words or less. And if it's not your tongue, then it's the way you look at them. Do you remember poor Jeffrey Harris?"

Emily rolled her eyes upward. "Don't remind me."

"The man would've attempted to walk on water for you, but you always looked through him as if he didn't exist. And it never seemed to bother you that he went on to become one of the youngest federal judges in the state."

"It didn't bother me because, number one, he was your brother's friend, and number two, I was in love with Christopher Delgado."

Sara hadn't wanted to meddle in her brother's personal life, but Emily had just provided her with the perfect opening. "Speaking of Chris, where is he? The last I heard was that he'd left Mom and Daddy a note telling them he was going to Ocho Rios."

Staring down into her cup, Emily forced back a smile. "When I left him in…" Her words trailed off; she had almost said *Mexico*. "He took a later flight."

"Why didn't you come back together?"

"Chris refuses to fly on the ColeDiz jet. He claims it would be tantamount to accepting a personal gift or a campaign contribution."

"He's right about that. Rumors are flying that this race between him and Savoy will be nothing like the last one. I've just signed on with the Las Cruces office as legal counsel. At least you and I will get to see each other when Chris comes down to campaign."

"It's not going to happen, Sara."

"Why not?"

Emily repeated what she had told Chris about Richard Adams's reassigning her to cover William Savoy's campaign. A rush of blood darkened Sara's deep brown face as she struggled to control her temper.

"Does your boss know that he's playing directly into William Savoy's hands? How much information do you think Savoy is going to disclose to you when he realizes your association with his opponent? And the fact that I'm married to his late lover's widower makes it even more bizarre.

"Grace Clark was involved with William Savoy while she was still married to Salem. The affair ended only when Salem initiated divorce proceedings. However, Savoy refused to marry Grace once she discovered she was carrying his child, and she freed everyone from their obligations when she took her life, along with Salem's son and the unborn child in her womb."

Emily placed her cup on a table. Pressing her head against the back of the chair, she closed her eyes and combed her fingers through her short hair, pushing the wayward curls off her forehead before she opened them. Determination shimmered from their depths.

Sara had just confirmed what Salem had confided to her a week before he married her best friend. Emily had heard the rumors about William Savoy's proclivity for conducting affairs with married women, yet no one had been willing to publicly verify them.

"William Savoy will not stop me from reporting the facts."

"I want you to be careful with him, Emmie. He preys on vulnerable women, and he's not above using his political connections to seduce the unsuspecting, who usually are taken in by his charismatic personality. After he lost to Chris two years ago, rumors were flying that he promised he would stop at nothing to become governor of New Mexico."

Emily's expression was impassive, her eyes a frosty green. "I'm neither vulnerable nor that naive. Which means that William Savoy doesn't frighten me." She didn't tell Sara that at present, despite her reassignment, she was more in control of her career than her private life.

"I'm not saying he should. It's just that I don't want anything to happen that would jeopardize your career."

"What's he going to do if I report what I hear or see? Threaten my life? I don't think so, Sara. I don't know what he said or did to Grace Clark to make her take her own life, but I'm not her."

A shiver of apprehension swept up Sara's spine, but she dismissed it. "Enough about William Savoy. What's happening between you and my brother?"

Lowering her gaze, Emily could not stop the flood of heat sweeping over her face, neck and chest. "I'm glad I waited for him," she admitted softly, smiling.

"Hallelujah," Sara crooned, pressing her palms together. "I'd almost given up on the two of you."

Emily sobered quickly. "I want you to promise me something."

Vertical lines appeared between Sara's eyes. "What?"

"I don't want you to breathe a word about Chris and me. We want to wait until after the election before we go public."

Sara's eyes crinkled in a knowing smile. She had tried playing matchmaker for years, yet it was Keith Norris's announcement that had spurred her brother into action. Her anxiety about Emily joining Savoy's campaign was overshadowed by her best friend's apparent joy.

"Of course, Emmie. You can count on me to keep your secret." The sound of a door slamming caught the women's attention. Sara glanced at a clock on the mantel. It was only two-ten; Salem was early. Within minutes he walked into the room, a warm smile

softening the lines of exhaustion lining his forehead and ringing his mouth.

Tall, slender and broad-shouldered, he presented a dramatic figure in black: wool crepe jacket, slacks, cashmere turtleneck sweater and low-heeled boots.

Placing her cup on a side table, Emily rose from her chair. "Belated Happy New Year."

He dropped a kiss on his wife's waiting lips, then closed the distance between himself and Emily. He gathered her in a strong embrace, bending down and brushing his mouth with hers. "Happy New Year." Holding her at arm's length, he looked her over. "From the looks of you, I'd say you had a wonderful vacation." Her tanned face was proof that the sun worshipped her.

"It was excellent." She affected an attractive moue. "You look great, Salem." And he did. His long, straight black hair, secured at the nape of his neck, was streaked with a few silver strands. The overall effect was stunning. The deep red undertones in his brown face were the perfect foil for his dark, slanting eyes, long, thin nose, high cheekbones and a firm mouth that was full enough to be thought of as sexy. He had inherited the very best physical characteristics of his Navajo and African-American parents.

Inclining his head in acknowledgment, he said, "You can thank Sara for that. Thanks to her, I've become quite a contented husband and father." His penetrating gaze swept around the room. "Where's Isaiah?"

"He's still asleep," Sara said. "I plan to wake him up around two-thirty."

Salem smiled at his wife. "I'm going to change my clothes, then I'll wake him up. The little prince and I are going to hang out for a while."

"Don't hang out too far," Sara warned her husband. "Remember, Mom and Daddy are coming for dinner."

He glanced at his watch. "What time do you expect them?"

"Seven."

"We'll be back before six."

"I'll get him up while you change your clothes," Emily volunteered. She was lucky if she saw her godson half a dozen times a year.

She walked out of the room and made her way up the staircase to the upper level. Her footsteps were muffled in the deep pile of the plush carpeting lining the wide hallway. Soft lights reflected off the baseboards along the hallway. She walked into the nursery and found Isaiah lying quietly on his side, facing a window.

Emily crept silently toward the crib but was surprised to find the child wide awake. His large hazel eyes regarded her for several seconds. Rolling over, he caught hold of the railing and pulled himself up. Extending his arms, he smiled. Isaiah hadn't forgotten her. He had a few more tiny white teeth than he'd had when she last saw him.

"Arriba."

"Of course I'll pick you up." Reaching down, she lifted him from the crib, pressing her lips to his inky black hair.

Even though Isaiah was eighteen months old, he rarely spoke in full sentences. However, when he did, it was to issue demands. Sara was troubled by what she thought was delayed speech, but Salem reminded her that their son was exposed to so many different languages that he hadn't decided which one would predominate. Sara spoke English to him, Salem a Navajo dialect and Matthew and Eve Sterling Spanish.

Emily inhaled the clean, intoxicating scent exclusive to babies. "Daddy's home," she crooned against his velvety cheek. "And he wants to take you out."

Isaiah hugged her, his chubby arms tightening around her neck. "Pot-tea, Titi," he giggled close to her ear.

Pulling back, she stared down at the round, rosewood-brown face. "Potty?"

"Sí, Titi. Potty."

Isaiah laughed uncontrollably as she raced toward the adjoining bathroom while struggling to take off his disposable diaper.

The diaper dropped to the tiled floor, but she wasn't quick enough. Within seconds the front of her shirt and jeans were soaked through, while Isaiah pointed to his little potty chair.

She stared at him staring numbly back at her. "Oh, oh, Titi."

The look on his face was so serious that she burst out laughing. "It's all right, sweetheart. Titi will clean it up."

Isaiah called her Titi, aunt in Spanish. Little did the child know that she had actually become his aunt.

Is this what I have to look forward to when I become a mother? "Probably," she mumbled under her breath as she removed his undershirt and placed him in the bathtub.

She wanted to share with Chris what Sara and Salem had: a home, a child and a love that promised forever.

Chapter 19

Chris spied Grant Carsons first. Bespectacled Grant was the epitome of conservatism—from his dress to his deportment. An only child, Grant had grown up privileged. His mother had become pregnant for the first time after twenty-three years of marriage, and Drs. Benjamin and Eulalie Carsons's lives changed forever. Eulalie resigned her position at a municipal hospital in a small Los Angeles suburb to devote all her time to her son.

Chris and Grant had met on the Stanford University campus when they pledged Kappa Alpha Psi fraternity, and their friendship was cemented once they shared an apartment while attending law school.

Grant had married after graduating, but the union didn't last a year. The woman he'd married claimed he wasn't ambitious enough because he refused to join one of the top law firms in Los Angeles who had offered him a mid-six-figure starting salary. Benjamin and Eulalie's son had graduated number-one at Stanford and Stanford Law School, and had earned an almost perfect score on his bar exam. He loved the law, but not enough to spend more than sixty hours a week writing briefs and billing client hours. He signed on as legal counsel with a local community organization who offered their services free of charge to low-income citizens.

What the ex-Mrs. Grant Carsons did not realize was that Grant's desire to study law was not to earn a lucrative salary or become a partner, but because he wanted to help the disenfranchised. He was persuaded to leave his not-for-profit organization to spearhead his fraternity brother's bid for a state senatorial seat. After helping Chris win his first elected office, he returned to Los Angeles. However, two years later, he was back. He'd promised Senator Delgado that he would deliver the gubernatorial seat—and this time Chris would win by a greater victory than sixty-four votes.

Chris walked up behind Grant, tapping him on the shoulder of his cashmere topcoat. Grant shifted, his intelligent gaze widening behind the lenses of a pair of wire-framed glasses.

"Welcome home." He slapped Chris on the back. "As much as I hate to admit it, you look great." Two weeks in the sun had tanned his face to a rich chestnut brown, and relaxation had filled out the hollows in his cheekbones.

Chris returned his rough embrace. "The next time I disappear, I'll check in periodically."

Pulling back, Grant shook his head. "There's no next time, Brother Delgado. At least not until after the election."

"There may have to be an exception."

A slight frown furrowed Grant's smooth nut-brown forehead. "Why?"

"I plan to return to Mexico to see my father."

The campaign manager's mouth tightened in frustration as he bit back acerbic words. He wanted to impress upon his candidate that they were behind schedule. Savoy would capture the media spotlight by hosting his kickoff fundraiser two weeks before Delgado's, and the whispered rumors about Chris's father's activities were beginning to surface.

Reaching for the leather Pullman at Chris's feet, Grant picked it up. "I'm parked in the lot. I thought we'd either go back to your place or mine. It doesn't matter."

Adjusting a matching leather garment bag over his shoulder, Chris shook his head. "I'd rather find a quiet place here in the airport to talk. If that's not possible, then we can check into the Best Western Fred Harvey for a couple of hours. I'm scheduled to take a four-fifty flight to Las Cruces."

"Something wrong with your folks?" Grant's frustration escalated. He needed more than a couple of hours to confer with Chris.

"No. It's just that I left rather abruptly. I need to take care of a few things before I return to Santa Fe."

"There's a restaurant at the end of the terminal that has a private area in the back. We can talk there," Grant conceded.

The two tall, well-dressed men made their way down the terminal, ignoring the surreptitious glances thrown their way.

"You've got my vote, Senator Delgado," an attractive young woman called out when she recognized Chris. He smiled, nodding in acknowledgment. The woman stopped, watching the sweep of his dark gray raincoat swirl around the trousers of his charcoal-gray suit. "Nice," she whispered under her breath. "Very, very nice."

Chris walked into the main house at Sterling Farms, encountering complete silence. It was apparent that his parents had gone out. Making his way to the wing of the large one-story house to the bedroom he had claimed when growing up, he placed his luggage next to a wall-to-wall walk-in closet. A clock on the mantelpiece chimed the hour. It was exactly seven o'clock.

He experienced a momentary disappointment, not seeing his mother or father, but shrugged it off as his own fault. He'd been out of the country for two weeks and hadn't called either of them during that time.

Slipping out of his raincoat and suit jacket, he placed them over the back of a chair. Within minutes he was naked, striding toward an adjoining bathroom.

The image of Emily's face—her demure smile, the color of her eyes after they'd made love—and the silkiness of her flesh under his tongue lingered in his mind while he shaved and showered. The sound of her sensual voice sang in his ears as he dressed. He was smiling when he made his way to the garage, where he'd left his Saab. Everything about his wife swept over him as he headed south.

Blazing lights in the sprawling house illuminated it like a jewel in the desert, while the sounds of laughter resounded off the walls and floated upward to the towering cathedral ceilings.

"You're spoiling him," Salem whispered close to Emily's ear

when she picked up Isaiah and cradled him on her slim hip. "He can walk."

"How often do I get a chance to be with him?" she countered in the same hushed tone.

Curving his long fingers around Emily's neck, Salem pressed his mouth to her ear. "You live less than three hundred miles from here. And you know you're always welcome to come to visit—at any time. Now, let his feet hit the floor, Miss Kirkland."

Pulling out of Salem's loose grip, Emily rolled her eyes and walked away, leaving him frowning at her back.

Salem encountered the same problem whenever his mother or Eve Sterling interacted with their grandson. They spoiled the child so much, Isaiah usually overdosed with their indulgences, leaving Sara to deal with his tantrums until he eventually settled back into his usual routine.

Making her way into the dining room, Emily saw Sara studying each place setting to make certain they contained the same number of sterling-silver forks and spoons.

"Do you need help with anything?"

Sara glanced up, the lights from the chandelier overhead highlighting the brilliant gold-green color of her eyes. She shook her head. "No. I believe everything is ready."

Emily smiled at her hostess. "I like you with longer hair." Sara's raven waves were swept off her face, falling sensuously down the nape of her neck. The style was both sophisticated and very feminine.

"It's not long by choice. I don't have the luxury of a lot of free time anymore. I'd like to think that I'm in control of my life, but there are days when I feel as if I'm drowning in an abyss of futile activity."

Moving closer, Emily stared at her friend. "Are you saying marriage and motherhood isn't what you thought it would be?"

"No, Emmie. It's just that I haven't decided what I want to do. I love Salem, and I love my son. But being a wife and mother doesn't quite do it for me. What I'm trying to say is that I miss my career."

"What you probably miss is the excitement of preparing for

trial. You miss the rush when you walk into the courtroom, where all eyes are focused on you. And if you're truly honest with yourself, you'll admit that you miss being onstage."

Sara went completely still. "How did you know?" Her voice had lowered to a hushed whisper.

"I know because I go through the same thing whenever I'm in front of the camera, knowing that millions of people are watching me, listening to my words, believing me. I could sit there and tell them lies, and because I'm Emily Kirkland, political analyst for KCNS Metromedia News Twelve, they believe me."

An expression of relief softened Sara's delicate features. "You're better than a shrink, Emmie. Salem and I are talking about having another baby, but I told him that I had to think about it. I'm only thirty-one, so I have a few more years before I'm considered high-risk. But he's thirty-eight, and he says he doesn't want to wait too many more years."

"When do you plan to start trying?"

"Probably August. By that time Isaiah will be two, and hopefully completely toilet-trained. I'd like him to attend preschool for a couple of hours each day so he can socialize with other children his age. It will also allow me time for myself before I go back to breast-feeding, teething and toilet-training all over again. I'd really like the next one to be a girl. I think having a girl will settle me down."

"Everything will work out fine, Sara. You have a wonderful husband, a gorgeous son and a beautiful home. And you can always resume your career whenever you want." Emily remembered Chris saying that he wanted to start up a practice with his sister.

"You're right, girlfriend." Curving her arms around Emily's neck, she pressed her cheek to hers. "Thanks for the pep talk."

The doorbell rang, echoing melodiously through the large house. "I wonder who that can be?" Sara said. Her parents had arrived at seven, and she knew Salem hadn't invited anyone else.

"I'll get it," Matthew Sterling said, making his way to the front door.

"Whoever it is, please try to make it quick, Daddy. We're

ready to sit down to eat," Sara informed him as she walked back to the kitchen to help her husband, who had offered to carve the succulently herb-roasted leg of lamb.

Matt Sterling opened the door, his curving eyebrows meeting in an angry scowl. "I should beat the crap out of you," he hissed through his teeth, "for what you've put your mother through these past two weeks. Where the hell have you been?"

Chris smiled, the tiny lines around his penetrating dark eyes deepening. "Hello to you, too, Dad." Curving an arm around the older man's neck, he kissed his cheek. "I'd prefer you beating the crap out of me to Mom's tongue-lashing."

Matthew Sterling smiled. "You're right about that. Even after being married to the woman for thirty-two years, I do everything possible not to get whipped by her tongue."

The two men hugged each other in a rough embrace, then moved into the house. "Look who I found," Matt announced when they walked into the living room.

Eve Sterling rose gracefully from a love seat, her stunned gaze fixed on the tanned face of her firstborn. "You're back."

Chris closed the distance between them quickly, pulling his mother's still-slender body to his. Lowering his head, he kissed her cheek. "I'm sorry, Mom, about leaving so quickly. But there were a few things I had to take care of."

Easing back, Eve looked up at her son. She had to admit that he looked magnificent. She didn't know why, but at that moment Christopher reminded her of his father—the man who had inflicted such pain—a pain that had lessened with age but left scars that would never vanish.

Placing a hand on his cheek, she smiled a smile so reminiscent of his own. "We'll talk later."

He gathered her to his chest again, brushing his mouth over hers. "Thanks." His head came up and he went completely still as his gaze met Emily's. He missed his nephew cradled in her arms, seeing only her radiant beauty as she offered him a secret smile.

Eve felt the muscles in his arms tense, and she turned to

glance over her shoulder. Her perplexed gaze registered the silent entrancement between her best friend's daughter and her son.

Emily moved closer, handing Isaiah to his grandmother when she held out her arms. "Welcome home, Chris. You wear your vacation well."

Inclining his head, he smiled. "So do you. How…" His words trailed off when Sara walked into the room, arms extended.

"Hey, bro!"

"Hey, sis." He picked her up, swinging her around. "I owe you one," he growled in her ear.

"About what?" Sara asked innocently.

"About me being a *man*." He held her at arm's length. "And I can assure you that I am very much a man," he said.

Sara kissed his mouth, then wiped away the streak of color from her lipstick with her thumb. "Sorry about that remark, bro. I had to do something to galvanize you into action. It worked, didn't it?"

"No comment, counselor."

Salem walked into the living room, announcing that dinner was ready, but hesitated before going into the formal dining room with the others when he saw his brother-in-law. He greeted him warmly, then stared at Chris with a strange look on his face.

"What's the matter, Salem?"

The veterinary surgeon closed his eyes, then opened them. "If you don't protect her, then you're going to lose her, Chris," he said cryptically.

Chris's left eyebrow rose a fraction. "Who are you talking about?"

Salem leaned closer. "You know damn well who I'm talking about. Your wife? And no, she didn't tell me. She didn't have to," he added.

It was Chris's turn to close his eyes. "Does Sara know?"

"If she does, she hasn't said anything to me."

Opening his eyes, he stared at his brother-in-law. There had been a time when he hadn't wanted to believe Salem's predictions, but he knew he spoke the truth. He had been given the gift of sight, and on more than one occasion his prophecies were manifested.

"Hire a protection specialist, Chris," Salem continued in a soft whisper. "If not, then you'll find yourself placing flowers on her grave." Resting an arm over the younger man's shoulders, he patted his cheek. "I don't know about you, Governor Delgado, but I'm starved. Let's sit down and eat."

The fact that Salem had referred to him as governor paled when Chris sat down at the table next to his mother and opposite his wife. No one at the table suspected his connection to Emily Kirkland because Salem's warning made the breath solidify in his throat, not permitting him to speak.

He answered questions directed at him, responding like an automaton, while Emily's mood was buoyant. Her luminous eyes sparkled in amusement when Isaiah picked up a spoon and managed to feed himself without dropping a morsel.

"Is it good, Isaiah?" she crooned softly.

The little boy's head bobbed up and down. He closed his eyes and opened his mouth to display its contents. "See food," he said clearly once he swallowed.

Sara frowned at her son. "Isaiah is suppose to eat food, not show it."

Eve touched her daughter's hand. "Let him be, Sara. He's just being a child."

"You never let us behave that way at the table."

"You've got that right," Chris mumbled, concurring with his sister.

Eve Sterling sat up straighter, the brilliant prisms of light from the chandelier glinting off her curly silver hair, creating a halo effect. She would soon celebrate her sixty-seventh birthday, and her exotic beauty had not diminished with age. "It's different with grandchildren."

Salem shook his head in a hopeless gesture. "Why is it always different with grandchildren?"

"Because it is," Matthew and Eve chorused in unison.

He winked at Sara. "I rest my case."

She gave him a *you-should've-known-better-than-to-ask* look at the same time she forced a smile. She and Salem tried not to spoil Isaiah, but all their efforts were in vain.

Dinner became a leisurely, festive affair as several different wines were served, along with a flavorful lobster bisque, a walnut salad in endive, a mixed green salad with a cider vinaigrette dressing, thinly sliced leg of lamb with roasted herbs, marinated asparagus spears, cabbage stuffed with mushrooms, walnuts, and bulgur and homemade yeast rolls.

Salem and Matt cleared the table, Chris and Emily washed and stacked dishes for the dishwasher, and Eve stored leftovers in refrigerator containers, while Sara took Isaiah upstairs to bed.

Emily pushed several buttons on the dishwasher just as the telephone rang. Salem answered the call, then extended the receiver to her.

"It's your mother," he said quietly.

She took the receiver and placed it to her ear. She heard the words and saw four pairs of eyes staring at her. "Yes, Mom. I'll let everyone know. Uncle Matt is here," she continued, as if she were in a trance. She extended the telephone. "Uncle Matt."

Closing her eyes, she tried to keep her legs from shaking. The waiting was over. Her grandfather had died in his sleep.

Chris moved quietly to her side, his arm going around her waist as he eased her gently to a chair. "What's the matter?"

Her gaze locked with his. "Grandpa is gone."

Ignoring the others, Chris pulled her face to his chest and held her. Emily Kirkland adored her grandfather, and he her. Samuel Cole had been known to say that Emily was his favorite grandchild, his favorite because she most resembled the woman who at one time he had loved more than his own wife.

Matt covered the telephone's mouthpiece with one hand. "Chris, what's on your schedule for the next few days?"

Turning and looking over his shoulder, Chris said, "Nothing. Why?"

"You, Salem?" Matt asked his son-in-law.

"Nothing my backup can't handle."

Matt's glowing eyes swept around the kitchen, like a large cat searching out its prey. "We're all going to West Palm Beach for a funeral. The ColeDiz jet will pick us up at the Las Cruces airport at six in the morning."

Rising to his feet, Chris stared at Matt. "I can't travel with you."

"Why not?" Matt barked.

"I'll take a commercial flight."

"Bull…"

"I will not discuss it," Chris shot back, cutting him off. A vein in his temple throbbed noticeably.

Eve looked at her husband, then her son. "Chris," she said softly, "it's not a pleasure trip, darling."

He turned and stared at her, and she took a step backward. His expression was so like Alejandro Delgado's that she thought she had gone back more than thirty years in time.

"I'll meet you there," he said with a finality that chilled everyone in the room. Turning on his heel, he walked out of the kitchen and out of the Lassiter house.

Raising the receiver to his ear, Matt said quietly, "We'll be ready at six."

Chapter 20

Chris had been in Florida for more than eight hours when the ColeDiz jet touched down on a private airstrip at the West Palm Beach Airport. He'd called Grant and informed him that he had to leave the state to attend the funeral of a family friend, promising to check in every day.

He hadn't slept on the red-eye flight, but after the jet touched down in Florida he rented a car, drove to a hotel, checked in and left a message for a wake-up call for nine that morning.

Dressed in a lightweight dark wool suit, white shirt and dark gray tie, he drove along a boulevard, then turned off onto a private street leading to the Cole estate.

He was met at a set of decorative iron gates by a man with a two-way radio. Lowering the window in the car, he leaned out. "Christopher Delgado."

The guard checked his name off on a list, then waved him through. "Stay to your right until the end of the drive. Someone will park your car."

"Thank you."

He drove slowly, his gaze sweeping over the magnificence of the showplace property. It was styled in the Mediterranean tradition, overlooking a lake and constructed to take advantage of both natural light and water views. Visitors were met with the grandeur of twin staircases leading to the upper level and four apartment suites. The house was filled with the priceless objects the Coles had acquired over several generations, and it was in their boxwood garden that he had kissed Emily Kirkland for the first time.

Thinking of his wife eased the lines of tension around his mouth. He had only touched her once since their return from Mexico, and that was to comfort her. He wanted to touch her in passion, taste her lush, sweet mouth and hold her while counting the strong, steady beats of her heart.

She had come to him untouched, a virgin, yet he found more delight in her body than he had in any of the other women he had slept with. When she crawled atop him and whispered in his ear what she wanted him to do to her, his whole being was flooded with a desire that made him forget who he was. Emily was the only woman who took him to heaven and back.

Another man stood at the end of the driveway, motioning for Chris to stop. He applied the brake and put the rental car in park. His gaze shifted beyond the valet, lingering on the tall, white-haired man he recognized as Martin Cole.

The valet moved forward and leaned into the open window. "I'll take it from here, sir." He opened the door, and Chris stepped out of the car.

Martin met him as he made his way toward the entrance. He extended his hand. "Thanks for coming."

Ignoring the proffered hand, Chris embraced Emily's uncle. "Think nothing of it. After all, we're family."

Martin laid his head on Chris's shoulder. "You're right about that."

We are family, Chris wanted to tell him. He'd married the man's niece. Arm in arm, they entered the house, where other members of the family had gathered soon after word that Samuel Cole had died was announced.

"How's your mother holding up?"

Martin shook his head. "Not well. I had to have a doctor sedate her. At ninety-six, she's quite frail."

Chris stared at Martin Diaz Cole. He would celebrate his seventy-fifth birthday on January 31 and had aged like fine wine. Tiny lines were clearly visible around his dark eyes, and deep slashes in his cheeks and along his nose were a testament to his aging. There wasn't a trace of black in his gleaming silver hair, yet his large body hadn't gone soft like so many men his age.

Martin led Chris into the library. Four generations of Coles crowded chairs, love seats and sofas, and many of the younger generation sat on the priceless Aubusson rug covering the inlaid parquet floor.

Martin's eldest daughter, Regina Spencer, crossed the room and hugged him. "Thank you for coming, Chris."

He kissed both her cheeks. "I'm sorry about your granddad."

She nodded. "He died in his sleep early yesterday morning. Aaron convinced Daddy and Uncle Josh to have him transferred to a hospital because he was having trouble breathing. They put him on a ventilator, but it was too late."

Chris offered Regina a comforting smile. "He's resting now."

"It's my grandmother I'm worried about. She was so distraught that she had to be sedated. Aaron's with her now."

Regina and her husband, Dr. Aaron Spencer, lived in Bahia, Brazil, with their teenage son and daughter but traveled to North America several times each year to spend time with the Coles, and to visit their retreat south of Mexico City.

Regina, an Oscar-nominated actress, had given up her career to marry a man much older than she out of deep gratitude. After his death, fate brought her late husband's son into her life, and everyone teased her because when the young widow married Aaron Spencer she didn't have to change her name.

Regina was as stunningly beautiful at forty-five as she had been the day she married Aaron. And despite being ten years her junior, Chris had more gray hair than she.

"Where's your mother?"

"She's on the loggia with Daddy's sisters. They've been inconsolable. Uncle Josh and Uncle David are at the funeral home, finalizing arrangements. They want to eulogize and bury Grandpa tomorrow."

"Will that give everyone time to get here? I don't see Michael Kirkland."

"He's on his way. And we expect Uncle David's Gabriel by six tonight."

Regina wound her arm through Chris's. "Come, let me introduce you to the latest Cole."

"Who does this one belong to?"

"He's Aunt Nancy's great-grandchild. At least Grandpa lived long enough to see his first great-great-grandchild."

Not only were the Coles very wealthy, they were also very prolific. He had argued with Emily about their children being Delgados and Sterlings, but after seeing all the Coles gathered together under one roof to mourn the passing of the patriarch, he realized 2,000 miles was hardly enough distance to keep his children from connecting with their East Coast relatives.

Emily did not see Chris when she walked into her grandparents' home. She consoled and was consoled by her many grieving relatives before she made her way upstairs to her grandmother's bedside. Aaron Spencer excused himself, leaving her to sit and hold the frail hand as she listened to the elderly woman's reminiscence about her seventy-fifth wedding anniversary celebration. Marguerite-Josefina Diaz Cole's soft voice was barely audible as she struggled to surface from the lingering effects of the tranquilizer she had been given.

Leaning over, Emily kissed the woman's cool forehead. "Why don't you rest, Grandma? I'll stay here with you."

A satisfied smile parted M.J.'s pale lips. *"Gracias, nieta."*

Emily gazed fondly at the woman whose exquisite beauty had not faded despite the fact that she was nearing the century mark. Her enchanting dimpled smile had been inherited by several of her children, grandchildren and great-grandchildren, filling every space in the twenty-four-room structure.

Emily felt a presence. Turning, she saw her brother's broad shoulders filling the doorway. Raising his hand, he beckoned to her.

Her eyes fused with his as she approached him. She suspected he had come directly to the house without stopping to change his clothes, because he was still in uniform.

"Hi," she whispered, reaching for his hand.

"Hi," he crooned, leaning down and kissing her gently.

"How's Washington?"

A frown twisted his handsome face. With the exception of his coal-black hair, he was an exact replica of his father. Newly promoted Captain Michael Kirkland's perfect symmetrical features were almost as delicate as a woman's—high cheekbones blending into a lean jaw and a strong chin, a firm mouth that was neither too full nor thin and clear green eyes framed by long black lashes that were captivating and hypnotic.

"Don't ask," he muttered angrily. "You're wanted downstairs," he continued, smoothly shifting the topic. "Dad and Uncle David are back. They want to let everyone know about the final arrangements."

Emily was aware of her brother's silent undeclared war with his employer—the U.S. Army. Less than four months earlier he'd been ordered back to the States from a post in Japan and reassigned as a special assistant to the Joint Chiefs of Staff in Washington, D.C. His superior officer's rationale had been that a high-ranking general had taken a special interest in him. First Lieutenant Michael Kirkland was now Captain Kirkland, but the promotion failed to elicit a modicum of excitement for the young career officer. He much preferred the shadowy world of intelligence to the mundane predictability of Washington's military machinations.

Hand in hand, they walked the length of the hallway and down the curving staircase. Emily's gaze swept over the throng that had gathered in the living room, searching for Chris. She found him standing off in a corner, watching her descent. Lowering her lids in acknowledgment, she greeted Ana Cole, David's nineteen-year-old daughter, with a comforting smile.

Then, her luminous gaze searched and found her father, who also had followed her progress as she descended the curving staircase. Her mother sat next to Eve Sterling, talking softly.

There was a hushed silence before Martin Cole began speaking, his soft drawl carrying easily in the large room.

"As many of you know, my father was very controlling—even to the very end." There were nods and smothered smiles. "And I'd like to adhere to his last wishes. To spare my mother additional grief, there will be no wake. I'd like to request everyone's presence at St. Michael's Cemetery tomorrow morning at seven o'clock for a graveside ceremony. Then we'll return to the house for breakfast.

"At eleven forty-five tomorrow morning John Edge will conduct a formal reading of Samuel Claridge Cole's last will and testament. Once Mr. Edge was informed of Samuel Cole's death, he instructed me to contact everyone who is currently in this room. I ask that you delay your departure until after the reading of the will. I've just been told that the caterers have arrived and will be setting up tables in the rear of the house. My mother's home is available to anyone who wishes to stay, and my sisters and brothers have also opened their homes for our out-of-town family. Thank you."

Emily hadn't realized she was holding her breath until she felt a tightness in her chest. Her gaze swept around the living room, lingering briefly on Salem and Sara Lassiter, Matthew and Eve Sterling, then her husband. When her mother had called her and told her that Samuel Cole had passed away, she had specifically asked to speak to Matt. Only Samuel Cole's personal accountant had been privy to his personal wealth; however, it was apparent that the former founder and president of ColeDiz International Ltd. intended to share his vast wealth with those outside his immediate family.

The room was filled with the babble of voices as adults discussed lodging arrangements. Samuel Cole's two daughters, Nancy Cole-Thomas and Josephine Cole-Wilson, conferred with their husbands, deciding who would stay with them and who would be put up in nearby West Palm and Palm Beach hotels.

Emily wove her way through the crowd toward Chris. "Meet me in the garden in five minutes," she said quietly as she moved past him.

Bright Florida sunshine greeted her as she made her way out of the house toward the gardens. Blinking furiously, she wished she had stopped to retrieve her sunglasses. It was half past noon and the temperature was a balmy sixty-five degrees.

The Cole property encompassed twelve acres of land, nearly a quarter of which was made up of gardens: tropical, exotic Japanese and boxwood. Emily entered the boxwood, meticulously cut hedges rising upward to more than fifteen feet around her. Turning to her right, she stopped and waited.

Within minutes she came face-to-face with Christopher. She found herself in his arms, her face pressed against his warm brown throat.

He buried his face in her fragrant hair. "I've changed my mind."

Pulling back, she stared at the anguish in his obsidian gaze. "About what?"

"The pretense, Emily. The subterfuge. I don't intend to live a lie where…"

Placing her fingertips over his lips, she stopped his words. She knew what he was going to say. "It's not a lie, darling."

He pulled her hand away from his mouth, struggling to control his temper. "What the hell else is it? We're legally married, Emily. Why can't I tell my family that you're my wife."

"Because we can't. You know my situation."

"What situation?"

"My job at KCNS."

"Your job is more important than our marriage? Is it?" he taunted when she averted her gaze.

Her temper flared when she realized he wanted her to choose between him and everything she'd worked so hard to achieve.

Straightening her shoulders under the jacket of her black wool gabardine suit, she glared up at him. "Don't ask me to choose right now, because you may not like my answer. Let me go. I should get back to the house."

He released her, watching as she disappeared around the hedge. Pressing his back against the unyielding foliage, he closed his eyes. He'd thought it would be easy—he and Emily could return to New Mexico and live out their separate lives until after the election. But Salem Lassiter's warning had changed everything. How could he protect her from unforeseen danger if they were separated by hundreds of miles?

He had taken an oath before God to love, honor and protect her. But the words were false, empty, because he couldn't claim her openly.

Chapter 21

A canopy protected chairs lined up in precise rows like soldiers at a dress parade. Another canopy shielded the freshly dug grave that would be Samuel Claridge Cole's.

The smell of wet soil hung in the air as the mourners filled the seats in the softly falling rain.

Martin and David supported their mother's limp body. Martin's wife, Parris Cole, stepped into the first row, along with her daughter, Arianna, and her son, Dr. Tyler Cole. Regina, Aaron, Clayborne and Eden Spencer followed.

Serena, David's wife, and their children were next. Ana clung to her twin brother Jason, while Alexandra Cole sobbed quietly against her older brother's broad shoulder. Gabriel's recent joy in receiving five Grammy nominations and an Oscar nomination for a movie soundtrack was tempered by his grandfather's death.

Nancy, her husband, children, grandchildren and great-grandchild filled three rows, while Joshua, Vanessa and Michael Kirkland sat behind them. Emily saw her parents glance around for her, but she did not move from Chris's side.

Josephine Cole-Wilson and her family members were next, followed by Matthew and Eve Sterling. Chris sat beside Emily, while Salem held Isaiah until Sara was seated, then handed her the sleeping child.

Emily heard the words, the prayers, but they were drowned out by her husband's query of the day before: *Your job is more important than our marriage?*

His words had taunted her when she returned to the house after their encounter in the garden. They lingered as she tried falling asleep in a bedroom at her parents' Palm Beach condominium and resounded in her head when she rose to prepare herself for her grandfather's funeral.

She wanted to blame Chris for her uneasiness, but she couldn't, even when she attempted to rationalize that she had been forced into marrying him. She had to be honest with herself; no one could force her to do anything she didn't want to do. It had not mattered what Alejandro Delgado-Quintero wanted. And it had not mattered whether Chris wanted to give in to a manipulative man's dying plea to see his son married. She'd married Christopher Blackwell Delgado because she loved him. Had loved him for so long that she couldn't remember when she did not love him.

She knew she had defied protocol when she elected to sit with him and his family; not only were Matt, Eve, Sara, Salem and Isaiah his family, but also hers. She hadn't missed her parents' questioning look when she hadn't joined them, but that no longer mattered. All her life she had challenged her parents for complete independence, and the red-hot streak of rebellion had surfaced again today.

Her father had taken a pledge that he would always protect her. What Joshua Kirkland didn't know was that she did not need his protection any longer. That responsibility was now her husband's.

Joshua Kirkland couldn't remember the last time he'd lost his temper. Those who knew him well said that he showed as much emotion as a robot—none.

His stride was determined as he walked into the Cole living room and waited for Christopher Delgado. Pale green eyes caught a pair black as pitch as Chris strolled into the room, his arm around Emily's waist.

Motioning with his head, he turned, expecting Chris to follow him. He was not disappointed when, a moment later, the young politician stepped into the cloistered seclusion of the library.

Even though Joshua was sixty-eight, it was nearly impossible to pinpoint his age. He had the same lines around his pale, penetrating eyes that he'd had at forty, and had managed to retain a slim, hard body, while his hair had silvered until it was a startling white against his golden-brown flesh.

Crossing his arms over a crisp white shirt, he glared at Chris. "What the hell are you doing with my daughter?" Though spoken softly, his words sliced the air like a knife.

Assuming a similar pose, Chris supported his back against a wall. Lowering his chin slightly, he met his father-in-law's lethal gaze with one of his own. "Do you actually expect me to tell you?"

Joshua's arms dropped to his sides. "You bet your ass I do."

Chris pushed off the wall and headed for the door. "Not today. Not ever."

"Christopher!"

He went completely still when his name exploded off the walls. Within seconds his face became a glowering mask of rage. "If you have something worthwhile to say to me, Joshua, then you'd better say it. Otherwise, stay the hell out of my face."

"What's going on in here?" A familiar Texas drawl captured the attention of the two men as Matthew Sterling walked into the library.

"That's what I want to know," Joshua snarled between compressed lips.

Matt's gaze shifted from his best friend to his stepson. "Am I missing something?"

Chris pointed a finger at Joshua. "Ask him. It appears as if he's a little perverted when it comes to Emily."

Joshua moved toward Chris, but Matt stepped between them. "No, Josh," he warned softly. "Not my son."

Tension shimmered in the room. Loyalty and a lifelong friendship hung in the balance as the three men faced off in what they knew could become a duel to the finish.

"What are you guys doing in here?" The three turned to find Eve and Vanessa in the doorway. There was complete silence. "I'm certain you all understand English," Eve continued, hands cradled on her hips. "If not, then I'll repeat it in Spanish."

"Nothing," Matt mumbled, not taking his gaze off Joshua.

Vanessa Kirkland pushed into the room. She looked at her

husband, then at Chris, knowing instinctively that something wasn't right between them. And knowing it had something to do with her daughter.

"Whatever it is that has you old gray fools acting like rutting bulls, you'd better solve it before you leave this room." Her dark, angry gaze seared her husband's impassive face. "We're here to mourn your father, not destroy a lifelong friendship."

Chris wanted to kiss Vanessa. He did not want to see nearly fifty years of friendship shattered because he and Emily were hiding their private passions.

"Am I included as a gray fool?" he asked glibly.

"If the shoes fits, then wear it, Senator Delgado," Eve snapped. "You ought to be ashamed of yourselves." She shook her head, her eyes filling with tears. "Mateo, I can't believe you'd dishonor a dead man's house by brawling like a drunken lout."

"I'm not drunk," Matt sputtered, turning away from Joshua.

"Well, you should be," Eve countered. "At least you'd have a good excuse for acting like a fool."

"Eve…"

She held her hand in front of his face, stopping his words. "Don't, Mateo. There's no way Vanessa or I will let you and Joshua destroy the covenant between our families because of your macho nonsense."

Still beautiful, elegant Vanessa Blanchard-Kirkland moved to her husband's side and took his hand. "She's right, darling. We've got to let go. We can't hold on to our children forever. They need to find their own way in this life. We've given them a wonderful start, and we're going to have to trust them to make the best of their lives."

Joshua smiled down at Vanessa, then cradled her to his chest. "But it's different with a girl."

"Emily's a woman," she reminded him softly.

Joshua stared over his wife's head. He knew she was right. He couldn't allow his concern for their daughter's well-being to threaten a lifelong friendship. He had saved Matthew Sterling's life, and Matthew his. Matt had risked his life to save the life of his younger brother, and he had also assisted the Cole family in rescuing Regina from her kidnappers. They'd shared too much for him to throw it all away because he believed that Christopher Delgado was taking advantage of Emily.

His gaze shifted, meeting the direct stare of his best friend's stepson. A vague light of compromise and understanding passed between the two men as they each registered the other's barely perceptible nod of acquiescence.

Lowering his head, he smiled at Vanessa. "You're right, angel. As usual."

"Don't you dare try to placate me, Joshua Kirkland."

His broad shoulders rose and fell as he shook his head in amazement. "I'm damned if I do and I'm damned if I don't."

Matt placed a large callused hand on his friend's shoulder. "Don't even try to figure them out. After thirty-two years of marriage we should know better."

Eve wound an arm around her husband's waist. "You're going to pay dearly for that little remark," she whispered softly.

He pulled her to his chest. "How?"

She wrinkled her pert nose. "I think I'm going to have a headache for the next month."

Slipping his hands into the pockets of his trousers, Chris rocked back on his heels. The women had successfully defused what had been certain to become a volatile confrontation.

"I told you guys before that you're too old for that," he teased his mother and stepfather.

"At least I don't need to take a little blue pill," Matt countered, deadpan.

Chris registered the gasps from his in-laws. "He's just kidding. He is," he insisted, when Joshua and Vanessa looked at him skeptically. "Damn you, Dad." Turning on his heel, he stalked out of the library, peals of laughter following him.

A smile crinkled his slanting eyes as he made his way to the formal dining room to look for Emily. He found her sitting on a chair, holding one of her many cousins, cradling the child to her chest as she held a bottle to the baby's mouth.

He walked over to her, leaned down and whispered, "I love you."

She smiled at his departing figure. She was still smiling when her parents walked into the dining room to find Chris sitting beside her, feeding her morsels of food from his plate while the child in her arms concentrated on sucking every ounce of milk out of the bottle.

The scene was imprinted on Vanessa Kirkland's brain. It looked as if she was finally going to get her grandchild.

There was a stunned silence, then hushed whispers as John Edge shook hands with Martin Cole. It had taken the attorney less than a quarter of an hour to read the will of self-made billionaire Samuel Claridge Cole. The contents had made all Samuel Claridge Cole's grandchildren, great-grandchildren and great-great-grandchild multimillionaires. Trust funds had been established for those under twenty-five. Samuel's thirty shares of ColeDiz International Ltd.'s privately held stock, along with thousands of shares of other stocks and bonds worth more than $600 million were to be evenly divided between his three sons and two daughters. All eyes were trained on Matthew Sterling when his name was mentioned. Samuel, wishing to thank him for his selfless sacrifice for the Coles, had added a codicil, leaving him a gift of $5 million. Eve Sterling closed her eyes and leaned against her husband's solid shoulder when John Edge stated that Christopher Blackwell Delgado and Sara Sterling-Lassiter would be given a gift of $2.5 million each. The Cole mansion would go to Martin Diaz Cole after his mother's death. Samuel's will had stipulated that the property remain in the Cole family for a minimum of 100 years.

Samuel's widow lay on a divan covered in aubergine-and-burgundy-striped silk, eyes closed and lips parted in a dimpled smile. Her Sammy had spent his life taking care of his family, and that would continue for generations to come. He had done well—very, very well.

Chapter 22

February 4
Santa Fe

The low babble of voices, punctuated by an occasional laugh, floated upward in the brightly lit ballroom at a Santa Fe country club. Black tuxedos provided a dramatic contrast to the brilliant colors of gowns molded to feminine bodies. Precious and semi-precious stones, fastened to scented necks and wrists, competed with the light of thousands of tiny crystal facets from four enormous chandeliers.

Emily stood in the lobby, her head lowered, and spoke into the tiny microphone attached to the bodice of her strapless gown. "I'm in."

"I read you," came a strong male voice through her earpiece. The man sat in a van with the network's logo painted on both sides, parked in a lot cordoned off for the media.

She removed her earpiece and microphone, concealing them inconspicuously in the upper portion of her gown. A fully charged battery pack was strapped to her right thigh with Velcro.

She and other members of the press had met with William Savoy's press secretary earlier that morning. He had cleared them to attend his fundraiser but had insisted they appear unobtrusive. And that meant no visible press badge, microphone, earpiece or handheld tape recorder. She had left the meeting glaring at the rigid man, while silently cursing him for being a spin doctor. He'd sought to control the flow of information about his candidate in order to strengthen William Savoy's image. The technique, used many times by political strategists, sometimes proved detrimental to a candidate's quest for victory.

Returning a formally dressed couple's smile with a casual nod, she made her way toward the bar and ordered a seltzer. Ignoring the flirtatious bartender, she sipped the cool liquid, her gaze sweeping around the room. In another two weeks the same ballroom would be filled to overflowing with Christopher Delgado supporters.

A secret smile curved her lush mouth as she thought of her husband. Chris had returned to Santa Fe the day after the funeral and reading of Samuel Cole's will to confer with his campaign manager and political strategists. She'd waited a week and then flown back to Las Cruces to find him at Salem and Sara's, waiting for her return.

They'd shared six glorious days and nights, recapturing their youth. She'd sat a horse for the first time in years, exulting in the feel of the wind caressing her face as she raced Chris across the flat landscape that made up Sterling Farms. They spent hours playing chess and listening to music, and crossed the border into Mexico to stay overnight in Juarez after a day of shopping. That was the first time they'd made love since their wedding night in Puerto Escondido. It had become a frantic, desperate coupling that left Chris gasping for breath and her close to tears. Both knew it might be their last time together until after the election.

"Good evening, Miss Kirkland. I'm pleased you could make it tonight."

Turning, she looked up into a pair of gray-blue eyes belonging to William Savoy. He was flanked by two men wearing buttonhole microphones and earpieces who were obviously members of his security staff.

This was her first time coming face-to-face with him since he'd lost the state senatorial election to Chris. Time had favored Savoy. There was something in his bearing that indicated that he had changed from the man who had campaigned vigorously for his first elected office. The man standing before her radiated charm, confidence and power.

William Alan Savoy was very tall—almost six-four—slender and imposing. The thirty-eight-year-old bachelor had been graced with a full head of brown, wavy hair, with natural streaks of gold from a distinctive widow's peak to the crown. A sun worshipper, his face was usually deeply tanned year-round. His features were ordinary—all except for his eyes. They were a penetrating blue-gray that changed color with his mercurial moods.

Despite the rumors as to his penchant for sleeping with married women, it was well known that he was one of the savviest politicians in New Mexico. He'd served as a special assistant to the state's attorney general while his father was lieutenant governor. He had distinguished himself during a high-profile case involving the death of several prisoners while in police custody. He had shattered the blue wall of silence to convict half a dozen rogue police officers who had earned the reputation of being "untouchable."

He inclined his noble head, a thick wave falling attractively over a high, intelligent forehead.

Extending her hand, Emily offered a polite smile. "Mr. Savoy."

He grasped her fingers, bringing them to his mouth, and dropped a light kiss on her knuckles. "I'm pleased that your boss took my advice and assigned you to cover my campaign. I can't think of a more professional journalist in the business today."

Her expression did not change. She'd blamed the wrong man. Richard Adams had reassigned her because William Savoy had requested her. Did he actually think she would fall into bed with him because her boss had served her up on the proverbial silver platter?

"I'm certain it's going to be a very interesting campaign." Her voice was neutral.

Savoy arched a sandy eyebrow as he leaned closer. "I can assure you that it's certain to become a memorable one."

Emily pulled her hand out of his loose grasp as his gaze lingered on her impassive face before easing down to her bared shoulders, then even lower to the soft swell of tanned breasts rising above the décolleté of her midnight-blue satin gown. It caressed the length of her long, silken neck before returning to her mouth.

William was unable to conceal his overt interest in Emily

Kirkland. He'd met her for the first time more than two years earlier and had been intrigued by her then. But she had changed. Gone was the business attire and the curly hair falling to her shoulders. He much preferred her sophisticated haircut and formal gown. Her eyes were mesmerizing, pulling him in and refusing to let him go.

She was perfect.

Emily raised her glass to her lips, taking a sip of the cooling liquid, her gaze fusing with Savoy's over the rim. Forcing a smile, she said softly, "If you can find time for me in your busy schedule one day next week, I'd like to conduct a personal interview."

Savoy smiled for the first time, attractive laugh lines fanning out around his eyes. "Of course. I'll tell my press secretary to call you and set up a time. Would you be opposed to a dinner meeting?"

This time her expression changed as she shifted her sweeping black eyebrows. "No."

He inclined his head, his smile widening until he displayed a mouth filled with large white teeth. "Good. I would like to linger and talk, but unfortunately I can't. I have to thank my constituents for their overwhelming generosity. Again, it's been my pleasure, Miss Kirkland."

Nodding, Emily stared at his broad back as he walked over to a gushing couple who appeared honored that he'd acknowledged them by name. The two men flanking him stood off to the side, their sharp gazes sweeping around the room. She wondered about them—how much did they actually know about their client? How much were they paid to protect Savoy? And how much to keep their silence?

"Emily Kirkland—fancy meeting you here. I'd thought you'd be on the other side of this political fence."

She turned at the sound of a familiar female voice. Her gaze brightened when she saw a woman who'd shared a number of graduate journalism courses with her. Bettina Gibson was now a feature writer for an entertainment magazine.

"Tina," she said, bending slightly to press her cheek to the tiny blonde's scented one. "When did you start covering the political circuit?"

Bettina blushed attractively, averting her gaze. "I'm here in an unofficial capacity." She managed a surreptitious glance at Emily. "You look fabulous. What's happening with you at KCNS? I couldn't believe you didn't get the weekend anchor slot." The words rushed out as if she was on drugs.

Emily gave her a critical squint. Something was wrong with her ex-classmate. "Are you okay?"

"Of course," she replied a little too quickly. Her deep blue eyes darted over Emily's shoulder. "I have to go. Call me at the magazine on Monday. We should get together and do lunch. Catch up on old times."

"Sure," Emily mumbled, watching Bettina push her way through the milling crowd. Her petite, compact body was swathed in a short, fitted black slip dress that hugged her curvy frame like a second skin.

Leaving her half-filled glass on the tray of a passing waiter, Emily moved through the lively crowd. Savoy's press secretary had reported that all the tickets for the $2,500-a-plate affair had been sold within a week of their mailing. They had estimated that the event would generate an additional $2 million to the candidate's already burgeoning campaign war chest.

She glanced at the slim gold bracelet watch on her wrist. The cocktail hour would end in another quarter of an hour, then everyone would file into another ballroom to eat. She hoped she was assigned to a table with a few interesting people. There was nothing worse than suffering through a catered affair with a dining partner or partners who rambled on about the most mundane topics—weather, sports or movies. And the only thing worse than the aimless chatter was a string of boring speeches extolling the merits of the esteemed candidate.

A slight frown appeared between her eyes when Emily spied Bettina walking up a flight of winding stairs to the second story of the opulent country club. She hadn't missed the woman's furtive gaze when she glanced around to see if anyone had noticed her.

Emily's reporter's instincts surfaced. Something was wrong with Bettina. Without hesitating, she followed the blond woman. Smiling at a man whom she knew was part of the security staff, she held the flowing skirt of her gown in one hand as she climbed the staircase. The midnight-blue satin shimmered against the warm brown flesh on her bared arms and flawless shoulders, highlighting the gold undertones in her skin. The man shifted his position, coming to stand at the foot of the stairs. She didn't notice a pair of blue-gray eyes following her ascent, while measuring the fluid grace of her slender body. Halfway up, she looked down and felt the iciness of the gaze. Slowing her steps, she found herself trapped in a cold, penetrating glare.

Her attention was diverted as an older woman, clinging to the arm of a much younger man, mumbled a greeting. She responded, holding the hem of her gown high enough to display a pair of slender ankles and shapely calves in three-inch dark blue pumps.

Making her way down a dimly lit carpeted hallway, she looked into several unoccupied rooms, searching for Bettina. The sound of voices came from a room at the end of the hallway. There was a man's voice, raised in anger, then a woman's. She tried discerning whether the woman's voice was Bettina's but couldn't; she was too far away.

Emily gasped and then went completely still when she recognized the distinctive sound of a gunshot, followed by a scream. There was an explosion, a scream, and then complete silence.

Closing her eyes, she pressed her body against the wall, waiting. She opened her eyes, unaware that she was shaking uncontrollably. She was the only one in the hallway. Someone other than herself had to have heard the gunshot.

The silence shouted at her as she registered the runaway pounding of her heart roaring in her ears. Moisture swept over her face like a fast-moving fog rolling in off the water. She hadn't realized it, but she was counting silently, the seconds adding up in her mind. Shock had rendered her mute and motionless. She continued to wait—to see if someone would step out into the hallway—if someone would come up the stairs to investigate the sound of the gunshot.

She had no idea how long she stood with her back pressed to the fabric-covered wall, wanting to move but unable to do so. All she had to do was walk another twenty feet and peer into the last room at the end of the hallway and look for Bettina, as she had done in all of the others.

Her runaway pulse slowed, her legs stopping their uncontrollable trembling and she moved off the wall, her fingertips tracing the design of the wallpaper. The bugle beads on her evening purse bit into the tender flesh of her right hand as she clutched it in a deathlike grip.

Biting down on her lower lip, she inched along, then found herself standing outside the room. The door was ajar, the opening large enough for her to see a wall of drawn burgundy-colored drapes. Her gaze glazed over, the drapes suddenly resembling a waterfall of rushing blood. She hadn't known why the thought of blood came to mind, but it did not take her long to realize why.

Lying on her back, eyes closed, lips parted in a silent scream, was Bettina Gibson. She looked as if she could have been asleep, except for the blood pooling in her left ear, spilling onto the cream carpeting and staining her pale-colored hair. Within seconds of seeing Bettina, Emily's shock turned to fear. What if the person who'd shot the magazine reporter was hiding in the room? Had he caught a glimpse of her through the narrow opening in the doorway? Even though the odor of cordite lingered in the room, it could not conceal the distinctive fragrance of a popular men's cologne. Her trembling fingers searched for the small audio devices. Shifting, she glanced over her left shoulder, pressing her back to the wall. The hallway was still empty. Slowly, methodically, she withdrew her earpiece and microphone, slipping them into place.

"Jimmy!" she hissed into the microphone. *Oh, please let him be in the van,* she prayed silently.

"What's up, Kirkland?"

She was certain he heard her intense sigh of relief. "Trouble," she whispered. "Big trouble. Someone shot Bettina Gibson."

"Who?"

"Never mind," she snapped angrily.

"Who shot her?"

"I don't know."

"Is she dead?"

"I don't know."

"Get out of there, Kirkland!"

"Jimmy…"

"Get the hell out of there *now!*"

"Call the police. They'll need medical backup."

"Get out of there or I'm coming in after you!"

"I'm coming. And call the station and tell them we're going to do a live hook-up."

"Get out…"

Whatever James O'Brian was going to say was lost when she ripped the earpiece from her ear and the microphone from her bodice and pushed them between her breasts.

She did not remember retracing her steps down the hallway or descending the winding staircase. No one seemed to notice her as she elbowed her way through hundreds of formally attired bodies to the lobby. Searching the depths of her small bag for the ticket for her jacket, she found it and slapped it on the counter of the coat check. If it hadn't been the beginning of February, or if the temperatures weren't just above freezing, she would've walked out without her jacket.

An elderly woman gave her a questioning look. "Leaving so soon, Miss Kirkland?"

"I'm on assignment tonight." She did not intend to explain her early departure.

"That's too bad," the woman mumbled, shaking her head. She turned and disappeared into the coat room to locate the pretty reporter's garment.

Emily felt a surge of adrenaline as she spied her jacket in the woman's arms. She needed to get back to Jimmy and the van. She had to make certain he'd called an ambulance for Bettina. *Please, please don't let anything happen to her.* The plea echoed over and over in her head as she placed a tip on the counter, pushed her bare arms into the sleeves of a matching quilted satin jacket, and raced out of the country club to the parking lot.

Plumes of gray vapor from her parted lips disappeared into the blackness of the night as she quickened her pace. She saw Jimmy standing outside the van, his video camera cradled on one shoulder. Her eyes were unnaturally large as she rushed over to him.

"Did you call for help?"

"They're on their way." As soon as the words were out of his mouth the sound of sirens shattered the stillness of the night.

"Did you call the station?"

"They're ready whenever we are."

James O'Brian waited for Emily to insert her earpiece, then he handed her a microphone. Within seconds he activated his camera, checked the audio and adjusted the light as he viewed the composed features of Emily Kirkland through the lens of the video recorder.

Waiting for Jimmy's signal, Emily stared directly at the camera. "This is KCNS Political Correspondent Emily Kirkland, bringing you a late-breaking event only minutes after it occurred here at the San Rafael Country Club. A young woman has been shot by an unknown assailant. She's lying in a pool of blood on the carpet in a private room on the second floor of this very affluent social establishment. The police have just arrived, along with emergency medical assistance. We don't know the woman's identity, her medical condition or who is responsible for shooting her. What we do know is that she is one of hundreds who came here tonight for a fundraising event for gubernatorial hopeful William Savoy. We will bring you more information as soon as it is available. This is Emily Kirkland, KCNS-12, Metromedia News, reporting live from the Santa Fe San Rafael Country Club."

Jimmy gave her the signal, ending the taping, and she closed her eyes, swaying slightly. He was at her side, one arm going around her waist to steady her.

She had lied to the viewing public. She did know who the

woman was. And whoever had shot her wanted to kill her. You didn't shoot someone in the head to wound or frighten them.

Jimmy tightened his grip. "Are you all right?"

Leaning against his shoulder, she nodded. The stubble on his chin scratched the tender skin on her forehead and she pulled back. "I'm okay now. I have to go back in."

The cameraman shook his head, a long graying ponytail sweeping over the worn wool fabric of his vintage pea coat. "Don't you think you've seen enough?"

"I'm a witness, Jimmy. Not an eyewitness, but I have to tell the police what I know."

He placed his fingers over his right ear, listening intently. "They want us back at the station. Governor Savoy just called Richard."

"I can't. Tell Richard I'll be in after I talk to the police."

Jimmy mumbled an expletive under his breath as she handed him the microphone. He watched the gentle sway of the hem of her gown as she made her way back to the entrance of the country club. Blue and white lights lit up the night as the wail of sirens screamed incessantly.

It was going to be a long night for veteran cameraman James Francis O'Brian. A very, very long night.

Chapter 23

"Hey, Chris, come over and take a look at this."

Chris didn't move as he studied the large map of New Mexico spread out on the conference table. Grant Carsons and one of the strategists stood in front of one of the many television monitors set up in the hotel suite that doubled as his principal campaign headquarters. Most of them were tuned to the major networks, each on mute.

"What's going on?" His voice was void of emotion. He had spent the past four hours with his campaign staff, scheduling his personal appearances for the next nine months. On average, he was expected to visit as many as ten cities each week. The mode of transportation varied: train, bus, private jet and car.

Someone increased the sound on the monitor, and the distinctive contralto voice belonging to Emily Kirkland filled the space. It caught Chris's attention immediately, and he moved away from the conference table to stand with the others in front of the television screen.

"Holy…" Grant swallowed an expletive, turning and staring at Chris. "He's toast."

Chris couldn't pull his gaze away from the image of his wife as she reported that a young woman had been found shot in a private room at the country club where gubernatorial candidate William Savoy was holding a fundraiser. Emily appeared calm, but something in her eyes said differently.

He'd slept with the woman, married her and had come to know her in the most intimate way possible. He had also watched Emily report the news for years, memorizing her body language, her speech patterns and her inflection. Now, she spoke slowly, too slowly. It was as if she had to measure every word to make certain she didn't say the wrong thing.

Removing his glasses, Grant ran a large hand over his face. "Savoy doesn't need anyone to screw up his campaign, he manages to do that all by himself."

"Who says he's to blame for this one?" Chris asked.

"Come on, Chris, don't be so naive," one of the strategists drawled sarcastically.

"Who's being naive?" he countered. "Billy Savoy's morals may be suspect, but I don't believe he'd become embroiled in a scandal that could derail his campaign before it actually begins."

His gaze was glued to the television monitor tuned to KCNS. He leaned closer. There was something in Emily's eyes that registered an uneasiness that usually wasn't there when she delivered the news. It was the same awkwardness that had lingered behind her stoic demeanor when he'd come to see her after she had been stalked by a man who sought to kill her because she hadn't responded to his cyber-marriage proposal.

He had known her all her life, yet not once had she ever shown him a modicum of fear. A slight shiver raced up his spine. How was she able to put on a mask of indifference, successfully concealing her emotions from him and the world? When had she become such an accomplished actress?

Chris stared at her expressionless face as she summed up her report. *She's just like her father.* It wasn't the first time he'd realized that Emily Kirkland-Delgado was exactly like the man who'd challenged him about his association with his daughter. He had no doubt that if his stepfather hadn't come between him and Joshua in the Cole library, the confrontation would have destroyed a friendship that spanned a generation, while also straining his own secret marriage.

He had made a mistake. He thought he knew everything there was to know about his wife—but her impassive expression on the monitor said otherwise. The woman he'd married had become a stranger—a stranger who frightened him.

Her image disappeared, replaced by Calvin Robinson's. He

updated her story, reporting that the woman had been flown to an Albuquerque hospital that specialized in head trauma cases.

"What do you think?" Grant asked close to his ear.

Without taking his gaze off the television screen, Chris shook his head slowly. "I don't know. It looks ugly—very, very ugly."

Grant leaned closer. "I'm going to have my contact follow up on this. And don't worry," he added when his candidate turned to stare at him, "it'll be discreet." He knew Chris was adamant about running a campaign free of slander, libel or scandal. Reaching for the small cellular phone in his shirt pocket, he dialed a series of numbers. Turning his back, he spoke softly into the mouthpiece. "Max, see what you can come up with on the girl." Pressing a button, he terminated a call that had lasted less than fifteen seconds. Placing a hand on Chris's shoulder, he whispered, "You're much too ethical for politics, my friend."

Giving his campaign manager a long, penetrating look, Chris forced a smile. "I don't want to know anything about this."

He didn't want to be privy to whatever Grant's informant came up with on the woman and Savoy—if, indeed, there was a connection between them. What he had to do was finalize his campaign schedule, then go to Emily. He had promised her that they would not have any personal contact with each other until after the election; however, this time he would have to break his promise.

Even though he had taken Salem Lassiter's advice and contracted with a private agency to protect her, as her husband, it was his responsibility to protect her emotional well-being.

Emily lay on the floor in her living room, her head resting on a mound of pillows, staring at the flickering flames in the fireplace. The subdued light complemented candles resting on several tables in the living and dining rooms. She'd pushed the thermostat up to eighty degrees, lit a fire, bundled herself in sweats and thick cotton socks, and yet she was still cold. It had taken hours for the shock of seeing Bettina lying in her own blood, her lips parted in a silent scream, to finally affect her.

She and Jimmy had returned to the station after the police had taken her statement and she had been met with another shock. Governor Bruce Savoy was livid that the KCNS correspondent had reported the shooting without clearance from his son's press secretary. Minutes after the governor's call, a fax had been forwarded to the station stating that Emily Kirkland had been removed from the press corps list for William Savoy's campaign.

The wording of the fax was veiled, but it was obvious that Bruce Savoy believed that Emily Kirkland had deliberately sought to sabotage his son's bid to become governor because of her personal association with his political rival.

Richard had suggested she take a couple of days off to give him time to reassign her, then congratulated her for being the first to report the shocking news. Not once had he shown any concern for Bettina Gibson's condition, or the fact that her own career was now in jeopardy. He was only concerned with ratings, while she knew she had made a powerful enemy in Governor Savoy.

The popping sound of burning wood, followed by a shower of falling embers behind the decorative screen of the fireplace shattered the silence in the enormous space. The clock on the mantelpiece chimed the hour. It was one o'clock. Closing her eyes, Emily bit down hard on her lower lip and prayed that Bettina would make it through surgery successfully.

The buzz of the intercom jolted her, and she sat up. The guard in the gatehouse was ringing her. Pushing to her feet, she walked over to a wall phone and picked up the receiver.

"Yes?"

"It's Senator Delgado, Miss Kirkland."

"Let him in, Jack."

She hung up the phone, pressing her back to the wall. What was she going to say to the guard—*Don't allow my husband access, because I don't want to compromise my position at the television station by interacting with William Savoy's political rival?* Well, she didn't have to worry about compromising herself; she was off the Savoy campaign.

She unlocked the front door, opened it and waited for Chris to pull into her driveway. A sweep of headlights came into view, then the outline of his Saab. A minute later she found herself in his arms as they moved from the foyer into the living room. She could feel his heart thudding against her own. His nearness was so overwhelmingly protective that she was able to temporarily forget the sound of angry voices, the explosion of a gunshot and Bettina's scream of terror.

Pulling back, Chris cradled her face between his hands, trying to see her expression in the wavering light. He inhaled the moistness of her breath when he lowered his head and drank deeply from her sweet mouth.

"Why didn't you call me?" he asked as he placed soft, nibbling kisses at the corners of her mouth.

Emily returned his kiss, her fingernails digging into the soft fibers of his sweater. "Hold me," she whispered, her voice breaking with emotion. "Just hold me."

One hand made soothing motions up and down the length of her straight spine. "It's all right, baby. Everything's going to be all right."

Pressing closer, she buried her face against the side of his neck. "It was terrible, Chris. I saw her lying there, her hair stained with blood. It—"

"You saw her?"

Emily uttered a small cry of protest when Chris eased her back. The look on his face frightened her. "Yes."

He tightened his grip on her upper arms. "You witnessed the shooting?"

Closing her eyes briefly, she shook her head. "No. But I heard someone arguing with her moments before she was shot."

His eyes blazed like burning coals as fear and anger formed a knot in his chest. "What were you doing there?"

"I'd followed Bettina."

His fingers were like manacles around her arm as he pulled her over to the love seat. He sat, pulling her down with him. "Tell me about it, Emily. And you'd better not leave anything out."

She closed her eyes. She couldn't fight with him now. The police interrogation and her meeting with Richard Adams had drained her. "Please don't bark at me, Christopher."

"I'm not barking at you," he retorted, his voice softening slightly. "I just need to know how involved you are."

"I am *not* involved." Slowly, methodically, she related everything she had seen and heard from the moment she walked into the country club.

"Did you see Billy Savoy go upstairs?"

She shook her head. "No." Vertical lines appeared between her eyes. "You don't think William Savoy tried to kill Bettina?"

Threading his fingers through her slender ones, Chris leaned closer and pressed his mouth to the side of her neck. "It doesn't matter what I think, baby."

Emily pulled her hand from his grip. "What matters is that some creep put a bullet in the head of a woman I went to graduate school with, a woman who shared field assignments with me, a woman who, if she survives, may live out her days in a vegetative state. Somebody's going to pay for doing this to her, and I'm not going to stop until I uncover who did it."

Chris's body stiffened in shock. "Let the police do their job."

"The police can conduct their own investigation. I'll conduct mine."

"Why?" The single word exploded from his mouth. "Have you forgotten that you're a political analyst, not an investigative reporter?"

"Right now I'm neither," she shot back. "I'm barred from covering the Savoy campaign because Governor Savoy complained to my boss about me not clearing my report with his son's press secretary. He had the nerve to label an attempted murder as an *incident*. Why, Chris? Because they wanted time to concoct a cover-up to protect their candidate from negative publicity? Meanwhile, I've been ordered to stay home and wait for my next assignment."

She didn't mention the accusing tone of Bruce Savoy's fax, or his suggestion that she had leaked the story to besmirch his son's reputation. He knew that even though she'd been assigned to cover William Savoy's campaign, her loyalties were with his opponent.

Reaching up, Chris cradled her head. Her silken curls wound

their way around his fingers. He lowered his head and stared down at her, his gaze calm. "Let it go, Emily. Let the law enforcement officials do their job."

"But what if there's a cover-up?"

"Let it go, baby," he crooned softly.

"What you're asking of me is impossible."

"Why, Emily?"

"You know why," she shot back.

"No, I don't know why."

She swallowed back her rising anger. He didn't want to understand; he refused to understand her. And she knew Chris was close to losing his temper; a vein throbbed in his temple.

"I stand to lose my job because I reported the truth."

"Your job!" The two words were thrown at her like large stones smashing into her face. "Is that all that matters? Your damn career. What about you? What if whoever shot Bettina saw you? What if he decides to come after you because he thinks you've seen too much? What about me? Us? I didn't marry you to become a widower."

Sitting up straighter, she shifted her eyebrows. "I care about us."

His lips twisted in a sardonic sneer. "You have a perverse way of showing it."

His mocking tone snapped the last thread of her self-control. "What the hell do you want from me, Chris?"

"I want you to be my wife." His tone had softened, becoming almost pleading.

"I am your wife."

His mood shifted abruptly. "No, you're not! You're too busy being Emily Kirkland, political analyst for KCNS-TV News."

"And what are you, Mr. Politician?"

"I am Christopher Blackwell Delgado, madam. Or, as our marriage certificate reads, Cristobal Blackwell Delgada-Quintero."

Snorting delicately, she shook her head. "Don't you mean Christopher Blackwell Delgado, wannabe governor?"

"No, wife. I'm your husband. I've wedded and bedded you, but I'm beginning to feel like your whore, Emily."

She went completely still, her eyes paling until only the dark pupils were visible. "How dare you say—"

"I dare anything," he snarled, interrupting her. "Don't," he warned softly when her hand came up quickly.

She ignored his warning, her arm arcing toward his face. He caught her wrist in midair, pulling her to his chest. Her heaving breasts were molded to his as she lay half on and half off his body. The very air around them shimmered with repressed rage, frustration and lust.

His hot breath seared her face. "All I want," Chris whispered between clenched teeth, "is to go to bed with you at night and wake up with you beside me in the morning. I want to be able to share breakfast and dinner with you. I don't want to have to watch you get dressed, then close the door behind you when you leave me, not knowing when I'll get to see you again. I think I've been reasonable, reasonable and very patient. But I rue the day we agreed to this sham of a marriage."

A thick lump rose in Emily's throat, not permitting her to swallow without difficulty. He was sorry, sorry he'd married her. He claimed he loved her, yet he regretted marrying her.

"If you want, we can annul the marriage." A spasm of pain gripped her as soon as the words were said, and she didn't recognize her own voice.

His frown deepened. "I'm not talking about an annulment, Emily."

A flicker of hope flared. "What are you talking about?"

"The secrecy. The pretense. The sneaking around and having to hide my feelings for you. If my father hadn't intervened after the memorial service for your grandfather, I doubt whether we'd be sitting here having this conversation, because I would've punched out my own father-in-law."

"What are you talking about?" she asked for the second time in less than a minute.

"Your father confronted me about us." Her eyes widened,

an expression of complete surprise freezing her features. "He wanted to know what I was doing with you."

"Daddy?"

"Yes, Daddy," he drawled sarcastically.

"What did you tell him?"

"Nothing."

"Why?"

"Did you want me to tell him that I'd taken his daughter's virginity? That I had married her in Mexico? And that we'd sworn an oath not to tell anyone that we're husband and wife because to do so at this time would jeopardize our *careers?*"

She wanted to tell Chris that she, too, was tired of hiding her feelings. That she wanted to tell the world that the man she had fallen in love with the year she turned twelve was now her husband. That she, too, yearned to go home at the end of the day and be with him. They'd shared only one night of unbridled ecstasy since their wedding night, the night they stayed in Juárez. She felt Chris's frustration as surely as if it were her own.

Resting her forehead on his shoulder, she whispered, "What do you want from me?"

His arms curved around her midriff, holding her close. "One week, baby girl. Am I asking too much from you when I ask for one week?"

She knew she didn't have a week. "I'm waiting to be reassigned. I may not have a week."

"Then ask Richard for a week off. Plead occupational trauma."

"You want me to lie?"

"You're falling apart, Emily. When I walked through the door, you were trembling so hard that if I hadn't held you, you would've collapsed."

"What if he won't give me the time off?" She shook her head. "You're asking me to sacrifice all I've worked for since graduating from college. What are you prepared to sacrifice in return?"

Easing her back, his dark eyes moved slowly over her flushed face, the fire radiating from them searing her delicate skin. "I'd give up anything you'd ask of me. I love you just that much."

She blinked slowly, digesting his statement. "You'd give up this election? The chance to become governor of New Mexico?"

He stared at her, unblinking. "Yes, Emelia. Just say it and I'll call Grant and tell him that I'm dropping out."

Shaking her head, she went limp against him. "No," she moaned. "You can't."

"Why not?"

"Because you're so close," she whispered into the soft texture of his sweater. "You've wanted this all your life."

"I've wanted *you* all my life."

Closing her eyes, she felt hot tears well up behind her lids. A wave of helplessness overwhelmed her. She had married a man she'd loved for more than half her life, yet she was willing to sacrifice that marriage for her floundering career.

"Okay, Chris."

"Okay?" He tightened his grip on her waist.

"A weekend," she conceded. "I can give you a weekend."

Chris wanted to shake her senseless. Shake her until she pleaded with him to stop. She was the most stubborn, single-minded, determined woman he'd ever met, but he loved her. Loved her enough to agree to anything just to be close to her.

He dropped a light kiss on her parted lips, inhaling her moist breath. "Why do I have to be a beggar with you?"

Emily gave him a sensual smile. "Because you love me."

"That I do."

She sobered, her smile slipping away. It was replaced with an expression of determination. "I'll make it up to you, Chris. I promise."

He placed his fingertips over her mouth. "Don't promise, baby. Just show me."

She pulled his hand down. "I don't know if I'm going to be available this weekend. I have to wait for my reassignment."

"It can't be this weekend. I'm meeting with major supporters in Gallup and Farmington."

"So, it's begun."

"Yes." He sighed. Lowering his head, his lips touched hers with a tantalizing persuasion that fired her blood and left her wanting more—much more. But it ended as he raised his head. "I have to go. Keep your cell phone and laptop charged so we can communicate with each other."

"I'll try to find out my schedule for the next two weeks."

He nodded. "Once we settle on a weekend, I'll have someone contact you."

"Where are we going?"

Leaning forward, he dropped a kiss on the end of her nose. "Just bring yourself and warm clothes."

"Chris," she wailed, "I'm not skiing."

"I doubt if we'll find time to ski, Mrs. Delgado, because we'll probably be too exhausted to get out of bed."

Emily couldn't stop the heat from stealing into her face when she remembered the last time they'd shared a bed. Her husband's sexual appetite had been insatiable.

He rose from the love seat, then extended his hand to her. She caught his fingers, and he pulled her to her feet in one strong motion. "I have to go. I have a breakfast meeting with Grant and Reanna."

She felt a rush of jealousy at the mention of the publicist's name. "Is she beautiful?"

"Who?"

"Reanna."

Chris grimaced. "She's hideous."

Emily landed a soft punch to his chest. "Liar."

"If you know what she looks like, then why did you ask me?"

"I just wanted to know what you'd say."

Moving closer, he cradled her face between his hands. "You don't ever have to concern yourself with me and another woman, Emelia. I'll never be unfaithful to you."

"Or I you."

His eyes tilted upward in a beguiling smile. "I know that, baby. Maybe it worked out for the best that you won't be covering Savoy's campaign, because if he ever came after you, I would kill the man."

"Please, Chris. I don't want to hear you talk about killing someone. You forget that someone tried to kill me."

He touched the minute scar along her hairline, then kissed it. If it had been a bullet instead of a piece of glass that had become embedded in her head, he never would have claimed Emily Teresa Kirkland as his wife.

"I'm sorry." He gave her a hard kiss. "I'll be in touch." He kissed her again. "Love you."

Emily clung to him, inhaling his scent, feeding on his strength. He released her and she turned her back. It wasn't until she heard the soft click of the door closing that she turned around. Tears filled her eyes and stained her face.

She loved Christopher Delgado, but he loved her more. He loved her enough to sacrifice becoming governor for her, while she wasn't willing to give up wanting to become lead anchor for a television news station for him.

When had she become so selfish? So stubborn? So very ambitious?

Now she knew what Sara Lassiter meant. Sara had married a man she loved, had given birth to a beautiful son, yet she wanted more—a career outside of her home.

What Emily had to ask herself was what would happen if Chris did become governor. Would she be content to assume the role of first lady of the state, or would she forfeit that title to continue as a television journalist?

Without warning, all of the events of the day came crashing down on her, and for the first time in her life she wanted to escape—escape to a place where no one knew her. A place where she and Chris could forget everything in their lives except each other.

But she couldn't leave Santa Fe—not yet. She had to wait to see if Bettina would recover from her injury. She would call Bettina's parents, then plan for her weekend with her husband.

Chapter 24

February 5

Emily was never given the opportunity to contact the Gibsons about their daughter's condition; Bettina had succumbed to the gunshot wound eight hours after a team of neurosurgeons attempted to remove bone fragments from her brain. The single bullet had splintered bone and tissue, lodging itself in the left side of her brain. Even if she had survived, the woman would have been severely brain damaged.

Emily spent the morning in front of the television, flipping from one station to another. Every network covered the same story, while each correspondent added his or her own dramatic touch. None of them mentioned her name, but she was reminded that she was the only witness when her telephone rang. She answered it, listening to the authoritative voice of the detective who was assigned to gather evidence on the murder of Bettina Gibson. She agreed to meet with him in her home at three o'clock that afternoon.

Homicide Detective Vincent McGrady's dark blue gaze hadn't strayed from Emily Kirkland's face more than twice in the three quarters of an hour he'd sat on the love seat in her living room. She wasn't wearing any makeup—not even lipstick—but he was still awed by her incredible natural beauty. He watched her as she studied a stack of photographs she'd balanced on her knees.

"The medical examiner found traces of gunpowder on Ms. Gibson's right hand."

Emily pulled her gaze away from the image of Bettina sprawled on the rug. "Don't tell me you're ruling this a suicide!"

"Not yet."

"What do you mean, not yet?"

"We don't have a suspect, Miss Kirkland."

"Bettina wasn't alone in that room. There was a man with her. I heard his voice."

"You heard his voice, yet you didn't see him?"

She took a deep breath. "If I'd walked into that room, then I can assure you that I wouldn't be sitting here talking to you." Her gaze shifted to the photographs. "The medical examiner found gunpowder on her right hand?"

"Yes. Why?"

"Bettina is right-handed. What did she do, reach across her chest and shoot herself in the left temple?"

"It could've been an accident," the detective said, deciding to play the devil's advocate.

Emily gathered the photographs, handing them to the police officer, who slipped them into a large manila envelope. "How close were you and Ms. Gibson?" he continued.

"Not close at all. We met in graduate school. Tina and I shared several classes and interned together, but after graduating we lost contact. We ran into each other a couple of times during the past few years, shared lunch or dinner, but that was it. She had her career and I had mine."

"How about the men in her life?"

Arching a brow, Emily gave him a narrowed stare. "Shouldn't you be asking her parents about who she was seeing?"

"I did."

"And?"

"They said they didn't know."

She shook her head. "I'm afraid I can't help you either."

"Did she appear upset? On edge when you saw her?"

"She wasn't herself."

"What do you mean?"

"She seemed uneasy. She was talking a mile a minute, and that wasn't like her. Tina told me that she'd stuttered as a child, and after many years of speech therapy she'd forced herself to speak slowly. If she was rambling, then I suppose you could say she could've been upset by something or someone."

"Upset enough to take her own life?"

"You're finished here, Detective McGrady." She rose gracefully to her feet. "Someone murdered Bettina Gibson, but you want to rule it a suicide. Who got to you, Detective?"

Vince McGrady stood up, his jaw hardening. "What are you accusing me of?"

"Nothing at all," she spat out. "A word of warning," she continued when he turned and headed for the door. She was several steps behind him. "Don't risk your pension by becoming involved in a cover-up. You'll only come up a loser in this one."

Halting, he reached into a pocket of his jacket. Turning, he extended a small white business card. "If you remember anything else, call me at the number on the card." She took the card, staring at the number. It was missing the familiar logo of the Santa Fe Police Department. "It's the number to my cell phone."

Emily nodded. She wasn't disappointed when he returned her smile. The gesture transformed his rugged features, making him a very attractive man.

"Thank you, Detective McGrady."

"Vince."

"Vince," she conceded.

"You're wrong about me, Miss Kirkland. Like you, I don't believe she killed herself."

"Thank you." The two words were barely a whisper.

Walking to the door, she opened it, waited for Vincent McGrady to leave, then closed it quietly behind his departing figure. Shaking her head, she returned to the living room and sat down. The images of the crime scene were vividly imprinted in her mind. The police wanted to rule Bettina Gibson's death a suicide. Well, they were wrong; the woman had come to the Savoy fundraiser to meet someone, and that someone had killed her.

She decided to wait until after the funeral before approaching the older Gibsons. Perhaps they would have the answers she needed to assist the police in apprehending their daughter's murderer.

Tension gnawed at Chris's confidence during the flight from Albuquerque to the Juan N. Alvarez International Airport, and when the jet landed in Mexico he doubted whether his quaking knees would support his body. His overwhelming confidence had been the result of an enthusiastic meeting with his Gallup and Farmington supporters. Both headquarters were ready to begin a vigorous campaign effort on February 18—the day following his fundraiser celebration.

However, moments after he'd returned to Santa Fe and walked into his apartment, the telephone rang. The feminine voice speaking Spanish on the other end of the wire had shattered his euphoria. His aunt tearfully informed him that Alejandro was declining rapidly, and that his doctor had had him transferred to a hospital, where he was resting comfortably after having been sedated.

He hadn't hesitated, telling Sonia he would be there as soon as he secured a reservation. He called Emily and left a message on her cell phone voice mail that he was leaving the States for Mexico. His next call had been to Grant Carsons, who expressed his sympathy and promised to keep the other three people who made up the inner circle of the campaign committee abreast of their candidate's personal crisis.

He slipped into a taxi outside the airport terminal, instructing the driver to take him to the hospital his aunt had mentioned. Twenty minutes later, the cab pulled up in front of the hospital, and the driver removed his passenger's garment and carry-on bags. Chris paid him, adding a generous tip and rushed into the small hospital. After securing a visitor's pass from a clerk who provided patient information, Chris took the stairs to the third floor instead of waiting for an elevator.

He hadn't realized how fast his heart was beating until he stood outside Alejandro Delgado's room, peering at his father's gaunt body and colorless face, blending with the pristine linen. Clear, measured drops of liquid dripped through a tube and into the needle inserted into a vein on the back of his right hand. Even from that distance, Chris could see the dark bruises from the intravenous feedings. The distinctive sound of a machine monitoring vitals shattered the silence in the room.

Taking several steps, he moved into the room just as an elderly nurse, sitting on a chair in a corner, rose to her feet. She seemed startled to see him but recovered quickly.

"He's resting, señor."

Chris nodded. "How long has he been asleep?"

"His doctor prescribed a morphine drip earlier this morning to ease his pain." She glanced at her watch. "The attending doctor will return in another hour."

Placing his luggage in a corner near the door, Chris walked over to the side of the bed. "I'll wait for him."

The older woman offered a polite smile. "There's a waiting room at the end of the hall."

"I'll wait here," Chris insisted, stressing the last word.

This time the nurse nodded. Turning, she walked back to the chair she'd vacated, sat down and picked up a magazine. She knew the young man was the patient's son. Alejandro Delgado's sister had informed her that he was expected to arrive from the States sometime that day. Well, he had come, and there was no doubt that he was a Delgado. Not only did he look like his father, but he sounded like him. When they had brought the patient in, he had demanded to be taken back home, where he could die with dignity. However, his protests were ignored, and it wasn't until the needle was inserted into his hand, filled with a solution of life-sustaining nutrients and a powerful painkiller, that his objections were overridden. Within minutes he had succumbed to the narcotic that permitted him to sleep peacefully.

Running his fingers over the paper-thin flesh on his father's cheek, Chris leaned closer. "I'm here, Dad." He pressed his lips to Alejandro's cool forehead. "Everything's going to be all right."

He took a chair next to the bed, knowing he'd lied to the sleeping man. Everything wasn't going to be all right. Alejandro Delgado-Quintero was dying. When he had leaned over the inert body, Chris had heard the death rattle in his father's chest. And like his mother had more than thirty years before, when she waited for the return of her son, he waited for his father to draw his last breath.

Closing his eyes, Chris tried to recall his wife's face. His wife. A secret smile curved his firm mouth when the image of her face seeped into his mind. He still found it hard to believe that he and

Emily Kirkland were married. Legally they were husband and wife, yet despite the fact that he'd slept with her, nothing much had changed between them. And, unlike most newlyweds, they were living separate lives.

He hadn't lied to Emily when he said he would walk away from the campaign to save his marriage. When he'd walked into his sister's house after returning from Mexico and saw her cradling his nephew to her breasts, the scene jolted him like an electric shock. In that instant it wasn't Isaiah Lassiter in her arms but their son. A son he hadn't realized he wanted until after he'd exchanged his wedding vows. He wanted to be governor of the state, but not as much as he wanted to be a husband and a father.

Moving the chair closer to the bed, he reached out and laid his right hand over Alejandro's left. Closing his eyes, he willed his mind blank. He was still in that position when his father surfaced from his drug-induced sleep to find his son sitting at his bedside, holding his hand in a protective grip.

Alejandro tried to focus on his son's profile, but the tears in his eyes would not permit him to see clearly. He pulled his hand away, and Chris woke up.

Black eyes surveyed him critically. "Dad? Are you in pain?"

Shaking his head slowly, Alejandro moaned as a spasm of pain gripped him in a tight fist, refusing to release him. "No," he lied. He didn't recognize his own voice. His throat hurt, as if he'd been yelling for hours.

Chris glanced up at the bag. It was nearly empty. He looked for the nurse, but she had left the room. "I'm going to call for a doctor to change your IV."

Alejandro clawed at his hand. "No, Chris. Don't. Not yet."

"Why not?"

His eyelids fluttered wildly when he tried to compose his thoughts. He couldn't think clearly because his body was being poisoned by the narcotics flowing into his veins.

"I want to talk to you. Just this last time before I die."

A frown creased Chris's forehead. "You're not going to die."

A knowing smile curved Alejandro's mouth. "You should be ashamed of yourself, lying to a dying man. And your father at that."

"When did you become a comedian?"

Alejandro sobered quickly, inhaling sharply as the knot of pain held him in a savage grip, held him hostage. He had to talk—and talk fast. Closing his eyes, he prayed for strength.

"I want you to tell your mother that I'm sorry for everything. Tell her that I still love her. She is the only woman I've ever loved." His narrow chest rose and fell heavily with each labored breath. "Is she still beautiful?"

Chris managed a trembling smile. "Yes, she is."

The confirmation elicited a smile from Alejandro. "I knew she would be. I always wanted to grow old with her, but it was not to be. She told me that I was a better boyfriend than a husband, because once we married I couldn't remain faithful to her.

"I didn't sleep with the other women because I wanted to. I did it because I was afraid of loving Eve too much." He opened his eyes, his gaze wavering. "Loving your mother frightened me. It was as if I couldn't control myself with her, so I took other women. With them I was always in control.

"Then she left me. She left me and took my son with her. The judge in the American court told me that I could only see you on certain days." His mouth twisted into a sneer. "The supercilious buffoon told me, Alejandro Delgado-Quintero, that I had to have you back at your mother's house at a certain time or she could call the police and have me arrested for kidnapping.

"I hated the American justice so much that I decided to challenge it. That's when I took you. It was so easy that I couldn't stop laughing. Then the laughter stopped when you began crying for your mother. Nothing I could do or say could stop you when you cried yourself to sleep night after night.

"I've spent many years atoning for my sins, though I know I can't erase your pain, or your mother's." He took a deep breath, then let it out in a ragged sigh. The death rattle echoed above the beeping sounds coming from the ventilator.

Chris patted his hand. "I'm going to get the doctor."

"No, not yet. I don't have a lot of time, but I want you to promise me one thing."

"What is it?"

"When you have a son, name him after me."

"Dad."

Turning his head slowly, Alejandro glared at his son. "Promise me, Christopher."

He wanted to scream at his father that he was a master manipulator. That even on his deathbed he wanted to control other people's lives.

"What if I have daughters?"

"You will have a son," Alejandro stated defiantly. "The Delgado-Quinteros will not end with you. Promise me, then go get the doctor and tell him to fill my veins with his poison."

Chris stared at him, wanting to hate him, yet he couldn't. No matter what he'd done, he couldn't hate him. "I promise."

A satisfied smile parted the older man's lips. "Good. Now, kiss me before you go and get the doctor."

Rising to his feet, Chris sat on the side of the bed. He laid his hand alongside his father's face. Leaning close, he pressed his lips to the dry cheek. "I love you, Daddy." Without warning, his eyes filled with tears, falling and splattering over Alejandro's face.

"Gracias, mi hijo. Te amo," he whispered. Tears leaked from under his closed lids, mingling with those of his son. "Go!" he gasped in English.

Chris rose from the bed, reaching for a handkerchief. He managed to wipe away the moisture staining his face before he walked out of the room. His aunt was coming down the hall, flanked by a doctor and the same nurse who had sat by Alejandro's bedside.

Sonia's expression brightened when she spied her nephew's tall figure. He met her, cradling her gently in his embrace while the doctor and nurse saw to their patient's needs.

"Thank you for coming, Cristobal. I prayed you'd get here before he left us to sleep with the angels."

Tightening his grip on her waist, he led her back into the room. They stood motionless, their gazes fixed on the flat line on the monitor. Alejandro was gone.

Chapter 25

Santa Fe

It was another four days before Emily heard her husband's voice again. It was the second message he'd left on her cell phone voice mail, and this one was profound and pregnant with emotion: *Alejandro's gone. I'll be in Las Cruces if you need me.*

Unlike the first one, when he'd notified her that he was going to Mexico, there was no declaration of love or that he missed her, and something whispered to her that she was losing her husband. Their marriage had not even begun, yet they were apart more than they were together.

She was no longer officially assigned to cover Savoy's campaign, so it wouldn't matter if she and Chris went public with their marriage. Shaking her head, Emily quickly dismissed the notion. They couldn't—not until the police apprehended Bettina's murderer.

Law enforcement efforts were hampered because, after a private memorial service, the Gibsons cremated their only child, then listed their home with a Realtor. Bettina Gibson had been dead exactly eight days when her parents left Santa Fe without leaving a forwarding address or telephone number. Detective Vincent McGrady had called her to see whether she knew of their whereabouts, and she'd informed him that the Gibsons had refused to take her calls, or to see her when she visited their home.

Richard Adams called her back to the station, reassigning her to edit copy and supervise a journalism student intern. She hadn't argued with Richard because she only saw the intern twice a week, allowing her time to help the homicide detective with his unsolved case.

The telephone on her desk rang twice, indicating that the call came from an outside call. Leaning over, she picked up the receiver before it rang again. "Emily Kirkland."

"Miss Kirkland, I'm going to make this quick. Don't interrupt me or I'll hang up. I think I know who killed Bettina Gibson."

"Who are you?" she asked the woman.

"Goodbye, Miss Kirkland."

"No…please. I won't interrupt again."

"I'll contact you again."

"Don't call me here." Emily lowered her voice. "Take down my cell phone number."

"Give it to me."

She whispered the number into the receiver, repeating it. Then she heard a dial tone. The woman had hung up.

Her hand was steady when she replaced the telephone on its cradle, though her stomach muscles had contracted tightly. Closing her eyes, she tried to steady her erratic pulse.

I think I know who killed Bettina Gibson. The woman had said that she *thought*—not that she knew for certain. The call had provided her with a lead—a slight lead. One that was worth following up.

Las Cruces

Chris dropped his mother's hand, draping an arm over her shoulders and pulling her closer to his side. Lowering his head, he pressed a kiss to her silver hair.

"I've spent the past three days in Mexico," he began softly.

Her head came up slowly, eyes so much like his own widening in shock. "What were you doing there?"

He hesitated, his gaze sweeping around the room. It lingered first on his stepfather, then sister, then returned to his mother. "Burying Alejandro Delgado."

Eve Blackwell-Sterling's soft gasp was audible in the swollen silence. "How long had you been communicating with him?"

Chris stared over his mother's head at Matthew Sterling. There was no mistaking the icy contempt in his gaze.

"A month."

Eve's lashes fluttered wildly. "Why didn't you tell me before?"

"There was no need."

"Why now, son?"

Chris turned his attention to his stepfather. "Because I had questions about my father—questions Mom refused to answer. The rumors about Alejandro Delgado being a Mexican traitor are running rampant through the Savoy camp, and it's only a matter of time before they'll go public with them."

"But Daddy's your father," Sara stated, speaking for the first time since she walked into her parents' family room. She was overly protective of the connection between her father and brother. She never thought of him as her half-brother, or Matt Sterling as his stepfather.

Chris glared at his sister, who seemed to shrink under the withering stare. "That's not what Billy Savoy gleaned from my birth certificate."

Eve pulled her lower lip between her teeth. "You contacted him because of the rumors?"

"That was the only reason."

Reaching for Chris's hand, she threaded her fingers through his. Alejandro Delgado was gone, and so was everything they'd ever shared—everything except the child they'd created.

"You did what you had to do."

"Did you get your answers?" Matt asked.

"Yes." His expression brightened, a smile crinkling his eyes. "Alejandro's death isn't the only reason I wanted to meet with everyone. Mom, Dad, I know the two of you plan to sell Sterling Farms at the end of the year, so I'd like to offer a bid."

Sara sat up straighter, the brilliant lights in her gold-green eyes sparkling. "What are you talking about?"

"I want to buy Sterling Farms."

"Sterling Farms?" the other three chorused in unison.

"Only the ranch house," Chris said quickly, staring at his

sister. "I know you and Salem were talking about starting up a stud farm."

Sara nodded. "Salem and Daddy are just talking."

Leaning forward and resting his elbows on his knees, Matt gave his stepson a direct look. "Why the house? Don't you plan on living in the governor's mansion?"

"Yes, I do," he replied confidently. "But I need a permanent residence once my term is over."

"What about your loft in Santa Fe?"

"I plan to list it with a Realtor after the election."

"You don't plan to continue your political career?" Sara asked, her gaze locking with his. "I thought your ultimate goal was the State Supreme Court."

"I've changed my mind about a lot of things over the past month." He missed the questioning gazes that passed between his sister and parents. "I'd hate to come back to visit Sara, Salem and my nephew and catch a glimpse of strangers living in the house where I grew up. It just wouldn't be right."

What he did not tell his family was that Alejandro Delgado had bequeathed him and Emily the Delgado-Quintero property in Puerto Escondido. The house and surrounding land had belonged to the Delgados for more than 400 years, and the terms of Alejandro's will made certain the tradition would continue for centuries to come. Chris did not want to claim the lands of a man who was his father only because they'd shared a bloodline, while denying the legacy of the man who had become his father in every way possible.

Matt looked at his wife, and she nodded. "That settles it. The house is yours."

Rising to his feet, Chris extended a hand to Matt, who also stood up. The two men exchanged a rough hug, then pounded each other's back.

Sara rose gracefully from the love seat. "When are you going back to Santa Fe, bro?"

"Tomorrow morning. Why?"

"Why don't you spend the night with us, then leave with

Salem in the morning? He's flying up. Besides, Isaiah would love to see his uncle again."

Chris smiled at his sister. "You've got yourself a deal."

He kissed his mother tenderly, promising to call her in a few days, hugged his stepfather, went into his bedroom to retrieve his luggage, then followed Sara out to her car.

Sara drove slowly away from Sterling Farms, her gaze fixed on the dark road. It was a moonless night, and the car's headlights provided the only illumination.

"What was that all about back there?"

Shrugging a broad shoulder, Chris stared straight ahead.

"It's exactly what you heard. I want to buy the house."

"Why?"

"Because I want to grow old here. Is there something wrong with that?"

"No. It's just that I've never heard you say anything about moving back to Las Cruces, that's all."

What he wanted to tell his sister was that after attending two funerals in less than a month, he was reminded of his own mortality, and the realization was sobering. That he wanted more from life than the ambition that drove him to consider a career in politics.

"What's the matter, sis, you don't want me as your neighbor because you're afraid that I'll see you and Salem when you guys run around naked outside at night?"

Sara's mouth gaped for several seconds. "We do nothing of the sort!"

"That's not what my brother-in-law told me."

Heat flared in Sara Lassiter's nut-brown face. "Both of you are full of it."

Curving the fingers of his left hand around his sister's neck, he caressed the hair on her nape. "And I love you."

Giving him a quick glance before she returned her attention to the road in front of them, Sara smiled. "Love you back, bro. What's happening with you and Emmie?"

"We see each other occasionally."

"Only occasionally?"

"Not enough," he admitted.

"You still love her?"

"More than I thought I could ever love a woman."

"Will she ever become more than godmother to my children?"

"What more do you want?"

"Try sister-in-law and neighbor."

Warm sparkling lights from the Lassiters' expansive two-story house lit up the desert. Less than a minute later, Sara maneuvered into the driveway that led to the three-car garage.

Chris turned his head, concealing a secret smile. "Have patience, little sister."

Sara wrinkled her delicate nose. "I'm trying, Chris." She pressed a button on the visor of the car and the garage door slid up smoothly. Pulling into a space beside her husband's truck, she put her car in park and turned off the engine. She touched her brother's arm, stopping him as he attempted to alight from the car. "I want to apologize."

Turning, he stared at her over his shoulder. "For what?"

"I didn't mean to sound so unsympathetic at Mom and Dad's."

"What are you talking about, Sara?"

"Alejandro Delgado. Your father. I'm sorry."

Leaning over, he pressed his mouth to her forehead. "Thank you, baby sister."

Two minutes later they walked into the kitchen arm in arm and found Salem Lassiter cradling his sleeping son in his arms. A smile softened the brilliant veterinary surgeon's stoic expression. Overhead lights glinted off the ebony and silver strands falling around his broad shoulders.

"Hey, Chris. How long are you going to hang out with us?"

"Only for the night. If you don't mind, I'd like to fly up to Santa Fe with you in the morning."

"Of course I don't mind. You know you owe me a rematch."

Whenever the two men got together they spent hours over a chessboard.

Chris wagged his head from side to side. "You're going to lose."

"Not tonight," Salem predicted. "Let me put the little prince to bed, then you get ready to weep."

"You wish."

Sara walked over to the counter, a smile curving her lips. She would put up a pot of coffee for the chessboard gladiators before she settled down to review a brief for a small Las Cruces law firm. She'd walked into their office a week before and volunteered her services. One of the partners stared at her, bewildered, until she placed her résumé on his desk. Two days later he called, asking if she would review a brief. It wasn't the courtroom, but that didn't matter. It was the Law.

Chapter 26

Emily maneuvered her Corvette out of the parking lot, waited until traffic slowed, then drove quickly, expertly, along the wide avenue. Each time she recalled the mysterious telephone call her pulse raced. She wanted to discover who'd shot and killed Bettina, and she also wanted to redeem her slightly tarnished professional reputation.

Some of her colleagues hadn't approached her, but rumors were flying about the office that she was guilty of journalistic sabotage when she reported the shooting without first clearing it with Savoy's press secretary. The rumors were compounded by everyone's knowledge that she was a personal friend of Savoy's opponent. No one had openly expressed an iota of sympathy for the murdered reporter or her family, and for the first time since she'd become a journalist, Emily regretted her career choice. She'd been taught that her first priority was reporting the news truthfully and accurately. That was what she'd done, and the result had been an unofficial demotion and ostracism.

Her right foot bore down on the gas pedal, sending the racy car forward in a burst of speed as she moved into parkway traffic. She hadn't gone more than a quarter of a mile when she heard a siren. Glancing up at her rearview mirror, she spied the flashing lights from a car belonging to the highway patrol. Slowing just under the speed limit, she moved over to the right. The car moved over with her.

Cursing softly under her breath, Emily maneuvered to the shoulder, then waited for the officer. He stopped, pushed open his door and strolled over to her. She knew she had been speeding, but not by much. This time she was only ten miles an hour over the limit.

Pressing a button, she lowered the driver's-side window. Her lush mouth parted in a friendly smile. "Yes?"

"License and registration, ma'am."

Sighing heavily, she turned and reached into her purse on the midnight blue leather passenger seat. The firm set of the police officer's sable brown jaw indicated that he meant business. This was one time when she wouldn't be able to flutter her lashes and talk her way out of a speeding ticket.

She handed him the requested documents, then settled back to wait for him to return to his cruiser. The eerie glow of headlights from oncoming traffic reminded her of films depicting a fleet of flying saucers filling the nighttime sky. She hadn't raised the window and a raw dampness in the winter air hinted of snow.

The familiar strains of a musical composition coming from the car's sophisticated sound system caught her attention. It was one of her cousin's Grammy-nominated songs, from Gabriel Cole's soundtrack. The album had been nominated for Album of the Year, Record—Single, New Artist and Male Pop Vocal Performer. Her uncle David, Gabriel's father, had received a nomination for Producer of the Year—nonclassical. Her very talented musician cousin had also garnered an Oscar nomination for Original Dramatic Score for "Reflections in a Mirror."

"Miss, your license and registration?"

Her head came around and she looked at the police officer bending over the low-slung sports car. She took the papers from his hand, stuffed them into her handbag. He had given her a ticket. "Thank you." There was no warmth in her voice.

He angled his head, his dark gaze moving slowly over her composed features. "Drive carefully, Miss Kirkland."

Forcing a supercilious smile, Emily nodded. He returned to his car and she eased out into traffic, watching the speedometer. She didn't exceed the speed limit until she exited the parkway and took the local road that led to her housing development.

Five minutes later, she pulled into the driveway of her house. She retrieved her mail, then opened the front door. Warmth and soft lighting enveloped her as she left her handbag, a stack of bills, magazines and catalogs on a table in the foyer. The top portion of the parking ticket was visible, and she withdrew it to see whether she would be able to pay the fine by mail or would have to appear in traffic court.

Her mouth gaped slightly when she read what the officer had written on a blank sheet of paper: *If you are free this weekend, I'll pick you up on Friday afternoon at five. I'll be waiting in the lobby of your office building to take you to CBD-Q. If you're committed to something else, then beep me to cancel. The number is on the back. Steve.*

She turned the page over and stared at the number. Throwing back her head, she laughed. Chris had said he would contact her about their weekend getaway, but she never thought their go-between would be one of Santa Fe's finest.

Emily was still smiling when she unbuttoned her coat and hung it up in a closet in the foyer. She had only three days before she would be reunited with her husband. Three days she prayed would pass quickly. Walking into the half bath off the living room, she washed her hands, splashed water on her face, then blotted it dry. She stared at her reflection, not recognizing the person she had become. Her face appeared thinner, almost pinched. Since she'd become an earwitness to Bettina's murder she hadn't been able to sleep undisturbed through the night, and not sleeping and eating had taken its toll. It was a good thing she didn't have to appear in front of the camera. The makeup person would be hard-pressed to conceal the obvious exhaustion mirrored by the deep hollows in her cheeks and the dark circles under her light-colored eyes.

The sound of the angry voices and the explosion of the gunshot wound their way into her dreams, shocking her into wakefulness. However, it was the sight of Bettina lying in her own blood that had provoked several nightmares.

She sat up at night, with all the lights on, shaking uncontrollably. It was only when exhaustion claimed her tense body that she was able to sleep—albeit fitfully, though she was grateful for even a few moments of tranquility.

Staring at her bare fingers, Emily was reminded that even though she was married she wore no evidence of her marital status. She'd returned Keith Norris's ring via a bonded courier, while the ring Chris had slipped on to her finger now lay in a safe concealed under a floorboard in her bedroom.

She, like Chris, was tired of hiding and couldn't wait until they were able to reveal to everyone that they'd pledged their futures to each other. Closing her eyes, Emily prayed that moment would come quickly; she didn't know how long she would be able to conceal their private passions.

Emily didn't recognize the police officer when he walked into the lobby of the building that housed the network's offices. He looked taller, much more muscular out of uniform. A short black sheepskin jacket, jeans, boots and a turtleneck sweater failed to conceal a hard, well-conditioned body. His smooth dark skin shone with good health, while his features were even, pleasant. She liked his eyes and mouth. A neatly kept mustache outlined his full lips.

His penetrating dark eyes spied her overnight bag resting next to her booted feet. If he looked different, then Steve Washington thought the same of Emily Kirkland. She was casually dressed in a pair of navy blue wool slacks, a matching pea coat and a turtleneck cashmere sweater. Her hair was brushed off her rounded forehead and over her ears. Large yellow stones sparkled in her pierced lobes, and as he neared her he recognized them as rare multifaceted diamonds.

Leaning over, he pressed his lips to her cheek. "Hello, Emily." He hadn't realized she was that tall. Her head was only several inches below his.

"Hello, Steve," she whispered, a gloved hand going to his shoulder.

He smiled down at her. "Are you ready?"

She nodded. "Yes."

Bending down, he picked up her large calfskin bag, then cradled her hand in his. Anyone who saw them together would think they were a young couple who were planning to spend the weekend together. And that was exactly what Highway Patrolman

Steve Washington wanted them to think as he escorted Emily out of the building to his Jeep, parked two blocks away.

A biting wind stung their exposed faces and he curved an arm around Emily's waist to share his body's heat. She stiffened slightly when the outline of his automatic handgun, clipped to the belt around his waist, pressed into her flesh, but she recovered quickly.

"So, Steve," she said, glancing up at his strong profile, "do you have a last name?"

He smiled. "Washington."

"How do you know Chris?"

"We went to the same high school." It was his turn to look at Emily. He liked her voice and her perfume. It was a heady, spicy scent.

"You grew up in Las Cruces?"

"No, I grew up here in Santa Fe. My family moved to Las Cruces during my last two years of high school. They still live there. I decided I needed a little bit more excitement, so I came back here to attend college. I graduated with a degree in Criminal Justice, then joined the police department."

They arrived at his Jeep, and he helped her in. She waited until he sat down beside her, then teased him about police entrapment. Steve laughed, saying he was certain she would forgive him because everything had been done in the name of love.

She sobered, wondering how much he knew about her and Chris. Did he know they were husband and wife?

Twenty minutes after she and Steve walked out of the office building, Emily found herself belted in as she sat in a twin-engine private plane. He told her he would be waiting to take her back home on Sunday night.

Emily was the only passenger as the pilot taxied down the private airstrip in preparation for liftoff. Closing her eyes, she waited for her stomach to settle as the propeller-driven aircraft rose smoothly off the runway.

It appeared as if they had just taken off when she felt the aircraft descending. Glancing at her watch, she realized the flight had lasted less than half an hour. They touched down, and she peered through the small window, encountering darkness.

She unbuckled her belt, retrieved her single piece of luggage, and followed the pilot as he opened the door and lowered the steps. Standing in the shimmering glow of a pair of headlights was Christopher Delgado.

Quickly closing the distance between them, he pulled her into his embrace, holding her close to his heart for a second before his head came down. His mouth devoured hers with a hunger that left her gasping for her next breath.

"Baby. Oh, baby," he chanted as plumes from his warm breath disappeared into the blackness of the night. "Let's go. We have so little time together before you have to go back."

Waving to the pilot, Chris picked up Emily's bag, then led her to a sport utility vehicle. He had kept the engine running while awaiting the arrival of the plane.

Sitting in the warm vehicle, she asked, "Where are we?"

"We're about fifty miles west of Cowles."

Her eyebrows lifted. They weren't far from a ski resort.

Chris glanced at Emily's profile. Diffused light from the dashboard shimmered on her face. The first thing he'd noticed when he held her was that she'd lost weight. He wondered what had happened to her since their last meeting.

"If it's all right with you, I'm going to stop and get us something to eat."

"Do you have food at the place where we're staying?"

"Yes. Why?"

"I'd rather eat in."

"You're more than aware of my culinary skills, so that means you'll have to do the cooking."

"We can eat out tomorrow," she argued softly. She knew she sounded selfish, but she wanted to spend all their time together alone with each other.

Chris nodded. "Okay."

He concentrated on navigating the dark, narrow, unpaved road. His ears popped with the higher elevation, and as they neared the small log cabin snow began to fall, covering up his footprints and the tracks from the SUV from earlier that afternoon.

He stopped under a carport. "We're here."

Emily registered the deep timbre of his voice, and a warmth spread over her body, settling between her thighs. She held her breath. Emily wanted Chris, wanted him with a hunger that nearly overwhelmed her.

She didn't move as he stepped out of the vehicle and came around to assist her. He opened the passenger-side door, extending his arms. Light from the cabin reflected on the snow as it fell, settling on his hair and jacket.

"Come, baby," he urged softly.

The sound of his voice broke the spell, and she curved her arms around his neck as he lifted her effortlessly. He set her on her feet, then reached in and took her bag from the backseat.

Hand in hand, they walked to the cabin as the silently falling snow blanketed the night with pristine beauty. He unlocked the door and opened it. Table lamps and a smoldering fire in a massive fireplace provided warmth and light for a space that was much larger than it had appeared from the outside. Her gaze moved up to a second-story loft. She walked in, followed by Chris, who closed and locked the door behind them.

"It's perfect," she whispered when she felt him move behind her. Pressing closer, his warm breath swept over the top of an ear.

"You're perfect, Emily Kirkland-Delgado," he whispered. One hand curved around her neck, pushing aside the soft cashmere fabric of her sweater to reveal the silken flesh on her nape. Lowering his chin, he kissed the side of her neck, eliciting a slight shudder and a smothered groan from his wife.

"Chris."

Her whispering his name fired his blood. He wanted her. Wanted her more than he had ever wanted any woman or *anything*.

Curving his arms around her waist over the short jacket, he held her to his heart, burying his face against her sweet, fragrant-smelling short hair. He didn't know when he had first fallen in love with her, but now he was thinking of the distinct changes in her the summer of her eleventh birthday. She had begun growing taller—several inches within months—and her body had begun to blossom.

She and her brother had come to Las Cruces to spend the summer. Chris, Sara, Michael and Emily Kirkland, and Billy Hall, the live-in housekeeper's son, were inseparable. They rode horses, camped out in the desert, and, on several occasions, went hunting with Matthew Sterling.

Late one afternoon, during a violent thunderstorm, he and Emily sat out the storm in the barn. She'd sat on the floor, gathering pieces of hay until she had a fistful. Then, without warning, she'd grasped the collar of his shirt and pushed the hay down his back. He'd reacted quickly, pushing her down and straddling her body, threatening to retaliate if she didn't apologize. She stubbornly refused, and he'd lowered his body over hers until their faces were only inches apart.

A shaft of light from the partially closed door swept over her face, highlighting her eyes when lightning lit the darkened skies, and he was mesmerized. It was as if it was the first time he'd realized their color. They'd become pinpoints of brilliant green against her chestnut-brown face. Neither had moved, both entranced by an awareness that hadn't been there before. He'd felt the faint stirring of sexual arousal and scrambled off her prone body. Not wanting Emily to see him in a state of arousal, he'd walked out of the barn and into the fury of lightning bolts bouncing off the wet earth.

She screamed for him to come back, but he'd ignored her until he was once again in control of himself and his body. It would be another four months before he celebrated his sixteenth birthday, but it had become a summer to remember. A time when the mere sight of the slim, long-legged, curly-haired girl reminded him that he'd been born male. It was also the first time he understood the unrestrained frenzy of the stallions when they encountered a mare in heat. He'd wanted to mate with his childhood friend. A rush of shame and guilt assailed him after he regained control of his runaway passions. Shame that he lusted after a girl whom he had always thought of as a younger sister. Guilt that he wanted to sleep with her when she'd trusted him to protect her.

And now, almost twenty years later, he still lusted after her. But now she was his wife. A wife he couldn't sleep with, touch or talk to whenever he wanted to because of the divergent paths their careers had taken. However, they had been given a weekend—hours wherein they could shut out the outside world to become reacquainted and share their love and passion.

"I love your smell," he crooned close to her ear.

Emily closed her eyes and smiled. "Thank you." Her sultry voice had lowered to a seductive whisper.

He moved closer, molding his chest to her back. "Are you hungry?"

A dreamy expression crossed her face. "Which hunger are you talking about?"

A deep chuckle rumbled in his chest. "Will I find Emily Kirkland-Delgado on the menu tonight?"

Turning in his embrace, she offered him a saucy look. "Yes."

"Entrée or dessert?"

Her lashes came down, hiding the desire she was unable to conceal from him. "Both."

Chris threw back his head, laughing. "Well, if that's the case, then I suggest we go upstairs and dine."

Chapter 27

Emily wasn't certain why, but suddenly she felt shy when she stood in the middle of a large bedroom with a king-sized bed as its focal point. The bed's iron and steel frames, black goose-down comforter and earth-tone throw pillows hinted of a masculine touch. A fire in the fireplace had been reduced to smoldering embers. The odor of fragrant burning wood chips lingered in the air.

Her gaze was fixed on Chris's tousled graying hair as he concentrated on unbuttoning her jacket. "Who owns this cabin?"

His head came up as he gave her a direct stare. She noticed an emerging stubble on his cheeks and cleft chin and wondered if he'd shaved earlier that day.

"It belongs to Steve Washington."

"Mr. Highway Patrol."

Chris pushed her jacket off her shoulders, dropping it on the padded bench at the foot of the bed. "He told me you were very calm after he pulled you over."

She shrugged her shoulders under the cashmere sweater. "It's not the first time I've been stopped."

"How fast were you going this time?"

"Only about ten miles an hour over the limit."

Cradling her face between his hands, he dropped a kiss on her pouting lips. "When are you going to stop speeding?"

"I wasn't speeding."

"What do you call speeding?"

Pursing her lips, she appeared deep in thought, then said, "Ninety."

Chris's nostrils flared as he let out his breath through tightly compressed lips. "Emily, don't."

"You know I'm an expert driver." And she was. Her father had given her tactical training, navigating obstacle courses at high speeds once she'd earned her driver's license.

"That's not the point. Please don't make me worry about you, baby girl."

"Please don't lecture me, Chris," she countered in a quiet tone. "Not tonight." Moving closer, she pressed her full breasts to his chest. "I thought we were going to make love."

Bending slightly, he swung her up in his arms and carried her to the bed. Placing his knee on the side of the bed, he lowered her to the mattress, his body following.

"Stay here while I fill the bathtub. I thought we'd share a bath." He placed a light kiss on the end of her nose before he left the bed and made his way to an adjoining bathroom.

Emily lay in the semidarkness, staring up at the shadows on the ceiling, trying to sort out the turns her life had taken. She'd married the man she had loved for more than half her life, yet she couldn't reveal to the world that gubernatorial candidate Christopher Delgado was her husband. Another man had acted as a go-between in order that she could spend less than seventy-two hours with a man with whom she'd exchanged vows.

I'm living a lie, a silent voice whispered in her head. She hadn't told her parents, brother, relatives or friends that she was now Emily Delgado, wife of Christopher Blackwell Delgado. Hot tears sprang up behind her lids and she squeezed her eyes tightly to stop them from spilling down her cheeks.

Meeting Chris in an out-of-the-way place for a few hours was not what she wanted. It was she who had insisted they keep their relationship secret because of her career. And it was Chris who perpetuated it once he proposed marriage.

She covered her face with her hands, trying vainly to stave off a swell of hopelessness, berating herself for slipping into a morass of despair. All her life she'd prided herself on being in control—of everything. But since she'd become an earwitness to murder, she was more unnerved than she was willing to admit.

Her mother had called her after she'd read an account of Bettina's murder in a Florida newspaper, and she had minimized her involvement in reporting the story. Only William Savoy, his chief advisers, Governor Savoy, KCNS news chief Richard Adams and the Santa Fe Police Department knew she was the last one to see Bettina Gibson alive.

In the past Emily never would have withheld anything from her parents—especially her mother. It was as if Vanessa Blanchard-Kirkland claimed an inherent gift that told her when someone was lying to her.

She had remained in West Palm Beach for a week following her grandfather's funeral, while the Sterlings and Lassiters departed the following day. Chris had flown back to Santa Fe that evening.

Her father had been quiet and distant, and she thought it was because he was grieving his father's death. She hadn't known that Joshua Kirkland had confronted her husband about their association. When she'd sat with Chris during the memorial service for Samuel Claridge Cole, it seemed the most natural thing to do. After all, he *was* her husband.

Turning over on her side and cradling her head on her arm, she closed her eyes. A hissing sound shattered the silence as minute pieces of burning embers sent up showers in a brilliant orange-yellow glow as Emily concentrated on listening to her own heartbeat. Her pulse had slowed.

She hadn't realized she had dozed off until she registered the familiar scent of Chris's aftershave. He shook her softly while calling her name. Rolling over, she tried making out his features. He'd turned off the bedside lamp, and the only illumination came from the adjoining bathroom. The side of the bed dipped with his added weight.

"Wake up, baby. I want to undress you."

She did not protest when he removed her boots, socks and slacks. Her sweater, bra and finally her bikini underpants followed. The tender graze of his fingers feathering over her breasts and down her rib cage caused her to hold her breath. His magical hands continued their foray on her naked body, communicating and awakening her dormant passions.

Sitting up, Emily curved her arms around his neck, pressing

her cheek to his. The stubble was missing; he'd shaved. Burying her face against his throat, she kissed the firm flesh, the side of his strong neck, then lower to the mat of crisp hair on his chest. Jolts of electricity shot through her breasts when they made contact with the silk fabric of his kimono-styled bathrobe.

The pulse in his throat quickened with her sensual assault, and Chris swept her off the bed and carried her into the bathroom. She was lighter, weighed much less than she had before, and he wondered how she had lost so much weight in such a short period of time. He would only have her for two nights, but during that time he would make certain she ate.

Emily gasped aloud when Chris stepped into the bathroom. Lighted candles burned on a window seat, around the ledge of a sunken, cream-colored marble tub and a matching marble dressing table. The ledge also held two fluted crystal glasses, a matching vase filled with a profusion of pale peach roses and a bottle of champagne in a silver bowl. The calming scent of vanilla wafted in the air. The only other illumination was from a fire burning behind a decorative grate to a fireplace carved into the same wall from which the tub was built. It was a place where peace and quiet met.

Jets pulsed in the tub as Chris lowered her into the warm, swirling waters. Her gaze, locked with his, revealed her surprise and delight. The soothing water lapped up around her breasts.

"What a wonderful way to celebrate a reunion." Her voice was pregnant with emotion.

Removing the black silk robe with embroidered Japanese characters indicating love and peace, Chris dropped it to the floor and stepped into the tub. The oversized tub was large enough to accommodate four adults.

Moving closer to Emily, he settled her between his legs, his chest pressing against her back. "I'd like to think of it as our celebrating our first anniversary."

She glanced at him over her shoulder. "We've only been married a month."

Lowering his head, he kissed her ear. "That's what we're celebrating—our first month."

Her eyes crinkled in a smile. "Is this what I have to look forward to every month of my life with you? Aren't you afraid of running out of innovative ways to celebrate each month?"

Cradling her breasts between his hands, he massaged the firm globes of flesh until they grew heavy against his fingers. "I want to celebrate every month the first year, then every year thereafter."

Smothering a moan, Emily tried to ignore the gentle massage of his fingers sending currents of desire through her. Resting the back of her head on his shoulder, she closed her eyes, reveling in the passion only Chris could elicit from her.

Her hand moved between his thighs and grasped his maleness. It was his turn to moan when she held him captive, his swelling flesh hardening against her fingers as she stroked him in a strong, measured rhythm. She released him long enough to turn and straddle his thighs. Before Chris could recover, she reached between their slick bodies, seizing him again, while her breasts flattened against his damp, hair-covered chest.

He curved an arm around her waist and within seconds joined her body to his. Every element added to the sensual coupling: the burning candles, smoldering fire, warm swirling water and dammed-up passions.

The water in the tub added a buoyancy to their lovemaking that hadn't been there before. Emily tightened her grip on her husband's neck. Her long legs circled his waist and she rode the waves of ecstasy. Her eager response matched his own, and both sought a penetration so deep that they ceased to exist as separate entities.

His mouth was everywhere—her neck, throat, shoulders. It was as if he wanted to devour her—whole.

Curving her arms under his shoulders, Emily concentrated on the swollen flesh pushing against the walls of her womb with each unrestrained upward thrust. Closing her eyes, she shuddered uncontrollably when the first spasm shook her.

"Chris!" His name was a desperate whisper against his ear. She called him again.

He was past the point of no return. Nothing mattered. Not

the campaign, William Savoy, or the fact that, as governor of New Mexico, he would have more authority than those of most states. As Governor Delgado he would have the usual powers of pardon, reprieve and veto; in addition he would appoint most of the state boards, departments, agencies and commissions. Consequently, he would be the virtual master of patronage and the state's political organization.

But all that really mattered was the woman he'd claimed as his wife. He loved Emily with an intensity that frightened him. Now he knew how Alejandro had felt about Eve Blackwell; whenever he was with Emily he wasn't in control of himself or his existence. It was she who unknowingly held the power to destroy him. All she had to do was open her mouth and tell him to drop out of the race and he would. She possessed the power to tell him to come—and he would. Go—and he would.

While buried deep in her soft, scented body he became whole again. She'd become his past, present and future.

Their bodies were in exquisite harmony with one another as their passions peaked, exploding in a deluge of fiery sensations that took them beyond themselves. Emily's gasps of wonderment matched Chris's deep groans of fulfillment. Her eyes opened. He stared at her, an expression of savage carnality radiating from his black gaze. He'd become someone she did not recognize. The man to whom she had offered her virginity and married had transformed himself into a complete stranger.

Closing her eyes, Emily collapsed against his chest, struggling to slow her pounding heart. They lay together, limbs entwined, Emily suddenly aware of the import of this coupling. Her husband had not protected her. Christopher Blackwell Delgado had waited for her most fertile time of the month to make love to her without contraception.

A soft smile curved her mouth. It didn't matter. Nothing mattered anymore. Chris had just buried his father, and if he had gotten her pregnant, then the blood of Alejandro Delgado-Quintero would continue to flow in his grandchild.

She lay in the comforting arms of her husband, feeling the

strong pumping of his heart against her breasts. "Happy anniversary, darling."

Raining kisses along the length of her neck, Chris chuckled. "Happy anniversary to you, too, wife." Pulling back, he stared at her upturned face. Moisture dotted her face, lashes and hair. "Will you share a glass of champagne with me?"

Her lips parted as she offered him a sensual smile. "Of course."

Chris was loath to withdraw from her, but he did so reluctantly. Moving across the tub, he uncorked the bottle of champagne, filling the flutes with the pale, bubbling wine. Emily eased closer, accepting the glass from him. They touched glasses, then sipped. The bubbles tickled Emily's nose as she stared at her husband over the rim.

Placing his glass on the ledge, Chris reached for Emily's left hand. She stared, motionless, when he reached around one of the candles and withdrew a ring. The flickering light bounced off the three large stones in the platinum band. He slipped the circlet with its central oval diamond flanked by two slightly smaller ones on her third finger. Her gaze was fixed on the magnificent three-stone anniversary band.

"You deserve to wear a ring that no other woman has worn before."

She knew he was referring to the wedding band he'd slipped on her finger, which had belonged to his paternal grandmother. And she also suspected he hadn't forgotten that Keith Norris had given her a ring.

The magnificence of the stones were apparent even in the diffused light. Her head came up slowly, her eyes filling with tears that turned them into another kind of jewels.

"It's beautiful, Chris." Her tantalizing voice had lowered, sending a shiver of desire along Chris's nerve endings.

"I love you, Emily. I know I tell you that, but somehow it doesn't seem like it's enough."

She shook her head, tears flowing down her silken cheeks. "It's enough," she whispered.

Pulling her against his body, Chris held her gently as she

rested her head on his shoulder and cried. He lowered his head and touched his mouth to hers, tasting her salty tears.

"I promised Alejandro that if we have a son I would name him after him." Emily nodded, not saying a word. "Do you want a baby, Emily?"

There was a moment's silence before she said quietly, "Yes."

"We can start trying this weekend."

The warmth of his champagne-scented breath and the soft, soothing sound of his voice swept over her. "I'd like that very much."

Chris released Emily long enough to refill their glasses. Tilting his head at an angle, he smiled at her. "Here's to another generation of Coles, Kirklands, Sterlings and Delgados," he said in Spanish.

She touched her glass to his, smiling broadly. *"¡Salud!"*

After their bathtub coupling, Chris and Emily washed, dressed, then searched through Steve Washington's freezer, selecting two large-mouth bass that had been cleaned and vacuum-packed in plastic bags. The vegetable bin yielded several baking potatoes, and the vegetable crisper in the side-by-side refrigerator-freezer green, yellow and red peppers that were still fresh. Looking for something green, she decided on a package of frozen spinach. A further foray in a pantry turned up a spice rack with the ubiquitous garlic powder and olive oil. She would sauté the spinach.

Chris slipped several Maxwell CDs on the carousel of the powerful mini-stereo system resting on a kitchen countertop, and whenever one of his favorite selections came on he pulled Emily away from her task to dance with him. What should've taken her an hour to complete stretched into twice that long. It was nearly ten when they finished eating, cleaned up the kitchen and returned to the loft.

Emily lay beside her husband on the large bed, her fingers threaded through his. He'd only mentioned Alejandro once, and that was to tell her that her now deceased father-in-law had requested that their son carry his name.

Squeezing his fingers gently, she turned on her side, facing him in the darkness. "Did Alejandro suffer?"

Inhaling deeply before letting out his breath, Chris shook his head. "No. The doctor made certain he was comfortable, even to the end." Reaching over with his free hand, he pulled her smooth leg over his hair-roughed one. "He left us the house in Puerto Escondido, all of the surrounding property and enough money to last us well into old age."

There was profound silence before she spoke again. "Why?"

"Who else was he going to leave it to? Distant cousins? Sonia's husband has provided for her, so it was either us or the church. And the church did receive a very generous donation."

She thought about the amount of money she'd inherited from her grandfather, and now Alejandro. Money she wouldn't be able to spend in her lifetime even if she squandered half of it.

"What are you thinking about, baby?" Chris asked after a prolonged silence.

"I was thinking about the money my grandfather left me."

"What about it?"

"I'd asked my mother to invest it for me."

"Has she?"

"Not yet. I think I'd like to take half of it and set up a foundation to offer college scholarships for African-American students who are considering a career in journalism."

Releasing her hand, Chris reached out and pulled her effortlessly atop his body. His arms curved around her waist. He placed light kisses on her mussed hair.

"I should've thought of that myself. Call your mother and have her put Samuel Cole's money into a foundation that will make it exempt from the exorbitant inheritance tax."

"Would you be opposed to setting up a foundation honoring the memory of Samuel Cole and Alejandro Delgado?"

Tightening his hold on her body, Chris kissed her forehead. "Of course not. I think that's a wonderful idea."

"I think so, too," she teased without a hint of modesty.

"I think you're wonderful, Mrs. Delgado."

Cradling his lean, clean-shaven cheeks between her palms, she searched for his mouth, covering it with hers. She moaned softly as she felt his hardening flesh stir against her belly.

"Haven't you had enough?"

Without warning, he reversed their positions, looming above her. "How can I get too much of something I don't get enough of?"

She wasn't given the opportunity to ponder his question as he pushed into her body without his usual foreplay. She knew this coming together would be different from any other they'd shared.

They utilized every inch of the large bed, rolling and reversing positions as they tried to get close enough to meld into one. Mouths joined, fingers entwined, Chris and Emily tore at each other as their passions rose higher and higher. She arched, meeting each relentless thrust of his powerful hips. Moans, groans and grunts punctuated the silence, escalating with the lust spinning out of control.

Love flowed through Emily like heated honey, and when they reversed positions she sat astride him, threw her head back, cried out her release, then melted all over him. Slumping to his chest, she lay there spent while he exploded, leaving his seed planted deep within her womb.

She didn't, couldn't move, staying sprawled over his body, waiting for sanity and reason to return. Moisture from her face and hair dripped onto Chris's sweat-covered body. They'd made love as if it would be their last time together. Each time they came together they refused to hold anything back, not knowing when or if they would make love again before the first Tuesday in November.

Chapter 28

Emily was thoroughly bored. She'd spent the past hour reading newspaper accounts of Chris's successful fundraiser.

She felt her mind wandering as her gaze shifted to the typed copy on her desk. Her intern wasn't scheduled to come into the KCNS office until the following day, so she'd spent the morning editing copy. She had approached Richard Adams about reassigning her, but he would not relent. Her desk assignment would continue until further notice.

In two days she would turn thirty-one, and Emily looked forward to traveling to Las Cruces to celebrate the occasion with the Lassiters and Sterlings. Her parents had planned to fly to New Mexico from Florida but had canceled their return. Vanessa was diagnosed with the flu, and the Coles' physician recommended she remain in Florida until she made a full recovery.

Light from the desk lamp glinted off the stones of the ring on her left hand. Once she returned from her weekend tryst with her husband, she refused to remove the ring. Several people at the station mentioned her "nice ring," then waited for her to offer an explanation. When none was forthcoming they whispered among themselves, speculating as to who might have given it to her.

The small, flip-top cell phone in an open drawer in her desk chimed softly. Picking up the palm-size instrument, she pushed a button. "Hello."

"It's me."

Her heart lurched. It was the mysterious woman. This was only the second time she'd called. "Yes?"

"I want you to meet me."

"Where?"

"Church of the Savior. Get there before the twelve-twenty mass. Sit in the middle of the church. Don't go up for communion or turn around. I'll be sitting behind you. Ignore these instructions and you'll never hear from me again."

"I understand."

The call ended and Emily stared at the phone. A knowing smile curved her lips. "You're a liar," she whispered.

It was obvious the woman knew Bettina personally or she wouldn't have contacted her to elicit her help in solving the murder. It was also obvious that she might have been privy to secrets Bettina hadn't told her parents. Glancing at her watch, Emily noted the time. She had to leave now if she intended to make it to the church before the afternoon mass.

Shoving her wireless phone and a beeper into her purse, she scribbled a note for the receptionist to page her if Richard Adams needed to contact her.

Taking the elevator to the parking lot, she slipped into her Corvette. The morning sun had disappeared, leaving behind gray, overcast skies. Winter had tightened its grip on New Mexico's northern region, with heavy accumulations of snow in the mountains. Skiers were coming to the resorts in record numbers.

A rush of adrenaline made Emily almost light-headed with anticipation as she drove toward the church. It had been exactly three weeks since someone had murdered Bettina Gibson, and when Emily called Detective McGrady he'd reported that his investigation had come to a complete standstill. Without the elder Gibsons' cooperation and any new leads, he was ready to label the case unsolved.

It had taken all of her self-control not to scream at him for his lack of enthusiasm in solving the case. She told him that if the victim had been the governor's wife, she doubted whether he would be so laid-back in his attempt to apprehend the murderer. Not waiting for his response, she hung up. She thought of contacting Steve Washington but changed her mind. The highway patrol officer was her only link to Chris, and she didn't want to compromise his friendship by drawing him into a murder investigation.

She drove quickly, making certain to stay under the speed limit. Glancing up at the rearview mirror, she noticed a dark, four-door sedan behind her. The driver was too close, nearly tailgating her. Her gaze narrowed as she slowed and changed into the left lane. The driver of the other car moved over to the left, dropping back several car lengths. Without signaling, she depressed the clutch, shifted into a higher gear, then moved across two lanes of traffic and turned off at the next intersection. It had taken less than ten seconds, but she lost her pursuer when she sped down a one-way street, turned off into a two-way, then reversed direction. The shrill of rubber hitting the roadway disturbed the quietness of the working-class residential neighborhood. Three minutes later, she maneuvered into the tiny parking lot abutting the small Roman Catholic church.

There were at least half a dozen cars in the lot, which meant parishioners had already arrived for the weekday noon mass. Gathering her purse, she opened the door, glancing around to see if she was still being followed. There was no other vehicle in sight along the street. Letting out her breath, she walked the short distance from the parking lot to the church entrance.

Flickering candles behind red and blue chimneys, along with votive candles in the same colors, winked in the cloaking shadows of the baroque-style structure. She sat down in the middle aisle. The pews in front and behind her were empty. She noticed that all of the worshipers were elderly men and woman. Most carried rosaries that were laced between clasped hands.

Without turning around, Emily felt a presence behind her. A shiver raced up her spine. Her sensitive nose detected a familiar masculine cologne. Why would a woman wear a man's fragrance? She did not have long to ponder the question.

"Bettina Gibson was pregnant," announced a soft male voice.

Emily stared straight ahead, her gaze focused on the altar. Her pulses were racing with excitement. "Whose baby was she carrying?"

"That's for you to uncover, Miss Kirkland."

"Who are you?" she whispered, rising to her feet as a young priest made his appearance.

"A friend of a friend."

"A friend of the woman who has been calling me?"

"I'll be in touch."

She felt movement behind her but didn't turn around. The informant had given her information that elicited a modicum of uneasiness. She didn't know why, but Grace Clark's name came to mind. Was there a connection between Salem Lassiter's late wife and Bettina Gibson? Had both women become involved with William Savoy? Were they both carrying his child when they died? Emily planned to call Detective McGrady and corroborate the information her contact had given her. He would be privy to the results of Bettina's autopsy—if the Gibsons had agreed to an autopsy.

Detective Vincent McGrady rose to his feet at Emily Kirkland's approach. She looked vastly different from their first encounter. She wore a dark green sheepskin swing coat, a pair of low-heeled black riding boots, a slim, black, midi-length wool skirt and a matching cashmere twinset. Her curly hair was brushed off her face and forehead, while a light cover of makeup highlighted her beautiful face. She'd called his private number the day before, leaving a message that she wanted to meet with him, and he'd suggested a small Italian restaurant in a Santa Fe suburb.

Extending her gloved hand, Emily offered him a warm smile. "Thank you for taking the time to meet with me."

He shook the proffered hand, returning her smile. "Your message said you might have some information for me." Moving to her side, he assisted her in removing her gloves and coat.

Emily nodded when Vincent sat down opposite her. "Yes, I do."

"If you don't mind, I'd like to talk over dinner. I highly recommend the ziti."

She hadn't planned to eat because she had at least a four-hour drive ahead of her. She wanted to tell the detective what she'd uncovered before she left Santa Fe for Las Cruces. Glancing at the menu on the red-and-white-checked tablecloth, she perused the selections.

"I'll just have a seltzer."

Vincent raised his sandy eyebrows. "Are you on a diet, Miss Kirkland?" His dark blue eyes moved slowly over her upper body.

She ignored his backhanded compliment, placing both hands on the table. The light from an overhead fixture caught the blue-white flash of diamonds on her left hand.

He shifted uneasily in his chair. He'd made a mistake. Keith Norris had held a televised press conference, revealing that he and Emily Kirkland had called off their engagement, but the ring on her finger indicated that they might have changed their minds again. The awkward moment passed when a waiter came to the table to take their orders.

Emily waited until the man walked away, then said, "Are you aware that Bettina Gibson was pregnant when she died?"

Vincent's expression did not change. "You told me that you didn't know whether Ms. Gibson was seeing a man."

"I told you the truth. But you didn't answer my question, Detective McGrady. Did you know she was pregnant?"

He nodded. "An autopsy revealed that she was at least two months into her term. Only the Gibsons and my office were privy to the medical examiner's findings. How did you come by your information?"

"That's privileged."

"If it's so privileged, why are you telling me?"

"I needed you to corroborate what my source told me."

"Who's your source?"

"That's also privileged."

Resting his elbows on the tablecloth, Vincent McGrady gave Emily a long, penetrating look. "What else has your source told you?"

"That's all for now."

"It appears that your source knows a little something about Bettina Gibson's private life."

The waiter returned with their beverages and all conversation ceased until he was far enough away not to overhear their discussion.

Emily took small sips of the seltzer, then moved the glass aside. "I'll be in touch with you when I get more information. I suggest you talk to her coworkers at the magazine again. I'm certain there is someone who might have seen Bettina with a man outside the office."

Vincent took a long swallow of his sparkling water. "I'll follow up on it."

He stood when Emily pushed back her chair, coming around to help her with her coat. He'd hoped to share dinner with her—get to know her better. His own marriage had ended eighteen months earlier, and the ensuing divorce had turned ugly. In all that time, he hadn't thought about dating a woman until now.

Emily flashed her recognizable smile. "Thanks, Detective McGrady. I'll be in touch."

He nodded, staring at her departing figure until she was out of his line of vision.

Emily pressed a button on the car radio for an all-news station. She listened absentmindedly as the newscaster updated the evening's rush-hour traffic but became suddenly alert when he offered the political news. Her fingers tightened on the leather-wrapped steering wheel as she heard the news Chris had been anticipating.

"Investigators hired by gubernatorial hopeful William Savoy have uncovered information that his opponent, State Senator Christopher Delgado's biological father was charged by Mexican authorities with trafficking in marijuana and cocaine more than thirty years ago. Mexican police records reveal that Alejandro Delgado, a former diplomat, fled Mexico before he could be apprehended. After he was diagnosed with cancer, he was permitted to return to Mexico where he died earlier this month. There has been no response from Senator Delgado or anyone at his campaign headquarters."

Emily mumbled a savage curse under her breath. The mud-slinging had begun. The threat that Savoy would expose Alejandro Delgado's past had manifested.

Concentrating on the taillights in front of her, she whispered a silent prayer that her husband's brilliant strategists wouldn't wait too long to call a press conference to give their candidate the opportunity to reply to the insinuations.

Politically astute Savoy had begun a blitzkrieg of television ads, while Chris's image was visible on billboards and campaign buttons. She'd noticed a number of vehicles with bumper stickers bearing his name, but his image was not as visible as she would've liked it to be.

What were his strategists waiting for? They had to know that voters were fickle *and* unpredictable. The slightest hint of a scandal could sway the most staunch supporter.

The word *scandal* was branded on her mind, along with Bettina's murder. Savoy's press secretary had released a report that the alleged suicide of Bettina Gibson at his candidate's fundraiser was an attempt to malign William Savoy's impeccable reputation. When asked why the journalist might have elected to take her own life at the country club on that particular evening, the response was that no one would ever know because dead people don't talk.

How true, Emily thought. Bettina had come to the event with a purpose. She suspected she was there to meet someone—and that someone was probably a man. A man she'd been arguing with, a man who had killed her to keep her from talking.

Maneuvering into the lane for southward traffic, Emily's delicate jaw hardened with determination. Bettina was dead, her own career was in limbo, and her husband's personal life was about to be dissected by the press.

The only bright light was her love for Chris and his for her. Even if Bettina's murderer was never brought to justice, or if Chris lost his election bid, they still would be victorious. Their love for each other was strong enough to sustain any loss or disappointment.

Her dark mood lifted when she saw the signs indicating the number of miles to Las Cruces.

Chapter 29

Emily entered the town limits of Las Cruces at nine forty-five and drove into the Lassiter drive at ten-ten. She'd made the 350-mile trip in less than three and a half hours. Once she'd left the interstate, she was able to speed undetected by many of the highway police who lay in wait for drivers who ignored the state's speed limit.

Twisting the ring on her finger, she dropped it into the depths of her leather purse before stepping out of the Corvette. Shadow greeted her arrival. The hybrid wolf-dog sniffed her, whining softly once he recognized her familiar scent.

She scratched the canine behind his ears. "Hello, Shadow." Her voice, though low and soft, carried easily in the desert night. The front door to the two-story structure opened, and the outline of Sara Sterling-Lassiter's tall, slender body appeared in the doorway.

Emily made her was up the flagstone path, through a central atrium, then into the massive foyer. Dropping her weekender to the highly polished wood floor, she hugged her friend.

Sara tightened her grip around Emily's neck. "Welcome back, Emmie."

"Thanks, Sara."

Sara eased back, her gold-green gaze taking in everything about Emily Kirkland in one sweeping glance. "You look wonderful."

"You look pretty good yourself for a housewife."

"Bite your tongue," Sara chided softly. She closed the door, picked up Emily's bag, and led her through the sculpture-filled foyer. "I'm working several days a week now."

"Where?"

"I'm not really working but volunteering. I'm reviewing briefs for a local law firm. And I manage to put in a few days a week at Chris's campaign office."

Emily stopped, staring directly at her sister-in-law. "Did you hear the news report that Savoy's people put out about Alejandro Delgado?"

A slight frown marred Sara's smooth forehead. "It was splashed all over the local evening news tonight."

"How are your parents taking it?"

"Mom's spitting mad. Dad's not saying much."

"Have you heard from Chris?"

Sara shook her head. "No. But he's expected to be here tomorrow afternoon. Have you eaten?" she asked, quickly changing the subject.

"No."

"I'll fix you a plate."

"Let me go upstairs and change into something more comfortable. Where's Salem?" she asked when they reached the staircase leading to the upper level.

"He's in his study putting the finishing touches on a research project for a veterinary journal. He'll probably be up half the night."

"And where is my godson?"

"He's in Taos with Salem's folks. They offered to take him for a few days to give Salem and me some quality time together. They're coming down tomorrow for your birthday."

Emily smiled, her luminous eyes crinkling attractively. "It'll be good seeing them again." She liked Salem's parents but hadn't seen the artist couple in nearly a year. Reaching for her bag, she eased it from Sara's loose grip. "I'll be down in a few minutes."

She climbed the stairs slowly, thinking of how different this coming birthday would be from the others she'd had. She would celebrate her thirty-first birthday with her husband and his family instead of her parents. And only Chris would know that legally she was Emily Delgado, not Emily Kirkland.

It was now the end of February, and two months had passed quickly. She just hoped the next eight would pass as fast. Notwithstanding, the outcome of the election would not change the promise she and Chris had made to each other. It would be on election night that they would finally get to reveal their private liaison to the world.

Chris took a red-eye commuter flight from Gallup to Las Cruces. A driver was waiting for him at the airport when he touched down. His strategists were prepared for the news about Alejandro Delgado's alleged drug trafficking, and his press secretary promised the media that his candidate would address the allegations in a televised news conference the following week. Grant had urged him not to wait, but Chris wanted to see his mother before he went public with the information he'd gleaned from his father.

The driver reached for his bags. "How was your flight, Senator Delgado?"

Chris flashed a tired smile. "Very good." He ducked his head into the spacious car, collapsing onto the rear seat. He was exhausted. His day had begun at dawn, when he visited several construction sites, a high school and a senior citizens' center where he shared lunch with more than 200 elderly men and women before he attended an ecumenical dinner with clergy from more than half a dozen religious groups. He'd planned to spend the night in Gallup and return to Las Cruces the following morning but changed his mind. He was impatient to see his parents and his wife.

His mouth curved into an unconscious smile when he thought of Emily, recalling their last time together. The weekend at the cabin had become a magical interlude, surpassing the one they'd shared in Ocho Rios.

They made love with a wild abandonment that was indescribable. When he'd asked Emily whether she wanted a baby the question had been a reckless impulse. He didn't know what had prompted him to ask her, but it was as if he hadn't been able to rid himself of the image of Alejandro's lifeless body. Emily had buried her grandfather and he his father, and he wanted to celebrate life—a life he would create with her.

The driver pulled away from the curb, and he closed his eyes. The smooth motion of the automobile lulled him into a comforting, dreamless slumber.

"Senator Delgado, we're here."

Chris came awake immediately, sitting up straighter and glancing out the window. The driver held the back door open for him. He was back at Sterling Farms. His luggage sat on the loggia next to the front door.

"Thanks." The single word mirrored his weighted fatigue. Reaching into the pockets of his slacks, he withdrew a money clip and tipped the driver, who gave him a wide smile.

"Thank *you*."

Mission lanterns placed strategically along the loggia provided enough light for him to unlock the front door without fumbling with the key. A small lamp on a drop-leaf table in the entryway cast a golden glow in the quiet house. It was after three and his parents were asleep. Leaving his luggage on the floor near the table, he made his way to his bedroom. He'd been awake for twenty-one hours and he still wanted to shower before he retired for bed.

Walking into the bedroom he'd occupied while growing up, Chris closed the door, undressed quickly, then retreated to the bathroom. He managed to brush his teeth and shower in ten minutes. Not bothering to dry his body, he returned to the bedroom, lay across the bed and fell asleep.

Emily woke early. She left Sara a note, telling her where she could find her, then walked to Sterling Farms. The early morning temperature was cool and crisp, and by the time she'd crossed over onto Sterling property the rising sun had fired the eastern slopes of the Organ Mountains. Dressed in a pair of jeans, boots, a pullover sweater and a lightweight jacket, she welcomed the exercise. Shadow had accompanied her until she crossed the bridge spanning the narrow stream separating the two properties. The wolf watched her until she disappeared, then loped back to patrol the Lassiters' vast Mesilla Valley acreage.

Pleasant memories assailed Emily as she surveyed the land Matthew Sterling had purchased several years before he'd married Chris and Sara's mother. Matt and Eve owned twelve hundred acres of prime land on which they'd amassed a fortune breeding champion Thoroughbreds.

There was a time when Sterling Farms had become her home-away-from-home. The summers she and Michael spent in Las Cruces they'd learned to ride, shoot, hunt and survive off the land. The summers Chris and Sara stayed with her family in Santa Fe included visits to museums, ballets and concerts. They became fierce competitors when they swam in her parents' Olympic-size pool or squared off on their tennis court. They'd all grown up without the angst most adolescents experienced, lamenting that they never wanted to grow up because they were having too much fun.

Emily had grown up thinking her feelings for Christopher Delgado would change once she entered college. She dated other men, but she could never bring herself to like any of them as well as she liked her best friend's brother. After a while she just stopped trying when she realized she was hopelessly in love with Chris.

She met Joseph Russell as he came from the opposite direction. The longtime Sterling Farms horse trainer's gray hair bore little traces of what had once been flaming red hair. A widower, he had moved in with Marisa Hall six months after Salem and Sara had exchanged vows, hoping the divorced, middle-aged mother of an adult son would accept his marriage proposal. Marisa had agreed to live with him, while stubbornly refusing to marry again.

"Good morning, missy," Joe called out. "Good to see you again."

She flashed him a friendly smile. "Good morning, Mr. Russell."

Minute lines fanned out around his brilliant topaz-blue eyes. "Risa told me that you're celebrating a birthday today. She's planning to bake your favorite cake. But don't let on that you know."

"I promise I'll act surprised. Is anyone up yet?"

"Risa's up preparing breakfast. She was kind of surprised to find that Chris had come in last night. We wouldn't have known he was in except that he left his bags in the entryway."

The pulse in her throat fluttered as she schooled her features not to reveal her delight. "Sara told me he wouldn't be in until this afternoon."

Joe sucked his teeth loudly. "I suppose he wanted to get here early to see his special lady."

"Special lady?" Her voice had risen slightly.

"You."

This time her eyebrows lifted. "Me?"

"Aw, missy, you have to know that you have Christopher Delgado's heart." He moved closer, peering at her shocked expression. "You don't know, do you?" When Emily didn't respond, he said, "You forget that I watched you kids grow up. I saw things you didn't think I saw. I knew that your brother would either go into the military or law enforcement, because I've never seen someone shoot like him. I couldn't believe it when he shot a quarter dead-center at three hundred feet.

"I knew Christopher and Sara would become lawyers because they were obsessed with Perry Mason. You, I hadn't figured out so well. But I knew Chris always had a thing for you because of the way he took care of you. He protected you more than he did his own sister."

"That's because Sara was a little tougher than me."

"Don't sell yourself short, missy. It was you who used to tangle with the boys, not Sara."

The horse trainer was right. She had a quicker temper than Sara and thought nothing of challenging Chris, her brother or Marisa's son to a fight. Most times they laughed at her and walked away, saying they would never fight a girl. And if they had, they would have her father to answer to. Even though William Hall didn't know his father, he wasn't exempt from the punishment Matthew Sterling meted out to his own children.

She nodded, unable to conceal a knowing smile. "I'm going to go in and get a cup of Miss Marisa's coffee. Are you going to join me?"

Crossing his arms over a wide, muscular chest, Joe shook his head. "Naw. I have to check a fence in the north pasture. I'll be along directly."

"I'll see you later."

Joe nodded. "Don't mention about the cake."

"I won't."

Emily walked up to the front door of the expansive one-story ranch house, pushed it open and stepped into the entryway. Chris's bags sat on the floor beside the antique table. She was amazed how fast her pulse was beating as she stood there staring at them.

She and Chris would spend the next two days together while in the company of his family. Would they be able to fool everyone again? She hadn't confirmed Joe Russell's assertion that Chris liked her, but she hadn't denied it either. Who else beside Joe and Sara knew? Could they afford to tell their families?

The questions continued to attack her as she walked into the kitchen. The man she loved and married sat at the table in an alcove drinking a cup of steaming black coffee. He placed the cup on its saucer, rattling it loudly, his hand shaking slightly at the same time he rose to his feet.

A soft gasp escaped Chris, and Marisa Hall turned to look at him. She followed his gaze and saw Emily Kirkland standing under the arched entrance to the large kitchen. The young couple seemed impervious to her presence as a silent, sensual entrancement passed between them.

Emily registered everything about Chris in one penetrating glance: his long damp hair, the dark stubble of an emerging beard on his brown jaw, the attractive shadows under his deep-set eyes and the prominent display of cheekbones in his lean face. Never had he appeared more virile. He was dressed in a pair of jeans that had been washed so many times that they'd appeared more pale gray than blue. The color was almost a perfect match for the sweatshirt bearing the logo of his college alma mater.

Marisa cleared her voice, capturing the young couple's attention. Emily's eyes crinkled into a smile as she turned her attention to the Sterlings' live-in housekeeper and cook.

"Good morning, Miss Marisa." Her soft, sultry voice was a shivery whisper.

Petite, fifty-eight-year-old Marisa Hall's round, dark brown eyes sparkled in delight as she surveyed Emily. "Good morning, Emily. Even after all of these years, you still haven't changed, have you?"

Emily's confusion was apparent when her eyebrows raised inquiringly. "About what, Miss Marisa?"

"You still get up before the chickens."

The running joke at Sterling Farms was that whenever Emily stayed over there was never a need for an alarm clock. She always got up before dawn. Most times Marisa found her in the family room, showered, dressed and watching her favorite videos.

"I'm not the only one who's up with the chickens," she teased, giving Chris a knowing look.

Marisa nodded. "You two make a perfect match. Our esteemed state senator just told me that he got in after three," she continued, as if Chris weren't in the room. "Yet he's up at six prowling around and looking for coffee."

Folding his arms over his chest and lowering his head slightly, Chris blew the housekeeper a kiss. "Can I help it if I love your coffee?"

Marisa waved a hand, shaking her graying chemically straightened hair. Her smooth coif swayed around her delicate jawline. "Save the pretty words for campaigning, Senator Delgado. What you need is a wife and a couple of kids to settle you down and keep you from prowling."

Emily and Chris stared at each other. He did have a wife—a wife he couldn't openly claim. A wife he saw occasionally, a wife he loved beyond description, a wife who stood several feet away. Yet he was unable to go to her to kiss her in the manner he wanted to.

"If you don't mind, I'll have a cup of coffee," Emily said.

She walked over to the alcove and sat down at the table. Chris retook his own chair, his burning black gaze moving slowly over her face.

"You still take it with lots of milk and one sugar?" Marisa asked.

"Yes, ma'am," Emily replied, returning her husband's direct look. "Sara told me you wouldn't be back until this afternoon," she whispered to him.

Leaning back in his chair, Chris stared down at the half-filled cup of black coffee, a sweep of long black lashes concealing the hollows under his deep, penetrating eyes. "Once Savoy released the news about Alejandro I decided to come back to talk to Mom. I got up early, thinking she would be up already."

"Sara said she's spitting mad."

Chris glanced up at her without raising his head. "She's probably a bit more emotional than spitting mad, kid. I'd be the first one to say that Alejandro Delgado was a debaucher, a kidnapper and a son-of-a-bitch, but not a drug trafficker."

"How are you going to reply to the allegations?"

He waited until Marisa placed a cup of coffee on the table in front of Emily and walked away, then said, "I want to talk to Mom and Dad before giving my strategists a statement for the media."

Picking up her cup, Emily nodded. She took a sip of the excellently brewed coffee, her gaze meeting Chris's over the rim. She replaced the cup gently on the saucer.

"I want to tell my parents about *us*."

Chris was certain Emily heard his quick intake of breath. When had she changed her mind?

"Why?"

"Come walk with me," she suggested in a soft whisper.

They rose together and walked out of the kitchen, leaving Marisa staring at their departing figures. Her sparkling eyes narrowed as she smiled to herself. She'd always thought her employer's stepson and the daughter of his best friend were perfect for each other. It was too bad they continued to relate to each other much like her own William did to Sara, Emily, Michael and Christopher—like siblings.

Chris held Emily's hand as he led her out of the house and in the direction of the pasture, where the horses were turned out to run free to graze. The rising sun turned the lush landscape into an ethereal prism of shimmering yellows, oranges, heathers and russets.

Curbing an urge to pull her to his body, he concentrated on placing one foot in front of the other. "What made you change your mind?"

"It was probably what you said to me the night Bettina was shot. About you being my whore. I feel the same way, Chris. We sneak around and meet in hideaway places to make love. You're a thirty-five-year-old man and I'm a thirty-one-year-old woman. We're both too old for that type of behavior. I married you because I love you. And even if we decide not to go public until after the election, I still want our families to know that we're married. What if I'm pregnant? What—"

"Are you?" he asked, interrupting her.

She shook her head. "I don't know, I was due two days ago."

Stopping, he turned and stared down at her. The rays of the sun caressed her flawless brown skin and brilliant eyes. Never had he seen her more lush than she appeared at that moment. It was as if she had turned on an inner light that shimmered and radiated her feminine sensuality.

"Will you let me know—one way or the other?"

She smiled. "Of course."

"When are you going to tell your parents?"

"I'm going to call them when we get back to the house." The two-hour time difference would make it nine o'clock in Florida.

"What about my folks?"

Moving closer, she pressed her breasts against his sweatshirt-covered chest. "You tell yours."

Gathering her to his chest, Chris lowered his head and kissed the side of her neck. "Thank you, Emelia. You've just given me what I need to make it to November."

She shivered slightly when her mind registered his cryptic statement. Had he considered dropping out of the race? Had he been willing to give up all he'd sought since he'd graduated from law school because of her?

"I love you, Christopher Blackwell Delgado-Quintero.'

"And I you, Emelia Delgado-Quintero," he whispered seconds before he moved his mouth over her waiting lips.

They retraced their steps to the ranch house, Emily retreating to Matthew Sterling's office, while her husband made his way to his parents' bedroom. Both felt as if they'd shed a heavy burden. The love and support of their families would make it easier for them to conceal their private passions until after the election.

Chapter 30

Emily dialed the area code, then the number of her parents' Palm Beach residence. There was a break in the connection after the third ring.

"Hello?" The strong, powerful voice of her father came through the receiver.

"Hi, Daddy."

"Happy birthday, baby girl."

She froze, her response locked in her throat. It was the first time she realized her father and husband used the same endearment for her.

"Emily? Are you still there?"

"Yes. Thanks, Daddy. How's Mom doing?"

"She's still coughing. But it doesn't sound as deep as it was a couple of days ago."

"I'm calling you because I need to tell you something." This time there was no response from her father. "Daddy?"

"I'm here," Joshua Kirkland replied.

"Please put Mom on the extension. This is something I want both of you to hear at the same time."

"What the hell is going on, Emily?"

"Get my mother, please!" Biting down hard on her lower lip, she realized she'd just shouted at her father. "Don't make this more difficult than it needs to be, Daddy," she continued, this time in a softer tone.

"Hold on."

Closing her eyes, Emily heard the runaway beating of her heart in her ears. She had to tell them. At 12:01 a.m. she'd turned thirty-one, and she was about to claim complete independence from her parents, even though she'd been living on her own since her senior year in college.

"What's the matter, Emily?"

She didn't recognize Vanessa Blanchard-Kirkland's raspy voice. "How are you feeling?"

"Much better than I did last week. I was going to call you later. Happy birthday, sweetheart."

"Thanks, Mom."

"Your father said you have something to tell us."

Inhaling deeply, Emily let out her breath slowly. "I do. I want you to know that I'm married." A chorus of gasps rippled through the wire. "Chris Delgado and I were married in Mexico on January tenth."

"Why did you wait this long to tell us, Emily?" Joshua was the first to respond to her startling announcement.

"Chris and I promised each other that we wouldn't tell anyone until after the election. We thought it best since I was covering William Savoy's campaign. Then, of course, everything changed when I reported the shooting death of Bettina Gibson."

"I can't believe you cheated me out of giving you a wedding," Vanessa said, her voice breaking before she lapsed into a hacking cough.

"Where's Christopher?" Joshua asked. His voice had taken on an authoritative edge.

"He's with his parents, telling them what I'm telling you."

"This is wonderful news, isn't it, darling?" Vanessa crooned into the receiver.

There was a pregnant pause before Joshua spoke. "Yes, it is. This marriage will link the Kirklands, Coles and Sterlings forever. Congratulations, baby girl."

Emily felt her eyes fill with hot tears. "Thank you, Daddy."

"We have to celebrate," Vanessa said quickly. "When do you think you and Chris can come to Florida for a little gathering? David is throwing something next weekend for Gabriel winning his three Grammys. Maybe we can combine the two."

Emily wiped away her tears of joy with her fingertips. "I'll ask Chris if he can get away. Arrange for me to be picked up

Friday night in Albuquerque. And don't forget to call Michael." She wanted her brother with her when she shared her joy with her other family members.

"Joshua, have Martin or Parris call Regina, Aaron and their kids," Vanessa told her husband on the extension.

"I will," he promised.

"Thanks, guys," Emily said softly. "You're the best."

Her father's deep laughter came through the receiver—and it wasn't often that anyone heard Joshua Kirkland laugh. "Thanks. We're proud of you, baby girl. And tell that son-in-law of mine that we're proud of him, too."

"Let Eve know that I'm going to call her later," Vanessa said, her voice filling with rising excitement. "She, Serena and I need to talk about how we want to go about this."

"Mom, Daddy, you've just given me the best birthday present I've ever had."

"What's that?" the elder Kirklands chorused in unison.

"Your love and support. I'm going to hang up now before I start bawling my eyes out. I'll talk to you again before next weekend."

She rang off, replaced the phone on its cradle, then sat for a few minutes staring at the wall. She was free—freer than she had ever been in all her life.

Feeling a presence behind her, she turned to find Chris in the doorway. Lowering his chin, he gave her a sidelong glance before his mouth curved into a grin.

She arched her sweeping black eyebrows. "Well?"

"Mom had a few choice words about us sneaking behind her back before she burst into tears."

Emily stood up. "Aunt Eve's crying?" The running joke was that beautiful, elegant Eve Blackwell-Sterling was as tough as they come and only resorted to tears when enraged. "She's angry with us?"

Shaking his head, Chris walked into the room and pulled his wife into a protective embrace. "No, baby. She's deliriously happy."

"What about your father?"

"He was a little smug when he said he's been waiting a long time for the Sterlings, Kirklands and Coles to become one family."

"That's what my father said. David and Serena are putting together a celebratory gathering for Gabriel next weekend. My mother would like us to be there. She says because everyone is coming they all can celebrate our marriage at the same time. How's your schedule for next weekend?"

He kissed the tip of her nose. "Whatever I have scheduled can wait. I'll meet you in Florida."

Curving her arms around his neck, she pressed closer and kissed him. She wasn't disappointed when he tightened his hold on her waist, communicating silently how much he loved her.

March 5
Palm Beach

The six passengers aboard the 1998 GIV Gulfstream readied themselves for landing as the aircraft began its descent over the Palm Beach International Airport.

Arrangements had been made for Matthew and Eve Sterling to share Joshua and Vanessa's two-bedroom condominium in Palm Beach, while Emily, Sara, Salem and Isaiah would have their own bedrooms at the Cole mansion in West Palm Beach.

Martin and Parris Cole now claimed two residences—the West Palm Beach mansion and their beachfront home in Fort Lauderdale. All their children had left home: Regina lived in Brazil with her husband and children, Dr. Tyler Cole resided in Georgia because of his work with the Atlanta-based Centers for Disease Control and Prevention, while thirty-two-year-old Arianna Cole had moved to Paris to live with her Moroccan-born dress-designer boyfriend. Arianna had called Florida the moment she heard of her cousin's musical achievement, telling everyone she would return to the States for Gabriel's party.

David and Serena Cole had secured ground transportation for everyone to their Boca Raton home for a noon cookout on Saturday.

Emily glanced out the large oval window, staring at the sparkling lights over the opulent Florida city. She'd spent most of the flight on a sofa that folded out into a bed, refusing anything to eat. She managed to swallow a glass of seltzer with a sliver of lemon, but it failed to relieve what she'd first thought were premenstrual cramps.

You're feeling queasy because you're pregnant, a little voice whispered in her head. She was a week late. Since she'd begun menstruating, her menses had arrived every twenty-six days of every month of every year.

The diamonds on her left hand winked at her under a halogen reading light. The day the Lassiters, Sterlings, Marisa Hall and Joseph Russell gathered to celebrate her thirty-first birthday and the news that she and Chris were married, she'd given him the ring to slip on to her finger for a second time.

Salem returned from the cockpit to sit beside his wife. As a licensed pilot, he was enthralled with the private jet, which boasted 6,500 miles. That was enough for a nonstop 14-hour flight from New York to Tokyo. The aircraft had a forty-foot cabin that was configured for eleven to thirteen passengers, with sofas that folded out into beds, a full galley and rest rooms.

Emily turned her head, watching as Matt pressed a button on a remote, turning off one of two flat-screen televisions. Reaching for his wife's hand, he squeezed her fingers gently. If her suspicions were right, then the Sterlings would have another grandchild before the end of the year.

The nighttime temperature was in the low fifties when the New Mexican residents stepped out onto the tarmac on a private airfield at the Palm Beach Airport.

Two Mercedes-Benz limousines were positioned on the other side of a fence. The rear door to one of the limos opened and the platinum head of Joshua Kirkland appeared under the lights.

Emily waved to her father, temporarily forgetting about her unsettled stomach. He returned her wave, quickening his long strides. Moments later she found herself in his arms.

"How was your flight?"

She kissed his smooth cheek. "It was good."

His pale gaze examined her face. "How are you?"

Shaking her head, she decided not to lie to her father. She had deceived him and her mother enough these past few months. "I'm not sure."

"What's the matter?"

"I think I'm pregnant."

Joshua went completely still. He stared at her, unblinking. "You haven't been to a doctor?"

She shook her head again. "Not yet. I'm only a week overdue, Daddy."

Tightening his hold around her waist, he kissed her forehead. "It's okay, baby girl. Tyler's coming in tomorrow morning, and Aaron's already here. One of them can look at you."

"I'm not going to let them examine me."

"Why not? They're doctors."

"They're my cousins."

"So?"

"So? They're family. I'd feel uncomfortable having them look at me."

"Why don't you have Parris or Serena call their doctors for an appointment?"

"Okay," she conceded.

Joshua released his daughter and extended his arms to Matt Sterling. The two gave each other a warm embrace. "Welcome to the family."

Matt patted Joshua's back. "It's the Sterlings who are welcoming the Kirklands and the Coles."

"Sorry, buddy. It's the girl's family who gives the wedding. Therefore, *we* welcome *you.*"

"I'm older than you by a year," Matt rationalized, "therefore I do the welcoming."

Eve shook her head. "Why don't you two give it up?" Her voice was filled with repressed laughter. "The older you get the sillier you become. All that matters is that our children are married." She glanced around her. "Where's Vanessa?"

Leaning down, Joshua kissed Eve's cheek. "She's home waiting for you."

Eve kissed Emily, Sara, Salem and a sleeping Isaiah. "I'll see you all tomorrow at David's."

She walked to one car with her husband and Joshua, while Emily and the Lassiters climbed into the other. The luxury automobiles left the airport, cruising smoothly in a northwest direction to West Palm Beach.

Martin and Parris were at the house when they arrived, both smiling when they saw their niece and her in-laws. Martin kissed Emily on both cheeks. He cradled her to his side as he greeted Salem Lassiter's family. A network of fine lines fanned out around his large black eyes as he flashed a dimpled smile.

"Welcome to Florida and to the family. I'm glad that this time we can all come together for a more festive occasion."

Parris Cole reached for Isaiah, taking him gently from his father's arms. "Come with me and I'll show you where he'll sleep. It's been a long time since there's been a baby in this house."

"Where are Regina and the others, Aunt Parris?" Emily asked.

"They all went out to a movie. They claim they miss American movies. They'll probably be in before midnight."

The driver brought in the luggage, taking the bags to the assigned rooms. He conferred with Martin Cole, who confirmed the time for his return the following day.

Emily climbed the curving staircase to the second-floor bedroom suites and walked into the bedroom where she'd slept many times before. She managed to brush her teeth and wash her face. Then she climbed onto the bed, fully dressed and fell asleep.

Chapter 31

March 6
Boca Raton

Temperatures had climbed to the low eighties by the time most of the Coles, Kirklands, Sterlings and the various members of Gabriel Cole's band assembled at David and Serena's seaside home.

At sixty-three, David Cole was still breathtakingly handsome. A faint scar along the left side of his face, running from the spheroid bone to mid-cheek, failed to minimize his masculine beauty. His silver hair was short and lay against his scalp, while tiny diamond studs sparkled in his lobes. He'd had his right lobe pierced for his sixtieth birthday, declaring that it was the last impulsive act of an aging musician.

He and his wife, Serena, a former nurse, had four children. Gabriel had followed in his father's footsteps, becoming a musician, while his nineteen-year-old twin sister and brother, Ana and Jason, were completing their first year of college. At twenty-four, Alexandra was close to completing her graduate work as a historical architect. Ana and Jason had elected to attend a local college because they couldn't bear separating from one another. All of David and Serena's children had inherited the characteristic Cole dimples, and their mother's mesmerizing golden brown eyes. The boys claimed their father's height, the girls their mother's diminutive stature.

Emily spied her uncle as he directed a few of the members in his son's band in setting up their equipment on the patio, overlooking a heated pool. She waited until he turned in her direction, then she smiled at him.

Closing the distance between them with long, fluid strides, David Cole swept his niece up in his arms, lifting her off her feet. "Congratulations, Emily." He kissed her soundly on her mouth.

Curving her arms around his neck, she hugged him. "Thanks. Congratulations to you, too, for winning a Grammy. How many do you have now?"

He set her gently on her feet. "Three." David and his former band, Night Mood, had earned several awards when he played percussion in his mid-twenties. He glanced at his watch. "Your husband should be arriving at any minute. His plane touched down around eleven-thirty."

She smiled. *Your husband.* It was the first time anyone had referred to Chris that way. "Where's Serena?"

"She's in the house, barking orders like a drill sergeant."

"Who's a sergeant?" asked a familiar deep voice.

Emily turned to find her brother Michael standing behind her. His brilliant green eyes were hidden behind a pair of sunglasses. Even though he wore a pair of black linen slacks with a matching shirt and Italian-style loafers, he still looked like a soldier. His posture was ramrod straight.

"I'll see you kids later," David said, returning to the house to see if his wife needed his assistance.

"Hey, Michael," Emily said softly.

Reaching for her right hand, Michael brought it to his lips. He kissed each one of her fingers before he hugged her, rocking her gently.

"Dad told me that you and Chris got married in Mexico just after the New Year. How long have you two been together?"

Pulling back, she stared over his broad shoulder. "Less than ten days before we married. He came to see me in Ocho Rios when he thought I was going to marry Keith Norris."

Michael frowned. "You really weren't thinking about marrying that idiot, were you?"

"He's hardly an idiot. He just happens to have an inflated ego."

Her brother flashed a wide grin. "I can't believe it."

"Believe what? Me married?"

"Not that as much as you as the first lady of New Mexico."

That was something she did not want to think about. Not yet. "Even if you can't get back home to vote, remember to send in your absentee ballot," she reminded her brother.

But Michael wasn't listening to her. His attention was fixed on a young woman who was probably a member of his cousin's band. The Florida sun glinted off her satiny, sable skin. Her natural hairdo was cropped close to her scalp, while a body-hugging tank dress exhibited an inordinate amount of smooth flesh. She leaned down to pick up several pages of sheet music, giving her admirer a generous display of her full breasts in a revealing neckline.

"Who is she, Emily?"

"I don't know. Do you want me to find out?"

"No. I believe I can handle that." Leaning down, he kissed his sister's cheek. "I left a wedding gift for you and Chris in the house."

Emily watched as her six-foot-four-inch brother strolled casually across the patio, removed his sunglasses and extended his right hand to the young woman. She appeared stunned as she stared up him, then extended her hand. They were still holding hands when Gabriel moved over to formally introduce them.

Regina Spencer walked over to Emily, curving an arm around her cousin's waist. "Your brother looks like he's on the prowl."

"That's because she's his type—tall and dark with long legs."

"She's beautiful."

"Stunningly so," Emily concurred.

Childish voices and giggles filled the air when Nancy Cole-Thomas crowded the patio with her husband, children and many grandchildren.

Minutes later, Josephine Cole-Wilson and her family joined the others. Some of the younger children stripped off their shorts and T-shirts and jumped into the heated pool, despite their parents' protests.

The smell of grilled meat filled the air as Martin, Joshua and Aaron Spencer lined three grill carts, each with a rotisserie, with marinated meats. David and Serena had wanted to cater the affair but had changed their minds when informed that Christopher and Emily Delgado sought to keep their marriage a secret until after the November election. The men decided they would do the grilling, while Vanessa, Parris and Serena opted to prepare all the main and side dishes.

The nausea Emily had experienced the day before had subsided after she'd eaten breakfast and had yet to return. She had examined her nude body earlier that morning in front of a full-length mirror, finding her breasts fuller than they'd ever been. There still hadn't been a sign of her menses, so she continued to suspect that she was carrying Chris's child.

She spied Chris coming out of the house with Tyler Cole. She tried not to be caught staring at him, but the depth of her love for her husband radiated from her gaze. He was as casually dressed as the other men—lightweight slacks and a short-sleeved shirt. He pumped hands and kissed cheeks wherever someone stopped to congratulate him.

He stopped several feet from her, lowered his chin slightly, and smiled. "Good afternoon, Mrs. Delgado. You're looking well."

"So are you, Mr. Delgado. How was your flight?"

"Uneventful."

Tyler Cole shook his head ruefully. "Damn. If this is the way newlyweds interact with each other, I'm never getting married."

Chris placed a hand on Tyler's broad shoulder. "You don't expect me to ravish her in public, do you?"

Tyler smiled, displaying a set of twin dimples. "You can kiss her, cousin."

Needing no further prompting, Chris swept Emily up in his arms and devoured her mouth. There was a spattering of applause that grew louder once everyone realized what was happening. Emily pushed against Chris's chest, trying to extricate herself. She felt her head spin when she couldn't breathe, going completely limp in his arms.

Chris's head came up, a triumphant grin on his face. Emily buried her nose against his neck, flames of embarrassment flaring and heating up her face.

"Put her down, Chris," Tyler suggested once the clapping stopped. "I want to take her into the house and examine her."

"What for?"

Tyler stared at Emily, then her husband. "You don't know?"

"What am I missing here?" Chris asked.

"Your wife could be pregnant."

Emily felt the burning anger of Chris's accusing gaze adding more heat to her already warm face. "I'm not sure. I felt sick on the flight last night."

Tyler placed a hand on her arm. "Come on, Emily. After I examine you and test your urine, you'll know one way or the other."

"Put me down, Chris." He complied, and she gave her cousin a beseeching look. "Tyler, I'd rather not."

Grasping her hand, he squeezed her fingers gently. "This is no time to be embarrassed. It's either me or Aaron. And I think I'm better qualified because I'm the OB-GYN."

She knew he was right; Aaron was a pediatrician. "Can Chris be there?"

Chris stared at his wife's cousin. Tyler was the quintessential male Cole: tall and broad-shouldered, with black hair, dark eyes, a dimpled smile and rich olive-brown coloring.

Tyler shrugged a shoulder. "I have no objection."

Chris and Tyler led Emily into the wing of the large house David and Serena had set aside for their guests. Vanessa moved beside her husband, watching the trio disappear into the house.

Resting her head on Joshua's shoulder, she smiled up at him. "What are you thinking about?"

Reaching up, Joshua smoothed back several strands of straightened graying hair from his wife's cheek, tucking them behind her ear. "I'm thinking you'll finally get your wish."

"And that is?"

"You're going to get your grandchild."

Vanessa affected a slight frown. "Don't take that tone with me, Joshua Kirkland," she chided softly. "I'm not the only one who wants a grandchild."

He raised a pale eyebrow, giving her a look that spoke volumes. "I know you're not talking about me."

"Yeah, you, Mr. Kirkland. Matt told me that you said you wanted to be a grandfather."

"Matt talks too much."

Rising on tiptoe, she pressed her lips to his clean-shaven cheek. "Do you?"

"What?"

"Want a grandchild?"

He gave her a tender smile. "Of course I do, angel. But what I really wanted was another child."

"Don't even try it, Joshua. You're lucky you got two children out of me. I'd warned you about your secret missions." She'd threatened to divorce him if he returned to his former career as a military intelligence officer.

Joshua might have wanted another child, but he was content. His life had gone better than he could've ever expected. Vanessa was a perfect wife and mother. He loved her, his daughter and his son. And now they could look forward to grandchildren. A satisfied smile curved his mouth as he basted slices of grilled chicken breast and butterflied lamb.

Emily sat numbly on the bed, allowing Chris to help her dress. Tyler had just confirmed her suspicions. She was pregnant and could expect to deliver sometime around November 8. Her due date was Election Day.

Mixed emotions assailed her. She'd agreed to having a child with Chris, but the import of their decision to begin their family wasn't apparent—until now.

Was she really ready for motherhood?

Was she willing to give up her career—a career that had been stymied by unfounded charges?

And did she really want to be a politician's wife?

She chided herself, staring down at the salt-and-pepper hair covering her husband's head as he knelt down to slip her sandals on to her bare feet. Had her love for him masked reality?

In less than three months she'd rejected one man's marriage proposal, accepted another's, married him and now become pregnant.

And in less than three months her professional life had also been turned upside down. A vindictive boss had reassigned her, she had become an earwitness to a murder and because she'd reported the incident her professional ethics had come under close scrutiny.

She'd become mired in a morass of uncertainty, while the only true thing was that she was the pregnant Mrs. Christopher Delgado.

Going to his knees in front of her, Chris grasped her cold fingers, holding them gently. "Are you all right?"

Forcing a smile, she nodded. "Congratulations."

Moving closer, he placed his head on her lap. "*Gracias, mi amor.* Thank you for making me so happy. And thank you for making my life so complete."

She pulled her right hand away and placed it on his head. "Aren't you forgetting about becoming governor?"

His head came up slowly as he stared at her, unblinking. "There was a time when becoming governor was as important to me as drinking water to sustain my life."

"And now?" The two words were barely a whisper.

"Now that's not important. Nothing is more important to me than you and this baby."

Closing her eyes against his intensity, Emily mumbled a silent prayer for strength, because at that moment his sentiments did not echo her own. She did love him, but the realization that a child was growing inside her had not yet become a reality. And like Sara Lassiter, she wanted more than being a wife and mother. What she had to discover was what that more was.

Resting her cheek on Chris's head, she pressed her lips to his hair. "Go get our parents. It's time we give them some more shocking news."

Leaning forward, he kissed her. "I'll be right back."

After he left the room, Emily moved over to a rattan chair. The fabric on the back and seat cushions matched the comforters on the twin beds.

Closing her eyes, she tried to stop the rush of tears welling behind her eyelids. What was wrong with her? All her life she'd fantasized about marrying Chris and having his children, so why was she having seconds thoughts now? What was it that kept her from sharing his joy?

She opened her eyes, successfully stemming the flow of unexpected tears. She was back in control when Eve and Vanessa walked into the bedroom, followed by Matt, Joshua and Chris.

Rising to her feet, she affected a bright smile. She looped her arm through Chris's when he moved next to her. "Chris and I have something to tell you." She glanced at him, inclining her head.

He cleared his throat, then announced, "Emily and I are expecting a child. We estimate that the birth will coincide with Election Day."

Vanessa and Eve clapped hands over their mouths, then turned and hugged each other. The two expectant grandfathers gave each other rough embraces, pounding each other's back.

Matt turned to his stepson, pulling him roughly to his chest. Leaning down, he kissed him on both cheeks. "Nice job, son."

"Thanks, Dad."

Extending his arm to Emily, he pulled her to his side. Joshua and Vanessa moved closer, forming a circle as the six people held hands.

Chris gave each one a calm look, saying softly, "Emily and I would like to keep this news between us for the time being. I'll respect her decision as to when she's ready to make the announcement." There was a unanimous nod from all those assembled.

"I think this calls for a celebratory toast," Matt said.

"Amen to that," Joshua concurred.

Vanessa turned and hugged her daughter. "Your father and I will return to Santa Fe with you and the others."

Emily went completely still. "I thought you and Daddy had planned to stay here until the end of April."

"Our plans have changed. You might need us—especially with the baby coming."

She held up a hand. "No, Mom. I'm only a few weeks into this pregnancy, and the baby's not due until early November."

"But Emily—"

"But nothing, Mom. I'm going to be okay. I'll see my own doctor as soon as I get back home. And I'll call you. Every day. I promise."

Vanessa pressed her forehead to her daughter's. "I love you so much."

"I love you, too."

"Can I tell Connie when she gets back from vacation?"

"Yes, you can tell Aunt Connie."

Constance Blanchard-Childs's husband, a newly retired cardiologist, had taken his wife, their two sons, daughters-in-law and preschool grandchildren on a family vacation to the South Pacific for three weeks. The Childses were scheduled to spend time touring Australia, New Zealand and Tahiti.

Vanessa Kirkland's large dark eyes crinkled as she displayed an alluring smile. Emily thought her mother was aging beautifully. Her thick black hair was liberally streaked with gray. Parted off-center, the soft, curling ends floated under her delicate chin and around her long, slender neck. She hadn't gained more than eight pounds since she had married Joshua Kirkland, but the additional weight was distributed in all the right places.

Emily couldn't remember her mother ever raising her voice. She had managed to make herself obeyed not by how she said something, but what she said. Vanessa was the only person Emily knew who struck fear in her father. A warning glance or a softly spoken threat usually had Joshua scrambling to do her bidding.

She wondered how it would be between her and Chris. They were married, yet they did not live together. She had time—eight months—before she delivered the baby—in which she would come to know her husband in every way possible.

Emily offered a smile so reminiscent of Vanessa's. "Let's get back to the others before they suspect we're hatching a secret mission."

"Don't you dare mention secret missions to me," Vanessa retorted, giving her husband a warning glare.

Joshua threw up his hands. "What?"

"Don't even think about it."

Mumbling under his breath in Spanish, he switched fluidly to French, then German. Shaking his head, he stalked out of the bedroom, his wife's triumphant laughter following him.

Emily spent the afternoon talking to relatives. She chatted with Arianna Cole, questioning her about her life in France. The Olympic gold-medal swimmer regaled her with tales of the inner workings of the European fashion industry, the many glamorous parties she attended with her boyfriend and the cities she'd visited since meeting Salih in Milan, while on holiday. She reported that she had secured a position at a Parisian private school, teaching French to English-speaking children. After everyone had eaten, Arianna entertained the younger children by racing them across the pool. She hadn't swum competitively for more than ten years, yet she hadn't lost much of her speed.

Bright lights lit up the perimeter of the Cole property, and chairs and tables were repositioned for live music and dancing under the stars.

Gabriel Cole held a microphone, tapping it gently to garner everyone's attention. Brilliant spotlights created a halo around his cropped black hair. Dressed entirely in black, two sets of small gold hoops in each ear and strutting much like his father had years before, Gabriel Morris Cole had become David Claridge Cole all over again.

Unlike his father, who played percussion, piano and guitar, Gabriel possessed the facility to play every instrument in an orchestra. He wrote and played music, and he was also gifted with a wonderful baritone singing voice.

"I'd like to thank everyone for coming to my parents' home to help me celebrate what has become the best that life has to offer me as a musician."

"You're the bomb, Gabe," a young voice called out from a crowd of people sitting with their feet dangling in the warm waters of the swimming pool.

Gabriel flashed a dimpled grin. "Thanks, Casey." He'd recognized his aunt's granddaughter's voice. "What I've achieved would not have been possible without the support of my mother and father." He turned, inclined his head, positioned his hands over his heart, then pointed to David and Serena, who stood side by side, their arms around the other's waist.

"Today's celebration is not only for me, but for two other family members. In case you haven't heard, Emily and Chris have finally come to their senses and decided to get married." There was a thundering round of applause and whistling. "New Mexico State Senator Christopher Delgado happens to be a serious Maxwell fan. Yeah, Chris, Emily told me." Chris raised his right hand in acknowledgment. "The band and I would like to celebrate your recent nuptials by playing a Maxwell composition, which just happens to be a favorite of mine. Ladies, gentleman, here's Maxwell's 'Fortunate.'"

Emily looked at Chris as he rose to his feet. He extended his hand, pulling her up gently. "You know they expect us to dance with each other."

He led her to the patio and cradled her in a close embrace. She curved her arms around his neck, smiling up at him. Gabriel and the attractive girl who had captured her brother's attention leaned toward each other and sang the sensual words of the love song that echoed the emotions of the couple who, despite being married and having created a new life, continued to live their separate lives.

Chapter 32

It was the middle of June when the employees at KCNS first became aware that Emily Kirkland was going to have a child. She had been gaining weight slowly, putting on a pound a month. Then, without warning, she awoke one morning and found a firm rounded mound of flesh where her slightly distended belly existed the night before.

She spent more than half an hour trying on everything in her closet to accommodate her burgeoning body, but the attempt was fruitless. She called the network offices to say she wouldn't be in, pulled on a pair of sweatpants and one of her brother's shirts, then headed for the nearest mall to purchase a new wardrobe.

Her life hadn't changed much since she'd returned from Florida in early March. She'd continued to supervise the intern until two weeks earlier, and Steve Washington was her constant companion and go-between, facilitating her assignations with Chris. They managed to see each other on an average of once every two weeks. His campaign schedule had him crisscrossing the state, visiting as many as eight cities or towns each week.

The increased activity was taking its toll. He'd lost weight, and whenever the camera captured his image it revealed an intensity that hadn't been apparent before he entered the gubernatorial race.

His strategists had countered Savoy's claim that Alejandro Delgado was a drug trafficker by securing declassified documents from FBI files showing that the former Mexican diplomat had assisted with the capture and demise of a quartet of powerful

Mexican drug lords. Word had filtered from the Savoy camp that the incumbent governor was livid that his son's investigators had failed to delve deeply enough into the elder Delgado's activities.

Emily checked with Detective McGrady every week, but the homicide detective hadn't uncovered any more information concerning the murder. Emily couldn't feed him more leads because she hadn't heard from her mysterious informant since late February.

Maneuvering into a parking space at a downtown mall, Emily walked into the air-cooled, two-story structure and headed for a specialty shop that sold lingerie. She had to purchase bras in a larger size. She'd found Chris leering at her whenever she undressed in front of him; her fuller breasts now spilled out of her very impractical lacy bra cups.

The morning passed quickly as she purchased undergarments and picked up six mix-and-match coordinates from a maternity shop before she stopped to eat a salad at one of the counters at the food court.

She left the mall with four shopping bags, stored them in the trunk of the Corvette, then sat in the car trying to decide what to do next. Reaching into her purse, she retrieved her cellular phone and dialed the number of her husband's cell phone. She heard his voice after the second ring.

"Yes?"

"Hi, lover," she crooned.

"Where are you?"

"I'm at the mall."

"Are you going back to work?"

"No. I didn't go to work today because I had to shop for clothes for my very misshapen body."

He laughed softly. "I think your body's very cute."

"You really think so?" she asked.

"Yeah, I do. Why don't you come over and model your purchases?"

"Where are you, Chris?"

"Home."

"What are you doing there?"

"Resting up before I attend a dinner with ninety members of the American Legion this evening."

"Do you think it's wise for me to come to your place?"

"Look, Emily, you're not covering Savoy's campaign, so there shouldn't be a problem."

"Right now, I'm not covering anything at the station."

"Come on over, baby girl, and keep me company."

Chris stood at a window, watching for Emily's car. He would be able to spot her as soon as she came down the street. The industrial building had stored corn and other grains in the late nineteenth century, but had been abandoned for years when the storage company moved to Texas. The owner subdivided more than 35,000 square feet into three separate lofts, and he was the third and last person to purchase more than ten thousand feet of living space.

A slight smile deepened the lines around his eyes when he spied Emily. She was driving much more slowly than she had been before her pregnancy. She'd said she was practicing to become a responsible mother.

Walking across the living room, Chris pressed a button on a wall panel, activating the garage door on the street level. His cell phone chimed softly. He pressed another button, disengaging the lock on the door inside the garage, which led into his apartment. Emily would be able to let herself in.

He retrieved the phone. "Yes?"

"She's on her way to your place," came a soft male voice.

"I know. She's here. Thanks."

Chris ended the call. The man he'd hired to protect Emily had planted a tracking device under the right wheel well of her car. The man had been the best in his field before an untreated case of strep throat resulted in a heart condition, which led to his retirement from the FBI. The former special agent monitored Emily's every move and who she met, and reported his findings by cell phone or laptop computer.

Chris moved over to the door and opened it, smiling as Emily walked up four steps and into his apartment. His gaze made love to her, sweeping over the black shiny curls falling around her long, graceful neck. Her on-and-off-again bouts of nausea prevented her from keeping her regularly scheduled beauty salon appointments. The result was that she'd affected a hairstyle that was less sophisticated but made her appear softer, more feminine.

Leaning closer, she pressed her mouth to his. "Hey."

Curving an arm around her thickening waist, Chris returned her smile. "Hey, yourself."

Emily cradled his lean face between her palms, noting the changes in her husband's appearance immediately. The photographs had been kind. Up close and in person he looked emaciated.

"Did you eat today?"

His gaze lowered, long lashes sweeping over the sharp ridge of his cheekbones. "I had a couple of slices of toast and a cup of coffee this morning."

"It's looks as if I'm the only one in this family who's putting on weight. You look horrible, Chris."

"I love you, too, baby."

"I'm serious. You look sick." Taking his hand, she pulled him in the direction of the kitchen. "You're so intent on campaigning that you're neglecting your health. Our baby has a right to grow up with both parents. From the look of you, you seem intent on starving yourself to death."

Releasing his hand, she walked over to the refrigerator and flung open the door. She went completely still. A bottle of orange juice, half a loaf of bread and a small plastic dish with no more than a pat of butter on it rested on the top shelf. The other shelves were bare.

Slamming the door with a resounding thud, Emily turned to face Chris. "Where are your takeout menus?"

"I'm going out to eat at the VFW tonight."

"What? Rubber chicken, raw bloody beef and putrid fish?" She extended her hand. "Give me the menus, Chris."

"Aw, come on, baby."

Her eyes lost their vibrant color. "Now!"

His temper exploded. "Dammit, Emily!"

"Watch your mouth, Christopher Delgado." She pushed past him, heading for the door.

"Where are you going?"

"Out. To buy some food for this place."

Chris raced across the large space, his fingers curling around her upper arm, stopping her retreat. "Okay, Emelia."

Turning, she stared at him, seeing the strain he tried vainly to conceal from her as her heart turned over in compassion. Closing her eyes, she swayed slightly.

"I love you, Chris. More than you know. And because I love you, I worry about you. I don't know what I'd do if something happened to you."

His strong hands circled her waist, pulling her flush against his body. He wanted to tell her how much he worried about her. He hadn't ignored his brother-in-law's warning to protect her; he'd taken Salem's suggestion and hired a protection specialist. Even though the man tracked her every move, Chris found that he was unable to relax until he received his daily report that she was safe.

"Shhh, baby. Nothing's going to happen to me."

She didn't know him. She was in love with him, married to him, yet she did not know him at all. He wasn't eating regularly because he hated eating alone. It was at fundraising dinners that he consumed the rubber chickens, half-raw prime rib and smelly fish plates.

"Have you eaten, baby?"

"Yes. Why?"

"I'll order something, but only if you'll share a few bites with me."

She laughed, the soft, sensual sound bubbling up from her throat. "I can assure you that right now I'm eating more than a few bites."

He placed a hand over her belly, his fingers splayed. He was missing so much—going to the doctor with her, massaging her legs when they cramped, bringing her the herbal tea she'd begun drinking to offset her nausea.

The next one, he thought. It would be so different with the next baby.

Chris retrieved several menus, and they selected a number of healthy dishes. Their selections were delivered forty-five minutes later.

Emily shared a chicken and blue cheese salad made with baby salad greens and sliced pears, served with a warm bacon vinaigrette dressing, along with slices of sourdough bread and chilled mineral water. Dessert was a cup of chilled mango mousse with a tart raspberry sauce.

Pushing away from the table, she made her way slowly up a circular flight of wrought-iron stairs to the upper level. The master bedroom was a repeat of the rooms on the first floor— shuttered windows, brick walls and herringbone-designed wood floors. She was full and very sleepy.

She removed her sweatpants, shirt and bra, leaving on her panties, and crawled under the sheet on Chris's king-size bed. She didn't know when he crawled into bed beside her, one hand resting over the mound where their child moved vigorously in her womb.

It was late afternoon when Emily rolled over and found Chris asleep on his back, one arm thrown over his head, the other resting on her belly.

He'd half-closed the shutters against the bright late-spring sun, but beams of light had inched across his eyes and forehead. She examined him feature by feature, a smile curving her lips. Every time she looked at Chris she wondered whether their baby would look more like him or her. She was certain it would have very dark hair, because they both did. Would it inherit his eye color, or would it be a lighter brown? Whether girl or boy, it was certain to be tall. Chris was an even six foot, while she was five-nine. Without warning, he opened his eyes, his gaze fusing with hers before it moved lower.

Emily felt the heat from his perusal, wanting to pull the sheet up over her bare breasts to hide them from his hungry eyes. She gasped when he placed a hand over the swollen, ripened flesh, squeezing gently.

Rising on an elbow, he moved over her, supporting his weight on his forearms. "You are so beautiful." He'd stressed each syllable.

Reaching up and curving her arms around his neck, Emily pulled his head down. "Liar," she whispered against his lips.

He shook his head. "No, I'm not."

Lowering his head, he caught a tender nipple between his teeth, and she gasped aloud, arching off the mattress. He suckled one breast, then the other. Liquid love vibrated and flowed even before he entered her quivering flesh.

Chris loved her—every inch of her sweet, fragrant, flesh. And as her desire rose, his met and matched hers. They'd been apart too long; he hadn't gotten enough of her. She didn't know how much he craved her: every day, hour, minute, second.

Emily's passion spiraled out of control, and she knew this was one time when she would climb the peaks of ecstasy before her husband. She couldn't control her cry of delight as she gave in to the rush of passion exploding and shaking her until she lay motionless, spent.

Chris felt the familiar tightening in the sacs carrying his seed, but he fought the urge to explode in his wife's body. He didn't see her enough, have enough of her, for it to end so quickly.

Gritting his teeth, he tried concentrating on everything else but the soft pulsing of the hot, moist flesh closing around his throbbing sex. But it was in vain, and he surrendered to the sexual hysteria that gripped him in a vortex that pulsed violently, refusing to release him until he collapsed on the body beneath him.

He rolled off her, not wanting to injure their unborn child. Waiting until his pulse returned to normal, he sat up, scooped Emily up in his arms and carried her to a sunroom where he'd erected a sylvan shower.

The sunroom, enclosed by frosted glass, was an oasis filled with tropical plants, flowers and ferns. The shower, erected from a metal frame, flowed into a small pool that emptied into the city sewer system via a series of pipes built under the floor.

Emily felt as if she were in a primordial jungle when she stood under the flow of lukewarm water with Chris. He lathered her body with a lime-scented body wash, his hands and fingers exploring the hidden places and reviving her passion all over again. They made love a second time, this coupling a desperate coming together that reminded them that it might be the last time for a long time.

She rinsed her body and washed her hair while he walked across the slate floor to shave for his dinner with the veterans. Stepping out of the shower, she sat down on a wrought-iron love seat, blotted beads of water off her body with a thirsty bathsheet, then returned to the bedroom to retrieve her clothes.

She didn't wait for Chris to let her out, and she didn't see him watching from a window as she drove away from his building, fighting tears.

Chapter 33

Emily made her way to Richard Adams's office, her pace slower now that she was midway through her third trimester. Everyone at the station deferred to her because of her *condition,* while many assumed she was engaged to Steve Washington because of the ring on her left hand and the baby kicking vigorously in her belly. She hadn't reported any personal changes in her marital status to the human resource department, not even concerning her medical benefits.

She considered herself lucky if she saw Chris more than twice a month, while Steve had elected to take her out to dinner or to a movie even when he wasn't directed to take her to meet her husband. The police officer wasn't very forthcoming with information about himself, but after a while he felt comfortable enough with her to reveal that he was divorced but wasn't dating anyone at present. He confessed that he was looking for quality, not quantity, when it came to women. As spring became summer and summer turned to fall, she and Steve became good friends. She had come to realize that she hadn't had a good male friend since Christopher Delgado.

The summer had passed quickly. She found herself spending more time with her parents at their Santa Fe Hills home, and visiting with her aunt and uncle. She'd traveled to Las Cruces with her parents to visit with her in-laws and the Lassiters over the Fourth of July weekend. Though the desert heat never bothered her before, she couldn't wait to return to Santa Fe with its cooler mountain breezes.

Emily arrived at Richard's office. The door was open and he sat behind his desk, half turned to gaze out the window. She rapped lightly to get his attention.

Swiveling on his chair, Richard stared at her for several seconds before he rose to his feet. "Please come in and close the door." He moved around the desk and held out a chair for her.

Emily sat down, thanking him. "Your secretary said you wanted to see me."

It was the first time in more than seven months that he had requested her presence.

Richard stared at her, noting the flawlessness of her skin, and her longer raven-black hair falling over her forehead and around her delicately made face. A rust-colored smock dress artfully concealed her advancing pregnancy. His gaze dropped to her fingers. The large diamonds on the ring on her finger had cost someone a small fortune. He was aware of the rumors that the father of the child in Emily Kirkland's womb was a Santa Fe highway police officer. First a ballplayer, now a cop. He thought she could've married better.

"Yes. I know you've been waiting for an assignment since you were dropped from the Savoy campaign."

Dropped! She wanted to tell Richard that it was more like she had been banished from the campaign and ostracized by her own network.

"I've decided to let you represent KCNS when Savoy and Delgado face off for their televised debates."

Her fingers tightened on the arms of her chair to keep herself from springing to her feet to kiss Richard. "I appreciate the offer."

Richard managed to look contrite. "I didn't want to pull you off Savoy's campaign, but I didn't have any choice. The governor called the head of the network, and the rest was history."

Emily nodded. "Most political journalists want access to campaigns for information. What Savoy thought I wanted was controversy. All I wanted to do was cover the campaign, then let the public form its own opinions."

"I know," Richard said softly. "There will be a series of three debates, the first on Monday. Do you think you have enough time to prepare?"

He had given her only six days, but she would be ready. "Yes."

"Good luck, Emily."

She flashed her famous smile. "Thank you."

"How do you feel?" he asked as she pushed to her feet.

"Wonderful."

"When's the baby due?"

"Election Day."

"Do you know the baby's sex?"

"Yes. It's a boy." The Kirklands and Sterlings were overjoyed that she was carrying a boy.

"Congratulations. A man always needs a son to carry on the family name."

"How right you are," she said softly.

Her step was quicker, lighter when she retreated to her office. She had been given the opportunity to face Savoy again. This time they would be in front of the camera together. Picking up a pen, she began making notations on a lined pad. Even though she hadn't been covering either of the candidates' campaign, she had followed it closely, viewing every bit of video she could.

She looked forward to questioning the man who'd nearly derailed her career.

Emily stared at the screen, listening intently to William Savoy's response to a question about the regulation of drug prices. The ringing of the cell phone on the table beside her shattered her concentration.

She picked it up, pushing the Talk button. "Hello."

"I have something for you."

It was her mysterious informant. It had been months since she'd heard from her. "What is it?"

"Meet me at the church."

"At what time?" She glanced at her watch.

"In ten minutes."

"That's impossible. It'll take me ten minutes to get out of this building and retrieve my car."

"Ten minutes, Miss Kirkland."

"Wait!"

The call was disconnected.

Shutting off the monitor, Emily returned to her office and gathered her purse. The elevator came only seconds after she rang the bell, and she prayed it would take her directly to the lobby without stopping. Her prayers were answered, and she quickened her pace, holding the underside of her belly. A slight pain radiated along the muscles in her groin.

She knew ten minutes had already passed when she eased the seat belt over her swollen body. Her contact had probably already left the church.

It had been months since she'd driven beyond the speed limit, but a rush of excitement made her reckless. Shifting into a higher gear, she took a corner on two wheels, then sped down a one-way street. Twenty-two minutes after the call, she pulled into the church's parking lot.

The church was empty, except for a cleaning man pushing a dust mop over the marble floor and a tiny woman kneeling at the altar. Emily sat where she'd been directed the first time, staring straight ahead. She waited for what seemed like an eternity until she felt a presence behind her. This time her nose detected the scent of a woman's perfume.

"You're late," the voice said accusingly.

"I told you that you didn't give me enough time." It was the same woman who'd called her. "Where's the guy?"

"That's none of your business, Miss Kirkland."

Emily swallowed back an angry retort. "What do you want to tell me?"

"Bettina Gibson was sleeping with Savoy. It was his baby she was carrying."

"How do you know this?"

"Ask me another question and I'm gone."

"Act snotty with me and I'll be the one walking out of here," Emily countered. She waited several seconds, then said, "There were rumors that Savoy was sleeping with another woman who was also pregnant with his child when she killed herself. Is there any truth to that rumor?"

"It's true. Her name was Grace Clark. She was a model who was married to a Navajo doctor."

Closing her eyes, Emily let out an audible sigh. The woman had just confirmed the fact that Salem's first wife was carrying William Savoy's child when she committed suicide.

"What is it you want me to do?"

The woman leaned close enough for Emily to feel her moist breath on the back of her neck. "I want you to go public with what I just told you."

She curbed the urge to turn around. "I can't. Not without proof."

"Why not?"

"I'd be sued for slander."

"Doesn't it matter that Bettina's dead?"

"Of course it matters. Remember, I was the last one to see her before she was shot."

"I've given you enough information, Miss Kirkland. It's up to you to figure out what to do next."

"Give me something else to go on. *Anything*."

There was a strained silence before the woman spoke. "He goes either way."

Emily took several seconds to register the statement. "Are you saying he's bisexual?" She waited and waited for a response but encountered silence. Then she turned and saw a petite figure walking quickly out of the church. She caught a glimpse of a dark, long-sleeved T-shirt, jeans and a black or navy-blue baseball cap that concealed her hair color. The only thing she knew for certain was that the woman was of European descent. Her coloring was very fair.

She lingered in the church, stopping to light a candle and to say a prayer for Bettina's departed soul. Walking slowly out of the church, she tried to sort out what she'd just been told. Bettina had been sleeping with Savoy and he had gotten her pregnant. But was he sleeping with Bettina and men at the same time?

Pondering his bisexuality triggered memories of another incident from the past. Sara Sterling was once engaged to a man who had disclosed his bisexuality, sending her into a maelstrom of doubt and mistrust.

Emily searched her memory for his name. *Eric Thompson!* Sara ended their engagement, and they had attended different law schools. Sara went on to become an assistant U.S. attorney in New York, while Eric had become a partner in a prestigious law firm in Las Cruces. He had also dabbled in politics, running unsuccessfully as an alderman from his district.

An expression of satisfaction showed in Emily's eyes.

Emily returned to her office and called an administrative assistant to bring her a telephone directory for Las Cruces. Within fifteen minutes, she had located the law firm.

She identified herself and the television station's call letters, saying, "May I please speak to Mr. Eric Thompson."

"I'm sorry, but Mr. Thompson is out of town."

"When do you anticipate his return?"

"Next week."

"I'd like to speak to Mr. Thompson to schedule an interview," she half lied. "May I leave my name and number, just in case he calls in?"

"Of course."

Emily hung up, hoping she would be able to gather enough evidence to implicate William Savoy in Bettina's murder. She thought about contacting Vincent McGrady with her new information, but decided against it. She'd wait until after she spoke to Eric Thompson.

She walked into her office early the next morning to a ringing telephone. She picked up the receiver before the call switched over to her voice mail.

"Emily Kirkland."

"Miss Kirkland, Eric Thompson. I was told you called my office looking for me."

Massaging the middle of her back, she eased her bulk down

into a chair. "Yes, that's true. I don't know whether you remember me, but—"

"I remember you, Miss Kirkland," he interrupted. "You're Sara Sterling's friend."

"She's now Sara Lassiter," she reminded him.

"Yes, that's right. What can I do for you?"

"I'd like to meet with you so we can talk privately."

"What about?"

"It's a very personal matter."

There was a moment of silence. "How personal, Miss Kirkland?"

She decided to be direct. "Alternative lifestyles. Not yours, but someone you're familiar with."

"Do you actually expect me to talk about someone else's lifestyle?"

"Yes, I do, Mr. Thompson."

He laughed softly. "You're really ballsy, aren't you, Miss Kirkland?"

"I don't think so, Mr. Thompson. I happen not to have that particular body part."

He laughed again. "I like you, Emily."

It was her turn to laugh. "Thank you, Eric."

"When and where do you want to meet?"

"It's your call."

"Have you had breakfast?"

"I had a glass of juice and oatmeal."

"I know a place that makes the best waffles in the state. I can pick you up at your office."

"That won't be necessary. Tell me where you want me to meet you."

Eric gave her the address of the restaurant, and she told him she would meet him there within twenty minutes.

She'd just hung up when the phone rang again. It was Grant Carsons, Chris's campaign manager. He wanted to meet with her to go over some of the topics she intended to cover in the upcoming debate. Checking her daily planner, she scheduled a meeting for four that afternoon.

Chapter 34

It was the first time Emily Kirkland had seen Eric Thompson in ten years. She had to admit that time had been very kind to him. Tall, slender and exquisitely attired, she recognized what had drawn Sara to him. Classically handsome, he exuded breeding and power.

She registered his surprise when his startled gaze dropped to the swell of her belly under a tent-styled navy blue knit dress she had paired with matching sheer hose and a pair of low-heeled leather slip-ons.

He cupped a hand under her elbow. "I didn't know you were in the family way."

"Not too many people are aware of it because I haven't been in front of the cameras this year."

"How much more time do you have before d-day?"

"Six weeks."

He raised his thick black eyebrows. "You don't look that far along."

"It's the dress."

He led her into the restaurant and they were shown to a table in a corner. "I hope you don't mind sitting here? It's the only spot that lends itself to a modicum of privacy."

She shook her head. "It's fine."

Eric seated Emily, then sat down opposite her. She looked different from the last time he'd seen her in person. Her face had changed. Her eyes reminded him of Sara's, except that hers were lighter, clearer.

Emily waited until Eric placed their orders. She leaned as close as her stomach would permit her. "I've heard rumors that William Savoy likes to work both sides of the aisle."

Eric's expression did not change. "Who told you that?"

"Someone. I don't know her name."

"You don't know her name, yet you're asking me about William Savoy because of something she said? Why, Miss Kirkland? Why do you think I would know about Savoy's sexual proclivity?"

"I know why Sara broke her engagement to you."

"Because I told her that I preferred men?"

"Yes."

"Sara was wrong and you're wrong. I've never been with a man."

"Then why did you tell her—"

"I told her what I needed to tell her to get her to break the engagement," he said, interrupting her.

Emily's shock was apparent when her jaw dropped. "You deliberately lied to her?"

Running a large, manicured hand over his clean-shaven face, Eric nodded. "I was sleeping with Sara and another woman at the same time. I thought I was very careful, but she came to me with the news that she was pregnant. Suddenly I was faced with a dilemma. I was engaged to one woman, while another was pregnant with my baby. I decided to do the right thing, end the engagement and marry the other woman. But everything backfired, because the next day the other girl fell down a flight of stairs and miscarried. Within a matter of hours I'd lost the only woman I'd ever loved and a baby. So if you're asking me if I'm gay or bisexual, the answer is no."

Emily's eyes paled. "You low dog! You lied about your sexuality to get out of marrying Sara."

He flashed a wry smile. "You don't think I'm sorry for what I did?"

"No, I don't."

"Then you're wrong, Emily."

She placed her napkin on the table. "I think I just lost my appetite." She picked up her handbag and walked out of the restaurant.

If she'd turned around, she would have noticed a man sitting at a nearby table move over to claim the chair she'd just vacated.

Emily's temper had cooled down by the time she left for her appointment with Grant Carsons at Chris's Santa Fe campaign headquarters.

She plucked a parking stub out of the machine, then waited for the wooden arm in the underground parking garage to go up. It lifted, and she drove up a steep ramp, downshifting to keep from rolling backward. The garage was nearly filled to capacity. She finally found a vacant space on the top level.

Pocketing her keys, she walked a short distance to the elevator that would take her back down to street level and the entrance to the high-rise office building.

She pressed the button for the elevator. Before the doors opened she felt herself jerked backward. Too frightened to scream, she turned and swung her shoulder purse at her attacker. It hit him in the face, causing him to release his grip on her neck. Within seconds he grabbed her again; however, she had retrieved her keys from the hidden pocket in her dress and aimed for his eyes.

She found her mark and he bellowed in pain. Struggling to make it into the elevator before he came at her again, she raised her knee, aiming directly for his crotch. Her knee smashed into his delicate organs, but instead of doubling over in pain he came at her, enraged. His large, hamlike hands caught the back of her dress and he jerked her savagely, causing her to lose her balance. She fell, her hands cradling her belly to protect her unborn child.

She felt the heat of his breath through the opening where his mouth was visible through a ski mask when he leaned over her. She watched helplessly as he seemed to draw back his hand in slow motion.

"Mind your business about the dead hooker," he hissed. He slapped her with an open hand and repeated his warning twice more, punctuating each one with a hard slap that left her head roaring with the rush of blood.

"Hey, buddy! What are you doing?"

The sound of another male voice ended her torture and she heard her attacker running away. She knew her eyes were swelling rapidly when she tried opening them to focus on the face looming above her.

"Chris Delgado," she whispered. "Get Chris Delgado."

"Hold on, lady. I'm going to get help."

Grant Carsons looked at the clock for the umpteenth time. It was after four, and Emily Kirkland was late.

Chris walked into Grant's office, a tie hanging loosely from the collar of his shirt. "Is she here yet?"

"No." The single word mirrored Grant's frustration.

"It's not like Emily to be late."

"Well, she is," Grant snapped.

A volunteer rushed into the office. "Someone attacked Emily Kirkland on the roof of the garage. The police are all over the building."

Chris raced out of the room, pushing the young man aside. He hadn't realized how fast his heart was pumping until he pushed open the door to the stairwell and jumped down three and four steps at a time to reach the building lobby. Perspiration soaked his shirt as he sprinted to the stairwell that led to the parking garage roof.

His heart felt as if it was going to explode in his chest when he saw a phalanx of uniforms bending over a body on the concrete floor.

He moved closer, but a strong hand stopped him. "Don't come any closer."

Roaring in rage, he shoved the officer aside. His action caused several others to reach for the guns on their hips. One of the officers recognized him.

"Senator Delgado."

They all froze, staring at him as he stepped forward, staring down at his wife's motionless form.

"Is...is she all right?"

Emily heard his voice and opened her eyes. She managed a sad smile. "Chris."

He went to his knees, his fingers touching her bruised face. "Hold on, kid. We're going to get you some help."

Her lids fluttered wildly. "The baby. Am I losing the baby?"

Leaning over, he kissed her forehead. "No." Curbing the urge to touch her stomach, he held her hand, his thumb caressing the ring he'd put on her delicate finger. He turned his desperate eyes on one of the officers. "Where the hell are the EMTs?"

The question hadn't left his lips before the sound of sirens drowned out his words. Mumbling a silent prayer, Chris hoped they weren't too late. The color staining his wife's dress was blood.

Chris sat at Emily's bedside, holding her hand as she slept. She had been rushed into emergency surgery. The medical team had successfully stopped her bleeding.

He saw movement out of the corner of his eye and turned to find his father-in-law standing in the doorway. Releasing her hand, he rose slowly to his feet and stepped out of the room.

Joshua gave him a cold look. "What happened to her, Christopher?" He moved closer. "She's your wife," he said between clenched teeth. "You are supposed to protect her."

"How dare you come here and preach to me about protecting her?"

"I dare anything," Joshua countered.

"Not anymore. She's *my* wife, and therefore my responsibility."

"Dammit, man, act responsible then!"

Grasping Joshua's arm, Chris pulled him into the corridor. He told Emily's father about Salem's warning and the steps he'd taken to protect his wife. He finished, saying, "I've done all I know how to do. If there's something else, then please let me know what it is."

Joshua shook his head, closing his eyes. "You've done what you could." He opened his eyes and shook his head. "When you called me it was like déjà vu, after that moron tried to kill her because she wouldn't respond to his online marriage proposal."

"Don't, Joshua. Just be thankful that she's going to be okay."

"The baby?"

Chris smiled. "He's fine."

"That's good."

"Did you tell Aunt Vanessa?"

"I couldn't. Not yet."

Resting an arm over Joshua's shoulder, Chris stared down at the floor. "Tell her Emily had an accident and that she's going to be okay. As soon as they release her, I'm going to arrange for her to be taken to Las Cruces. I'll bring her back after there's no threat of further bleeding and her bruises fade."

"Thanks…son."

Emily was whisked out of the hospital two days later, after the attending physician confirmed that she was no longer in danger of hemorrhaging. Salem Lassiter flew up from Las Cruces to take her back with him. Chris kissed her bruised face tenderly, then watched the small plane as it lifted off.

Emily lay on a chaise in the Lassiters' family room, watching the televised debate. Pride swelled in her chest at her husband's intelligent responses to the questions from three network journalists. He had a natural gift for communicating effortlessly.

William Savoy did not fare as well. He exhibited an awkwardness that usually made the viewing public uncomfortable. He stammered and stuttered and, on two occasions, lost his temper. The debate ended with the score Delgado one, Savoy zero.

Sara rose to her feet, applauding. "He was magnificent."

Running her tongue over a healing split lip, Emily nodded slowly. "Awesome." She attempted to push off from the chaise but froze. A slight contraction gripped her lower abdomen.

Salem stared at her. "Are you all right?"

Rubbing her belly, she breathed in and out through her parted lips. "I felt a contraction."

Sara crossed the room and sat down on the foot of the chaise, reaching for Emily's hands. "I can't wait to see my nephew."

"You're not the only one who's impatient. I'm beginning to feel like a beached whale."

"You're a lot smaller than I was in my eighth month."

Emily wrinkled her nose. "I've gained fourteen pounds."

"I gained twenty-four overall," Sara admitted.

Salem stood up. "Well, ladies, I'm off to bed." He walked over and kissed his wife, then Emily. "Good night."

Sara stared at her best friend and sister-in-law. She bit down on her lower lip as she surveyed Emily's battered face. The swelling was fading over her left eye, her split lip was healing, but the purple bruises on her jaw and chin were constant reminders of the vicious attack.

"Why do you think that man attacked you?"

Emily shrugged her shoulders. "I don't know," she lied smoothly. She hadn't told anyone about her attacker's warning. *Mind your business about the dead hooker.* She would remember his threat to her grave.

He had to be talking about Bettina, and she wondered if the man who'd killed her also wanted Emily dead because he thought she knew too much. But she didn't know too much. In fact, she'd only gathered the small pieces of information her informant had deigned to feed her.

She heard a male voice from the television and peered around Sara to see Governor Bruce Savoy, offering his comments about the televised debate, claiming that both candidates were highly intelligent and had demonstrated that they were aware of the problems facing the citizens of the state.

Closing her eyes, Emily listened to the cadence of his speech, trying to figure out why his voice was so familiar. Her eyes opened, widening. Now she knew. It was the governor's distinctively gravelly voice she had heard in the room in the country club the night Bettina was shot.

It was Bruce, not William, who had gotten Bettina pregnant. And it was Bruce whom she had seen, not William. While William had strolled around the first floor, greeting and thanking his supporters, Bruce waited upstairs for his mistress.

Her heart was pumping so loudly, Emily was certain Sara could hear it. She had to make contact with the governor. She had to confront him and hear his side of the story. Had he shot Bettina, or did she actually shoot herself?

Swinging her legs slowly over the side of the chaise, she planted her feet on the floor. "I'm going to bed, Sara." Leaning over, she hugged her. "Thanks for everything."

Sara returned the hug. "Love you, Emmie."

"Love you back."

She stood up, a hand going to the small of her back as she made her way slowly out of the room. The way she felt, she doubted she would last until Election Day.

Chapter 35

Emily returned to Santa Fe after spending twelve days in Las Cruces, recuperating from the parking garage assault. Chris flew down the morning following his first debate to be with her. He campaigned in his hometown for several days, coming back to Sterling Farms each night. At last they were able to experience what it meant to be a married couple when they took up residence at one of the cabins on the property that had been built for live-in employees of the farm.

Chris wanted her to go on medical leave from the station and remain in Las Cruces with his family, but she reminded him that her doctor was in Santa Fe.

However, when she awoke on October 15, her contractions were so strong that she called Richard Adams to inform him that she would not return to work until after the birth of her child. Two days later, three large cartons were delivered to her home, bearing gifts from the employees at the station. She opened the cartons to find every conceivable item she would need to care for a infant: disposable diapers, lotions, shampoos, a bathtub, undershirts, socks, blankets, crib sheets, one-piece rompers, sweaters, caps, terry-cloth robes and tiny towels.

Her parents had set up a nursery at their home because she'd planned to stay with them after the birth of the baby. She and Chris couldn't be certain where they would reside until after the election.

Governor Savoy's voice continued to plague her even though she didn't want to believe he was the one responsible for Bettina's death. The elder Savoy's personal life was impeccable. Married to the same woman for forty-five years, father of three, grandfather of two, there was never a hint of any impropriety or scandal in his past. On the other hand, she was certain that it had been Bruce's voice she'd heard in the room at the country club.

Picking up the telephone, Emily dialed the number of Governor Savoy's office. It took twenty minutes, but she was finally connected to his personal secretary.

She gave the woman her name, saying that she was calling from KCNS. She was placed on hold, then told that the governor would call her back. Much to her surprise he did call her, and when she heard his voice she knew with a 99 percent certainty that it was Bruce Savoy who had been in that room with Bettina.

"Governor, I'd like to meet with you to discuss a personal matter."

"How personal Miss Kirkland?"

"Extremely personal, sir."

"Would you like to come to my office? I can have my secretary schedule a time when it will be convenient for both of us."

"I'm sorry, Governor Savoy, but that won't be possible."

"What would be possible, Miss Kirkland?"

"A neutral place."

There was a moment of silence before he replied. "Name the place."

"There's a small motel outside town. It's only a few miles from the airport. If it's possible, I'd like to meet you there tomorrow morning at ten." She gave him the name of the motel.

"Okay, Miss Kirkland. I'll meet you at ten."

"Governor?"

"Yes?"

"I want you to come alone."

"I never travel without my state police escort."

"This time you will, Mr. Savoy. I think it's *incumbent* on you that you follow my wishes." She had stressed the word, reminding him that his tenure would end in less than three months.

"Okay, Miss Kirkland. I'll come alone."

"I'll register under another name. Ask the desk clerk for Miss Gibson." She smiled when she heard his labored breathing.

"Okay."

"Goodbye, sir."

"Goodbye, Miss Kirkland."

Emily hung up, unable to believe what she'd just orchestrated. She sat on the middle of the bed, stunned by her boldness. She reached for the telephone again and dialed Vincent McGrady's cell phone number. She left a message on his voice mail, telling him where he could find her the following morning at ten.

Emily woke up the following morning to a cold rain. She prepared her breakfast as usual, showered, then dressed for the weather. Pulling on a pair of black tights and an oversized tunic, she pushed her feet into a pair of black leather rubber-soled loafers. A short raincoat and a baseball cap completed her casual attire. The raincoat had deep pockets—large enough to hold a palm-sized tape recorder without being detected. It was half past nine when she drove her Corvette out of her housing development and headed for the motel.

She alternated turning on and off the car radio. When she couldn't stand the silence, she turned it on again. At 9:50 a.m. she pulled into the parking lot of the small motel. It was a popular place for couples who required a few hours of private time together. Rumors were rampant that the establishment's personnel were more tight-lipped than the CIA.

The young woman at the desk never made eye contact with her as she asked for a room. She placed two twenties on the counter, signed *E. Gibson* in the register, and picked up a key for a room with a view of the back parking lot.

She found the room after she'd taken a wrong turn. Not bothering to sit, she checked her watch. It was ten.

Minutes later, there was a light rap on the door. "Miss Gibson?"

Emily crossed the room, peered through the security eye, and saw the distorted face of the governor of New Mexico. He'd sought to conceal his identity with a pair of sunglasses and a baseball cap. She released the lock and opened the door. Her green eyes darted down the hall. It appeared he had come alone.

"Please come in, Mr. Savoy."

Bruce Savoy could not believe an obviously very pregnant woman had gotten him to meet her in one of the seediest motels in the city. However, he had to admit that Emily Kirkland was one of the most beautiful mothers-to-be he'd ever had the pleasure of seeing. He stepped into the room, closing the door behind him.

"Please sit down, Governor."

He inclined his head. "You first, Miss Kirkland."

"I'd rather stand, thank you." Standing helped her deal with the contractions that seemed to come and go without any regularity.

The tall, elegant politician sat on a straight-backed chair. He removed his glasses and cap.

"What do you want to talk about?" he asked directly.

Resting her hips on a table nailed to the wall, Emily studied his composed features. He and his son did not look alike. Slipping her hands into the pockets of her raincoat, she pressed a button, activating the small recorder.

"Bettina Gibson."

"What about her?"

"I know you were sleeping with her."

Bruce Savoy's expression did not change, but a throbbing vein in his forehead was an indictor that she had hit pay dirt.

"You know nothing of the sort, Miss Kirkland."

"Don't lie to me, *Bruce*." Emily deliberately stressed his name. "Not only were you sleeping with Bettina, but also Grace Clark-Lassiter. It was you who got them pregnant." Her green eyes narrowed. "Why? Why would you, a married man, sleep with a woman without using protection? Certainly you understood the risks."

Crossing his legs, Bruce tried to appear unaffected by the journalist's accusation. She couldn't prove anything. "You're speculating, Miss Kirkland."

"Am I? If I'm speculating, then why did you agree to meet me?"

"Curiosity."

"Wrong, Bruce. You're more than curious. You came because you're not certain how much I know about you. You're uncertain whether I'll go public about your double life. A life that includes you sleeping with young *men* and women."

He jumped to his feet, eyes wild with fear. "No!"

Emily pressed her attack. "Yes, Bruce. I know about that, too."

"That's too bad, Miss Kirkland, because you'll never walk out of here to tell anyone."

She straightened, removing her hands from her pockets. "Why did you do it?" Her voice was soft, coaxing. "Why did you shoot Bettina?"

"I didn't shoot her. We were struggling with her gun and it went off."

Her eyes widened. "Her gun?"

He nodded. "Yes. She came to me a week before she died, telling me that she was pregnant and that she wanted me to leave my wife and marry her. She told me if I didn't, she would expose me."

"How?"

"By going to the newspapers."

"To tell what?"

"That I liked…liked having…"

"Come on, Bruce, let's not be shy. We're both adults."

"I liked… I couldn't do it unless there was a third party present."

Emily's eyebrows shifted with this disclosure. "You mean you liked a ménage à trois?"

Walking over to the window, the highest elected official in the state stared out at the parking lot. "I'd watch them together." His voice trailed off. "After he left, I would have her."

Shaking her head, Emily felt a surge of pity for the middle-aged man. "What role did your son play in this?"

Spinning around, he glared at her. "None! He has nothing to do with any of this."

"But I was told that he was seen with Grace Clark-Lassiter on several occasions."

"That's because he was bringing her to me."

Any compassion she'd felt for the man fled. "You used your son to cover up your adulterous affairs?"

"Billy would do anything for me. I would do anything for him."

"It's over, Governor Savoy. You've destroyed two lives and who knows how many others?"

He walked toward her. "You say it's over, Miss Kirkland, and that's true. It's over for you. There is no way I'm going to let you walk out of this room with the information I've just given you. Something like this would destroy my boy's chances of becoming governor."

"Your *boy* is finished. He's an accessory in a homicide. He knows you shot Bettina Gibson but has deliberately chosen to conceal it."

Reaching into an inner pocket in his jacket, Bruce pulled out a small automatic handgun. Tilting his head at an angle, he leered at her. "I want to thank you for telling me to come alone, Miss Kirkland, because no one will know that I've been here. I'm going to do what the worthless piece of garbage couldn't do that day he met you in the garage."

Emily's blood ran cold in her veins when she realized what he'd said. He meant to kill her. It was he who had hired the thug to beat her up in the garage. Within seconds she saw her life flash in front of her. She didn't want to die—not yet.

She wanted to see her son born, live with her husband, celebrate holidays with her parents, family and friends. She wanted to live out her dreams.

She moved backward, the table stopping her retreat. Could she make it to the door before he shot her? Her fingers inched behind her, closing on a solid object. Its shape revealed that it was a ceramic dish or ashtray.

Emily knew she had to buy time or she would never make it out of the motel room alive. "You said you were struggling with Bettina for the gun and it went off. That's accidental homicide. I'm certain if you tell the police your story, you wouldn't be charged with her murder."

Bruce moved closer. "Sorry, Miss Kirkland, I'm not swallowing it. I'm not going to do anything that will jeopardize my son's chance to succeed me."

He leveled the gun at her chest at the same time the fingers of her right hand closed around the dish. Moving as quickly as her bulk would permit her, she hurled the heavy object at him. It struck him on his cheekbone and landed on the carpeted floor with a dull thud. His finger on the sensitive trigger squeezed, the sound of a bullet exploding in the small space.

Emily raced to the door. Bruce stood stunned, blood pouring from a gash in his cheek. She opened it and ran smack into a broad chest. Screaming, she pounded the chest, trying to escape.

"Emily! Stop! It's me."

She stared up at Chris. Closing her eyes, she tried to stop the world from spinning dizzily. "Chris," she moaned.

"It's all right, baby girl. You're safe."

Plainclothes officers rushed into the room as he eased his wife down to the floor, holding her close to his heart. He'd gotten there in time. A smile curved his mouth when he felt the kicking of his son in her womb against his middle.

"My pocket," Emily whispered. "Look in my pocket."

Reaching into the large pocket of her raincoat, he pulled out a small tape recorder. It was still running. "What's on this?"

"Governor Savoy's confession. He claims he wasn't directly responsible for shooting Bettina Gibson. He was just trying to stop her from shooting him.

Chris stopped the tape. "We'll let the police handle this." He pressed a kiss to her cool forehead. "Speaking of the police, Detective McGrady called me early this morning. He thought I should know what you were up to."

"How did he know you and I…" Her words trailed off.

"A friend of mine had a chat with him."

"What friend?"

"Someone I paid to keep an eye on you."

"What!"

"I'll tell you about it later."

Emily struggled to free herself. "Oh, no. You're going to tell me now."

Chris shook his head. "Later, Emelia."

"¡Ahora, Cristobal!" She gasped audibly when a contraction seized her, the pain radiating around to her back.

"Emily!"

Her eyes widened, filling with fear and pain. "Oh, Chris. I think the baby's coming."

He couldn't remember retrieving the small phone clipped to his waist, or how calm his voice was when he spoke to the 911 operator. What he could remember was the wail of sirens when he sat beside his wife in the back of the ambulance, holding her hand.

The most memorable sight was when he saw his son born. The quiet, trembling little boy was three weeks early, but he was perfect—as perfect as the woman who'd carried him beneath her heart. He remained with Emily throughout the day until a night nurse told him he would have to leave.

He called a press conference the next day, telling the residents of New Mexico that he'd become a father. There was a chorus of loud gasps when he revealed that he'd married Emily Kirkland earlier in the year, and that they'd decided to keep their marriage a secret because of professional obligations.

"How's your wife doing, Senator?"

"She's doing well, thank you."

Chris pointed to another reporter. "Yes?"

"Who does the baby look like?" the woman asked.

There was a smattering of laughter. Lowering his head, he smiled. "He happens to look like his grandfather."

"Which grandfather?" asked another reporter.

"His maternal grandfather."

Alejandro Delgado II looked nothing like his namesake. Somehow he'd inherited Joshua Kirkland's pale hair and green eyes. Emily reassured him that his hair would probably darken as he grew older, but Chris doubted it. However, it didn't matter who his son resembled as long as he was healthy. Besides, he and Emily had quite a few years to try it again.

Epilogue

Emily sat down at the kitchen table, running a letter opener under the flap of an envelope. The earrings that Eve Sterling wore for more than three decades sparkled in her lobes. The letter had been addressed to her at the governor's mansion. She was intrigued by the plain white envelope with no return address.

Her gaze raced over the page of single-spaced type:

Dear Mrs. Delgado:

Words cannot express my gratitude for your helping to solve my twin sister's murder. Bettina Gibson was my sister. I know you believed that she was an only child, but she wasn't. Our birth mother gave her up for adoption when she found herself single and pregnant with twins.

The Gibsons were looking to adopt, so they offered my mother enough money to take one of us. They took Bettina. It wasn't until I turned twenty that my mother told me that I had a twin sister. Bettina and I met for the first time when we were twenty-two. She didn't tell the Gibsons that she'd met me, so it became our secret. We bonded quickly, unable to believe that even though we weren't identical twins, we still looked a lot alike.

Bettina told me that she'd met Governor Savoy, and after a few months they'd begun sleeping together. It wasn't until she found out that she was pregnant that she disclosed his perversions. She said she didn't want to be like our mother. She didn't want to have a baby without a husband. She threatened Savoy that she would tell his wife if he didn't leave her, but he refused. That's when she decided to kill him.

Words will never convey my appreciation; you risked your life and that of your unborn child, and your career, to bring my family closure. I thank you, and our mother thanks you.
Pamela.

Emily handed the letter to her husband. She watched his impassive expression as his gaze moved slowly over the page.

Their lives were finally on track. Bruce Savoy had resigned as governor only months before his term was to expire. He was hospitalized, his doctors claiming a mental breakdown.

William Savoy surprised his supporters when he withdrew three weeks before the election to take care of his mother and father. Even though it was too late to remove his name from the ballot, he managed to get half a million votes—not enough to defeat Christopher Delgado.

And it wasn't until she had come home with Alejandro that Chris explained to Emily how he came to be at the motel with Detective McGrady.

She'd listened, stunned, when he told her of Salem's warning and his subsequent hiring of a former FBI agent to track her. The man met with McGrady after he'd observed her with him at a restaurant. The police officer agreed to inform him of any information she passed along to him.

Once McGrady received her message that she was to meet with Governor Savoy at the motel, the police department took action.

Chris placed the letter on the table, his dark gaze trained on his wife's smiling face. "You did good, Emelia."

She nodded. "I tried."

Rising to his feet, he came around the table and kissed her. "I'm only going to work half a day. You and I have an anniversary to celebrate."

It was their first wedding anniversary, and Vanessa and

Joshua had volunteered to take care of their grandson. It would be the first time the little boy wouldn't sleep under the same roof as his parents.

Chris had listed his loft with a Realtor. They were waiting for Matt and Eve Sterling to find a smaller house in Las Cruces before she and Alejandro moved to the expansive ranch house.

Newly elected Governor Christopher Delgado hadn't spent one night in the governor's mansion because he preferred living in his wife's home. He planned to commute between Santa Fe and Las Cruces every weekend until his term expired.

He and Emily had not talked about what they would do in another four years. They had time…time to celebrate the gift of life and their love for each other. And this time it would be played out publicly.

Emily walked Chris to the door, watching as he slipped onto the rear seat of the dark sedan parked in their driveway. She waved to him, then closed the door.

Good things come to those who wait. She'd waited a long time for Christopher Delgado and she'd claimed him as lover, husband and father of her child. He'd waited a long time for her and to be governor. He, too, had gotten his wish.

Life was good, she mused, smiling. Very, very good.

* * * * *